FOUR & TWENTY BLACKBIRDS

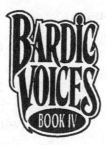

BARDIC VOICES

BOOK IV

BAEN BOOKS by MERCEDES LACKEY

BARDIC VOICES

The Lark & the Wren

The Robin & the Kestrel

The Eagle & the Nightingales

The Free Bards

Four & Twenty Blackbirds

Bardic Choices: A Cast of Corbies
(with Josepha Sherman)

The Fire Rose

The Ship Who Searched
(with Anne McCaffrey)

Wing Commander: Freedom Flight
(with Ellen Guon)

If I Pay Thee Not in Gold
(with Piers Anthony)

URBAN FANTASIES

Bedlam's Bard (forthcoming)
(with Ellen Guon)

The SERRAted Edge:

Born to Run
(with Larry Dixon)

Wheels of Fire
(with Mark Shepherd)

When the Bough Breaks
(with Holly Lisle)

Chrome Circle
(with Larry Dixon)

THE BARD'S TALE NOVELS

Castle of Deception
(with Josepha Sherman)

Fortress of Frost & Fire
(with Ru Emerson)

Prison of Souls
(with Mark Shepherd)

FOUR & TWENTY BLACKBIRDS

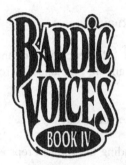

BARDIC VOICES
BOOK IV

MERCEDES LACKEY

Four & Twenty Blackbirds

This is a work of fiction. All the characters and events portrayed in this book are fictional, and any resemblance to real people or incidents is purely coincidental.

A Baen Books Original

Cover art by Darrell K. Sweet

ISBN 0-671-87853-0

Printed in the United States of America

Chapter One

Rain, cold rain, as icy as only a midwinter night could make it, dripped despairingly into the dismal streets of the city of Haldene. It should have cleansed the pavements, but instead it left them looking slick and oily; glistening with a dubious sheen, but not clean. There was a single lamp burning outside a warehouse two doors down, but although the flame burned bravely, it did little to illuminate anything beyond the immediate area of the door it hung above. The rain soaked through everything; the piles of refuse waiting for the rag-picker beside each warehouse and tavern door, Tal Rufen's waxed cape and the woolen coat beneath it—

—the limp and lifeless body of the street-singer at his feet—

More wavering light from his storm-lantern moved uncertainly across her pale cheek and gave her a cheating semblance of life. She sprawled in a strange, contorted snarl of limbs and wet garments, lying half on her back and half on her side, with her arms outflung to the uncaring sky. Her own ragged cape, a garment of the poorest and shabbiest kind, threadbare and patched and heavy with rain, had been thrown partially to one side as she fell. It had not given her much protection from the cold and rain when she had been alive, nor had the thin chemise that served her as a blouse, now soaked and clinging to her thin torso, nor the coarse-woven skirt, torn and muddy about the hem. Her feet, though not bare, wore "poor-man's boots" of thick stockings clumsily made of scraps of yarn salvaged and reknitted, and soled with leather likewise salvaged from some other article too worn to save. Harness-leather, Tal thought, judging from the wear spots on it; her feet were slim enough that pieces cut from a worn saddle-girth would be just wide enough to serve her as soles. Such make-do footgear wouldn't serve to protect from rain and not much from snow, but they would have served to keep the feet out of direct contact with frigid cobblestones.

Her instrument, a tambour-drum, lay a little way from her hand, skin-down in a puddle on the street where it had landed when she fell. It was a very cheap drum, quickly made, undecorated. A drum was the usual instrument of the poorest musicians because drums were the most inexpensive of all forms of music-maker. The rim was already warped by the rain; one of the cross-braces had popped out, and even the skin would be ruined by now. No longer useful, it was another piece of flotsam for the rag-pickers and scavengers, who would soon be quarreling over the rest of the girl's meager possessions.

She had been faintly pretty—would have been quite attractive, if poverty and hunger hadn't already left their marks on her in the form of bad teeth, a sallow complexion, and lank hair. The witnesses said she had a pleasant enough voice, but made up for all deficiencies of face and voice with a sunny, outgoing disposition. Unlike some, apparently she had never supplemented her street-singing with other sources of income; she'd never, at least in the course of cursory questioning of those who knew her, ever been known to sell herself as well as her songs. *She was too proud,* said one of the local stall-keepers who'd come to identify her body, a man who sold hot drinks and fried fish in the nearby fish-market where she made her usual stand. He'd meant that in the best possible sense and as a compliment, for the thin body beneath the threadbare clothing would only have attracted the attention of someone mistaking her for a preadolescent.

The cause of her death was obvious enough, even without the witness to the murder. Despite the rain, blood the color of black rubies still stained the front of her chemise and soaked into her skirt in a dark blotch; not just a stab-wound, a blow like this one told Tal a tale of rage, rage against the victim that a simple thrust of the knife could not purge. Her murderer had practically disemboweled her with a single stroke.

And that simple fact just did not *fit.*

The stall-keeper had seen her murderer accost her; he'd even overheard a little of the conversation. The man had offered a job, spoken of a gathering of friends in one of the more reliable dockside taverns who wanted a bit of lively music, and had even mentioned another musician who had agreed to come. So far as the stall-keeper knew, he was a stranger to this part of the docks; the girl had spent the last year or more at the corner in front of the stall-keeper's stand, and the fellow swore he'd never seen the man before today. Nor had the girl herself shown any sign of recognition when he'd spoken to her.

A piece that doesn't fit. This murderer was a stranger, by the accounts, and bloody work of this level of savagery only came from the desperate power of a wounded animal, or the rage of someone formerly close to the victim. How could a stranger have built up such a terrible anger against the girl? That level of anger needed reasons, and a long and careful nurturing, both of which required previous acquaintance.

The stall-keeper was somewhat in shock and hadn't been able to throw any light of knowledge on this terrible situation.

Nor could the single witness to the murder itself, a boy of about nine who sat a few yards away, shivering in the shelter of his mother's tavern—the one to which the girl had allegedly been invited—so traumatized he was barely able to speak. He rocked back and forth slowly with his arms wrapped around his thin torso. The boy only knew what he'd already told Tal; that the girl had been walking alongside a man as the boy waited outside the tavern for the bread-baker to make his delivery. The man had stopped and pointed to something on the river; the girl had turned to look. While she was distracted, the man had taken his knife from a sheath at his belt.

Then with no warning at all, the man stabbed her viciously, ripping upward with such force that he lifted her off the ground, caught on the cross-guard of his blade. His fist drove all the air from her lungs in a great, choking gasp, leaving her unable to cry out. Not that it would have done her any good, for she bled her life away too quickly for help to arrive. The boy had been completely paralyzed with shock and terror, able only to shrink back into the shadows in hopes that he had not been noticed, and certain he was about to be murdered on his own doorstep. That instinctive reaction might indeed have saved his life.

The man had shaken the girl off the knife *as if he was shaking off a bit of fish-gut.* That was the analogy the boy used, and it looked apt judging by the way the girl had fallen. She hadn't been dead when she hit the pavement, but she was dying. She'd made a single abortive attempt to rise, one hand clutching the wound in her stomach, before she fell back again, and died in a gush of blood.

The man had ignored her, just as if he didn't realize he had just murdered someone. He had looked around, his face frozen in what the witness said was "a horrible look." Tal wished he knew just what that "horrible look" was; the expression might have given him more clues.

Then the man had dropped the knife casually beside the body, walked straight to the edge of the dock, and kept going, falling right into the Kanar River. The current was powerful here and the water cold and deep. Not even a strong swimmer would survive long, and Tal expected to hear that they'd pulled the murderer's body out of the shallows by morning.

That was the point at which the boy had run for his mother, who had sent the tavern's peace-keeper for the constables rather than going out and investigating herself. You didn't live long in the wharf-district by throwing yourself into the darkness after a murderer. She and her son had stayed safely in the tavern until the constables arrived.

The witness had been very clear on one thing that had Tal very puzzled: the murderer had dropped the knife beside the body. Between his cursory examination and the witness's description, Tal judged that it was a very unusual knife, three-sided, like an ice-pick or a stiletto, with a prominent hilt. And here was the last of the pieces that did not fit, for the knife was gone. If someone had rifled the body in the time it had taken the boy to run to his mother, and his mother to get the constables, then why was the clothing completely undisturbed and why was the girl's meager pouch of coins still on her belt? Why steal a knife, especially one that had been used in a murder?

That was the real question; for most people, even the most hardened dock-rat, the idea of merely touching such a weapon would be terrifying. There was a superstition about such knives; that a blade that had once tasted a life would hunger for more, driving the unfortunate owner to more murders or to suicide.

All of these things were small, but they added up to a disruption of the pattern that should have been there, familiar and inescapable. But there was a pattern this case *did* fit: a series of four similarly horrific murders that had taken place over the past six months. All of the victims were women, all were poor, all were street-entertainers, and all were murdered between midnight and dawn.

All had been killed with a similar, triangular-bladed knife, and presumably all had been murdered for some reason other than money. He could not be sure of that last, because this was the first such murder to have a witness.

Three of the cases had been marked as solved. Two of the murderers had committed suicide on the spot, even before their victims were actually dead, and one murder was attributed to a man who'd been picked up the next day, raving and covered with blood, and quite mad. All of the women had lived alone, without lovers, husbands or children, in small coffin-like basement or attic rooms in tenement houses, rooms too small for a normal-sized man to lie down in. They owned little more than the clothing they stood up in, a rude pallet to sleep on, and their instruments. They eked out a precarious existence, balancing rent against food in a desperate juggling act played out day after day without respite.

They were like hundreds, thousands of others in the city, yet in this they were different. They had not died of cold, disease, or starvation; someone had murdered them, and Tal was convinced that there was more to these murders than simple random violence. There was suspicion of sorcery and enchantment being involved—there always was such talk around murders, more from superstition than actual suspicion. While he had seen the evidence of magic often enough, from the legerdemain of street tricksters to the awe-inspiring, palpable auras of "high magic," he preferred to look for more conventional explanations than the supernatural. Tal believed that it was wisest to look for the answers that came from what normal people could devise, afford, and enact, and kept his deductive powers "clean" since it was all too convenient to chalk up uncomfortable mysteries to dark forces.

"Tal, it's time to go." The words, uttered, he now realized, for the third time, finally penetrated his consciousness. He looked up, to gaze into the weary and cynical eyes of Jeris Vane, the constable who shared night-duty in this district with him.

"You aren't going to learn anything we don't already know," Jeris said, as if explaining something to a brain-damaged child, "We have a murderer, and he's already taken his punishment into his own hands. The case is closed. Let's go back to the station, fill out our reports, and make it official."

Tal shook his head stubbornly, holding up his lantern to illuminate Jeris's face. "There's something about this that's just not right," he replied, and saw Jeris's mouth tighten into a thin, hard line. "I know it *looks* cut and dried—"

"That's because it is," Jeris snapped, water dripping off his hat brim as he spoke. "There's no reason to pursue this any further. We have what we need—one victim, one criminal, one witness, one suicide, end of question."

"But why would—"

Jeris interrupted him again. "*Why* is not your job, or mine, or any other constable's. *What* and *who,* maybe, but not *why.* We don't worry about the reasons people do things. We catch them, and after we do, we hand them over to the Justiciars, the gaolers, and the executioners. Worrying about things that are not part of your job will only bring you trouble. I'll be at the station when you decide to straggle in from meddling in things that aren't your business."

With that, the unpleasant man turned, and splashed up the rain-slick cobbles towards the district station, leaving the scavengers to do their work. For a moment more, Tal hesitated, hoping he could glean just that tiny bit more information from the scene.

But he wouldn't, and in his heart he knew it. Even if he brought in a mage, at this point, the mage would learn nothing. Rain was running water, and running water washed away magic. Just as in the other four cases, which had all taken place on rainy nights (as if there was anything other than a rainy night this time of year!) there would be no trace of anything magical on or about this body.

That was one more thing that didn't make sense about any of these murders. People weren't murdered in the street on rainy nights, they were killed at home, or in rooming houses, inns, or brothels, where it was dry and at least a bit warmer than on the street—or they were killed in taverns and public houses, where it was dry and the chill made people drink more than they had intended to. But no one picked a victim, then took her out into the pouring rain to kill her. This was another odd circumstance that linked all five of these cases.

There was something very wrong here, and he wanted very badly to find out what it was before any more women were murdered.

He hesitated a moment longer, then followed Jeris back to the station. Perhaps by now they would have found the body of the murderer, and he would learn something more.

The rain showed no signs of letting up, and would likely continue until dawn. Rain, rather than snow, was the dominant winter weather pattern in Haldene, and there were some who longed for snow instead. Tal didn't; granted, snow did make it easier for a night-constable to do his job, for with a layer of snow on the ground, nights were brighter, and fresh snow made it possible to track a night-criminal in the less-trafficked parts of the city. Even if he got into an area where there was a great deal of activity at night, if he'd left prints in the snow, a constable could look for soles that matched those prints. Nevertheless, Tal didn't care for snow any more than he did rain.

What I would like would be to have a dry winter instead of a wet one—a winter where no rain fell until spring.

He lengthened his steps to catch up with Jeris without losing his dignity and running. It was foolish, but a great deal of status within the ranks of the constables depended on appearances.

"You called for the wagon?" Jeris asked, as Tal came up to him.

"Right after the woman sent for the constables and I responded," he replied—and as if to prove that he had done his job, the body-wagon rattled around the corner ahead of them, heading their way. The wheels rumbled on the cobblestones, and the cart itself rattled as the uneven surface jarred every separate board and bit of hardware. Those were the only noises it made; the pony hauling it, its rain-slick hide a mottled dark-on-dark, never made a sound, and the wooden horseshoes it wore were muffled (as per city ordinance for horses at night) by leather boots tied over the hooves. The driver, enwrapped in his regulation black-hooded cloak, spoke not a word as he drove past them. In a few more moments, the girl's body would be ingloriously tossed into the back of the cart, covered with a black-dyed bit of canvas, and taken away to the city morgue which was operated by the Church. In weather this cold, they'd probably keep her there for a week, hoping for some friend or relative to step forward, claim the body, and pay for the burial. At some point, however, they would give up, and with reluctance and scant ceremony, drop her pitiful remains into a shallow, unmarked paupers' grave in Church grounds at the Church's expense. As a murder victim, and not a suicide—and in default of any evidence that she was *not* a loyal daughter of the Church—she was the Church's responsibility. The only paupers that the Church was not responsible for were nonhumans, suicides, pagans, heathen, and heretics—all of *those* placed themselves out of Church hands by their beliefs or actions. If no relatives came to claim them, the city would dispose of them in Potter's Field, in the pits left after clay was dug up.

This assumed, however, that the medical college didn't need a subject for dissection. In that case, a priest would bless the body and hand it over, and the girl might have a real marked grave, although the bits and pieces that had once been a human being would not be reassembled before burial. It would be the medical college's job to pay for that burial and, to do them credit, *they* did not skimp on ceremony or expense.

In either case, he doubted that it would matter to her. She was done with the envelope of flesh, and what became of it could not concern her anymore, outside of a haunting. But assuming that there *was* something beyond that envelope—and assuming she had any reason to be concerned with anything in the "here and now" anymore—surely her only concern would be revenge. Or justice; there was a fine line between the two that tended to blur in most folks' minds, including Tal's. He was not convinced that she had or ever would have either revenge or justice, even if someone pulled up the body of the man who had killed her in the next few moments.

On those other four occasions of the past several weeks, someone had written "case closed" after a murdered woman's name because her killer had slain himself. And in a few more days or weeks, another woman had died in circumstances that were all too similar to the previous, supposedly-closed case. Either there was a sudden rash of murder-suicides going on in this city, or there was something very wrong with the deductions of the city constables.

"You're asking too many questions, Tal," Jeris said, as the wagon passed by. "The Captain doesn't like it. You're taking up too much time with this obsession of yours."

"Too much time?" He felt as if he should be angry, but he was too tired for anger. He weighed his next words down with heavy contempt. "Since when are *you* concerned with my private interests? Most of this has been on my own time, Jeris. The last time I looked, what I did with my own time, whether it was bead-work, plowing, or criminal investigation, was no one's business but my own."

Jeris grunted scornfully. "Charming hobby you have, Tal, and frankly, I don't give a rat's ass what you do on your time off. The only problem is that you've cooked up some half-crazed idea that there's a force out there, walking the night and murdering women. Even that would be all right if you kept it to yourself, but you can't do that, can you? You have to tell every gypsy bitch and street whore you meet why she should be more careful at night, as if a few stupid cows more or less in this town would make any difference to anyone."

Now anger did stir in him, dull and sullen, smoldering under a heavy weight of sheer exhaustion. It had been a long night before this happened, and the end wasn't in sight. Jeris's arrogance made him want to give the man a lesson in humility—and in how it felt to be the one under the hammer. "So far, there've been five murder victims that look enough alike to make anyone with a brain think twice about them. These murders are too damned similar to be coincidental, and these murders *don't* fit the patterns of anything I've ever seen before, not in twenty years as a constable. Just for one moment, why don't you play along with me and pretend I'm right? Don't the women who have to be out in the street to make a living deserve to be warned of danger?"

A sudden gust of wind blew rain into their faces. "They're street-trash, Tal," Jeris replied crudely, never once slowing down to look at him, just pulling the brim of his hat down over his face. "Anybody out on the street at night instead of decently home where she belongs is out looking for trouble. Try getting it through your head that scum doesn't deserve anything. They aren't worth considering, but decent, tax-paying citizens are beginning to get wind of your stupid idea, and they're getting nervous. The higher-ups don't like it when citizens get the idea that there's something dangerous on the street that the constables can't stop."

Tal's anger burned in the pit of his stomach, warming him more efficiently than his sodden cloak, but he knew better than to make a retort. Jeris was a boot-licker, but as such, he had the ear of the Captain, with an eye to making himself—Jeris-the-upstart—look better. Jeris had only been a constable for four years to Tal's twenty, but he was already Tal's equal in rank and probably his superior in advancement prospects because of his lack of personal modesty and his artistically applied hostility. Ordinarily, Tal wouldn't have cared about that; he'd never wanted anything more than to be a good constable, maybe even the best if that was how things turned out, keeping the streets safe, solving the cases that were less than straightforward. But Jeris-the-toady, interested only in what the job could gain *him,* grated on Tal's nerves and enraged his sense of decency. This was not the least because Jeris represented not only everything Tal found despicable in the city constables, but also precisely the kind of constable who would advance through ambition and eventually become Tal's superior in rank. Captain Rayburn was exactly like Jeris—and when Rayburn gave up the job, no doubt Jeris would be promoted into it.

So Jeris was only reflecting the sentiments of Those In Charge; "street-trash" didn't matter. Forget that those who Jeris and Rayburn styled "street-trash" were also tax-paying citizens; Rayburn would dismiss that simple truth with an unverifiable allegation that everyone knew that the "street-trash" cheated to avoid paying their taxes and so did not warrant service.

As if the "good citizens of Haldene" that Rayburn favored never did anything of the sort! How did he think some of them *got* their fortunes?

That didn't matter; really, nothing was going to make any difference to the Rayburns and Jerises of this world. The real fact was that the underdogs of the city had no power in the politics and policies of the city, and never would, and for that reason, Rayburn and his ilk discarded and discounted them, always had, and always would.

Tal slowed his steps deliberately, allowing Jeris to splash on ahead. Let Jeris, the ambitious, be the one to file the initial report. Let him get the "credit" for the case. Tal would file a second report, and he would see if Jeris could find a way to explain the missing murder-weapon, or the myriad of discrepancies and illogics in the story.

Then again, it probably wouldn't matter if he couldn't. This was just another inconvenient blot on the record, an "unfortunate incident" that no one would bother to pursue any further. Neither the victim nor the murderer were of any importance to anyone who mattered, and thus it would be simpler and easier for the authorities to ignore everything connected with them.

That realization—or rather, the final acceptance of something he had known in his heart of hearts—sickened him. If he had not been so weary, he would have been tempted to turn in his baton, badge, and braids as soon as he reached the station and find some other job in the morning, perhaps as a private guard for one of the wealthy merchants.

But he *was* tired; his head ached, his joints complained, his stomach was knotted into a burning ball, and the only thing he could really muster any enthusiasm for was the fact that his shift would be over in an hour or two and for half a day he would no longer have to tolerate Jeris and his ilk. In fact, by the time he reached the station, made out his report, and did the follow-up with the searchers at the river, it would probably be time to stop for the day.

He plodded on, head down for many reasons, through the cold wind and intermittent rain, and because he had deliberately lagged behind Jeris, when he arrived at the station he discovered that the other constable had already commandeered the single clerk on duty at this time of night. That meant Tal would have to write out his own report, instead of dictating it to the clerk.

One more miserable item in the long list of the evening's miseries. The station, a cramped, narrow building, three stories high with a basement lockup for violent cases, was unusually busy for a cold and rainy night. The waiting room was full, and the sergeant at the desk looked as haggard as Tal felt.

For a moment, he simply leaned against the wall and let the warmth and babble wash over him. With oil lamps along the walls and a small crowd pressed together on the benches, there was enough heat being generated to make up for the fact that one of the two stoves supposed to heat the place was cold. This was the Captain's idea, a means to economize during the hours that Rayburn was not on duty, and never mind that there were other people who were forced to shiver through the coldest hours of the night due to his economies. This was the only part of the building that the general public ever saw, but it was enough to make them nervous. No one ever came to the station who was not forced to.

The first story consisted of one main room and several smaller offices and the ward-room behind them all. The main room had a half dozen benches arranged in front of a desk; at the desk sat the Duty-Sergeant, and on the benches were ranged a variety of folk who either had complaints that needed a constable's attention, or were here to see about getting someone out of the general lockup on the second floor where drunks and minor troublemakers landed. They were the source of the nervous babble, and unfortunately, also of a variety of odors, none of them pleasant. Sweat, dirt, garlic, wet wool, beer, and wet rawhide; bad breath and flatulence; and a hint of very cheap perfume from the one or two whores waiting to register complaints—the people who came here at night were not among the city's elite by any stretch of the imagination, and they brought the "atmosphere" of their lives with them. Judging by the crowd out front, the offices were probably all full, either of constables interviewing witnesses or constables interviewing people with complaints. More accurately, given the attitude of the night watch, the truth was closer to *enduring* than *interviewing*.

The second floor was divided into the general lockup—a temporary holding area for drunks, vagrants, general "undesirables," and as many participants in a fight as could be rounded up—and a second ward-room. Third floor held the records. It would be quieter up there, but much colder. There was a clerk in the records-room by day who refused to work if the stove wasn't fired up, but there was no one to keep it stoked at night, and no one cared if the prisoners in the lockup were comfortable.

The harried Sergeant barely acknowledged Tal's presence as the latter entered and saluted. Since he was dealing with three different arguing parties all at the same time, Tal didn't blame him. Instead, he went in search of pen and paper to make his report, and a relatively quiet corner to write it in.

When he finally found both in the ward-room his headache was much worse and his jaw ached—and he realized to his chagrin he'd had it clenched tight ever since Jeris started in on him. It was enough to give him a deep throbbing at the root of his teeth, which faded slowly as intermittent shocks of pain until only a background discomfort remained.

By that time, the Sergeant had managed to throw out all three of the contending parties, which had cleared the waiting room considerably. While he'd been searching for writing materials, Jeris had finished his report. The Sergeant gave him a look at it, and as Tal had suspected, no mention was made of a missing murder-weapon or even that the weapon had been something other than the usual belt-knife.

He went up to the third floor in search of quiet. With his fingers stiffening in the cold, Tal rectified those omissions, wishing a similar headache and bout of indigestion on Jeris, who, according to the Sergeant, had chosen to go off shift early once his report had been written.

When he came back down, with his stack of closely written papers in hand, the Sergeant waved him over to the desk.

"The riverside search-team come in, Tal," he said with a gleam in his red-rimmed eyes. "They found the body of a man they figger was the murderer. What's more, they know who 'twas."

He handed the new report, a short one, to Tal, who read it quickly, his eyebrows rising as he did. The body certainly fit the description that the boy had given, and he had been identified almost as soon as he had been pulled from the water by a most extraordinary chain of coincidences.

Both the discovery of the body and the identification were exceedingly fortunate for Tal, if not for the prospects of turning in *his* shift early, for he had not expected the body to turn up until it floated by itself. But as luck would have it, a barge had gotten torn from its moorings this afternoon before he arrived for his shift; it had run up against a bridge-pier downstream, then sunk. Now the usual scavengers were out in force on the water with all manner of implements designed to pull cargo out of the water. One of the scavengers had netted the body and brought it up. As it happened, several of the river-rats had recognized who it was immediately, though they had no idea that the man had murdered a girl before drowning himself.

So now Tal had his identification, and the search-crew had happily retired from the scene, their job completed.

The Desk-Sergeant had the particulars. The murderer had been the owner of a shabby shop in Jeris's district, who made a living buying and selling secondhand goods. The scavengers had sold their pickings to him more than once, and knew him not only by sight, but by habits—and the one who had pulled him out was actually in the station waiting to be interviewed.

Although Jeris had officially declared himself off-duty, the Sergeant noted (with a sly smile) that he was still proclaiming his genius in the second-floor ward-room to the clerk and anyone else who would listen. "The boy come to witness wants out of here," the Sergeant said. "He's not likely to wait much longer." He did not offer to send someone after Jeris.

The Sergeant was as old a veteran as Tal, and with just about as little patience for boot-lickers. They both knew that since the shopkeeper was from Jeris's district, it would look very bad if someone else took the report because Jeris had gone off-duty early and had not bothered to check back at the desk.

"Any sign of Jeris checking back in, then?" Tal asked.

The Sergeant shook his head. "Not that it's *your* job—"

"No," Tal replied, deciding to get subtle revenge by grabbing the interview for his own report—which was, without a doubt, what the Sergeant had in mind. "But a good constable concentrates on the case, not the petty details of whose district the witnesses and victims come from."

"That's the truth," the Sergeant agreed. "Your witness is in the fourth crib along, right-hand side."

Tal collected more paper, left his initial report with the Sergeant, and found the man waiting patiently in one of the tiny cubicles in the maze of offices and interview-rooms in the back half of the first floor.

There were oil lamps here as well, and it was decently warm at least. Maybe too warm; as Tal sat down behind the tiny excuse for a desk at the back end of the room, he caught himself yawning and suppressed it.

He had brought with him a steaming cup of the evil brew that was always kept seething in a pot on another pocket-sized stove in the first cubicle. Allegedly, it was tea, though Tal had never encountered its like under that name anywhere else. It was as black as forbidden lust, bitter as an old whore, and required vast amounts of cream and whatever sweetener one could lay hands on to make it marginally palatable, but it did have the virtue of keeping the drinker awake under any and all possible circumstances.

The witness had evidently been offered a cup of this potent concoction, for it stood, cooling and barely touched, on the floor beside his chair. Tal didn't blame him for leaving it there; it was nothing to inflict on the unprepared and unprotected, and offering it to a citizen came very close to betraying the Constables' Oath to guard innocent people from harm. He just hoped it wouldn't eat its way through the bottom of the cup and start in on the floor, since he'd be held responsible.

"I understand you and some of your friends located the body of a man who drowned?" he said as he slowly dropped down in the chair, after setting his cup on the table within reach of his right hand. "Can you tell me how that came about?"

The young man, lean and sallow, with a rather pathetic excuse for a beard and mustache coming in, nodded vigorously. "We been salvagin', an' I hooked 'im. Knowed 'im right off. Milas Losis, 'im as got the secondhand story on Lily, just off Long, in the Ware Quarter."

Tal nodded; so the murderer had not even come from the same quarter as the victim, although Wharf and Ware were next to each other and in this district. Still, Lily Street was a considerable distance away from Edgewater, where the girl had made her usual stand. And more significantly, Edgewater held nothing to interest a dealer in second-hand goods, being the main street of the fish-market. With luck, this boy would know a bit about Milas Losis.

"Did Milas Losis have any reason to want to do away with himself?" he asked.

The boy shook his head. "Hard t' tell about some of these old geezers, but not as I think. Shop was doin' all right, old man had no family to worry about, an' never had no reason t' want one. Useta make fun of us that came in and talked about our girls—told us *he'd* be laughin', and free in a brace of years, an' *we'd* be slavin' to take care of a naggin' wife and three bawlin' brats, an' wishin we was him." The young man shrugged. "On'y thing he ever cared for was chess. He'd play anybody. Tha's it."

And I doubt that the girl was one of his chess partners. "Did he ever show any interest in music?" Tal persisted. "In musicians? In female musicians? In women at all?"

To each of these questions, the boy shook his head, looking quite surprised. "Nay—" he said finally. "Like I said, on'y thing he ever seemed to care for was his chess games, an' his chess-friends. He could care less 'bout music, 'e was half deaf. An' about wimmin—I dunno, but I never saw 'im with one, and there wasn't much in 'is shop a woman'd care for."

After more such fruitless questioning, Tal let the youngster go. The boy was quite impatient to be off doing something more profitable than sitting in the constable-station, and only pressure from the team searching for the body had induced him to come here at all. There were a few more hours of "fishing" he could get in before traffic on the river got so heavy that he would legally have to stop to allow day-commerce right-of-way and pull his little flat-bottomed salvage-boat in to the bank until night. He had money to make, and no reason to think that Milas had been the victim of anything other than an accident or at worst, a robbery gone wrong.

Tal sat at the tiny desk, staring at his notes for a moment, then decided to go prowling in the records-room again. This was a good time to go poking through the records, for during the day, the clerk defended them as savagely as a guard-dog, allowing access to them with the greatest of reluctance.

He took his notes with him, since the records-room was as good a place as any to write his addition to the report. Besides, now that he officially had the identity of the murderer, he wanted to check the file on current tax-cheats, debtors, heretics, and other suspected miscreants to see if Milas was among them. There was always the barest chance that the girl was a blackmailer who'd found something out about him that could ruin him. Not *likely*, but best to eliminate the possibility immediately, and leave Jeris no opportunity for speculation.

As he had expected, the old shopkeeper's records were clean. From the complete lack of paper on him, it would seem that this murderer had, up until this very night, led an amazingly boring life. There wasn't a file on him, as there would have been if he had ever been noticed during a surveillance or a raid on an illegal or quasi-legal establishment.

Interesting.

So, once again, he had the same pattern. The perpetrator was perfectly normal, with no previous record of violent or antisocial behavior, and no indication that he was under undue stress. He had no interest in weapons, music, or musicians, and none in women—and no obvious *dislike* of these things, either. He had no record of interests outside his shop except for chess.

In short, he had led an utterly blameless and bland existence, until the moment that he pulled out a knife and used it on the girl. He even had a perfectly good reason to have an odd knife; anyone who owned a secondhand shop would get all kinds of bizarre weapons in over the course of time.

Maybe I'm going about this wrong. Maybe I should be concentrating on the missing knife. It seems to be the one thing that ties all these cases together.

Very well, then; it was an unusually long knife, with a strange, triangular blade, a bit longer than a stiletto. Tal *had* seen knives like that, very occasionally, as part of the altar-furniture during certain holy days. No one ever touched the knives during the service, and they were evidently the remnants of some earlier, older ceremony. Tal was not particularly religious, but one couldn't help picking up a certain amount of religious indoctrination when one was in school, since the schools were all taught by Priests. He'd had the knack even then for putting things together that other people didn't particularly want put together, and his guess was that the knives were from an old, pagan ceremony of sacrifice that the Church had coopted and turned into a holy day. Good idea, that—if people were going to celebrate something, make them celebrate *your* ceremony. Keep them in the Church all day so they can't go out and get up to an unsanctified frolic in the woods and fields. . . .

Tal sat back in his chair for a moment, thinking about that. Perhaps it was the late hour, but his imagination, normally held in check, began to paint wild pictures for him.

Some of the more lurid tales that had given him goose-bumps as an adolescent rose up out of memory to confront him with bizarre possibilities. What if some of the knives in Church regalia were the *original* sacrificial knives of an unholy, blood-drenched ritual out of the ancient past? What if this one was one of those knives, one of the cursed blades out of legends, craving blood now that it was out of the safe hands of the Church magicians? Could it be taking over the murderers somehow, and forcing them to use it so that it could drink its fill of blood and lives as it used to do?

But why pick musicians as targets? And most importantly, where did it go when it wasn't killing someone?

More to the point, have I got the chance of a snowball in a bakery oven of convincing the Captain that a knife with a curse on it is going around killing people?

Not likely. Captain Rayburn believed wholeheartedly in magic, but in magic of the practical kind. Cursed weapons were a matter of legend, and not something to be found lying about in this city.

What do I have for proof? A handful of men who killed for no apparent reason, who all used, if not the same knife, a very similar knife. They all murdered women, who were also street-entertainers. Rationally, even I have to admit that killing entertainers could be nothing more than a matter of convenience and coincidence. The only woman who is likely to go off with a stranger is going to be either a whore or an entertainer, and of the two professions, a whore is going to be more suspicious than an entertainer. Finally, the murder weapon always vanishes, and the murderer often commits suicide.

Not a lot of "proof" for anything, and no proof whatsoever for the notion of a knife with a mind and will of its own.

Stupid idea. I must be getting light-headed from lack of sleep.

What were the possibilities that fit this particular pattern? The *reasonable* possibilities that is, not some tale-teller's extravaganza. The religious angle *did* have possibilities—a cult of some kind was actually possible. People would do some very strange things in the name of religious belief, including commit murder and suicide. Odd cults sprang up in the Twenty Kingdoms from time to time, and most of them were rightfully secretive about their practices and membership. The Church did its best to wipe out every trace of such cults once Church officials got wind of them, either directly or by threat of Holy Wrath. And while the latter might not impress anyone not born and steeped in the fear of the Sacrificed God, practically speaking, since every law-enforcement official in the Twenty Human Kingdoms was likely to be a loyal son of the Church, there was secular wrath to deal with as well as Holy Wrath.

That's a dangerous suggestion to make, though. Politically sensitive. It wasn't that long ago that there were people saying nonhumans were demonic, and accusing them of this kind of bloodletting. Claim that there are humans going around doing the same thing—Captain isn't going to like it if that comes up again.

Still, it was the most feasible and would explain the disappearance of the murder weapon, or weapons. Other members of the cult could be watching the murderer, waiting for him to act, then nipping in and stealing the ritual dagger when he was done.

That's more reasonable than a dagger with a curse on it. I'm more likely to get the Captain to believe that one, even if he doesn't much like it. I don't like it, though; what if he decides that it's nonhumans who've somehow seduced humans into their cult?

Another outside possibility was that there was a slowly spreading disease that drove its victim to madness, murder, and suicide. People who went mad often had a mania about certain kinds of objects or whatnot. He personally knew an account of a hatter who went about trying to bludgeon redheads, for instance—and that could explain why all the victims were musicians. Maybe the disease made it painful to listen to music!

But in that case, why were they all killed with the same kind of weapon, and where did it go afterwards?

His death-black tea grew cold, as his thoughts circled one another, always coming back to the mysterious, vanishing daggers.

Until tonight, there had been the possibility that the women were being marked by the same person, who also murdered men, possibly witnesses, to make the crimes look like murder-suicides. That possibility had been eliminated tonight by the presence of a witness who had not been detected.

Lastly, of course, it was possible that Jeris and the Captain were right. There was no connection; these were all acts of random violence.

But there were too many things that just didn't add up. There had to be a connection. All of his years of experience told him that there was a connection.

His resolution hardened, and he clenched his jaw. *I'm going to solve this one. No matter how long it takes, no matter what it costs.* For a moment, the anger and his resolution held him. Then he looked down at the papers on the desk and his cold tea, and snorted at his own thoughts.

Getting melodramatic in my old age.

Still . . . He picked up the pages of his second report and stood up.

Idiot. It's duty, that's what it is. Responsibility, which too damn few people around here ever bother to think about. I became a constable to make a difference; too many young asses these days do it for the uniform, or the chance to shove a few poor fools about. And the rest take up the baton as a quick road to a fat salary and a desk, and political preferment. Damn if I don't think Jeris did it for all three reasons!

He made his papers into a neat stack and carried them down to the Desk-Sergeant, who accepted them without the vaguest notion of the thoughts that were going through Tal's head. By now, it *was* quitting time; the constables for the next shift were coming in, and he could return to his two rooms at the Gray Rose, a hot meal, his warm bath and bed, and a dose of something that would kill his headache and let him sleep.

He could, and this time he would, for there was nothing more that he could learn for now.

He went out into the cold and rain with a sketchy salute to the Sergeant and the constables coming on duty. He hunched his shoulders against the rain and started for home.

But somewhere out in that darkness was something darker still; he sensed it, as surely as a hound picking up a familiar scent.

Whoever, whatever you are, he told that dark-in-the-darkness silently, *I will find you. And when I do, I will see to it you never walk free again. Never doubt it.*

The darkness did not answer. But then, it never did.

Chapter Two

There was no one waiting in the station as Tal came on duty two days later. Under other circumstances that might have been unusual, but not on this night. It wasn't rain coming down out of the sky, it was a stinging sleet that froze the moment it struck anything solid. The streets were coated thickly with it, and no one in his right mind was going to be out tonight. Tal had known when he left his rooms at the Gray Rose that this was going to be a foul shift. It had taken him half an hour to make the normally ten-minute walk between the inn and the station.

As a rare concession to the weather, both stoves were going in the waiting room. He stood just inside the door, and let the heat thaw him for a moment before stepping inside. *What got into the Captain? Charity?*

Before he left the inn, Tal had strapped a battered pair of ice-cleats on over his boots, and took a stout walking-stick with a spike in the end of it, the kind that was used by those with free time for hiking in winter in the mountains. Even so, he didn't intend to spend a moment more than he had to on his beat, and from the hum of voices in the back where the ward-room was, neither did anyone else. What was the point? There weren't going to be any housebreakers out on a night when they couldn't even carry away their loot without breaking their necks! Not even stray dogs or cats would venture out of shelter tonight. The constables would make three rounds of their beats at most, and not even that if the weather got any worse. A constable with a broken neck himself wouldn't be doing anybody any good.

The Desk-Sergeant crooked a finger at Tal as he took off his cloak and shook bits of thawing ice and water off it. Tal hung his cloak up on a peg and walked carefully across the scarred wooden floor to avoid catching a cleat in a crack. He couldn't possibly ruin the floor, not after decades of daily abuse and neglect.

"Got another mystery-killing this afternoon," the Sergeant said in a low, hoarse whisper once Tal was within earshot. "Or better say, murder-suicide, like the other ones you don't like. Want to see the report?"

Tal nodded, after a quick look around to be sure they were alone, and the Sergeant slipped a few pieces of paper across the desk to him.

Tal leaned on the desk as if he was talking intently with the Sergeant, and held the report just inside the crook of his elbow. In this position, he could read quickly, and if anyone came in unexpectedly he could start up a conversation with Sergeant Brock as if they'd been gossiping all along.

Brock wasn't supposed to pass reports along like this; they were supposed to be confidential, and for the eyes of the Captain only. Evidently Brock had gotten wind of Tal's interest, and had decided to give him an unofficial hand. Tal thought he knew why; he and Brock were both veterans, but Brock was considerably his senior, and would never get any higher than he was now. It would be almost impossible to discharge him, but his hopes of advancement were nil. He *could* have spent his time as a place-holder, and probably Rayburn expected him to do just that, but like Tal, Brock had unfashionable ideas about the duties and responsibilities of a constable.

And if someone tied a bag of rocks to the Captain's ankles and threw him in the river to drown him, we'd both consider it a fine public service, but a waste of good rocks.

Evidently, since Brock was no longer in the position to do any good out on the beat, he had decided to help out Tal, who was. And perhaps he was getting back at Captain Rayburn by offering tacit support of a "project" the Captain didn't approve of.

Somewhat to Tal's surprise, *this* murder had taken place at the very edge of the district, upstream, where the grain and hay-barges came in. Unlike this area of the docks, the barges were not towed by steam-boats nor sailed in; instead, they were pulled along the bank by teams of mules and horses. The presence of all those animals, plus the kinds of cargoes that came in there, gave the Grain-Wharf an entirely different atmosphere than this end of town, more like that of the inland farm-market. Tal didn't know the day-constable on that beat, but from the tone of the report, he was competent at least.

The Grain-Wharf played host to a completely different cross-section of workers than the down-river docks as well; a peculiar mingling of farmers and barge-drivers, stock-men, grain-merchants, and river-sailors. In some ways, it was a more dangerous place; grifters and sharpsters of all kinds and avocations were thick there, waiting to prey on naïve farm-boys just down to see the town. But there were businesses there you wouldn't expect to find on the waterfront, to serve the many interests that converged there.

Blacksmiths, for instance.

For the first time, the murderer was a plain craftsman, a Guild man. Even the secondhand store owner had been operating on the fringes of society, buying and selling things that, if not stolen, were certainly obtained through odd channels. This man had been one of Captain Rayburn's "honest taxpayers," though his victim had not. Perhaps *this* would get Rayburn's attention.

Tal read the report quickly, grateful that the author had a gift for being succinct—given the paucity of actual detail, there were constables who would have padded the text shamelessly, since a thin report could be construed as lax performance that pure word count might disguise. This time, though, there really hadn't been much to report; there were no witnesses to the murder, though there were plenty who had rushed into the smithy at the first cry, including the smith's two apprentices. By then, of course, it was too late.

This was the first murder, at least to Tal's knowledge, that had taken place in broad daylight, but it might as well have been in the middle of the night. It had occurred in the smith's back-court, where his wood and charcoal were stored; the court was open to the sky, but otherwise completely secluded. The victim was a known whore—a freelance, and not a member of the Guild or a House. Her official profession was "dancer."

But there's a tamborine and a set of bones listed among her effects, which means she had at least pretended to be a musician. There's the musical link again.

The smith had actually killed her with a single stab of a long, slender knife with a triangular blade—

There it is again!

—but this time, the victim was beaten unconscious first, and rather cut up before she died. She must have taken a long time to die, at least an hour or so. No one had heard any of this, probably because anyone who *might* have noticed the sound of blows would assume that one of the apprentices was chopping wood. Rain had been pouring down all day—

Again.

—and as dusk neared, it was just turning to ice. The smith had finished with the knife the job he had begun with his fists, and then went into the smithy, picked up a pitchfork he'd been asked to mend, took it back out into the court, braced it in a pile of wood, and ran himself up onto it.

He'd screamed as he did so, and that was the sound that had brought the apprentices and neighbors running. But he'd done a good job of killing himself; he hit numerous vital spots with the tines, and by the time they arrived, he was dead, and so was the girl.

There was the expected panic and running about before someone thought to summon the law. The knife was missing by the time the law arrived, a fact that the constable in charge carefully noted. This fellow was competent and thorough, giving the case his full attention. He stayed for several hours questioning those who had been at the scene about the missing blade. He'd even had the apprentices searching the entire smithy for the missing knife, and had ordered them to take the wood and charcoal out piece by piece until they either found it or had determined that it *was* gone.

Good for him!

Tal handed the report back to Sergeant Brock, who tipped him a wink. "I know you're a-mindful of this sort of affair. It's the sort o' thing a *good* law-man would find odd. Bodies are at the morgue," he whispered as he slipped the report back inside his desk. "And I've *heard* there's something peculiar about one of them." He shrugged. "Night like this, no Priest is likely to sit about minding corpses."

Tal nodded his thanks, and went back to the ward-room to see if there was anything in the way of orders at his locker. He didn't expect anything—the weather had been so miserable all day that it wasn't likely the Captain had bothered to stir from his own comfortable house just for the purpose of appearing in his place at the station. When he made his way past all the tiny cubicles and entered the ward-room, he found his assumption was correct.

The stove back here had another cheerful fire in it, and the desultory comments of those going off-shift told him that the Captain had indeed sent word by a servant that if he was needed he could be found at home today. No wonder all the stoves were fired up—the Captain wasn't here to economize!

Nice to be able to work from home when the mood hits, he thought sourly, for Captain Moren, Captain Rayburn's predecessor, had spent most of his waking hours at his post, and the only time weather had ever kept him away from the station was the ice-storm of the year he died. Even then, he'd actually set out for the station, and it was only the urging of the constables that knew his ways and came to persuade him to turn back that prevented him from trying to reach his appointed place.

But Tal kept those words behind his teeth; you never knew who was listening. "Anything I should know about?" he asked the constable he was relieving.

"Not a thing; nobody wants to move outside in slop like this," the man said, holding his hands over the stove. "I looked in on a couple folk I thought might be in trouble down by the docks, but they've got smarter since the last storm; families are moving in together to share fuel." He laughed sardonically. " 'Course, with twelve people packed in a room, they don't need much fuel to warm the place up. Even the joy-girls have doubled up until the weather turns. I guess they figure they might as well, since there won't be any customers out tonight, or maybe they think they'll get a tip to split if they're two at once, hey?"

Tal shrugged; there wasn't much he could say. Except that at least now some of those women he feared were in jeopardy would no longer be *alone,* not for the duration of this cold snap, anyway. And for tonight, at least, none of them would be on the street.

But the last one wasn't taken on the street, was she? I wonder what she was doing there; the girls who pose as street-singers don't usually visit blacksmiths. Futile to speculate; he could find out for himself, tomorrow. That was his day off, and he would be free to invade any beat he chose to.

Tonight he would take advantage of the storm to go a little out of his area and visit the Church morgue. Technically, there should be a Priest there at all hours, praying for the repose of the dead and the forgiveness of their sins—but as Sergeant Brock had pointed out, in weather like this, it wasn't at all likely that anyone would be there. The dead-cart couldn't go out in an ice-storm, for the pony might slip and break a leg, and no amount of roughing his shoes would keep him safe on cobblestones that were under a coating of ice an inch thick. So there was no reason for the Priest in charge of the morgue to stir out of his cozy cell, for he could pray for the souls of those laid out on the stone slabs just as well from there as in the icy morgue. If his conscience truly bothered him, he could always take his praying to the relative discomfort and chill of the chapel.

So Tal would be able to examine the bodies at his leisure, and see what, if anything, was true about the story the Desk-Sergeant had heard, that there was something strange about one of the bodies.

He got his uniform cape out of his locker, and layered it on beneath the waxed-canvas cape. His baton slid into the holster at his belt, his dagger beside it, his short-sword balancing the weight on the other side. Beneath the weight of his wool tunic and breeches, knitted shirt and hose, and two capes, he was starting to sweat—better get out before he got too warm and killed himself with shock, walking into the ice-storm.

He took his spiked staff in hand and clumped slowly back out, saluting Sergeant Brock as he headed for the door to the street. There was a constable at the front entrance handing out the storm-lanterns; he took one gratefully and hung it on the hook in the end of his staff. It wasn't much, but on a night like tonight, every tiny bit of light would help, and if his hands got too cold, he could warm them at the lantern.

He opened the door and stepped into the street. There wasn't much wind, but the pelting sleet struck him in the face with a chill that made up for the lack of wind. He bent his head to it, and told himself it could be worse. *It could be hail,* he reminded himself.

But it was hard to think of how anything could be worse than this; ice so thick that if he had not been wise enough to strap on those metal ice-cleats, he'd have broken an arm or his neck in the first few paces, and cold fierce enough to drive every living thing from the street tonight. It would be a bad night for taverns and families with an abusive member; no one would be going out for a drink, and people with bad tempers didn't take being cooped up well. More often than not, the abuser would take out everything on people who could not run out of doors to escape him. A colicky baby that wouldn't stop crying, a child with a cough that couldn't be soothed, or a woman with the bad luck to say the wrong thing at the wrong time—the triggers were many, but the results were all depressingly the same. There would probably be a few—children mostly—beaten to death before morning. Nights like this one brought out the worst in some people, as the inability to *get away* set tempers and nerves on edge.

Try not to think about it. There's nothing you can do to prevent any of what's coming tonight. You'd have to have a million eyes and be everywhere at once. Tal set the spike of his staff carefully, lifted a foot and stepped forward, driving the cleats into the ice before lifting the other and repeating the motion. His beat would take three times as long to walk tonight.

He was glad that he was not the morning man, who would be the one to deal with the bodies that would turn up with the dawn. Sometimes the perpetrator would manage to hide his crime by burying the corpse or dumping it in the river, but it would take a truly desperate person to manage that tonight. *They never learn; they call the dead-cart and say the mate or the kid "froze to death," the constable shows up with the dead-cart and sees the bruises or the smashed skull, and that's the end of it. Another battering, another hanging.* It generally never even came to a trial; a Justiciar would see the evidence and pronounce the verdict before the end of the day. An easy conviction, but Tal was weary of them, for nothing ever seemed to change, no matter how many batterers were hung.

Maybe that's because for every one we see and catch, there are a dozen that we don't, because they don't actually manage to kill anyone. They only cripple the bodies and kill the souls of their "loved ones," they never actually commit murder. And as long as the wife doesn't complain, we have no right to step into a quarrel or a parent punishing his child.

More than the weight of the ice on his shoulders weighed him down, and he wondered for the hundredth time if he should give it all up.

No, not yet. Let me solve this last one, then I'll give it up. It was all a noble motive; tonight he was ready to acknowledge that part too. Part of it was sheerest curiosity. *I want to know what can drive a man to kill someone he doesn't even know with a weapon that vanishes.*

As icy as the morgue was, it was warmer than being outside. The ice-storm had finally passed as Tal finished his beat, but its legacy would make the streets impassable until well after daybreak. Even inside his boots and two pairs of socks, Tal's feet felt like two chunks of ice themselves. At least in here he could walk without having to calculate each step, and he didn't have to worry about the cleats scarring the stone floor.

The morgue was a cheerless building of thick gray stone, with tall, narrow windows set into the stone walls, glazed with the poorest quality glass, thick and bubbly and impossible to see through. The anteroom was supposed to hold a Priest who would conduct visitors to bodies they wished to claim when such appeared, and otherwise he was supposed to be on his knees before the tiny altar with its eternal flame, praying. More often than not, he would probably be at his desk, reading instead. But just as Tal had assumed, there was no Priest here tonight, and the door had been left unlocked just in case the dead-cart ventured out onto the ice before dawn. The flame on the altar was the only other source of illumination besides his own lantern, but there wasn't much to see in its dim and flickering light. The morgue was not made for comfort, either spiritual or physical; the only place to sit besides the chair at the desk was on stone benches lining three of the walls beneath the slit windows. These benches, which were not softened by so much as a hint of a cushion, were intended to encourage the sitter to think on the chill of death and the possible destination of the one who reposed beyond the door. Two of the benches were single pieces of carved granite that stretched the entire length of the wall. The door to the street was framed by two more uncompromising structures, just as imposing though only half the length of the wall. The matching granite altar, kneeling-bench, and the door to the morgue proper were ranged with mathematical precision on the fourth wall, and the Priest's desk, holding the records of all bodies currently held here, sat right in the middle of the room. The desk was a plain, wooden affair, but it hid a secret, a charcoal brazier in the leg-well that would keep the Priest nicely warmed all day. Tal began opening drawers and discovered more secrets. One of the drawers held goosedown cushions and a sheepskin pad to soften the hard wooden chair. There was a stack of books, most of them having little to do with religion, and a flask and a secret store of sweets. Finally he found what he was looking for—the records detailing what body lay where. A quick glance at the book told him where to look for the smith and his victim. Tal put the book back, then turned and crossed the intervening space with slow and deliberate steps, disliking the hollow ring of his cleated boot-heels in the dim silence, and pushed the door open.

On the other side of the door, what appeared at first glance to be multiple rows of cots ranged out beneath the stone ceiling. But a second look showed that the "cots" were great slabs of stone, disturbingly altarlike, and the sheet-draped forms on top of the slabs were too quiet to be sleeping—although Tal had known a Priest or two, more iron-nerved or insensible than most, who would take a late-night nap among his charges on an overly warm night. It would almost be pleasant in here then; a special spell kept the temperature low, so that the bodies would not decompose as quickly. On one of those sweltering nights of high summer, when the air never moved and rain was something to be prayed for, the only place to escape the heat besides the homes of the ultra-wealthy was here.

The morgue was crowded; season and weather were taking their toll of the very young, the elderly, and the poor. Judging by the lumpy forms beneath the sheets, the Priests had laid out several children on each slab, and Tal swallowed hard as he passed them. He could examine the bodies of adults with perfect detachment, but he still could not pass the body of a child without feeling shaken. There was something fundamentally *wrong* about the death of a child, and even after twenty years as a constable he still had not come to terms with it.

His targets were at the very end of the morgue, a little apart from the rest, as if distaste for what had happened made the Priests set them apart from their fellows. Tal was mostly interested in the smith, but just for the sake of seeing if he spotted anything the first constable had not, he pulled back the sheet covering the girl.

The sight of her battered face shocked him, and he had not expected to be shocked. When he'd read that she had been beaten, he had not really expected that she'd been beaten nearly to death. He spotted three injuries that by themselves would have killed her in a day or less. He could hardly imagine how she had survived long enough to be killed with the knife—her jaw was surely broken, and there was a pulpy look about her temple that made him think the skull might be crushed there, broken ribs had been driven into lungs, and her internal organs must have been pulped. She was so bruised that he could not really imagine what she had looked like before the beating, and that took some doing. The places where she'd been cut up were odd—symmetrical, forming patterns. Her clothing was tasteless and gaudy, cheap, but not shabby, indicating that she was not as poor as the last victim. That was probably because the last victim had insisted on earning her bread in ways that did not involve selling her body. As so many girls had found, when men were willing to pay more for sex than any other kind of unskilled work, it was hard to say no to what they offered.

Not that I blame them. You've got to eat.

He couldn't spot anything that caught his attention, so he pulled the sheet back over her and moved on to the smith.

Even on a freezingly cold day like this one, the heat in a forge was as bad as the full fury of the sun in high summer, and most smiths were half-naked most of the time. This one was no exception; leather trews and a leather apron were his only clothing. And it was because of that lack of clothing that Tal saw immediately what made Sergeant Brock whisper that there were rumors that one of the bodies looked "odd."

In fact, if Tal had not known that the man's victim was a relatively frail woman, he would have sworn that the smith had been in some terrible fight just before he died. There were bruises all over his arms and shoulders, especially around his wrists.

That couldn't be post-mortem lividity, could it? The marks were so very peculiar that he picked up the man's stiff arm and rolled the body over a little so he could examine the back. No, those bruises were real, not caused by blood pooling when the body lay on its face. He opened the shutter of his lantern more, and leaned over to examine the bruises closely.

This is very, very strange. He wished that he was a doctor, or at least knew a Healer so he could get a more expert second opinion. He had never seen anything quite like these bruises before. . . .

The closest he could come had been in the victim of a kidnapping. The perpetrators had ingeniously wrapped their victim in bandages to keep him from injuring himself or leaving marks on his wrists and ankles. The victim had been frantic to escape, full of the strength of hysteria, and *had* bruised himself at the wrists, ankles, and outer edges of his arms and legs in straining against his swaddlings. The bruises had looked similar to these—great flat areas of even purpling without a visible impact-spot.

But no one had bound the smith—so where had the bruises come from?

Tal stared at the body for some time, trying to puzzle it out, before dropping the sheet and giving up. There was no saying that the smith had not had those bruises before the girl ever showed up at his forge. And in a man as big and powerful as this one was, no one would have wanted to ask him where they had come from if he himself wasn't forthcoming about it.

Some people have odd tastes. . . .

And *that* could have been what brought the girl to his business today. If she was a girl he'd picked up last night, no one would be aware that he knew her. And if she thought she could get a little extra business—or hush-money—out of him . . .

He grimaced as he walked back towards the door. All this way— and this could very easily be a perfectly ordinary killing, if murder could ever be called "ordinary." The girl ventured out into filthy weather because she needed money and he was the nearest source of it. And perhaps she threatened him in some way, hoping to get that money, or wouldn't go when he ordered her out, and he snapped.

But as he put his hand on the door, he knew, suddenly, that this was just too pat an explanation, and it all depended on the very fragile supposition that the smith was a man with peculiar appetites. Just as he could not be sure that the bruises had not already been present when the girl came to the forge, he could not be sure that they *were.*

Furthermore, that did not explain the strange suicide, nor the vanishing murder-weapon. Why would the man kill himself at all? The forge had been vacant at the time, but fully stoked; it would be more logical for the smith to throw the body on the flames and hope it incinerated before anyone looked in the furnace. The temperature required to smelt iron and steel was high enough to deal with one small human body. And why, with the variety of weapons and even poisons available in a forge, had he chosen the particularly excruciating death he had?

No, this was another of his mystery-crimes again; he had the "scent," and he knew it by now.

But for the moment, there was nothing more to be done about it except let it all brew in his mind. He stepped back out onto the icy street, and the sardonic thought crossed his mind that in weather like this, even murder came second to getting across the street without falling.

Weak sun shone out of a high sky full of even higher, wispy clouds, as it hastened across the sky towards the horizon. The only ice now was in the form of icicles hanging and dripping from most eaves; as if relenting a little for the battering the city had taken beneath the ice-storm, winter had worn a smiling face for the last few days.

And it was Tal's day off; with all of his leads gone cold, he was pursuing his private time, for once, in a little ordinary shopping. He needed new shirts, preferably warm—and having no vanity and not a great deal to spend, he was looking through the bins in one of the better secondhand clothing stalls. Although it was late for shopping in the "better" part of town, in the district where Tal lived, full of folk who had to work during most of the daylight hours, street-vendors and shopkeepers accommodated working folk by opening late and staying open past sunset.

"Tal!" A vaguely familiar voice hailed him from across the street, and he looked up. From beneath the overhanging eaves of the building directly opposite, Constable Kaelef Harden beckoned slightly.

The shirts he'd found so far weren't all that good a bargain, and there didn't seem to be anything better hidden in the deeper layers of the bin, so he dropped them back and made his way across the street to his colleague.

"Brock says you're collecting the murder-suicide, vanishing-knife cases," Harden said without any preamble whatsoever, and his voice seemed strained to Tal. "I had one first thing this morning, he said to come tell you about it. Little street-beggar girl got snuffed by a trash-collector, then he threw himself under the wheels of a carriage. Weird. Very weird."

"In broad daylight?" Tal asked, surprised. "Witnesses?"

Harden nodded. "Me, for one. I *saw* it, or most of it, anyway, and I couldn't stop it, it all happened so fast."

Now his voice had a tremor in it that Tal didn't like. He took a second look at Harden, who was one of the younger constables, less than a year on the job. Harden was white beneath his weather-tanned skin, and visibly shaken. Tal put a steadying hand on the man's arm, and Harden made no move to shake him off.

Hell. Poor lad's in shock. And he doesn't recognize it, because it doesn't occur to him that a constable could or would have any such weaknesses.

"Are you on duty now?" he asked.

Harden shook his head. "Just got off, and Brock was just coming on; he made a point of saying I should come talk to you, since Rayburn just threw the report in a drawer and didn't even glance at it. I checked at the Gray Rose and they told me where you'd gone."

Huh. Brock probably wants me to talk him through this one, and that's why he sent the lad to me, whether or not this case fits my pattern. It's an excuse to get him to a veteran. Still, Harden was a good man, and it was pretty obvious that Rayburn wasn't going to do *his* duty by the lad. The Captain was supposed to help a new man through things like this, but Rayburn—

Rayburn is too busy kissing feet to take care of his men, and that's the end of it.

"Come on back to the Rose," he replied. "We'll get something to eat, and you can tell me about it there."

"Not—I'm not really hungry," Harden said, his lips white, but he didn't pull away when Tal took his elbow and steered him back to the inn that was his home. There were never really crowds in this part of town, and a constable's cape always made traffic part as if there were flunkies clearing the way. Two constables together—even if one was out of uniform—prompted people to choose the other side of the street to walk on. It wasn't long before they paused under a wooden sign boasting a rose that might once have been red, but which had long since faded to a pale pinkish-gray.

The Gray Rose—which may once have been known as The Red Rose, when its sign was in better repair—was a modest little inn in a shabby-genteel part of town, and encouraged long-term residents in the dozen two-room "suites" in the third story. These were right above the single rooms normally let out by the night. For a price just a little more than he might expect to pay for private lodgings and food, Tal got the benefits of living in an inn—meals he didn't have to prepare himself, and servants cleaning up after him—and none of the disadvantages of living in a boardinghouse, where he might have had similar benefit. Granted, the menu never varied—a fact which he tried to look upon as "being reliable"—and the rooms were tiny compared to a lodging, but he had privacy that he wouldn't have gotten in a boardinghouse, he didn't have to tailor his hours to the preferences of a boarding-house keeper, he could bring home whatever visitors he cared to whenever he wanted, and he never had to come home to unswept floors and an unmade bed. During the day, the inn was quiet—all the really noisy activity associated with carousers and private parties in the rooms below his took place while he was on-shift. The girls cleaned his rooms as soon as he left them in the early evening, just before the evening rush and after cleaning everyone else's rooms. For their part, the proprietors appreciated having a constable in residence; that fact alone ensured that although things might get noisy, they never got past the stage of a generally happy ruckus. And knowing that there was a constable living here kept thieves from even *thinking* about trying their luck under the tiled roof.

He steered an obviously shaken Harden past the broad-shouldered Mintak who minded the door, and raised two fingers and an eyebrow at one of the serving-girls as he went by her. She nodded, responded with a quick mime of *eating*, then turned away after Tal nodded back. He led Harden up the stairs to his rooms, knowing that food for two would be arriving shortly. He preferred to supply his own drink; the wine here was cheap, and beer was not to his taste.

He unlocked his door and motioned Harden in ahead of him; the cleaning-girl had already been through this morning, so he knew that his sitting-room was presentable. There actually wasn't a great deal to tidy up; his needs were few, and so were his possessions. He had a single comfortable chair beside the tiny fireplace shared with the bedroom, a bookcase and a lamp standing next to it. A braided rag rug covered the worn boards of the floor, a wooden table and four stools standing on it, and a cupboard holding a few bottles of good wine, four glasses, knives, and plates, some preserved fruit, bread, crackers, and cheese, stood opposite the armchair. There was a chest just under the window that contained all of his other odds and ends, and a tiny desk beside it. As an awkward nod to the amenities, two mediocre landscapes purchased because he felt sorry for the artist decorated the yellow-white walls. One of the few women to ever come here as a guest had seemed surprised that there was so little that was personal in this room. "It's like your face, Tal," she'd said, as if she found it disturbing. "It doesn't tell me anything about you."

But fellow bachelors felt comfortable here, and Harden settled onto one of the four stools with what seemed like real relief. The room was, in every sense, a very "public" room, and right now Tal sensed that the younger constable would not be comfortable with anything that verged on the personal. He left the outer door slightly ajar as a signal to the girl that she should bring the food straight in, and set about making Harden feel at ease.

Hanging his cape and Harden's on once-ornamental pegs beside the door, Tal mended the fire and put fresh logs on, then fetched a bottle of wine and two glasses. Extracting the cork deftly, he poured both glasses full, put one in front of Harden, then took the other and sat on the stool opposite the younger man. He hadn't been there more than a moment when one of the serving-girls tapped on the door with her foot, and then pushed it open with her hip. She carried a large tray laden with bowls and plates, fragrant steam arising from most of them.

Dinner was, as usual, stew with fresh bread and butter, pickled vegetables, and baked apples. If Tal wanted anything other than the "house meal" he had to pay a little extra, and once in a while, for variety, he did so. But his tastes in food were plain and easily satisfied, and he doubted that Harden was going to pay very much attention to what he ate so long as it wasn't absolutely vile.

The girl maneuvered her heavy tray deftly in the cramped space; before Harden even reacted properly to her presence, she had placed his bowls of stew, pickles, and apples in front of him and Tal, plunked the plate holding a hot loaf and a pannikin of butter between them, and dropped wooden spoons in each bowl of stew. Then she was gone, empty tray held loosely in one hand, closing the door firmly behind her.

Harden blinked and picked up the spoon automatically. Tal cut slices from the loaf for both of them and buttered them generously. "You might as well eat," he said casually, gesturing with his spoon. "It's not bad, and it's hot. You may not feel hungry, but you need food."

By way of example, he dug into his own meal, and in a moment, Harden slowly began eating as well. Neither of them said a word until all their plates were empty, nothing was left of the bread but crumbs, and the wine bottle held only dregs. Tal collected the dishes and the empty bottle and put them outside his door, then returned to the cupboard for a second bottle of wine. He poured fresh glasses, then resumed his seat.

"All right," he said, as Harden took the glass in both hands but did not drink. "Now tell me what happened."

Harden shivered, his sober, angular face taking on a look both boyish and lost. "It was this morning," he began. "Late morning. I was on my third round; there's a little half-mad beggar-girl that always takes a particular corner, and I have to keep an eye on her, because sometimes she darts out into the street and starts dancing in the middle of the road. She scares the horses and holds up traffic, people get angry." He shrugged apologetically; Tal understood what he did not say—that when something like that happened, people always blamed the constables. But what were *they* supposed to do? You couldn't lock up every crazy beggar in the city, there'd be no room for real criminals in the gaols.

"So you kept an eye on her," Tal repeated. "She ever done anything worse?"

Harden shook his head. "Mostly she just sits like today and sings hymns, except she makes up words for them. You can tell when she'd be going to cause trouble, she acts restless and won't sit still, and she wasn't like that today, so once I saw that, I ignored her. She's harmless. *Was* harmless," he corrected himself, growing pale again. "No one ever minded her. I was on the opposite side of the street from her. I—I really don't know what happened then, because I wasn't really looking for any trouble. *She* wasn't going anywhere, and no one out in the street was going to bother her. I thought, anyway."

He sat quietly for a moment, and Tal sensed his internal struggles as the constable warred with the seriously shaken man. "All I can tell you is that the very next thing *I* knew was that people on the other side of the street were screaming and pointing, a couple were trying to run, and there was a rag-picker standing over her, waving a bloody knife in the air. Then he threw the knife away, and before *I* could move, he ran out into the street. And I could *swear,* honestly, he actually threw himself right under the wheels of a heavy water-wagon. The driver couldn't stop, the wagon turned over and the barrel burst and flooded everything, and by the time I got it all sorted out the rag-picker was dead, too." His hands were trembling as he raised his glass and drained it in a single gulp. "I—didn't do anything. I didn't stop him, I didn't even *see* him kill that mad girl, I didn't stop him from killing himself—" His voice rose with each word, and he was clearly on the verge of hysteria.

A natural reaction, but not at all useful. Better snap him out of this.

"Are you a mage?" Tal interrupted him.

Harden stopped in midsentence and blinked owlishly at him. Probably the question seemed utterly irrelevant, but Tal had a particular strategy in mind. "Ah—no," he stammered.

"Then you couldn't have done anything, could you?" Tal countered. "There was no reason to assume that a rag-picker was going to murder the beggar; they're normally pretty feeble-bodied and just as often they're feeble-minded, too. They don't *do* things like that, right? Rag-pickers wander along the gutter, collecting trash, and half the time they don't even see anything that's not in the gutter in front of them.

You had no reason to watch him, you didn't even know what he'd done until it was too late.''

"But after—'' Harden began.

"You said it yourself, it all happened quickly. How close were you? Across the street you said, and I'd guess half a block down.'' Tal shrugged as Harden nodded. "People were shouting, screaming, blocking the street—panicked. You couldn't possibly have gotten across to him with any speed. There was *certainly* no reason to think he'd throw himself under a wain! And short of using magic to do it, you couldn't have stopped him from where you were standing! Right?''

Harden nodded again, numbly. Tal poured his glass full and topped off his own. "That was a hell of an experience,'' he said, with a little less force. "A hell of a thing. Bad enough when you come pick up the pieces, but when it happens right in front of you, it's natural to think *you* could have done something the cits couldn't. But just because you're a constable, that doesn't give you the ability to read thoughts, move faster than lightning, and pick up water-wagons with your bare hands.''

Harden took a few deep breaths, closed his eyes for a moment, then took a small sip of the wine. "You're right, of course,'' he replied shakily. "I wasn't thinking—''

"No one could be, in those circumstances,'' Tal replied dryly. "Lad, most of the cits think we can do anything, and expect us to on a regular basis; that kind of thinking can get you believing you're supposed to really be able to. But you're just a man, like any of the cits—just you have a baton and some authority, people listen to you, and you can handle yourself against a couple of armed ruffians. And none of those things make you either a Priest or a mage, to save a soul or a body, either. Now, what made Brock think you should talk to me about this?''

"Well—I guess because it was another murder-suicide, and the knife is missing,'' Harden said after a moment of thought. "He told me about your theory, and it seems to fit. I suppose you could say that the beggar was a musician; at least, she was always singing. She didn't know the man, *I* had never seen him on my beat. Judging by the wound, it was a strange knife, too; like a stiletto, but with a longer blade. We looked for it, too, believe me. After he threw it away, it just vanished.''

From the moment that Harden mentioned the rag-picker throwing the knife away, Tal had the feeling that this murder *did* match his profile; now he was sure of it. Once again, the knife was gone, and he was already certain that it would never be found.

He was also certain that no links would be uncovered joining the beggar-woman and the rag-picker, no matter how diligently he looked. The rag-picker probably was not even from this part of town, and he normally would never have been on that street. It was the same pattern all over again; the same damnable, frustrating pattern.

The use of magic *could* explain it, some kind of compulsion-magic, perhaps operating through the medium of the knife, but *why*? All the victims were utterly insignificant!

What was more, all the victims were utterly unalike, especially the last three. A real street-musician, a whore, and a beggar—aside from being poor and female, and marginally connected with music, they had nothing in common.

He shoved it all into the back of his mind and concentrated on coaxing Harden to talk himself out. The wine helped; it loosened the boy's tongue to a remarkable extent, and once Harden started, he kept going until he ran himself out.

Just like I did, the night that fellow jumped off the bridge in front of me. . . .

He hadn't thought of that in many years now, but there had been a time when he literally could not get it out of his mind. Now he knew that his presence or absence would have had no effect on the man, but then—

Half the time I thought I'd somehow caused him to jump by just being there, and half the time I thought if I'd just tried harder I could have talked him out of it. In both cases, the guilt and self-recrimination were the same.

Now it was his turn to listen and say all the things that Harden wanted desperately to hear—things he *knew* were logical, but that guilt told him could not be true.

They emptied that bottle and another between them, though most of it went into Harden. At one point Tal ascertained that Harden lived alone, and had no woman or relative waiting anxiously for him to come home, and just kept replenishing his glass until he finally broke through the final barrier and wept.

That was what he had needed, more than talk, more than sympathy; he needed to cry, in the presence of someone who understood. Not all men needed the release of tears after something like this, but many did.

And may Rayburn find himself in this position one day, with no one willing to listen to him and pour the wine!

He came very close to hating his superior tonight, and only the fact that Rayburn was not worth wasting hatred on kept him from doing so. If the Captain himself did not feel capable of offering such important moral support to his men, it was his responsibility to find someone who could and would! It should not have been left up to old Brock to find someone!

And getting the lad drunk was not the most optimal way to get him to unload his troubles, but it is the only way I know, Tal thought glumly. *He should have been with someone who knows how to handle situations like this one, not with me. He's going to have a head in the morning, poor boy. On the other hand—*

He was Harden's senior. He could legitimately report him in sick. Rayburn would have to find a replacement for his shift—

Hell, Rayburn can walk the lad's beat himself and do some real work for a change!

Although emotion wore a good bit of the wine off, Harden was still not fit to leave the inn, either. So when the tears were over, the guilt somewhat dispersed, and Harden reduced to telling Tal what a fine fellow he was in slurred and half-incoherent speeches, Tal excused himself long enough to tap on the door of one of the two Mintak brothers who worked as peace-keepers in the bar downstairs. He knew Ferg would still be awake; they had the same taste in books, and the Mintak would often come tapping on *his* door about this time of the night if his own library ran dry. He liked Ferg and his brother, and if anyone ever said a word against nonhumans in general and these two in particular, he took care to let them know just how he stood on the matter. If he hadn't been a constable, that might have gotten him into a fight or two, but between his baton and the brothers' muscle, troublemakers generally took their prejudices elsewhere.

Ferg answered the door quickly enough to have been awake and reading, sticking his shaggy brown head out of the door cautiously. A pair of mild brown eyes looked down at Tal out of a face that was bovine, equine, and human, all at once. He opened the door a little further when he recognized Tal, and as if to confirm Tal's guess, there was a book in his broad brown hand, a thumb stuck in it to keep his place. "Got a friend who needed to get drunk tonight," Tal said shortly, knowing Ferg would understand. "I need to get him down to a room for tonight."

The Mintak nodded wisely. "Hold a moment," he said in that deep voice all Mintaks shared regardless of gender. "Let me put the candle somewhere safer."

He withdrew his head; there was a little shuffling, and he returned, without the book. "Nobody's using the guest-room," the Mintak offered. "Might as well put him there, and we won't have to move him down any stairs."

"That might be best," Tal agreed. "He's a good lad, but I'd just as soon not run up too big a bill on his behalf."

There was a single, very small room on this floor, a room not much bigger than a closet, that the tenants had—with the agreement of the proprietors of the inn—fixed up as a bedroom for their own guests. Sometimes it was used for visiting relatives, and sometimes for those who were in the same condition as Harden. Once or twice it had been used by quarreling couples, and on those occasions, the rest of the tenants were very careful not to ask any questions of either party. Those who were going to entertain visitors for more than a day were careful to schedule the guest-room well in advance, but at any other time it was open for spur-of-the-moment use.

Harden would be less embarrassed to wake up in what was obviously a guest-room removed from Tal's lodging than he would be if he woke up in Tal's sitting room. And Tal's charity did not extend to giving up or sharing his own bed.

Ferg followed Tal back to his rooms; Harden looked up at their entrance and squinted at the sight of the Mintak, who towered over Tal by a good several inches.

"Din' I shee you downshtairs?" Harden slurred.

"That was my herd-brother, good sir," Ferg replied calmly. "Do you think you can stand?"

"Not by m'shelf," Harden acknowledged ruefully, after an abortive attempt that left him staggering and finally sitting right where he'd begun. " 'm drunk, butsha couldn' tell by m' dancin'."

"All right then, old man," Tal said, slightly amused. "We're going to get you to a bed where you can sleep it off."

Harden nodded wisely. "Good—idea," he said carefully. " 'f I can' stand, I sure can' walk, eh?"

Tal and Ferg got on either side of Harden and assisted him carefully to his feet. Both of them knew better than to move abruptly with him; at the moment, he showed no signs of getting sick, but any too-sudden movements could change that, and neither of them felt much like cleaning the mess up.

"Right you are," Ferg said cheerfully. "Now, we'll take your weight and keep you balanced, you just move one foot in front of the other, and we'll get you safely into a nice, warm bed." Obediently, Harden began to walk, swaying from side to side, supported by Ferg and Tal. "Good, you're doing fine," Ferg encouraged. "Right. Left. Right. Left. Now through the door—into the hall—"

This was hardly the first drunk Ferg had assisted into a bed—the Gray Rose encouraged patrons who had a bit too much to spend the night if they weren't rowdy. It was good for all concerned—the inn got a paying customer overnight, and the customer found himself only a bit lighter in the pocket, rather than waking up in an alley or a worse place. The Mintaks, with their enormous strength, were usually the ones called upon to help the inebriated into their rooms, so Ferg had plenty of experience; either of the brawny brothers could have carried Harden on their own, but the companionability of Ferg and Tal doing this together would likely be important to Harden when he thought back upon it. In a much shorter time than Tal would have estimated, they had Harden down the hall, in the bed with his boots pulled off, and under several blankets, since the room was too tiny to have a fireplace of its own. Tal closed the door quietly and marked his name down on the schedule outside. There would be a linen charge and a cleaning charge, and since Harden was his guest, he would be the one responsible. Ferg nodded approvingly.

"A friend of yours?" Ferg asked. "A fellow constable? And what brought him to this pass?"

"A bad incident on his beat," Tal replied, grateful that Ferg knew enough of the constables to know what a "bad incident" was.

"Ah. His first, no doubt. Well, better to purge himself in the presence of one with the experience to advise him—but I misdoubt he'll be fit for duty in the morning. . . ." The Mintak cocked his head in obvious enquiry, and Tal had to chuckle at his curiosity. Tal never ceased to be bemused by the blazing intellect and extensive vocabulary possessed by Mintaks. Other humans too often dismissed Mintaks as being as stupid as the beasts they resembled, but Tal knew better.

"Oh, I plan to take care of that," Tal replied. "In my opinion as a senior constable, that boy has a touch of something. Food poisoning, maybe. I'll have a note run over to the station to that effect before I go to bed."

Ferg chuckled. "Mendacious, but reasonable. A good Captain would have excused him from his duty for a day or two anyway. It is a pity there is nothing in the rules requiring that absence from duty. Well, good night—and I have a history I think you might enjoy, when you have the leisure for it."

"And I have a Deliambren travel-book I think you'll like," he replied, and saluted the Mintak as he opened his own door.

He stayed up long enough to write sick-notes for both Harden and himself—after all, they *had* eaten the same meal, and they *were* both suffering similar symptoms.

Uh-hmm. We're both light-headed, dizzy, flushed, and in the morning we'll both have headaches and nausea. Well, Harden will. Brock will probably guess, but he won't let on to the Captain. Tal decided that if his hangover wasn't too bad in the morning, he would go ahead and appear for duty on his shift, but in case it wasn't, he was covered. He left a third note, telling Harden that he'd written him up for sicktime and not to go in on his shift, on the tiny table beside the bed, and sent one of the inn's errand boys around to the station with the other two notes. Harden, when he took a final look in on him, was blissfully, if noisily, asleep.

Tal nodded to himself with satisfaction, closed the door, and sought his own bed, after taking the precaution of drinking a great deal of water.

But when he finally lay in the quiet darkness, with only the faint sounds of creaking wood and faint footsteps around him, his mind wrestled with the problem of this latest case. It fit; it certainly did. There was no doubt of that.

But what did it all mean?

The whole thing is mad, he thought, tossing restlessly. *The pattern is there, but no motive.* Maybe that was why Rayburn was so stubborn about admitting that the cases were all tied together; there was no discernible motive to any of them. That was one of the first things drummed into a constable's head when they taught him about murder: *find the motive, and you find the killer.* But in this case, the killers were obvious; it was the *motive* that was missing.

Why? Why, why, why? Why these people? Why that particular kind of knife? What was there to gain? It has to be the same hand behind all of them, but what is the motive?

No the killer *wasn't* obvious, after all. The people who used the knife and spilled the blood couldn't be anything more than tools, hands to wield the blade, and nothing more. So, the law still held true.

Find the motive, and you find the killer.

So what was the motive? What could drive a man to use other people to kill like this? If there was a purpose, what was it? Where was the killer all this time?

And *who* was the killer?

Chapter Three

The next murder got the attention of the entire city; it was a nine-day wonder that kept the taverns a-buzz for long enough that even Tal got tired of it.

But this time, like some strange disease that strikes three homes in a row, then suddenly occurs halfway across the city, this crime happened so far outside of Tal's district he would never have heard of it, if the circumstances hadn't been so bizarre. Whoever, whatever was behind all this, "he" had moved his area of operation from the waterfront side of the city to the tenement district farthest inland.

Once again, the poverty of the murderer and victim should have relegated the incident to a mere item in a few records. Tal heard about it over his morning meal in the common-room of the Gray Rose, and his first, cynical thought was that if the deaths themselves had not been so outrageous, the entire package of murder and suicide would have been put down as a sordid little sex-crime.

Even so, the details were so unbelievable that he was certain they were exaggerated. It was only when he reached the station that he learned that if anything, the public rumors were less horrific than the truth.

And that was enough to send cold chills over him.

When he heard the official report for himself, he had one of the oddest feelings he had ever experienced in his long career as a constable. Part of him was horrified, part sickened—and part of him knew a certain sense of self-righteous pleasure. He knew what it was, of course. Hadn't he been *saying* something like this was going to happen? Well, now it had, and he had told them so. It was a base emotion, but—maybe it was justified.

As Tal read the report, though, he found it very difficult to keep his detachment. A jewel-crafter (too unskilled to be called a full Jeweler) named Pym, who made inexpensive copper, brass, and silver-plated trinkets, was the perpetrator. A Gypsy-wench called Gannet was the victim. And what had happened to the poor whore at the hands of the smith palled by comparison with what happened to the Gypsy.

Gannet showed up at Pym's workshop just before he closed, with a handful of trinkets she wanted him to purchase. That much was clear enough from a neighbor, who had probably been the last one to see either of them alive. The neighbor had been loitering about the area in front of Pym's shop and her own; other neighbors said she had "an interest" in Pym, and what they probably meant was that she had her mind set on inveigling him into marrying her. The neighbor was not pleased to see a younger woman show up at the shop, and drew close enough to hear the ensuing conversation. The Gypsy insisted that someone had sent her to Pym specifically to sell her goods, and although the jeweler seldom made such purchases, tonight he waved the wench into his shop and shut and locked the door behind her. That had been so unlike Pym that the neighbor suspected something illegal (or so she told the constables) and set herself to watch Pym's door.

Right, Tal snorted to himself, as he read that particular bit of nonsense. *More like, she suspected Pym of a bit of funny-business with a skirt, and was nosy and jealous enough to wait around for details.*

But the Gypsy didn't come out, although there were lights and shadows moving about in the back of Pym's workshop all night long. And in the morning, the neighbor, whose imagination had been running at high speed ever since the girl showed up, knocked insistently on the door on the excuse that she had smelled something burning. Then she called the constables when Pym didn't appear to open his shop or answer the door.

The constables, unable to rouse anyone, broke the door down. There was no one in the front of the shop, nor in the rooms above, but what met them when they opened the door to the workshop sent one of them running to empty his stomach in the gutter, and the other to rouse the entire station to come and cope with the scene.

What was left of Pym lay on the floor in a posture of agony at the foot of his workbench. The girl lay spread-eagled on the top of his biggest workbench, also dead. Pym had used the entire contents of his workshop to make a strange display-piece out of the girl, beginning by clamping wrists and ankles down to the table, filling her mouth with wax, then setting to work with copper wire, semiprecious stones, and most of his tools. She was quite chastely covered in a garment of wire and gems, all of it laced through her muscles and skin, and riveted to her bones to anchor it in place. Her eyes were wired open, her head covered with a wig of fine wire riveted to her head. The pain must have been excruciating, and because the wounds were so small, she wouldn't even have lost consciousness because of blood-loss. The knife he had plunged into her breast must have come as a relief.

Now the detachment Tal had been looking for finally came, and with it, that odd ability to analyze even the worst information. *If she'd lived, she would have been crippled for life. The amount of nerve-damage he must have done would have been impossible to repair, let alone whatever he did to her brain by spiking that wig into her skull.*

But she was not to be alone in her suffering, for Pym finished his night by drinking every drop of acid and poisonous chemicals in his shop. It was the horrified judgment of the Healer-Priest brought in to decide on the cause of death that Pym probably lived about as long as his victim before he died.

Once again, the girl had been murdered with a knife with a triangular blade, and once again, the knife was missing. The *official* version was that Pym had stabbed her with one of his files, but none of the files had even a trace of blood on them—in fact, the files were the only tools Pym *hadn't* used to make his "display."

Tal would have given five years of his life to see Pym's body, but unfortunately, the acid he had drunk had rendered it unfit even to be placed in the morgue. Or, as one of the constables with a mordant sense of humor said, "The only way to put him in the ground was to scoop him up in buckets and pour him in."

But I wish I knew if he had the same bruises as the others I've seen. . . .

The Gypsy-wench was buried the next day with all the pomp due a Guildmaster, a funeral that was paid for by donations. If she had any relatives, they were lost in the throng of spectators who came to gawk rather than mourn, searching for some sign of what had been done to her under the burial-gown of stiff snow-white silk that covered her from chin to toes. Tal didn't go, but Captain Rayburn made a prominent appearance.

The last murder took place right under Tal's nose.

He was making another attempt to find a decent set of shirts, because by now he needed more than one, and this time had gone much farther afield than his usual haunts. Lately, bargeloads of clothing came in at the southern end of the city on a semiregular basis, brought up out of places where a species of establishment called a *manufactory* was becoming common. There were manufactories in the High King's capital of Lyonarie, but only lately had anyone set them up along the Kanar River. Such establishments produced large quantities of simply-made garments in a limited range of sizes and colors, and shipped them off by water, since shipping them overland would have made them too expensive to compete with locally made garments. Tal was not certain that he would fit any of the sizes available, and he was more than a little dubious about the quality of such garments, but by now he was desperate enough to go look at them when word came that another shipment had arrived.

It was a pleasant enough day, sunny with no more than the thinnest of cloud-cover, and Tal took his time about reaching his goal. The only thing on his mind was the book that he'd just started, and a vague wish that he'd brought it with him to read if there was going to be a queue.

As he arrived, it was obvious that he had come to the right address by the crowd just outside the door, and he resigned himself to a wait. He was only one among a throng of customers at the dockside ware-house, and was met at the door by a man who looked him over with an appraising eye and sent him to stand in a particular queue, one of six altogether. The warehouse was only dimly illuminated by light coming in at some upper-story windows and by skylights in the roof. Enough of the people here felt compelled to chatter at the tops of their lungs that a confusing din echoed and reechoed through the warehouse, adding to the confusion, as Tal inched forward in his queue.

Never having been here before, he was a little bewildered about why the fellow had directed him into this line, until he arrived at the head of the queue and found himself confronting four piles of neatly folded shirts, each pile being shirts of the same size but a different color. His choices were brown, gray, blue, and white, apparently, and the man at the door was evidently practiced in sorting people's sizes out by eye.

Tal took two each of the brown and the gray, on the grounds that they would show dirt and wear less than the white, and fade less than the blue, and moved to one side quickly, for the man behind him seemed very impatient.

He shook out one of the gray shirts and held it against himself, then examined it carefully. Aside from the fact that the stitching was mathematically even—which was entirely possible even when sewn by a human rather than a machine, if the shirt was of high quality—he saw nothing wrong with it. It was just a trifle large, perhaps, but no few of his secondhand purchases were also oversized. There was no real "style" to it, and the pattern it had been made to was a very simple one, but a city constable hardly needed "style." Surprised and pleased, he took his prizes to the front of the warehouse where he paid about the same as he would have for four secondhand garments, even though there was no haggling permitted. The clerk wrapped his purchases into a packet with brown paper and string, and gave them back to him. Given that these should last longer than secondhand shirts which already had a great deal of wear on them, he had gotten quite a bargain, and left the warehouse with a feeling of minor euphoria.

In fact, he had enough left over for a decent lunch, so he decided to treat himself. He seldom got to see the wharfs in daylight; by night, they were dirty, dangerous places to walk, but by day it was no worse than any other mercantile area. There were several warehouses here where individuals were buying things directly; this was something new to the city, and he wondered how the merchants were going to take it.

It probably isn't going to bother them too much, he decided. *Nobody with any significant money is going to come down here and stand in lines when they can go to a fine, warm shop and be waited on, even fawned over.* There might be some loss of secondhand trade, but that would even itself out eventually. Those who bought secondhand garments would rightly point out that the market value of such goods had decreased and be able to buy them at a lower value than heretofore, and the very poor, who could not afford even cheap goods like these, would then be able to afford the second-hand goods. The merchandise leaving those warehouses wasn't what he would call luxury goods, either. Most of those who were buying these new items were those who would bargain fiercely, leaving a secondhand merchant with less of a profit anyway.

Taking advantage of the crowds, other vendors had set up shop along the street. There were no entertainers, probably because there was no room for them. Performing on the docks would be dangerous, with wagonloads of heavy goods going in both directions, and the wharfs on one side. Not only that, but the wheels of those wagons, rumbling on the wooden planks of the wharf, made it too noisy for anyone to hear an entertainer. But there were other peddlers and vendors, anyone who could set himself up in a small space. A flash of color caught Tal's eye, and he wormed his way through the press of people to a ribbon-seller. Midwinter Festival was coming up, and he liked to get small things for people who were decent to him.

He bought a bit of scarlet for the black hair of the little wench who cleaned his room, and the little blonde who usually waited on him in the tavern would receive a streamer of blue. Farther along, there was a candy-monger, an orange-girl, a man selling feathers, and a knife-sharpener with his grinder in a barrow. The candy-monger had a clean-looking cart and display, and little bags of candy would make appropriate gifts to the tavern errand-boys; Tal's mind was entirely on the complicated problem of different-but-equal bags of sweets as he wormed his way towards the cart, when suddenly the noisy but relatively peaceful scene changed dramatically.

He had looked down long enough to tuck his bits of coiled ribbon into his belt-pouch and make certain the antipickpocket flap was in place, when the crowd surged into him, knocking him off-balance. People screamed and surged into him again as they tried to escape from something just ahead.

Training went into effect as people tried to move, surged back and forth mindlessly, and generally made things worse all the way around. Reacting as a constable and not as a man in the crowd, he fought free of them with a few precisely placed kicks and elbow-jabs, and broke out into an open space for a moment, looking for the source of the trouble.

He didn't take long to spot it. Ahead of him, the knife-sharpener brandished a bloody blade in one hand, a woman covered in blood lying motionless at his feet. Tal's eyes went immediately to the knife and not the man, for it was obvious *who* the attacker was, and in this press of bodies, he would not be able to get away.

Though he only saw it for a moment, he knew he would be able to draw a picture of it from memory alone at any time in the next year. It was unusually long, with a wicked point; the cross-guard was minimal, the hilt undecorated, and the blade itself was exactly like a triangular file, except that it was polished to a satin-gleam on all three flat sides, and glinted razor-sharp on all three edges.

Tal dropped his package of shirts at the feet of the candy-monger and launched himself at the murderer. In spite of the fact that he was *not* frozen with shock or surprise, and in fact was already moving towards the man as his eyes and mind took in every detail of the murder-weapon, he was not fast enough to prevent the next scene of the tragedy. With the speed of the weasel he resembled, the knife-sharpener flung the blade wildly into the crowd, turned, and plunged off the dock into the murky, icy water of the river. And since he was wearing a belt encumbered with several pounds-worth of metal tools, even if he *could* swim, it wasn't likely he was going to come up again. Tal knew that even before the man hit the water and sank without a sound.

Tal ran to the edge of the dock anyway, but there was no sign of the murderer but a trail of bubbles. He debated plunging in after him—

and even teetered on the brink for a moment—when one of the dockworkers grabbed his elbow.

"Don't," the man said shortly. "The bastard's a goner. Won't last
a minute in that water, and neither will you."

"You're right," Tal acknowledged, and turned back to the woman's
body.

She was dead, and he was unsurprised to find that the woman had
been stabbed as viciously as the very first victim he'd seen. She had
probably died instantly; the amount of blood soaking the dock and her
clothing indicated that the knife-sharpener had used his blade with
brutal expertise.

Although it seemed to him that the better part of an hour had passed,
he knew it had only been a few minutes, and the crowd was still
milling about in panic. He took charge of the scene at once, getting
the crowd settled, separating out witnesses from those who only knew
that *someone* had died, and eventually dispersing all those who were
not direct witnesses. He also gathered up a few level-headed volun-
teers.

"You and you," he ordered, picking two large, steady-looking fellows. "You two go north and south along the river, and see if you
can't find the constables patrolling this district."

He turned to a smaller, soberly clad man, plain and ordinary. "You
go to the station and alert the constables there."

All three nodded, and went briskly off on their assigned errands.
That left him with four more, all dockworkers, who should know this
area. "You see if you can't find that knife," he told them, although
he knew it was a hopeless quest. The mysterious, vanishing blade was
going to vanish again, and there wasn't anything he could do about it.
"You saw him throw it away; something about it may tell us why he
went crazy that way."

The four looked at him a little oddly, but began their search the
moment he explained that he was a constable. He dealt with the murder
scene a few moments later, draping the girl's body with a tarpaulin
given him by a barge-man.

At least this time I saw it, and I know exactly what it looks like, he
thought bleakly. *I can describe it to knife-makers, armorers, smiths—
there* can't *be that many knives like that in this city. I can check with
secondhand stores and have people keep a watch for it. Maybe I can
track it down that way, or at least find out what kind of a knife it is.*

Or he would—if this was *not* some strange cult of murder and suicide, with special ritual blades of their own. There were not many

things more secretive than a religious cult, and doubly so in a circumstance like this one.

Still, someone has to forge these things. I'll check with smiths.

By the time the local constables arrived—more than a bit annoyed that an apparent outsider had so cavalierly taken over *their* crime—he had all of the information that really mattered to him. The girl was local; she cleaned and gutted fish at one of the salting-houses. The knife-sharpener was new; no one had ever seen him here before. The orange-girl, the candy-monger, and the fellow with the feathers were all locals as well, and knew the fish-cleaner by sight.

"Everyone knew her," the orange-girl sobbed, weeping messily into her apron. "She was always singing, whistling—so cheerful, her voice so pretty, we always told her she ought to go for a Free Bard—"

Tal froze inside, although he knew there was no sign of his reaction on his face. There it was, the music connection again! What was going on here?

He patted the girl on the shoulder, trying awkwardly to comfort her, then turned to the newly arrived constables. "I'm sorry to have barged into your territory like this," he began, knowing that if he apologized immediately, the new arrivals would stop being annoyed and start being grateful that he had done all the preliminary work for them. "I would never have, except that I know from my own experience that if you don't take over in a case like this, there's a panic. Wild tales spread like a fire in dry grass, and the next thing you know, you're getting reports of a wholesale massacre of fishwives. And if you don't herd all these people together at the start, they'll manage to wander off on their own errands before you can get any sense out of them."

He handed the man he judged to be the most senior his own notes. "Here's what I've gotten, sir, and I hope it will be of use to you," he continued, as frowns softened to reluctant approval. "The ones who swore they *had* to go, I got addresses for in case you have to do a follow-up. Any my statement is in the pile as well, and my own address."

"Oh, we know where to find you," the senior constable replied, with more approval showing when Tal made no mention of getting credit on the report, or indeed having anything to do with this other than be a witness. "You can go ahead and go now, if you like. We can take it from here."

Tal turned to go, and the candy-monger, with a display of honesty that was quite remarkable, handed the package containing his shirts back to him, undamaged except for a bit of dirt. "You tried, sir," the sad-eyed little man said. "Most wouldn't have done that for her. Than-kee."

Tal nodded, accepting the compliment in the spirit intended, and tucked his package under his arm, but his mind was elsewhere, planning the report he was going to write for Captain Rayburn. He had several cases now, including one with an impeccable eyewitness in the person of himself. Now the Captain *must* believe him!

Enthroned in splendid isolation behind the walnut bulwark of his desk, Captain Rayburn gazed down his long, thin, aristocratic nose at Tal with mingled contempt and disbelief. "Would you mind telling me what you were drinking when you wrote this bit of imaginative fiction?" he asked sarcastically. "I'd like to get hold of a bottle or two myself."

Tal considered any number of possible responses and confined himself to a civil one. "You can't argue with the facts, Chief," he replied. "All the murders are in the records; they were all committed with the same kind of weapon, which always disappears."

"They were all committed with a *knifelike object*," the Captain corrected. "We don't know what that object could be, and there is no evidence that it is the same or even a similar object in any two of the murders. The instrument of death could have been a file—or a piece of bar-stock—or an ice-pick—or, for that matter, an icicle! There is nothing connecting any of these murders except your half-toasted idea that the victims were all musicians of a sort, and that is too absurd to even credit. There is *also* no trace of magic involved in any of these deaths, and they *have* been checked by a reputable Priest-Mage."

Tal clamped his mouth shut on the things he wanted to say, for there was no point in going any further. He *wanted* to point out that the examinations of the wounds of the victims showed identical characteristics consistent only with a triple-edged blade, and remind Rayburn that none of the weapons had ever been recovered, much less identified. He wanted to tell the Captain that the Priest-Mage was less interested in finding traces of magic than he was in getting his unpleasant task over with as soon as possible, and that this particular man was hardly as reliable and reputable as Rayburn painted him. He wanted to say all of these things, but he said none of them.

The Priest in question is in his position because he is out of favor with the current Bishop, and liaison with the constables is the lowest position a Priest-Mage can have. But I'm not supposed to know that. Rayburn wants this thing covered up, and it suits him to pretend that

*the man is careful and competent. The only question is, why is he so
intent on covering this up?*

"I hope you aren't planning a new career in sensational storytelling,
Constable," Rayburn continued, tapping the pile of papers with his
index finger, "because this is too far-fetched to attract any publisher."

Tal dropped his eyes and studied the top of Rayburn's immaculate
desk, knowing that if he wanted to keep his job, he was going to have
to keep his temper.

*But I'm beginning to wonder if this is a job worth keeping. Why is
it worth Rayburn's while to sweep this under the rug?*

Rayburn waited for him to say something, and when he did not
speak, the Captain shook his head. "I would have expected a piece of
nonsense like this out of one of the green recruits, not out of a senior
constable," he said with an undisguised sneer. "Really, you make me
wonder if you are not ill with a brain-fever yourself! I hope you
haven't been spreading this nonsense about—"

"I've told no one," Tal replied stoically. *No one else would have
cared, you bastard, except a few idiots like me who want to do their
jobs right, and they don't have any power or influence. The rest are
all too busy playing politics, just like you.* "I saved it all for my
report."

"Oh, did you?" Tal's hands, hidden by the desk, clenched at Rayburn's tone. "In that case, I won't have to order some punitive assignment for you for spreading rumors designed to cause panic or
unrest." Rayburn drummed his fingers on the desktop for a few moments. "In that case, because of your fine record, I am going to forget
I ever saw this."

Tal looked up in time to see the Captain turn in his seat, take the
report that he had labored over for so long, and toss it into the stove
beside his desk. Tal stifled an oath as Rayburn turned back to him.

"Now, I *order* you to say nothing more about this," Rayburn said
with a cold core of steel underlying the false cordiality. "I won't have
wild rumors of death-cults or renegade mages circulating through the
streets. Do I make myself clear?"

The weak blue eyes had turned as icy and flat as a dead fish's, and
Tal said what he was expected to say.

Go to Hell, Captain.

"Yes, Captain," he replied, trying not to choke on the two words.

Rayburn settled back into his chair with an air of satisfaction. "This
district is quiet, and I intend to keep it that way," he warned Tal.
"Even if any of that nonsense *was* true, I would order you to hold
your tongue on the subject. Rumors like that are all that it takes to

spark a riot, and I *will not* have a riot on my watch.'' He waved his hand in a shooing motion at Tal. "Now, get out of here, and don't let me ever see anything like this report again.''

Tal shoved the chair back, watching Rayburn wince as the legs grated on the floor, and left the office before he could say anything he didn't want Rayburn to hear.

He won't have a riot on "his watch"! As if he paid any attention to his district at all!

He seethed all the way back to his rooms at the Gray Rose, and only long practice helped him to keep his stoic expression intact. Not even the Mintaks, notoriously sensitive to body-language and able to read trouble from the most subtle of expressions, had any idea that Tal was suffering from more than his usual moodiness.

When he reached the safe haven of his rooms, his first impulse was to reach for a bottle—but he did not give in to it. He *wanted* a drink— he wanted to numb his mind and his soul, wanted the oblivion that a bottle would give him, the few hours of respite when nothing mattered anymore. But that respite was a lie, and oblivion cured nothing, and he knew the depth and shape of the trap far too well to fall into it himself. Liquor had been the ruin of many a constable, in part because they needed to numb their feelings and their memories, and in part, he suspected, because more and more of late the good constables were not able to do their jobs properly.

You can drop into despair, or you can beat the bastards at their own game. I'll be damned if I let a pinheaded little shoe-licker keep me from doing my job.

Instead of reaching for that bottle, he sat down at his desk with pen and paper in hand. There was more than one mystery here, and the second one was a question that concerned him intimately.

Why had Rayburn suppressed all of this? Why was he so adamant that *nothing* was to leak out?

Sometimes it helped him to make physical lists, and he began two of them, writing slowly and carefully, with his tongue sticking out at the corner of his mouth as he concentrated. Writing did not come easily to him, although reading did, but working at a difficult task would keep him from doing something he might regret later. Like reaching for that bottle.

Murders he headed the first list, and *Rayburn* was what he put on the second page.

He started the second page first.

Rayburn is trying to cover up the murders, he wrote. *He's trying to make them appear perfectly common. Why?*

Why, indeed? The victims were all poor, insignificant; their neighborhoods were those where crime was, if not a daily occurrence, certainly not a stranger. Except for the Gypsy girl, whose death had not even occurred in his district, there had been no notoriety attached to any of the cases. And there were no relatives clamoring for any other solution than the "official" one. Maybe he shouldn't be looking at the victims for his answer—maybe he should be thinking about the hand behind the murders.

Who or what could be doing this? he wrote on the first page. *A disease of the mind—possibly spreading. A curse, or more than one. A mage.*

Now he returned to the second page. *Rayburn could be trying to prevent people knowing that there is a disease that makes them kill for no reason.* But that assumed that Rayburn would be aware there was such a thing. . . .

Huh. He might. There was that tainted-wheat scandal. Nearly two dozen people died raving mad from eating flour made from it. The moneyed in this town would not want anyone to know about tainted food, especially not if it was a common article, like flour.

A good reason for Rayburn's superiors to want it hushed up—the only thing wrong with that theory was that in the wheat scandal, there were a lot more victims, spread across all classes, for they had all bought their flour from the same merchants.

It could still be a disease or a taint, but it would have to be coming from something only the poor are likely to come into contact with. He racked his brains on that one. *Maybe the water?* The poor got their water from common well-pumps that stood on every street corner. The rich? He didn't know, and decided to let the idea lie fallow for the moment.

A curse is more problematic—I've never actually seen a curse that worked, but that doesn't mean it hasn't happened. Elven curses—everybody's heard of those. I can't imagine why a curse would take this particular form, though, unless it happens to be as undiscriminating in who it attaches itself to as any disease. Why a curse, why here, and why now? And why were all the victims of the poorer classes? It would make more sense for a curse to strike the rich and powerful—wouldn't it? Or was that just wishful thinking?

I suppose a curse or a cursed object would be able to work itself out no matter who was the victim, so long as they fit its qualifications. If the qualification is something as broad as "human," well, just about anyone would fit.

He made a note, but he didn't expect to get much information. He just didn't know enough about the subject of curses and cursed objects to ask the right questions.

But there was another question that was related. *Why did Rayburn keep talking about riots if any of this got out?* Did the Captain have some information, perhaps passed on from his superiors, that would make him think that there was a possibility of a riot if wild enough rumors began to spread?

It could be. There've been riots and near-riots over nonhumans recently. There was that nonhuman ghost that carried off a High Bishop! When people talk about curses that work, they usually claim they came from nonhumans. Elves and the like, most of the time, but still . . . people tend to lump all nonhumans into one group, and figure that if Elves work magic, they can all work magic.

There were a fair number of nonhumans working in this city, some of them quite prosperous, and the usual prejudices and resentments against them by those too lazy to make their way by hard work. Nonhumans were easy targets whenever someone wanted a scapegoat. Maybe Rayburn knew more about the riots and disturbances in other cities than Tal did—and maybe he was keeping a lid on this because he was afraid there would be more of the same here if rumors of curses and nasty magic got out.

That certainly fits in with all that talk of civil unrest and rioting. Oh, talk of a knife with a curse on it would certainly set people off, especially if they thought it was part of a plot! Things had been unsettled lately, and he doubted that they were going to get any calmer. There were a lot of changes going on, Deliambrens moving huge machines across the countryside, new mechanical devices showing up and putting people out of work as more machines replaced hand-labor, more and more nonhumans moving into the Twenty Human Kingdoms. That would make a lot of people unhappy and uneasy, and ripe for trouble. There were always troublemakers happy to supply the trouble. Maybe Rayburn wasn't as much of an idiot as Tal had thought.

And maybe he is, doing the right things for the wrong reasons. Keeping things quiet because he wants to make some rich patrons happy, instead of keeping things quiet so trouble-mongers don't have anything to work with.

He shook his head. Not enough information. Without knowing what Rayburn knew, and who (if anyone) had ordered him to keep all this under the rose, it was still most likely that Rayburn was being a sycophant and a toady.

Last of all on his list—what if it all was being done by magic, magic that was directed and purposeful, rather than random like a curse?

Well, that kind of magic meant a mage was working it, and that meant—what?

Elves are mages, they don't like humans, and we humans are encroaching more and more into their lands. If it was an Elf, or it was rumored that it was an Elf that was doing this, that would bring up more resentment against nonhumans. That just didn't feel right, though. As he understood it, when there was some indication that nonhumans were going to have their rights taken away, the rich were in favor of the move because they would have had first chance at confiscated properties and would have been able to purchase former free creatures as slaves. Rayburn's patrons would not want riots—unless the ultimate goal meant more profit—

Oh, I'm making this far too convoluted. I'm not certain any of Rayburn's patrons are that smart.

Who else could be working this kind of magic? *They say that some Gypsies are mages—well, Gypsies have some friends in questionable places, but I've never met a Gypsy that would have done to one of their own what was done to that poor girl. Of course, there are bad cases in everyone's family, and I suppose it* could *be a Gypsy mage. But that wouldn't cause any trouble with Rayburn's superiors.*

Gypsies, Elves—who else worked magic? Some Free Bards, allegedly, through music. But how would that figure in the fact that the victims were all musicians of a sort themselves?

Free Bards getting revenge on substandard minstrels? The idea made him smile reluctantly. *No, that's too far-fetched, even for me. Who else could it be? The only other mages that I know of are Priests. . . .*

Priests! Suddenly an entirely new range of questions opened up before him.

What if this is being done by a Priest who is a mage? he wrote on the first page.

Why? Well, by strict Church standards, every single one of the victims and their putative killers were unrepentant sinners. Of course, the Church would *never* condone murdering unrepentant sinners, but the Priest could be mad. He could imagine himself to be the punitive arm of a stern and judgmental God; could even believe that God was commanding him to do away with these people in fashions that would horrify other sinners into instant repentance.

Right. Assume it is a Priest. Assume that the Church doesn't know for certain, but suspects this is what is going on.

That would definitely fit the other question, which was Rayburn's behavior. One word from a Priest to Rayburn advising him to keep all of this quiet, and Rayburn would be scratching to cover it like a fastidious house-cat. If the Church didn't even have a suspect yet, there would *really* be a cat among the pigeons, as every Priest that was in on the secret watched his fellows with suspicion.

Next idea—assume they have a suspect or two, but don't have evidence yet. They'd have Rayburn digging holes to dump evidence, if they had to!

Next—they know who it is, and they have him locked up, but he's still doing this. A barred cell isn't going to stop a really determined magician, but I've never *heard of a Priest being executed. As far as I know, they can't be executed, only imprisoned, and nothing is going to stop a renegade mage but execution.* Certainly the Church would not want *anyone* to know that they couldn't keep a crazy Priest-Mage from killing people! The resulting scandal could rock the Church to its foundations, calling into question virtually every aspect of control now exercised by Church officials. There had been enough scandal already associated with the Church's *possible* involvement in the Great Fire at Kingsford, and the trickery and chicanery of High Bishop Padrick *had* caused great unrest.

Riots? There'd be riots over that one, all right. With the Church claiming its tithe and doing damned little for the poor with that tithe, all it would take would be a hard winter, bad storms, and food shortages. A real, full-scale riot directed against the Church would produce enough angry people to level every Church-owned structure in the city.

If the Priest *wasn't* mad—if he was doing this with Church sanction—

A chill ran down his spine. *Don't think that. Don't write it down.*

It could be some terrible experiment in magic gone wrong. And that would be another reason for Rayburn's superiors to want it nicely sunk in the bottom of the harbor. No one would want people to know that the Church permitted anyone to dabble in the kind of magic that would drive a man to murder a relatively innocent woman and then kill himself.

Something else occurred to him and he wrote that down under the *Murders* topic. *What if this isn't local? What if we aren't the only city to have this going on?*

Well, if it wasn't local, it *probably* had nothing to do with the Church. Not that the Church *couldn't* be involved, but mages couldn't work magic at great distance, and something that caused murders in more than one city couldn't be hidden for long if Church officials knew about it. Things like that leaked out, novices learned things they weren't supposed to know, spreading rumor and truth more effectively than if the Church was spreading the tales deliberately.

There is a bare possibility that this is a mad Priest, that the Church knows about it, and they keep moving him from town to town every time he starts doing things like this, trying to cover up the murders and hoping that at some point he'll just stop, or God will stop him for them.

Well, there was one way of telling if it was local or not.

He put his two lists aside and took a fresh sheet of paper, addressing it to *The keeper of the mortality lists, Highwaithe,* which was the nearest town upriver.

He sighed, and flexed his hand to ease the cramps in it, dipped the quill in the inkwell, then set the pen carefully to the paper again.

Good Sir, he began, *I am collecting mortality statistics in relation to the weather, and am particularly interested in the occurrence of murder-suicides over the past five years.* . . .

There. Let Rayburn try to stop him now.

The only thing that is going to stop me now, he thought wryly, *is my aching hand, and the number of letters I'm willing to write.*

About the time he began getting replies to his letters, the rash of murders ended, as inexplicably as they had begun.

There were no more street-musicians cut down with vanishing knives. The only murders occurring now were the sordid and completely uninteresting kind.

But Tal was not relieved—rather, he was alarmed.

Every one of the clerks to whom he had written had responded, and most had been delighted that *someone* was showing interest in their dreary statistics. He'd gotten everything he asked, and more—one enterprising fellow had even sent him a breakdown of his violent-crime statistics by moon-phase.

Tal had set up one corner of his sitting-room with a map pinned to the wall and his pile of return letters beneath it. He sorted out the letters that showed no real increase in the number of murder-suicides, then stuck a pin into the map for every occurrence in those towns and cities where the number *had* gone up. The result was a crooked line that began—at least as far as he could tell—at a small town called Burdon Heath. At first, the grisly trail followed the route of the Newgate Trade Road, then it left the road where it crossed the river and followed that instead. There was no doubt in Tal's mind, now that it was laid out in front of him. Whatever this was, it was following the course of trade. The pattern was quite clear.

And he knew that it was not over, although the deadly shadow was no longer stalking the streets of *his* city. The mind that had conceived of these murders in the first place was not going to simply stop needing to commit them.

He sat back in his chair and closed his eyes. His first partner had been a constable who had solved the case of a madman who'd gone about mutilating whores. Tal remembered what the man had told him.

"A man like this has a need in him, lad," the old fellow had said. *"It's a craving, like drugs or strong liquor. He* needs *what he gets from doing things like this, and what he gets is power. The ability to control everything that happens to these girls, the moment they get into his hands—what they feel, how much they feel, and the most important control of all, when and how they die. That's what he gets. When you've got to find the man who does things like this,* that's *what you look for—that's what'll tell you what he's made of, not how he does it. Look for what he gets."*

If ever there was a case that those words fit, this was it.

And Tal knew that the mind behind these crimes, the mind that craved the power he had over the victims, had not suddenly been cured of its particular brand of madness. Rather, that mind was aware exactly how dangerous that last death had been—and he had moved on before he could be caught. Being caught was no part of his plan.

He had to have been watching, somewhere—he won't get the thrill he needs just by hearing gossip. He must have seen and understood what was going on when I took over the situation, and recognized that I was a constable. He wasn't going to take any more chances at that point. The murderer knew how perilous it was that there had been a constable close enough to *witness* that last death, and to have seen the knife and know it had vanished for certain. Tal's attempt to find the knife only proved to the murderer that Tal knew what he was looking for. The murderer had probably taken himself and his associates (if any) to another hunting ground.

Mortality Clerks were both cooperative and incurious, a fabulous combination so far as Tal was concerned. They not only supplied him with the bare statistics he'd asked for, they usually gave him the particulars of each murder.

The "musician" connection was still there. And the dates were in chronological order.

The further a town is from here, the farther back the rash of murder-suicides goes.

There was no overlap of dates—no case where there were times when the deaths occurred in two different places at nearly the same date. The unknown perpetrator staged his deaths, no less than three, and so far no more than nine. Then, at some signal Tal could not fathom, he decided it was time to move on, and did so.

He was finished here. That was the good news. The bad news was that he had moved on.

Unfortunately, the most likely place was the one city in the entire Kingdom where his depredations would be likely to go completely unnoticed for weeks, if not months, due to the chaotic conditions there. The Kanar River was the obvious and easiest road; it flowed easily and unobstructed through a dozen towns between here and the place that must surely attract this man as a fine, clear stream attracted trout fishers.

The great, half-burned and half-built metropolis of Kingsford.

Chapter Four

Reading too long—especially letters with terrible penmanship—always made Ardis's eyes ache, and the Justiciar-Priest closed and rubbed them with the back of her thumb. Rank did have its privileges, though, and no one asked the Priests of her Order to sacrifice comfort in return for devoting their lives to Justice and God. Though plain *almost* to the point of austerity, Ardis's quarters were warmed by a fine, draft-free stove, her reading-chair comfortably cushioned, and the light falling on her papers was as clear as fine oil, a carefully-trimmed wick, and a squeaky-clean lamp could provide.

But I'm tired, overworked, and getting no younger. Briefly, she wondered what her life would be like if she had wedded according to her stature, as her family had expected her to. At this hour, she would probably be receiving callers in a luxuriously-appointed reception room, giving final orders for a sumptuous formal dinner, and thinking about which dress she would wear to the evening's ball or party.

I'd be bored, which would be worse than overworked; my mind would have gone to mush, and I would probably have joined some stupid group devoted to mystical rubbish out of sheer desperation for something different in my life. Or I'd be having affair after frantic affair, like so many of my female relations are doing, because they are shackled in loveless, lifeless marriages with nothing to occupy their minds.

"I could read those and give you a summary," said her secretary Kayne Davenkent, a clever and steady young novice that Ardis had plucked from the ranks of the scribes just last summer.

Ardis didn't immediately reply, but she smiled to herself as she recalled the occasion that the novice had been brought to her attention. Like most novices in the Order of the Justiciars, she had been assigned to the copying of legal documents from all over the Twenty Kingdoms; these copies were sent out to Church libraries everywhere, in order to keep everyone current on legal precedent in all of the Kingdoms. There were only two forces common to all of human life on Alanda, the Church and the High King; and of the two, only the Church substantially affected the life of the common man. Kayne had persisted in questioning the authenticity of a recently acquired document she was supposed to be copying, which had irritated her superior. Ordinarily, he would have taken care of the problem himself, but he was of the faction that had not been in favor of Ardis when she asserted her control over the Abbey of the Order of the Justiciars at Kingsford, and he delighted in taking the smallest of discipline problems directly to Ardis rather than dealing with them himself. He probably hoped to overwhelm her with petty details, so that he and his faction could proceed to intrigue her right out of her position while she was drowning in nit-picking nonsense.

Unfortunately for his plans, she was already aware of his intentions, and in particular this attempt to irritate his superior had backfired. Intrigued by the notion of a novice who stood her ground against a Priest's judgment, Ardis demanded the particulars, and discovered that Kayne was right and Father Leod was wrong. Further, she discovered that in disputes of a similar nature, Kayne was usually right and Father Leod wrong.

Intelligence, acute observation, courage, wit, and persistence, and the ability to think for herself rather than parroting the opinions of her superior—those were qualities all too often lacking in novices, and qualities that Ardis appreciated. Knowing the young woman was wasted in her position, she had snatched Kayne up for her own staff before Father Leod knew what was happening.

"I know you could give me a summary, and a good one too, but you know why I won't let you," Ardis replied, putting her head back against the padded leather of her chair, her eyes still closed. "I told you why a week ago when you made the same offer—which is appreciated, by the way, even if I don't accept it."

"Because a summary won't give you the sense of things they aren't putting down," Kayne repeated, with a little well-bred irritation of her own. "That sounds rather too much like mind-reading, and I can't see where it's all that important in personal correspondence." Her irritation showed a little more. "It also sounds, frankly, as if you simply didn't want me to see the letter, and if that's the real reason, I wish you'd just *tell* me instead of making something up."

Ardis laughed at that, and opened her eyes. Kayne was very young to be a novice, but her clever tongue, acidic wit, sharp features and sharper temper were unlikely to win her many friends, much less suitors, so perhaps that was why she never attracted a marriage proposal. Ardis appreciated her sharp tongue, but she was going to have to teach Kayne how to curb it. Kayne was really too intelligent to ever remain a mere secretary, but if it hadn't been for Ardis, she probably would have been kept in a subordinate position all her life, and she *would* remain subordinate if she made too many enemies to advance.

She might have done well enough in secular society, but she had told Ardis in her initial interview that there really hadn't had any choice but to go into the Church. She was too poor to become a merchant, and there were not too many Masters in the more interesting Guilds and Crafts who would take on an Apprentice without the Apprenticing Fee.

Not much like myself at her age—but I think she's going to go far, if the Church will let her. And it will, if I have any say in the matter and she can learn when it is better to keep your observations behind your teeth.

"It's not mind-reading, and it's not intuition either," Ardis told her. "It's all based on patterns that I have observed after many years of dealing with these same people. I know what they say, how they say it, and how they conceal things they don't want me to know by the way they choose their words. It's knowledge you can't describe briefly to someone else, but it's knowledge all the same. And it's all the more important in personal correspondence, when the people who are writing to me are the movers and shakers of their areas—like my cousin Talaysen."

Kayne's brow wrinkled as she took that in. "I don't suppose you could give me an example, could you?" she asked.

"As a matter of fact, I can, from this letter." Ardis tapped the sheet of thick, cream-colored vellum on the desk, just above the seal of Free Bard Master Talaysen, currently the advisor to the King of Birnam. "My cousin mentions that his King has had three visitors from Rayden—from *our* part of the kingdom, in fact—but goes into detail on only two of them. He knows all three of them from his life at Court, before he gave up his position as a Master of the Bardic Guild, although it seems that none of them recognized him as he is now. I know from things we have written and spoken about in the past that he believes that the third man, who appears to be an ordinary enough fop, is actually playing a much deeper game involving both secular politics and the Church; he's warned me about this fellow before. I also know from other sources that this fellow has said things about *me* in the past that are less than complimentary. My cousin doesn't like to worry me, and if he believes there is something going on that threatens me, he will take whatever steps he can to thwart it himself without involving me. Hence, this third visitor has said or done something that makes Talaysen think he is gathering information for possible use against me, and Talaysen is trying to spike his wheels—probably by feeding him misinformation.'' She raised an eyebrow at her crestfallen secretary. ''Now, assume you've read this letter. Would you have made those deductions from it?''

''No,'' Kayne replied, properly humbled. ''I probably wouldn't even have mentioned the visitors at all, thinking they came under the heading of social chit-chat.''

''*Nothing* comes under the heading of social chit-chat when people have managed to make a High Bishop out of you,'' Ardis corrected sourly. ''May God help me.'' That last came out with the fervor of the prayer it actually was. Ardis would have been much happier if no one had ever come up with that particular notion.

''I thought you wanted to become a High Bishop,'' Kayne said in surprise. ''How could you not?''

''What, how could I not want to become a bigger target for slander, libel, and intrigue than I already was?'' she responded tartly. ''If I were only the Abbess and the Chief Justiciar, I would have been much safer; as a woman, they would always underestimate me so long as I didn't intrigue for a high position. If I had the power, but not the title, I would not be nearly the threat to other power-holders inside and outside the Church as I am since I wear the miter. I am not so fond of fancy hats that I was pleased to put up with all that just so I could wear one.''

Kayne snickered at Ardis's designation of the High Bishop's miter as a ''fancy hat.'' Ardis leaned over her desk and fixed her young secretary with a stern look.

''If you are going to prosper in the Church, you'd better keep in mind that a woman is always in a more precarious position than a man,'' she said carefully. ''It is much better to hold power quietly, without trappings, than it is to make a show of it. The men will resent you a great deal less, listen to you a great deal more, and might even come to respect you in time.''

Kayne nodded, slowly. ''So that's why—'' She spread her hands, indicating the office.

''Correct. The appearance of austerity and modesty, the reality of a certain level of comfort.'' Ardis smiled. ''You should have seen this office when my predecessor sat here. It looked like a cross between a Cathedral and a throne room. I cleared most of that out, sold the expensive trash to pay for this, and donated the rest to one of the orphanages Arden established after the Fire.'' She chuckled reminiscently. ''Somewhere in Kingsford there are orphans bouncing on his overstuffed, plush-covered sofa and grinding muddy little feet into his appalling carpet, and I do hope he finds out about it.''

Kayne snickered again. ''Well, is there anything you'd like to dictate to me before I retire to my office and catch up on the last of the work from yesterday?''

Ardis considered the stack of correspondence before her. ''How are things coming across the river?''

By ''across the river,'' Ardis meant in the city of Kingsford, which had been half burned down by a disastrous fire a little more than two years ago. The fire itself was not natural; it had been set by conspirators hoping to murder Duke Arden who had joined forces (or so Ardis suspected) with members of Ardis's own Order in an attempt to usurp control of the Cloister and Cathedral of the Justiciars, and then take full control of all of the Church holdings in Kingsford and put the lot in the hands of a group of closed-minded fanatics.

Ardis only suspected that the two groups had been in league with each other, even though there was nothing but rumor to link them— the fires had certainly been started magically, in the rafters of the Duke's Theater while the Duke was attending a performance. So far as Ardis knew, the only humans in Kingsford and the surrounding area who could use magic were Priests of the Order of Justiciars. There had been any number of the fanatical faction preaching and stirring up trouble before the Fire, and there were a few witnesses among the actors and musicians who had seen a figure in the robes of a Priest loitering about the theater in a suspicious manner just before the fire. And the uprising within the Cloister walls had occurred so simultaneously with the fires in the theater that even the most skeptical were convinced that it could not be a coincidence. But a hot, high wind combined with the driest summer on record had contributed to spreading the fire out of control, while the uprising within the Cloister walls had ensured that there were no mages to spare to fight those fires, and when it was all over, the greater part of Kingsford lay in ruins. It was only the personal effort of Arden himself that kept the disaster from being worse than it was. The Duke had led the battle against the fire himself, working side by side with the lowest citizens of the city. His actions had earned him the undying loyalty of all of Kingsford, and the title ''Good Duke Arden.''

Two years later, the city was still partly in ruins, and Ardis felt very sorry for the Grand Duke. He had beggared himself to help pay for the rebuilding, with the intentions of creating an ideal city out of the ashes, a city with no slums, a city that was planned from the beginning, a city where residential districts would not sit cheek-by-jowl with tanneries, and sewers would not dump their noisome contents upstream from places where people drew out their water.

But the best-laid plans of men and Grand Dukes were subject to the whims of fate, and fate had decreed otherwise. Unwilling or unable to wait on the Duke's plans to rebuild their homes and businesses, those who had money of their own proceeded to put those homes and businesses wherever they pleased—usually building on what was left of their old property.

The result was that half of the rebuilt city was laid out along Duke Arden's plans, and the other half was laid out the same way it had been—in as haphazard a fashion as could be expected. The only real change was that he had been able to decree that streets would be laid out on a grid, so there were no more dead ends and cul-de-sacs, or meandering alleys that went nowhere.

"Arden finally got the fireboats he ordered," Kayne reported. "They arrived today. Whether they work or not—" She shrugged.

"If they don't, I'll make a point of assigning someone to get those pumps working by magic, providing Arden doesn't browbeat a Deliambren to come up with something better," Ardis replied. She still suffered from twitches of mingled guilt and anger when she thought of how easy it would have been for Church mages to halt the fire before it had spread more than a block or two. Not that *she* was responsible for the fact that they hadn't, but still—

I am a mage and a Justiciar, and what happened to the people of Kingsford was a gross miscarriage of Justice.

"He probably will; he already has them working on a system to pump water to every part of the city," Kayne observed. "What's a little thing like fixing the pumps on a fireboat, compared to that?"

Ardis nodded absently. *If the idiots that started those fires didn't perish in the conflagration, they had better be so far from Kingsford that humans are an oddity. Because if I ever get hold of them, they'll pray to be handed over to the Duke for punishment. He'll only hang them.* She had already taken care of those she had been able to catch. Recalling a magic transformation discovered and abused by another renegade Priest-Mage, she had put his discovery to better use. The miscreants were serving out life sentences, toiling under baskets of rubble and ashes, and wearing the forms of donkeys. Titularly the property of the Abbey, they were under long-term loan to the city.

And when all the rubble was cleared away, they would be hitched to the carts that carried away the dead. They were well cared for, housed in their own stable in the city, where a special Priest of one of the Service Orders—a close, personal friend of both Ardis and the Duke—who knew what they were had been assigned to their physical and spiritual needs. They were awakened every morning at dawn with prayer, put to bed in their stalls with prayer, and prayed over while they worked. They would have ample opportunity for repentance, redemption, and contemplation.

They were also performing the hardest physical labor they ever had in their lives, seven days a week, from dawn to dusk, in pouring rain, burning sun, or blinding blizzard. They would never be human again, for Ardis had locked the spell on them herself. No one knew of their fate except Ardis, the Grand Duke, and the young Priest assigned to their care, who was far more concerned with the state of their souls than the discomfort of their bodies. Even Duke Arden agreed that the punishment was sufficient. Ardis had similar fates planned for any more miscreants that turned up.

"As for the rest, Arden has given up on the Carpenters, and now he's trying with the Weavers and Dyers." Kayne looked thoughtful. "I think he'll have a bit more luck with them; they need water for their work more than the Carpenters do."

Arden was trying to persuade those who had built according to their own plans to tear down what they had put up, and rebuild according to his. He was having mixed success, and often it depended on the season and whether or not he had alternatives available while those who were displaced waited for the new construction to be completed. People who might not mind spending a month or two in a well-appointed tent in the summer, would get decidedly testy about the idea in midwinter, and those whose businesses required that their materials stay dry were not likely to give up a roof for the sky.

Ardis chuckled. "Poor Arden! He'll never give up, not as long as there is a single crooked street in Kingsford."

"Perhaps. Or perhaps he will find other things to occupy him," Kayne observed. "He can't stay out of politics forever, as you have pointed out in the past. Speaking of politics, have you anything you'd like me to take care of for you, since you haven't got anything to dictate to me?"

"Here—" Ardis handed the young woman a small packet of invitations. "Accept the invitation to Duke Arden's musical entertainment, give permission for the Novice's Choir to sing at the opening of the new Wool Guild Hall with the stipulation that no more than half the repertory be hymns mentioning sheep, shepherds, spinners, weavers, or wool, and decline everything else with my sincere regrets." She shook her head. "I never got this many invitations to dinners and parties when I was a maiden looking for a husband; I can't conceive of why I'm getting them now."

Kayne accepted the packet with a shrug. "I haven't the background to tell you," she said with callous frankness. "Maybe they hope God will judge their entertaining with charity when they die if you attend."

Ardis stretched, the heavy sleeves of her scarlet robe falling down around her elbows. "That's as good a theory as any," she replied. "Now, I'll just write a brief letter to my cousin, and you can pick it off my desk and address it in the morning."

Taking that properly as her dismissal, Kayne rose and made the ritual bows: a brief nod of respect to Ardis, and a deeper genuflection to the small altar in the corner of the room. When she was gone, Ardis picked up her pen and took a clean sheet of paper. It never took long to write to Talaysen; words flowed as easily as if she was talking to him rather than writing. No matter how long it had been since they last saw each other, or how many leagues lay between them, they were still closer than many siblings.

When she had finished, she sanded the letter to dry the ink, then set it aside in the tray for Kayne to take in the morning. There were more records to deal with, for record-keeping had not been a priority when there were people who were going to die of injuries or exposure if something wasn't done about their needs right that moment.

Ardis had never minded record-keeping or paperwork, unlike some of her colleagues. These days it gave her some time to herself, time when she was not the High Bishop. Even now, it still gave her a twinge when she realized that the title and all that went with it were hers. It was an honor and a responsibility she had not expected to attain before her hair was totally white, if ever.

She had known all along that the position would be as much trouble as honor, and she was resigned to dealing with the former. These records were a part of that; extremely sensitive information that she did not want in the hands even of her loyal secretary. These were the Abbey records that dealt with crime and punishment.

Priests who "failed the Faith"—the euphemism for criminals— were seldom turned over to secular authorities, and were never punished publicly. Every Abbey had a section of cells with locks on the outside of the doors—effectively a gaol—and some even referred to that section by that name. Others, like the Justiciars' Kingsford Abbey, were more discreet, and called the section by the term "repentance retreat." Those who stole, committed fraud, or violated Church canon law ended up there until they truly, sincerely repented. Sometimes, however, there were cases that were more serious and required a solution that went beyond simple incarceration. There had been four such cases locked in the cells at the time of the rebellion and Fire, three of whom had been mages, and like the others who had been down there, they had been released by the rebels. One had died in a mage-battle. The one who was not a mage had fled, though not to the rebels, but to Ardis's people and had earned a certain amount of forgiveness by warning them and fighting at their side. Two had vanished completely.

Since they had last been seen fleeing for the city, it was presumed that they were dead, but Ardis didn't much care for making such presumptions. Especially not where these two were concerned, since both of them, like her little donkeys, had been locked into forms that were not human. One of them was the renegade Priest-Mage named Revaner, who had discovered transformative magic in the first place, and his transformation was public knowledge, since it had occurred very dramatically at the Midsummer Faire.

It was a tale that had been made into more than one song. Revaner had lusted after a young Free Bard and Gypsy named Robin; she had spurned his advances, and in revenge, he had conspired with a Guild Bard named Betris to catch and confine her. When she was caught, Revaner transformed her into a huge, brightly-colored bird that he displayed as a curiosity and forced to sing for his guests at the Faire. Master Talaysen, his apprentice Rune, and another Free Bard called Heron had discovered what had happened to Robin and appealed to the Justiciars. Ardis had directed them to bring the bird before her; they had stolen the captive and after a long and dramatic chase through the grounds of the Faire, had brought not only the transformed Bard, but had brought Revaner who had been pursuing them. The Priest made the mistake of underestimating Ardis's power and had claimed the bird as his property; Ardis and the other two Justiciar-Mages with her had demonstrated by breaking his spells that the bird was the Gypsy after all.

They had been not only his judges, but the instrument of his punishment; in breaking his spells, they turned his magic back on him, and he was the one who was transformed. Ardis was senior enough to decree that this was fit punishment, and transformed he had remained until the day of the Fire.

There were two more rebellious priests who were among the unaccounted-for, although they were not mages. Ardis had spent the last several days going over the records of the unidentified dead from the

Fire, hoping to find matches for her missing miscreants. She frowned as she came up empty-handed.

This is not good. I would rather not contemplate the consequences of renegade Priest-Mages wandering about, feeding their own mad agendas. Granted, they had been stripped of their powers, but it hadn't been their magic powers that were the cause of their incarceration. They could still do harm.

They could set themselves up as Priests of some other Order out in the back of beyond, and go back to abusing those who are in their care. And we wouldn't know unless someone reported them, or the local Priest got curious because they stopped attending services in his chapel. Even then, we wouldn't know unless he made an inquiry—

She shook her head. The only thing that she could think to do was to send letters to the Clerks of the Records of all the other Orders, describing the runaways, advising that they might try to set themselves up in their own parishes, and asking that copies of any suspicious inquiries be sent to Kingsford Abbey.

If they dare try that and we catch them— She gritted her teeth. They would be made very unhappy.

I wonder how they would like serving the Church as oxen at one of the hermitage farms? That would be particularly appropriate in the case of Revaner.

She did what she could among the records, made a first draft of the letter she was going to have to send to the other Orders, and locked it in a drawer. She'd have to make some special preparations tomorrow, but this was one time when it made more sense to make copies magically than by hand. Someday, perhaps, she could allow Kayne to know this particular secret, but for now it was best kept as private as possible.

She turned back to the letter from her cousin, for the final paragraph troubled her. Talaysen very seldom asked her for anything, and the request he had for her this time was a disturbing one.

I have been receiving reports from Rayden of the murders of several Free Bards and Gypsies, he wrote. *Ardis, I will be the very first to admit that my people tend to get themselves into trouble of their own accord, and occasionally some of them do end up on the wrong end of a knife. But these have all been violent, senseless, horrible murders by absolute strangers; no one understands why or how they happened, and all the victims have been women. Some of my people are becoming very alarmed; they don't know how to explain it, but the ones with magic think that there is some power that is deliberately seeking them out to slay them. I don't know what you can do—but you are a Priest, a mage, and a Justiciar. Can you try to find out what is going on and put a stop to it?*

She smoothed her short hair back with both hands and stared at that last paragraph, cursing Talaysen for not sending her all the facts.

But that assumed that he *had* them; he might know nothing more than what he had told her. Still, if she had names, dates, places—she might have been able to start an investigation. It would be a great deal more difficult to do so with "information" that was this vague.

She had already told him, though, in an equally vague sentence at the end of her letter, that she would do everything she could to "help him with his problem."

She folded up his letter and locked it away with the other sensitive material in her special desk drawer. *I'll put it in the back of my mind and sleep on it,* she told herself, knowing that she often came up with solutions to difficult situations that way. *Right now, more than anything, I need a little time to myself. My mind feels as bloated and stiff as a cow-gut balloon.*

Now—now was her one hour of indulgence, the hour she kept solely for herself, when she could read in silence and peace, and not have to think of anything but the words on the page before her.

She'd only begun taking this hour for herself in the last few weeks; until now, things had been too hectic even to steal a single hour for herself. This was the quiet time she had been hoping for since the Great Fire; in the months that had followed the conflagration, she had been forced to do the work of four people. There had been the situation in her own Order to consolidate, by making certain that *her* allies in the Order were placed in every position of importance and those whose loyalties were in doubt were put in positions of equal stature, but where they could do her no harm—such as Father Leod. Occasionally, she had been forced to manufacture such positions, to avoid making an outright enemy by demoting him. Then there had been the relief effort in the city—the number of deaths had been appalling, and as the days passed, more and more of the missing had to be added to the rolls of the "presumed dead." The number of burned and injured was even worse than the number of dead, for at least the dead no longer suffered. The injured suffered terribly, for fatal burns made for a long, drawn-out, agonizing death when there were not enough painkillers to treat more than a fraction of those hurt. For those who were most likely to die anyway, she had had to make the unpleasant decision to give them the painkillers with the worst long-term side effects—since after all, they would not survive long enough to suffer them—but while they still breathed they could have less agony. Then there were the homeless

... and the illnesses that followed exposure to the elements, food and water that could not be kept clean, and of course the overwhelming shock and grief.

The one saving grace had been that it was summer rather than winter. The one miracle was that some of the warehouses where the tents used in the Kingsford Faire were stored had been spared. One of Ardis's first acts was to order the warehouses broken into and the tents erected on Faire Field to shelter the homeless, no matter who owned them. Her second had been to commandeer as much canvas as existed within several days' journey and arrange for it, rope, tools, and poles to be made available to the refugees. It was amazing how many of them acquired tent-making skills when the raw materials were left at hand for them to use. She had ensured that no avaricious profiteer could scoop it all up and sell it by having the canvas parceled into reasonable bits and rationed by armed guard.

All of the resources of the Church had been put to the task of making it possible for people to begin salvaging their lives again, and between the Church and their Duke, by that winter, most people had some sort of reasonable shelter to meet the snow.

And now, most people had real walls and roofs, and it was *their* duty to get their lives in order, and not the Church's. Things were not back to normal, and would not be for many years to come, but they were at the point where people could take over their own lives.

And Ardis could, at last, go back to some of her old habits. She might even be able to devote more of her time to reading than just that single hour.

Kingsford was not a jewel without a flaw; there were plenty of them. The Duke's coffers were far from bottomless, and he could not remedy every ill. He would very much have liked to build places where the poor could enjoy walls and roofs as solid as those of their "betters," but he had to budget his resources, and there were others with fewer scruples ready to supply the needs of the lowborn. Nor had the nature of the people who had lived there been changed by the Fire. So as a result, the new Kingsford was a great deal like the old Kingsford. There were blocks of ramshackle tenements that looked as if they would fall down in the first strong wind—but somehow managed to survive all the same. There were a few lawless places where even the constables would not walk at night. There were thieves, cutpurses, sharpsters, game-cheats, procurers, unlicensed street-walkers, and those who preyed upon their fellow humans in every way that had ever been thought of.

Ardis, who as a Priest was far more cognizant of the breadth of human nature than Duke Arden, could have told him that this would happen. She had also known that it would be useless to tell him, as this was the last thing he wanted to hear. So she had held her peace, and as Kingsford rose Phoenix-like out of the ashes, she did her best to counsel and console him when some of his city's new-grown "feathers" were broken, dirty, or stunted.

At least now that winter had settled in, there would be less violent public crime for her people to handle. Dealing with that was yet another task of the Justiciars, although they generally only were involved when a putative criminal was apprehended and not before. The death rate wouldn't drop off, for the very old, the weak, and the very young would succumb to the cold and the illnesses associated with the cold. Those deaths were the purview of the Charitable Orders in the city itself, and not of the Justiciars. Justiciars and Justiciar-Mages could and did work limited Healing magics, but not often, and it was not widely known that they could do so; the fact that the Justiciars worked magic at all was not exactly a secret, but detailed knowledge was not widely disseminated. The problem with doing magical Healing was that it was difficult to know when to stop—and who to help. It would be easy to spend all one's time or energy on Healing and get nothing else done.

That would certainly be a cause for rejoicing among the city's miscreants and criminals, who would be only too happy for the Justiciars to spend their time on something besides dispensing justice.

Well, they're all bottled up until warmer weather. When the winter wind howled, even the cutthroats huddled beside their stoves and waited for spring.

And just as they, she settled into her often-uneasy new position, huddled beside *her* stove, and took an hour's consolation each night in books.

This wasn't frivolous reading—she'd left all that behind her outside the Cloister walls—but she didn't often choose devotional works, either. Usually, it was law or history; occasionally, works on magic.

Today it was to be a very private work on magic which had arrived with her cousin's letter, written expressly for her by one of Talaysen's Gypsy friends, and to be destroyed as soon as she finished reading it. It was a short manuscript on Gypsy magic—or rather, the fashion in which Gypsies used the power that was magic. Another manuscript had come with this one, which had been hidden inside the larger tome—also written by a Gypsy, it described the means by which miracles could be faked. After some editing for form rather than content, Ardis intended to have this one published for the general public.

Then, perhaps, there will be less of a chance for another High Bishop Padrik to deceive the public.

She evened the manuscript and set it down on the desktop before her. But before she had read more than the introductory sentences, Kayne returned, a frown on her face.

"There's a fellow here who insists on seeing you," she said with annoyance. "He won't leave, and short of getting guards to throw him out, I can't *make* him leave. He claims to be a constable from Haldene, and he says he has information it's vital to give you."

Ardis sighed. "And it can't wait until my morning audience hours tomorrow?" she asked wearily.

Kayne shook her head. "He says not, and he won't talk to anyone else."

Ardis weighed duty against desire, and as always, duty won. "Send him in," she said with resignation, putting her manuscripts safely away in that special drawer, and locking it. She secured the lock with just a touch of magic as the importunate visitor came in, escorted by Kayne, who made no effort to hide her disapproval.

But Ardis was not so certain that Kayne's disapproval was warranted. The fellow was quite clearly exhausted, his plain, workaday clothing travel-stained, and his face gray and lined with weariness.

First impressions were important, and this man impressed her because of his physical state. If whatever he had to tell her was *not* really important, he would have taken the time to clean up and don his finest garments.

"Constable Tal Rufen of Haldene," Kayne announced with an audible sniff, and Ardis rose and extended her hand. Rufen took it, went to his knee in the appropriate genuflection, and pressed it briefly to his forehead in token of his submission to the authority of God and the Church. So he was a Churchman. Not all humans were—the Gypsies, for instance, held to their own set of deities, chief of whom was the Lady of the Night. Very different from the Church's sexless Sacrificed God.

"Sit down, Tal Rufen," Ardis said as soon as he rose to his feet. She turned to her secretary. "Kayne, please bring us some hot tea and something to eat, would you?"

Kayne's disapproval dropped from her like a cloak when she saw that Ardis was going to take the man seriously. "Yes, High Bishop," the young woman said respectfully, as Ardis's visitor dropped into the chair she indicated with a lack of grace that bespoke someone nearing the end of his strength.

Ardis ignored that and settled into her own chair, steepling her fingers together as she considered the constable before her.

The man was of middling stature and middling years; she would guess he was very nearly her own age, perhaps a year or two older. He had probably been a constable for most of his adult life; he exhibited his authority unconsciously, and wore his uniform tunic with an easy familiarity that suggested he might be more uncomfortable in civilian clothing than in his working garb. No paper-pusher this, he had the muscular strength of a man quite used to catching runaway horses and running thieves, wrestling rowdy drunks and breaking down doors. The lines on his face suggested that he didn't smile much, nor did he frown; his habitual expression was probably one of neutral sobriety. He had an oblong face with a slightly squared chin, high, flat cheekbones, and deepset eyes of an indeterminate brown beneath moderately thick brows. Gray in his brown hair suggested that he might be a bit older than he looked, but Ardis didn't think so.

He probably earned those gray hairs on the streets. He looked competent, and a competent constable took his duty seriously.

So what was he doing so far from Haldene?

"Tal Rufen of Haldene," she said, breaking the silence and making him start. "You're a long way from home."

The entrance of Kayne with a loaded tray gave him a reason not to answer, but Kayne didn't stay. Ardis caught her secretary's eyes and made a slight nod towards the door; Kayne took it as the order it was and left them alone. Ardis poured out tea and handed him a cup and a plate of cheese and unleavened crackers. Tal drank his cup off in a single gulp, asked permission with a glance, and poured himself a second cup that he downed while he wolfed crackers and cheese as if he hadn't eaten all day.

Perhaps he hasn't. Very curious.

But if he did his work the way he ate, his superiors would never be able to find fault with him; he was quick, efficient, and neat. Without being rude or ill-mannered, he made the food vanish as thoroughly as if he were a sleight-of-hand artist, and settled back into his chair with a third cup of tea clasped between his hands.

"I don't see very many constables from outside of Kingsford," Ardis continued, "And then, it is usually only in the summer. I would say that it must have been some very urgent errand to urge you to travel so far in the middle of winter."

"If you consider murder an urgent errand, you would be correct, High Bishop," the man replied quietly in a ringing baritone. "For it is murder that brings me here." He waited for her to interrupt, then went on. "I want to beg your indulgence, however, and allow me to tell you this in my own way."

"If your way is to begin at the beginning and acquaint me with the facts as you discovered them, then proceed," she told him, watching him from beneath lowered lids.

He nodded soberly and began his narrative. He was precise, detailed, and dry in a way that reminded her of a history book. That, in turn, suggested that he had more than a passing acquaintance with such books. Interesting; most of the constables she knew were hardly scholars.

She had interviewed any number of constables over the course of the years, and he had already stated it was murder that brought him here, so it was no surprise when he began with the details of a particularly sordid case. The solution seemed straightforward enough, for the murderer had turned around and immediately threw himself into the river—

But it can't be that straightforward.

Her conclusion was correct, for he described another murder, then a third—and she very quickly saw the things that linked them all together. The bizarre pattern of murder, then suicide. And the missing knife.

She interrupted him as he began the details of a fourth case. "*What is going on in Haldene, Tal Rufen?*" she demanded with concern. "Is there some disease driving your people to kill each other? I cannot ever recall hearing of that many murder-suicides in a single year in Kingsford, and this is a far larger city than little Haldene!"

He gave her a look of startled admiration. "I don't know, my Lady Bishop," he replied with new respect. "I did consider that solution, but it doesn't seem to match the circumstances. Shall I continue?"

She gestured at him to do so, and continued to listen to his descriptions, not only of the chain of murder-suicides in Haldene, but similar crimes that he had uncovered with patient inquiry over the countryside. They began in a chain of villages and towns that led to Haldene, then moved beyond.

Beyond—to Kingsford, which was the next large city in the chain, if the pattern was to follow the Kanar River.

He came to the end of his chain of reasoning just as she came to that realization.

"Interesting." She watched him narrowly; he didn't flinch or look away. "And you think that Kingsford is now going to be visited by a similar set of occurrences? That is what brought you here?"

"Yes, High Bishop," he told her, and only then did he raise a hand to rub at his eyes, wearily. "I do. And now I must also make a confession to you."

"I am a Priest," she said dryly. "I'm rather accustomed to hearing them."

She had hoped to invoke at least a faint smile from him, but all he did was sigh. "I fear that I am here under somewhat false pretenses. I *was* a constable of Haldene, but I'm rather afraid that I am no longer. I began investigating this string of tragedies over the objections of my superiors; I continued against their direct orders. When they discovered what I had learned, they dismissed me." He waited to see if she was going to react to that, or say something, and continued when she did not. "I would have quit in any case, when I saw where this—series of coincidences—was heading." He smiled, with no trace of humor. "There is a better chance that the King will turn Gypsy tomorrow than that my superiors would permit me to take leave to inform authorities in Kingsford about this. After all, the plague has left Haldene; it is no longer a problem for those in authority there."

"I . . . see." She wondered for a moment if he was going to ask her for a position. Had all of this been manufactured just to get her attention? "Have you gone to the Captain of the constables in Kingsford?"

"I tried," he replied, and this time he *did* smile faintly. "He's not an easy man to get to."

"Hmm. True." In fact, Captain Fenris was the hardest man to *find* in Kingsford, but not because he was mewed up in an office behind a battery of secretaries. It might take weeks before Tal was able to track him down. "I believe that at the moment he is on double-shift, training the new recruits. He could be anywhere in the city at any given moment, and his second-in-command is unlikely to make any decisions in a situation like this."

"More to the point, I'm hardly going to get a glowing recommendation from my former superiors in Haldene, if his second-in-command were to make an inquiry about me," Tal pointed out. "They'll probably tell him I'm a troublemaker with a history of mental instability."

Honest. And he hasn't said a word about wanting a position.

"I will admit that I'm becoming obsessed with this case," Tal continued, and then she saw a hint, just the barest glimpse, of something fierce and implacable. It gazed at her out of his eyes for a moment, then vanished. "Who or whatever is behind this, I want it stopped."

"And you want from me?" Ardis spread her hands. Now, if there was going to be a plea for anything, she had given Tal an opening.

He hesitated. "I want—authority," he said finally. "Credentials.

Not a great deal, just enough that if anyone asks me why I'm snooping around, I can say I'm acting on your behalf and with your knowledge. Of course, I'll keep you informed every day, even if I find nothing, and I won't actually *do* anything unless it is to stop a murder in progress. I won't search houses or people, I won't try and haul anyone off to gaol, I won't threaten or bully. I'll just observe and ask questions.''

Ardis graced him with her most skeptical look. "And that's all you want?''

"Well, obviously I'd *like* to have all of the Kingsford constables working on this, I'd *like* the services of a mage, and I'd *like* four or five personal assistants,'' he replied a little sarcastically. "But I'd also like to be made Captain of the constables, stop this madness before it infects Kingsford, and be rewarded with the Grand Duke's daughter. Obviously none of this is possible, so I'm asking for the least I need to continue to track this case.''

"And what had you planned to do to make ends meet?'' she asked bluntly. "I assume you aren't independently wealthy.''

He shrugged. "I was working on the case in my off-time anyway. I have enough muscle and experience to get a job as a private guard, or even a peace-keeper in a tavern. I can still work on it in my off-time, and without being harassed for doing so, if I can just get minimal credentials.''

So, he's willing to support himself in a strange city just so that he can continue following this—whatever it is. He's right. He's obsessed. I wish more people would become that obsessed when it is necessary.

"Let me assume for the moment that there really *is* a—force—that is causing these deaths. It occurs to me that alerting the entire constabulary to this case might also make that force go into hiding,'' she said aloud, not quite willing to answer his request yet.

"That could easily be true,'' he agreed. "Which is, unfortunately, a good reason *not* to inform Captain Fenris—or at least, to ask him not to inform the rest of the constabulary. And it also occurs to me that this force knows a great deal about how both investigation and magic operate.'' He raised one eyebrow at her. "It hadn't escaped my notice that every one of the suicides was either *by means* of running water or *under* running water—even the jeweler.''

Now she was surprised, for she had thought that last horrific case had all been perpetrated indoors. "How could the jeweler—''

"He worked with acids, and he had a kind of emergency downpour rigged in his studio,'' Tal replied. "He had a pipe coming down from his rooftop cistern that ended in the ceiling of his studio, with a valve on the end that was operated by a string with a drain beneath it. After he drank his acids and poisons, he staggered over beneath the pipe and pulled the string. When he was found, the cistern was empty—the initial investigation missed that, because by then the floor was dry." He looked at her expectantly.

"Obviously I don't have to tell you that running water is the only certain means of removing evidence of magic." She tapped the ends of her forefingers together and frowned. "This is beginning to form a picture I don't like."

"Because most of the *human* mages are in the Church?" Tal asked quietly.

Surprised, but pleased at his audacity, she nodded. "There is the possibility that it is not a human, but frankly—what you've told me fits no pattern of a nonhuman mind that I am aware of. At least, not a sane one, and the nonhuman races are very careful not to allow their . . . problems . . . to escape to human lands."

"Just as we are careful not to let ours escape to theirs," he corroborated. "Still. Elves?"

She shook her head. "Elves take their revenge in a leisurely fashion, and an artistic one. This is both too sordid and too hasty for Elves to be involved."

"Haspur aren't mages, nor Mintaks, nor Deliambrens," he said, thinking out loud. "It could be someone from a very obscure race— but then, I'd have known about him; he'd stand out in those neighborhoods like a white crow. What about Gypsies? I've heard some of them are mages."

Again, she hesitated. "There are bad Gypsies—but the Gypsies are very careful about policing their own people. If this is a Gypsy, he has somehow eluded hunters from among his own kind, and that is so difficult that I find it as unlikely as it being an Elf. I have information sources among them, and I have heard nothing of—"

She stopped in midsentence, suddenly struck by something. Her cousin's letter—

Tal waited, watching her expectantly.

"I was about to say that I have heard nothing of this," she said very slowly, "but I have had *some* distressing information from my sources. The victims—have they by any chance been Free Bards or Gypsies?"

Again, she got a startled look from him. "I can only speak for the cases in Haldene; I didn't get much detail on the ones in the other towns and villages, and frankly, I didn't spend much time investigating when I learned that the murders were going in the direction that I had feared. No Free Bards, and only one Gypsy," he told her, licking his lips. "But—perhaps this will seem mad to you, which is why I hesitated to mention it—every one of the dead women was either a musician of sorts, or posing as one."

Ardis pursed her lips. "So. There is a link between the victims, even when they seem disparate in everything but their poverty."

I don't like this. I don't like this at all. Ardis was not aware that she was frowning until she caught a brief glimpse of worry on Tal's face. She forced her expression into something smoother.

"I believe you, Tal Rufen," she said at last. "Anyone planning to hoodwink me would have concocted something less bizarre and more plausible."

The constable's visible relief conjured at least a tiny smile onto her face. "So you'll vouch for me if I have trouble getting information?" he asked hopefully.

"I'll do more than that." She pulled the bell-cord that summoned Kayne from the next room. When the novice arrived, eyes brimming with suppressed curiosity, Ardis motioned for her to sit down as well.

"Tal, this is Novice Kayne, my personal secretary. I suspect you will be working at least peripherally together." They eyed one another warily; a grayhound and a mastiff trying to decide if they were going to be friends or not. She hid her amusement. "Kayne, I am making Tal one of the Abbey Guards, and my personal retainer." She smiled a bit wider as they both turned startled eyes on her. "Please get him the appropriate uniforms and see that he has housing with the others. A room to himself, if you please, and a key to the garden doors; his hours are likely to be irregular. He is going to be a Special Inquisitor, so draw up the papers for him. No one else is to know of that rank for the moment except you and the Guard-Captain, however. To the rest, he is simply to be my Personal Guard."

Kayne's eyes danced with excitement; this was obviously the sort of secret she had hoped to be privy to when Ardis appointed her to her post. "Yes, High Bishop. At once. Guard Rufen, have you any belongings you wish me to send to your quarters?"

"I have a pack-mule in your courtyard, and a riding-mule," Tal said dazedly. "I left them tied to the post there."

"I'll see that they are taken care of." She rose quickly to her feet, and looked briefly to Ardis for further instructions.

"You can come back for him here," Ardis said. "Oh—and draw out his first quarter's pay, would you?"

"Of course, High Bishop." The young woman left in a swirl of rust-colored robes and anticipation.

Ardis settled back in her chair, secretly a little pleased to have so startled the stone-faced constable. "There are times when it is very useful to have no one to answer to but one's own self. So, Guard Rufen, you are now a Special Inquisitor. That means that no one can hinder you in whatever you wish to ask or wherever you wish to go. That which is told to you is under the same veil of secrecy as the Confessional; you may tell it to no one except your direct superior, which is myself, since you are the only Inquisitor the Kingsford Abbey now boasts. Within reason, and Kayne will tell you when you have transgressed those bounds, you may requisition anything you need from the Abbey resources. That includes bribe-money—"

She laughed at his shocked expression. "Oh, come now, Inquisitor Rufen—do you take me for a cloistered unworldly? You will have to bribe people; often only money will loosen the tongue when not even threat of eternal damnation will have an effect. Simply tell Kayne what it is for, and keep strict accounts."

"Yes, High Bishop," he said faintly.

"Come to Kayne for whatever you need," she continued. "Report to me once a day if you have anything new to report, to Kayne if you have nothing. Take your meals in the Abbey or in the city, as you prefer, but meals in the city will have to come under your own expenses. Wear your uniform as you deem advisable; *always* within the Abbey, but outside of the Abbey, you may choose to wear civilian clothing. As a Special Inquisitor, your duty is to investigate what *I* deem necessary, not religious irregularities. Those are for the General Inquisitors, of which this Abbey has none. The city constables will not interfere with you when you show them your papers—but in any event, once they know you by sight, they won't bother you. I'll tell Fenris only that you are conducting an investigation for me. Only Duke Arden's men might continue to impede you, and they won't after I send my cousin a little note. The people who will know your true rank will be myself, Captain Fenris, Captain Othorp, Duke Arden, and Novice Kayne. Any questions?"

Tal Rufen still looked as if he had fallen from a great height onto his head. "Ah—just one," he said, finally. "*Why?*"

As an answer, she tossed him her cousin's letter—for those who did not know Talaysen—or Gwydain, the name he had been born with—the contents were innocuous enough.

Tal read it through quickly; that answered one of her questions: he was obviously not only able to read, but fairly literate. *Which means he may well be an amateur scholar of history. I shall have to be sure to let him make free with the Abbey library.* He got to the last paragraph, and she watched him as he read it through twice.

He looked up at her. "This Talaysen—this is—?"

"Free Bard Talaysen, Master Wren, Laurel Bard, and advisor to the King of Birnam."

"And the leader of the Free Bards, as well as a person respected and admired among the Gypsies. I see." He handed the letter back to her. "I think we can probably assume that most, if not all, of the murders he speaks of bear the same signature as the ones I told you about."

"I would say so." She put the letter away in her desk. "You also asked for a mage; I can offer you two. The first is a fellow Justiciar who also has some other abilities—he can touch minds, and sometimes read the past from objects. His name is Arran, and he just happens to be another cousin of mine."

The corner of Tal's mouth twitched a little at that; the first hint that he had a sense of humor. "Are you related to half the Kingdom?" he asked.

She sighed. "Only a third. Oh, not really, but sometimes it feels as if I am," she replied feelingly. "Especially when they all seem to have favors they want granted."

"Well, it looks as if you are granting another," he observed cautiously.

She shook her head. "No. That wasn't what I meant when I handed you that letter. I would have done this if Talaysen hadn't sent that letter and that request. It was simply a confirmation of everything you told me, with the additional information that there were more victims than even *you* knew about. It is the duty of the Justiciar to see that all creatures have justice. Generally, miscreants are brought before us, but it is fully within our power to order investigations when the secular authorities are moving too slowly."

"Or not at all," Tal muttered bitterly, giving her a brief glimpse of how deeply his anger ran that he had not been heeded.

"Or not at all," she agreed. "It is our duty to see to it that *nothing* impedes an investigation that needs to be made. Not even when suspicion indicates a suspect within the Brotherhood of the Church."

Another startled glance from Tal made her nod. "This isn't the first time I have suspected a Priest-Mage of wrongdoing," she told him with brutal frankness. "The only difference is that all the other times I at least had actual suspects. Now I have only the—what did you call it?—the signature?"

"The signature," he confirmed. "The methods and the victims change, the settings change, but the signature stays the same. There are some very basic needs being addressed here. A great anger is being fed, and I suspect there is some—'' He hesitated.

"Sexual link?'' she asked shrewdly. By now he was over being shocked or surprised by anything she would say, and nodded. *Probably due to the fact that I suggested it could be a Priest.* "If it *is* a member or former member of the Brotherhood, that would not be a surprise. Sometimes the appearance of chastity is used as a disguise rather than being part of a vocation. Sometimes it is used as an escape. Sometimes it is a symptom of a great illness of the spirit, rather than being embraced joyfully.''

He nodded, his face very sober. "Domination, manipulation, and control; that's what drives these murders, for certain. Maybe revenge.''

"With the ultimate control being, of course, the control of the victim's life and death.'' She nodded her understanding. "Not one constable in a hundred thousand would have reasoned that out. I do not think my confidence is misplaced.''

She would have said more, possibly embarrassing the man, but Kayne returned at that moment. "Your belongings are in your quarters, as are your uniforms and your first-quarter pay, Inquisitor Rufen,'' she said as she came in the door. "Your mules are in the stables, and you will have just enough time to clean yourself and change into a uniform before dinner, where you will have an opportunity to meet the rest of the Abbey Guards. And by the time you are ready for dinner, your papers will also be ready and I will bring them to your quarters.'' She beamed at both of them, and Ardis rewarded her.

"Well done, Kayne, very well and efficiently done, and thank you.'' She stood up, and Tal Rufen did likewise, again making the genuflection when she extended her hand. "That will be the last time you need salute me in that fashion, unless we are in the presence of others, Inquisitor,'' she told him. "I do not stand on formality in private with my associates.''

He stood up, and gave her a half salute. "Thank you, High Bishop,'' he said, with more feeling than he had yet shown under any circumstance. "Thank you for—''

He was at a loss for words, but she already knew what he would have said if he could have. "Thank *you* for competence and courage,'' she replied. "Thank you for being ethical, even at a cost. Both of you. Those traits are too rare, and should be cherished. Now, if you would?''

Kayne took the hint, and so did he. The new Inquisitor followed her secretary out the door, and she resumed her chair, wondering what box of troubles she had just opened even as she turned her eyes towards her page.

Chapter Five

Ardis could no more have settled down to a book now than she could have renounced the miter and gone back to being a simple Priest. She rose from her desk, but rather than pace as she might have done when she was younger, she turned with a soft sigh of heavy woolen robes and went directly to the small altar in the corner of her office. She genuflected, then knelt there, and clasped her hands on the rail before her.

Put your body in the attitude of meditation, and your spirit will follow. That was the precept, and she had generally found it to be a true one. This time was no exception; as she stared at the Eternal Flame upon the altar, she found her mind slipping into the proper state where she could examine what she had just done without any emotion intruding. Now she played Justiciar for her own actions, answerable to her own conscience and the will of God.

Had she been too hasty in coming to a decision? Had she been so desperate for a way to shift the burden of Gwydain's request from her shoulders to someone else's that she had grasped at the first opportunity to be shed of that responsibility that presented itself?

The answer to the second question was *no.* Decidedly not. Murder was a dreadful thing, Tal Rufen was accustomed to solving dreadful crimes, and he *wanted*—in fact already had assumed—that burden. If he was forever after this night unable to solve these murders and stop the fiend responsible, he should be honored for that. That he had not been aware of the murders of Gypsies and Free Bards meant nothing; there was no point in launching a belated second investigation when Tal Rufen was already well along on his. All she had done was to make it possible for him to continue the work he was already doing— and it just so happened that her problem and his were the same.

I would make a very poor constable, just as I would make a very poor carpenter. Rather than solving this set of crimes—or building a house—it is far better that I give those whose business it is all of the means at my disposal to do what they are suited for. What was the point of having authority if you did not delegate it appropriately? What was the point of having rank if you did not exercise it in order to smooth the way for someone accomplishing something important?

No, she was not shirking her responsibility. If Tal Rufen got himself into trouble with Captain Fenris or Duke Arden she would bear the brunt of the blame. Not that this was likely, but she had known when she ordered Kayne to write up those papers that she would be answerable not only to the secular authorities, but to the Conclave of Bishops if anything went drastically wrong. That, too, was justice.

And now that she knelt here, she felt a deep certainty that none of this—Gwydain's letter, Tal's appearance, and all the rest of it—was a coincidence. When circumstances conspired to involve a Priest in some situation or other, it was her experience that it was never coincidental. When they moved to involve a Justiciar, that was doubly so, and when the Justiciar happened to be a mage as well, the odds against it being a coincidence were insignificant. Tal Rufen had been guided to her, just as she had been guided to the decision to make him a Special Inquisitor. Only a Justiciar could create an Inquisitor, and only the High Bishop, who was also a Justiciar, could create a Special Inquisitor. Tal Rufen was, in effect, a constable who was answerable to no secular authority for his actions, if he but knew it. If he left Kingsford now, with those papers in his hand, he could go anywhere and do anything he pleased.

But he won't; he's driven by this, as surely as the one behind this is driven in turn by his *needs.* The Hunter and the Hunted, and which was which?

Or perhaps—the Hunted, and the Haunted. Tal has his ghosts to exorcise, and I suspect, so does our unknown enemy.

Blessed God—the burden of the Justiciar, who would and must always see all sides to a problem. *And what kind of life must it have taken to drive this man to feed his hungers on such a dreadful feast of blood?*

And that *she* was now involved, with her link to the Gypsies and her experience with renegade clergy? What did that say about this situation?

She sighed and closed her eyes, bowing her head over her hands. *Let it not be that I have been blind to the faults of those who are my friends,* she prayed. It wasn't likely—there wasn't anyone in this Abbey that she could think of who had been in Haldene a month ago, let alone in all the other towns and villages Tal mentioned, but that was, she felt, her besetting sin. She was hard on herself, implacable with strangers, but with her friends—

Soft. Too forgiving.

She remained kneeling for the rest of the time left to her before dinner, praying. First, that she had not forgiven too much, been too compassionate. It was so hard to balance justice with compassion. . . .

Second, for the souls of all those unfortunates that she and Gwydain had not known about, as well as those that they had.

And third, for Tal Rufen. His way had been hard, and it was likely to be harder still, for even if he found and caught the person behind all of this, he would still have to come to terms with the fact that he had not caught this evil creature earlier, and forgive himself for all of those who had perished.

And so shall I, was her last, grave thought before the bell rang for dinner. *And so shall I. . . .*

Tal had never seen the uniform of a Church Guard before, and he was a bit taken aback by its jaunty splendor. He had expected something a great deal more sober—something all in dull black, perhaps, or dark gray. This bold scarlet trimmed and edged with black piping was more like the uniform he would expect to see on the Grand Duke's guards than anything the Guard of the clergy should wear.

He felt much the better for a hot bath and the bit of food the High Bishop had given him. His headache was almost gone, and he was finally warm again. With a good meal inside of him, he would feel better still.

After his bath and a change into the only clean clothing he had left, he had returned to his tiny room to find the Bishop's secretary and his new uniforms waiting for him.

"We don't have many Guards at the Abbey," Kayne observed as he picked up the wool tunic and sniffed at the scent of cedar that still clung to its folds. "We have the uniforms, of course, to fit just about anyone, but most of them have been in storage for as long as I've been here. That's lucky for you; that uniform has probably never been worn, but we novices get nothing but handed-down robes until we become full Priests." She chuckled. "I suppose that's to get us used to sharing with sweet Sister Poverty!"

She handed him his papers; he took them, still feeling altogether dazed by the High Bishop's swift and decisive actions. He hadn't quite believed that she had been serious, even though he had made free of her hospitality, tucked his belongings into the tiny cell of a room that Kayne had shown him, and used the Abbey's hot water and soap with abandon. Now though—with this uniform and two more like it waiting on the narrow, but comfortable bed—he had to believe it.

I'm a Church Guard. A Special Inquisitor. I've been assigned *to the hunt.*

The official papers only confirmed the reality. He looked them over carefully, but they simply reiterated what the High Bishop had told him.

"And here's your first quarter pay," Kayne added, handing him a black leather pouch that *chinked* softly as it went from her hand to his. "Ardis didn't tell you how much it is—she wouldn't of course, she never thinks about things like money—but I'm told it's not bad. Not as much as a specially licensed and bonded Bodyguard, but not bad. Ten silver a week for twelve weeks; enough, supposedly, to make you unbribable."

Since that sum was more than he had made per week after all his years on the force at Haldene, he hardly knew what to say except— "It is."

And with no personal expenses to speak of—it's quite *good.* Food, lodging, uniforms—the Church supplied all of these. What would he *do* with ten silver pieces a week?

She nodded briskly. "Good. Anything else you need to know?"

He held the tunic up a little. "This. It's not what I expected—" He flushed. "Actually, it seems a bit . . . gaudy. I thought I'd be wearing black or something."

Kayne laughed, her dark eyes sparkling with amusement. "That's because you've never been in an Abbey of the Justiciars before. You should see all of us in our ecclesiastical best—you'd think the room was on fire."

"Ah." He'd noted the red robe that Ardis wore, and the rust-colored one of the novices, but it hadn't occurred to him that these were their equivalent of working clothes. "So on an occasion like a High Holy Day, we Guards wouldn't stand out at all, would we?"

"In fact, you'll blend in," she assured him, "And if you wore, say, black—like the Guards of the Healing Orders—you'd stand out like crows against a sunset."

At that moment, a bell sounded somewhere, and Kayne cocked her head to one side. "That's the bell for dinner, and I believe I hear one of the other Guards coming to show you the way." No sooner had the words passed her lips than a shadow blocked the door, and a discreet tap on the frame proved that she was right.

She turned, as the biggest man that Tal had ever seen eased himself into the room. "Well, this is an honor, indeed! Tal Rufen, this is the Captain of our Guards, Herris Othorp."

The huge, black-haired man who was clearly several years Tal's junior gravely offered a ham of a hand to Tal to shake. Tal took it, and was pleased and relieved when the handclasp was firm without being a test of dominance. It seemed that Herris Othorp saw no reason to prove he was a better, stronger man than those under his command.

What a pleasant change!

"I am pleased to welcome the new Special Inquisitor," Othorp rumbled, actually *sounding* pleased. "I have told the High Bishop more than once that her office requires at least one. No one among the Guards has had any experience in investigation; I wouldn't have the faintest idea of where to start if I were assigned to a case."

"Don't be too pleased," Tal warned. "Maybe I have experience, but I'm not sure I'm any good!"

At that, Othorp laughed, a deep bass rumble. Tal decided that this man was going to be, not only easy to work with but a definite ally. "I think we should let God and Time judge that, and go to our dinner."

"And on that note, I shall take leave of both of you," Kayne said, and turned with that swift agility that Tal had noted in the High Bishop's office, and left them.

Othorp waited expectantly, and after a moment, Tal realized that the Captain was waiting for Tal to assume one of his new uniforms. Feeling a little self-conscious, Tal shed his old, worn canvas trews and knitted woolen tunic, and did so. When he belted the new tunic and pulled it straight, the Captain beamed with as much pride as if he had tailored the uniform himself.

"You make a fine show, Inquisitor, and that's a fact," Othorp told him. "When you aren't out investigating, I'd like to have you up in the front ranks at our major ceremonies, if you've no objection. It's a pity, but half the old fellows here are just that—old fellows, one short step from collecting their pensions. They look sad, that's the truth of it. What used to be their chest has gone south, you might say, and I'm afraid they think more of their dinners than they do of why they need to be in shape."

"And why do they need to be in shape?" Tal asked curiously as he preceded the Captain out the door and into the hallway. "Other than for ceremonial occasions, that is?" He coughed. "I hope you'll forgive me for saying this, but it would seem to me that an Abbey full of Justiciars would be the last place a troublemaker would care to go.

Constables in general reckon a position like Church Guard is a soft berth.''

Othorp's face darkened, but not with anger; he was very clearly worried. "You'd think that, wouldn't you." He made it a statement, not a question. "Think about it, though. Someone has a suspect, they want the truth out of him—they bring him to Justiciar Arran to see if Arran can use his magic to call it out. City constables have evidence, have a group of suspects, they call in the High Bishop or one of the other mages to link the two. And when it's Judgment time for misuse of magic, murder, rape, serious crimes, who is the one who sets the penalties if the Duke and his two Judges don't have the time or don't feel qualified to make a Judgment? Justiciars, that's who. And the more serious the crime, the more likely it is that it'll be passed here across the river.'' He shook his head as he walked.

Tal suddenly felt very stupid. "That's a lot of enemies," he said slowly. "The bad lads tend to put the blame on anybody but themselves for what happens to them.''

"And not all of them wind up doing the rope-dance. Some of them even see out their time and get turned loose." Othorp sighed heavily. "And do you think I can get *one* of them to believe that they might be the chosen target of some very bad people and take care about their movements?" He shook his head. "*That's* why I wish we could just retire our old men when they get too fat to run, but they're sentimental around here, though you wouldn't think it. They won't hear of sending a man off to pasture on half-pay and replacing him with someone younger.''

Tal shrugged; there wasn't much he could add to that. "Maybe you could urge it on appearances—it doesn't look good for Church Guards to look fat—like, aren't we supposed to be part of the chastity and poverty business?''

Othorp chuckled, and rubbed his heavy eyebrow with his forefinger. "I could try that. At the least, it might get the High Bishop to order some of these old fellows on a serious training regimen. Reducing diets won't work; most of them are steady customers of the inns across the river.''

By now they had reached the tall wooden door at the end of the hallway; Othorp pushed it open, and Tal looked into the refectory.

He'd had occasion to stay at Abbeys of the Wayfaring Order a time or two when he'd taken excursions into the country, and these dining-halls all looked alike. The one thing that struck him as odd about this one was the relative quiet. Beneath a high ceiling crossed with age- and smoke-blackened beams, tables and benches were arranged with mathematical precision on a plain, scrubbed wooden floor. At two of them, rows of scarlet-clad Guards were already waiting for their meal, talking in hushed voices. From another door, Priests in the scarlet robes of the Justiciars, and novices in the same rust-colored gowns that Kayne wore were filing in silently to take their places at the rest of the tables. They must have been wearing soft-soled boots or slippers of some sort, as their footfalls were barely audible.

All four walls were plastered white, with dark beams exposed. One wall held a huge fireplace, the opposite one nearest Tal and Othorp had three windows glazed with tiny diamond-shaped panes of glass in lead. There was a raised dais of dark wood at the far end of the room with a wooden lectern on it; beside the lectern was another table, this time with only a single bench behind it. Othorp led Tal to the second table full of Guards; there were wooden plates of bread and cheese already on the table, wooden spoons, mugs, plates, and bowls before each place. Someone—*probably Kayne,* he thought—must have informed the kitchen staff of his arrival, for there was an extra place laid ready for him. He and Othorp were the last of the Guards to arrive, and it was plain that Othorp had only spoken truth when he commented how important their dinners were to some of these men.

When the last of the Priests had taken his or her place at a bench, the High Bishop entered, followed by four other Priests, all male. All of them wore the standard cowled scarlet robe, belted with a black cord. The High Bishop wore a small round cap of scarlet on her short blond hair; the rest went bareheaded.

"That's Arran, Leod, Harden, and Cole," Othorp whispered. "Chief Justiciar, Chief Clerk, Chief Exchequer, and Chief Household. You'll only have much to do with Arran and Cole; you'll only see Harden if you need to draw out some extraordinary expense and Kayne can't handle it for you—and as for Leod, write your own letters, he has a knack for making a man feel like a chunk of street-scum."

Of the four, Arran and Cole looked the easiest to deal with. Ardis took her place in the middle of the table. Arran, a tall, raw-boned man with a mouth like Ardis's and the kindest eyes Tal had ever seen, took his place beside Ardis on the right. Cole, lean, bald, and good-humored, took the left. A novice stepped up to the lectern, opened the book there, and began to read aloud as other novices with white aprons tied over their robes passed among the tables, ladling soup into bowls and cooked vegetables onto plates. The Guards passed the bread and cheese up and down the table, ignoring the novice, who was reading some religious text; Tal, with the edge taken off his raging hunger, took a modest amount of both bread and cheese and passed the rest on. The soup proved to be pea, and the vegetables a mix of squash, beans, and root vegetables in a thick sauce.

"This is Tal Rufen," Othorp said as he tore off a hunk of bread for himself. "New man, High Bishop's own Guard from now on. Recommended by Justiciar Brune, from Haldene."

Tal gave Othorp points for giving him the story he should follow, and nodded affably at the rest of the Guards, hoping there would be no jealousy over what should have been a prime position going to an outsider.

"About time she got her own Guard," one man said without prompting, a fellow with a weathered face and graying black hair. "Stop messing up the duty-roster every time she takes a notion to go across the river. Hard on us, trying to reshuffle so that nobody gets stuck with double-duty."

The others nodded, in total agreement, and Tal was taken a bit aback for a moment. Then he realized what was going on—as Othorp had hinted, these men were used to a fairly set routine with very little variance, and resented any change in it. They had the soft berth that he had described.

As he listened to them talk, he had no doubt that most, if not all of them, would spring to the defense of their charges if one of the Justiciars *was* attacked—assuming some of them *could* spring anymore—but if there was no crisis, they simply didn't want to be stirred from their set ways.

"Don't envy you, Tal Rufen," said another, one of the very men Othorp had complained about, whose uniform tunic strained over a decided paunch that overlapped his belt. "High Bishop's always gadding here, gadding there—you'll miss half your meals, leave your bed early and get to it late. When you aren't running your legs off to keep up with her, you'll be standing around outside of doors for hours and hours."

"Oh, I'm used to that by now," he replied easily. "I was on third shift, dockside duty in Haldene. At least now, if it rains, I won't be spending a full shift out in it."

"There is that, but I wouldn't have lasted a year on a third shift," agreed the second man, and tucked into his food with a will.

There seemed to be plenty of that food; at least, the novices kept serving the Guards as long as any of them wanted further helpings, although the Priests and their fellow novices were apparently restricted to single servings. *More of that asceticism,* he decided, grateful that they did not impose their rules on their secular servants. At the end of the meal, all of the Brotherhood rose as one and filed out again, leaving the Guards to wipe their plates with the last of their bread and make a more leisurely exit.

"High Bishop will want to see you, I'd expect," Othorp said, as Tal hesitated just outside the door, not certain what he was expected to do next. "I doubt she finished with you before dinner. You remember the way."

He nodded; he would have made a poor constable if he couldn't remember a few turns and twistings of corridors. A constable was supposed to be able to negotiate an unfamiliar neighborhood in the dead of night.

They parted at the first intersection of hallways, and Tal made his way back to the High Bishop's office. There was no one outside, and he tapped tentatively on the door, wondering if he was supposed to have gone first to Kayne.

But it was Kayne who opened the door, and she seemed pleased enough to see him. "Come in, please," she said. "The High Bishop is just finishing up some business, but she has already mentioned that she wanted to talk with you before Evening Services."

Evening Services! He'd forgotten that part of Abbey life! His dismay must have shown on his face, for Kayne chuckled. "Oh, don't worry," she whispered, a conspiratorial sparkle in her eyes, "The Guards aren't expected to attend all the Services. Just one of the ones on Sevenday. It's like the rest of the Abbey life; *we* have vocations; we don't expect you to, and we don't expect you to abide by the rules made for those who do."

He sighed, just a little, and hoped his relief didn't show too much. Kayne gestured him inside and shut the door behind him.

He resumed the chair he had vacated only a few hours ago, and waited for the High Bishop to finish whatever she was doing. It seemed to involve a great deal of paperwork, and some whispering between herself and her secretary. Eventually, though, Kayne went trotting off with a huge sheaf of papers, and Ardis turned her attention back to him.

"This is a little backwards," she said with a crooked smile. "I usually know all about someone before I engage them, and I would like to rectify that situation now so I know what kind of man I am dealing with." She settled back into her chair, and clasped her hands in her lap. "So tell me, Inquisitor—what kind of a man *is* Tal Rufen? What does he care for? What does he despise? What makes him the man he is?"

Her shrewd gray eyes regarded him soberly from beneath winglike brows the same color of gold as her hair.

"Tal Rufen is a man who never wanted to be anything other than a constable," he told her. "As soon as I was old enough to play, I had a baton I'd made from an old broomstick and a constable's cape from a scrap of canvas. The others would play at robbers, and I'd capture them and hang them. When I got old enough, I learned everything I could about the job, and as soon as they'd take me, I applied. I've been a constable since I was sixteen, and if they'd taken me younger, I'd have gone. If you're looking for what drives me, that's it."

"And do you consider this position to be a step back for you?" she asked unexpectedly.

He had to think about that for a moment. "No—no, I don't think so. This is what being a constable *should* be like. You've put me in a position to be able to do my job again, which was more than my Captain was doing. When this case is over, though—"

"You're afraid it might turn into a glorified Bodyguard position," she stated, with a little nod.

He shrugged. "I don't know. I don't think I'd be satisfied to stand at attention at ceremonies for the rest of my life."

A brow lifted. "I don't think there will be any danger of that," she told him crisply. "You may not pursue investigations as ..." She paused to search for the correct word. ". . . as tense and distressful as this one. But you will be pursuing investigations; I have needed someone with your skills to aid me as a Justiciar for some time, and now that I am High Bishop, I need your skills more than before. Magic isn't always the right way to find the answers, and when it is useful, it doesn't always supply *all* of the answers. I mislike making a Judgment without all of the information."

He nodded grave agreement, and she continued. "Now, besides wanting to be a constable all your life, what else are you?"

"Dull." He laughed. "As a person, I'm afraid I tend to become my work. I don't have many interests outside of that. Games—skill games, not cards or dice. Reading. History, mostly."

She smiled at that, and he wondered why, but she made no comment. "Parents?" she asked. "Other ties?"

He shook his head. "Parents are both dead; I was a late-born child, came long after Mother thought she was past having any, and I don't think either of my parents was comfortable around a child. They both died a few years ago. No close friends, no women who cared to put up with the hardships of being a constable's wife."

"I understand." She contemplated him for a moment. "Perhaps you are more suited to our sort of life than I had thought. I was afraid it would be too dull for you; our entertainments are mostly mental. If you had a vocation, you could be one of the Brotherhood.''

She's right, actually. How many of the lads on the force told me that I lived like a Priest? "That may be," he agreed. "Since most of my life could be packed up on the back of a mule and carried off with me." He thought about that for a moment, and added, "The only things I'm really going to miss in Haldene are the books I left behind and the friends I left them with. A pair of Mintak brothers; we used to play castle-board and share books we'd read. Other than that—" He surprised himself with a bark of laughter. "Other than that, the only thing I'd like is to see the Captain's face if he ever finds out what I'm doing now. I have the feeling that as a Special Inquisitor, technically I outrank him."

A broad grin sprang up on Ardis's face, making her look very like a vixen in her coat of scarlet and little round red cap. "I sometimes think that the reason God demands that we leave revenge to Him is because He prefers to keep such delights to Himself," she said sardonically. "I quite understand. Well, Tal, before I send you off to the bed you very much deserve, I only want to tell you three things. Make free of the Abbey library; use of it is one of the privileges of being attached in service to the Abbey, and I think you'll be pleased by what you find."

He flushed a little and ducked his head, obscurely ashamed for some reason that his hunger for books had been found out, and her smile softened. "Tomorrow you can present your papers to whomever you think you will need to work with; trust me, no hour is too early for Captain Fenris, if you can find him. Use your own discretion as to who you inform of your true rank; I'll take care of notifying the Duke myself."

He started to object, and stopped himself. She was right; she had ways of getting to the Duke quickly, where he would have to wait days or weeks for an audience. "I'll probably tell this Captain Fenris, High Bishop, and I'd rather tell him in person, myself. I want him to see me, I want to see him, so we can—"

"So the two hounds can sniff noses and decide not to fight," she interrupted with an ironic look that dared him to say otherwise. And since that was pretty much what was going to happen, he couldn't deny.

"Well, we do have to know that we can trust each other," he pointed out. "Where I'm going to be prowling—well, I might need someone to come to my aid, and if I have to ask Fenris for help, I want him to be willing to send a man with me. He won't do that if he's never seen me."

"I rather thought that." She lost her smile. "That brings up the last point—remember that you can't track this murderer down if you're dead, Tal. This is a ruthless creature, and if he realizes that someone is tracking him, he may deviate from his chosen victims to remove you from his trail."

With a feeling of shock, he realized that she was right. It had not occurred to him, he had been so preoccupied with the pursuit, and so focused on the *female* victims, but she was right. Whoever this was, he was smart enough to not only elude pursuit, but to avoid it in the first place.

That meant he was not only clever, he was intelligent. Someone like that would be smart enough to watch for pursuit, and if he could not shake that pursuit from his trail, he would eliminate it, or at least try.

I'm going to have to think like someone who is stalking one of the Great Cats in unfamiliar territory. At any moment, it could be the Cat who becomes the stalker, and the former hunter becomes the prey. Tal had never been in a position like this. It gave him a very unsettled feeling, to think of himself as the hunted, rather than the hunter.

"I'll remember," he promised. "And I won't go picking up any strange knives!" She nodded, accepting that promise.

With nothing else to be dealt with, he took his leave; Kayne was waiting outside the door with another sheaf of papers, and hardly waited for him to clear the doorframe before entering the office. He wondered a little at this; did the woman never rest? It was long past the time when most folk would have considered that they had put in a good day's work.

When he returned to his little room, and sat down on the side of the bed, he realized that he had been working on nervous energy for some time. The moment he got off his feet, it ran out, leaving him exhausted.

For a while, he simply sat there, examining his new quarters. This was the first time he'd had a chance to get a good look at them.

As was to be expected in an Abbey, this little room, about the size of his bedroom back at the Gray Rose, was not what anyone would call luxurious. At least it didn't have penitential stone walls, though; like the rest of the Abbey, this room was plastered and painted white, with all woodwork and exposed beams stained a dark sable. There was a closet opposite the door; the closet stood open, and his bags were inside—obviously, he was expected to tend to his belongings himself. The narrow bed was set along one wall, and a small table and chair on the other. There was a bookcase—empty—at the foot of the bed, a nightstand with a candle alight in a pewter holder on it at the head. Except for a hook on the door and two more on the wall, that was all there was.

The bed was firm enough, with plenty of blankets, which would be welcome since the room did not boast a fireplace. But there were no windows, either, so at least there wouldn't be any drafts—though in summer, there wouldn't be any cooling breezes.

How are we supposed to deal with these woolen uniforms in summer? Or do they have a summer uniform as well?

He couldn't imagine the Priests wearing those long woolen robes in summer either, so perhaps the summer-weight clothing had been packed away for the season.

Well, if I don't get my things put up now, I probably won't get to them for days. Somewhere, he dredged up a last bit if energy, and got back to his feet.

The books he had brought with him all fit nicely into one half of the first shelf of the bookcase. He hung his civilian clothing up first, then his new uniforms. All the rest of his belongings, such as they were, fit into the two drawers of the nightstand.

Except, of course, for his weaponry. He had seldom employed it as a constable, but he kept in constant practice; a hand-crossbow and a belt-quiver of bolts went on one hook on the wall, his short-sword on the other. His various boot-, belt-, and wrist-knives he laid out on the table, along with his cudgel and a bag of lead shot. That last served double-duty, both as a weapon in and of itself and as ammunition for the sling tied to it. Over the back of the chair he laid his wide, stiff leather belt that served as kidney-protection, and the leather collar that protected his throat. His leather wrist-braces went on the table with his knives.

He'd worn none of this for his interview with Ardis; he hadn't known what kind of guards she'd have and how they'd take to a man bearing arms into her presence. But he had no doubt that someone had looked through his weapon-bag when they put it in this room, and that Othorp knew precisely what he'd brought with him—and that it all had that well-worn look.

He'd wear all of this tomorrow when he went into the city to find Captain Fenris. He got out of his new uniform, blew out the candle, and was surprised at how *dark* the room was without the light. There wasn't even a line of light from the hall under the door. He might have been inside a cave.

And it was quiet; unnervingly quiet to a man used to sleeping in an inn. He couldn't hear anything out there in the hall, and if there was someone on the other side of his walls, he couldn't hear any sounds from them, either.

He felt for the head of the bed, and climbed under the thick, soft woolen blankets. But once he was there, he kept staring up at the ceiling in the darkness, unable to quite get to sleep. Partly it was the silence, so thick it made his ears ring, but partly it was a belated state of nerves.

It was all catching up with him now, and he found himself a little dazed. He had come here to the Abbey on a whim when he'd been unable to locate the Captain of the Kingsford constables or the Kingsford Sheriff; everyone knew about the Justiciars, of course, and down in Kingsford he had heard stories about Ardis and had taken the chance that she might hear him out and perhaps get him an appointment with Captain Fenris. He had not expected her to take a personal interest in the case.

He had expected even less that she would turn around and coopt it and him. After trying to deal with the authorities in Haldene, he had really been anticipating that he would be put off. In fact, if his suspicions were correct, and a Priest or high Church official *was* involved in this, Ardis would have had every reason to deny him an interview at all. He'd been steeling himself for the long trudge across the bridge to Kingsford again, a scant dinner, and the cheapest room he could find. His resources, never large to begin with, were dwindling quickly.

And now—

Now he was beginning to get the feeling there was much more going on here than he had dreamed of, and he was afraid that the High Bishop was privy to more and more serious information than he had yet uncovered.

Was it possible that he was getting in over his head? Was *that* why everyone in Haldene had tried to put him off this case? Was it more serious than he knew—did it involve suspicion of someone with a *very* high rank?

It didn't have to be a noble, it could be a Priest, as he had suspected many times now—and it could be that she knew it, even had some suspects, but had no way to prove who it was. Perhaps that was why she had conscripted him so quickly. Oh, wouldn't that just open a box of beetles!

And I could end up being the scapegoat when I catch the man. He *could,* if Ardis was like other high-ranking people he'd worked under. But nothing he'd seen and heard so far made him inclined to think that she was. In fact, her reputation was that she protected her underlings from those who were higher in rank, provided that those under-lings were on the side of the angels.

So I just have to make sure I'm on the right side.

If it was a Priest, in one of the other Orders, say, he and Othorp and Fenris might end up having to go in and pry the fellow out, which could get very ugly. Then again, at least if it was a Priest, as a Special Inquisitor he wouldn't have the problems with bringing him to Justice that he would have had as a constable. A Priest could claim immunity from secular authority, but not from someone delegated by the Church.

I'm the enforcement arm of the Church. I can throw anyone I need to into gaol. It wasn't the heady thought it might have been; he'd never cared for the power of the baton, only for its use as a tool to get bad people put where they couldn't hurt anyone again. It only meant that there was nowhere he could not go in the course of this investigation; he hoped that he wouldn't need to use that authority.

The other complication was the one Ardis herself had briefly touched on. If his target was a Priest and a mage—or just a mage—well, he would know that Tal was coming, and who Tal was, long before Tal ever learned who *he* was, and there would be plenty of opportunity for "accidents" to occur. Magic opened up an entirely new set of problems, given that Tal really didn't know the full breadth of what a mage could and could not do.

This is no time to get cold feet, he chided himself. *You've never backed away from a case before; not when you had to go after mad drunks, murderers, and cutthroats. Any one of them could have disposed of you if you'd made the wrong move. She's already told you that you can go to her or any of the other Justiciar-Mages she thinks is discreet and get help, which includes finding out what a mage can do. And besides, the High Bishop is counting on you. She thinks you can handle this, or she wouldn't have given you the authority in the first place.*

Yes, and just what *had* convinced her to give him the authority? He'd like to think that he showed his own competence as clearly as she showed hers, but he doubted that was the case. How could he have looked like a professional, when he'd come in exhausted, travel-worn, in shabby clothing? He wouldn't have impressed himself, and he doubted that his outward appearance had impressed her.

I probably looked like one of her Gypsy friends. Then again, maybe that wasn't so bad. If she had contacts among the Gypsies and Free Bards, she must be used to looking past shabby clothing and weary faces.

It could have been his careful investigation thus far that had impressed her—and he'd really like to think that was the case. He *had* done good work, especially considering all the opposition he'd faced. He could have done more if he'd just had some cooperation, and she probably knew that as well.

But the reason why she trusted him could also have been desperation. If you didn't have the faintest idea where to start with a problem, wouldn't you take the first person who came along and said, "I know what to do" and throw the whole thing at him? She'd had that letter on her desk when he came in; she'd probably just gotten it. She wasn't supposed to track criminals, she was supposed to sentence them, and considering that the Bardic Guild had its Guild Hall in Kingsford, she might not get much cooperation from the Kingsford authorities in trying to hunt down a killer of Free Bards. For that matter—maybe the killer was some high-ranking, crazed Master Bard! Hadn't he heard it said, more than once, that Bards were supposed to be mages?

It might be that when he walked in her door with additional evidence, she'd been disposed to welcome him as God's answer to her difficulty.

Maybe so. But she didn't get where she is now by being incompetent to handle her own problems.

For that matter, why did he agree so readily to become her servant? Or the Church's servant, really, but it amounted to the same thing in this case. What in Heaven's name made him throw away everything he'd done to this moment to take this position? He'd *never* imagined himself serving the Church, not even as a secular adjunct. He never *wanted* to be a Guard, even one with other duties. He would have done so if that had been the only answer, but he hadn't even begun to explore his options in Kingsford. He certainly hadn't come into that office looking for a position!

It might have been the personality of Ardis herself that had persuaded him. Tal knew that, in some respects, he was a follower, not a leader. He felt more comfortable with someone competent in authority over him, for all of his cherished independence; and what was more, he was honest enough to admit it, at least to himself.

Competent—I'd say. She couldn't run this Abbey better if she was a general and it was a military barracks. Not that he'd been in a *lot* of Abbeys—but there were little signs when things weren't being run properly. Dirt in the corners, things needing repair, indifferent food, an aura of laziness or tension, a general sense of unhappiness.

A lot like the headquarters back in Haldene, as a matter of fact.

People weren't tense here, but they weren't slacking, either. Nobody was running around as if they were always forgetting to do things until the last minute, but no one dawdled. That novice, Kayne—she moved briskly, got things done, but there was no panic about it, no sense of being harried, and that went for every other person he'd seen. Even the rest of the Guards—though Othorp sighed over their condition, they *were* competent and they got their jobs done properly; their biggest problem was that they were set in their ways. They weren't lazy, just so used to routine that changes in it made them uneasy. When it came down to it, that would probably hold true for all the Priests as well, and why not? Routine was *part* of an Abbey. No, Ardis had this place well in hand. Maybe that was what he had responded to.

The moment I got here, I felt it. He hadn't even ridden all the way into the courtyard before someone came to greet him and ask his business—one of the Guards, he realized now. A stablehand had come to take his mules and tie them up for him, a novice had led him to a little chamber just inside the front door, and brought Novice Kayne to him. Kayne had questioned him briefly, and everything had fallen into place, and all without a lot of running about and fuss and feathers.

Not what I would have expected from a place being run by a woman. But just as he thought that, he knew it could just be prejudice on his part.

I don't expect much out of women when it comes to running things. But—really, look at the women he'd had the most to do with! You didn't expect much of women, when all you saw them doing was falling apart in a crisis. The women he saw on a day-to-day basis mostly seemed to be looking for men to take care of them.

And they weren't very bright. Or if they were, it had been starved or beaten out of them a long time ago. You could have some pity for the pathetic streetwalkers of the dockside district, you could have sympathy for all the hard work a tavern-wench had to do—but the women who took those jobs were not exactly the cream of the day's skimmings when it came to intelligence. So far as that went, most of the *men* he saw were not long on mind-power.

Well, more than half the battle in getting rid of a prejudice was in recognizing that it *was* one. Ardis would have been as formidable as a man; the Abbey would have been just as well run; hence, there were other women who were her equals in intelligence, and he had just never run into any before. Which was not too surprising, when you considered his social circle—or lack of one.

That brought him to the High Bishop herself; she seemed very young to be wearing a miter, and even younger to be wearing the gold miter. Most of the Bishops *he* had seen had been gray haired—and male. He might have a prejudice, but so did the Church; females in *any* position of authority were rare birds, indeed.

So how had Ardis, not only female, but relatively young, gotten where she was now? It couldn't have been an accident that she had been the highest ranking Priest in this Abbey when the previous High Bishop died—and even then, it wasn't the usual thing for a Priest to simply step into the vacancy. He vaguely recalled that High Bishops had to be elected by the Council of Bishops, which meant she had to pass muster before all of them—gray-haired men. *She can't be any older than I am, or not much,* he decided. *Not that I'm all that young, but I'm not all that old, either.*

Well, she was related by blood to a lot of important people, including Grand Duke Arden. After almost single-handedly saving Kingsford from a fire which—so rumor had it—renegade Priests had a hand in setting—well, if Duke Arden suggested that his cousin ought to be made High Bishop, he rather suspected that there were plenty of people on the Council of Bishops who would take that as a Very Good Idea.

The Great Fire might have had something to do with the decision. He hadn't been in Kingsford long, but stories about the Fire had spread all the way to the High King's capital. The Grand Duke was considered a hero—but Ardis was considered a saint for throwing herself and the Abbey into the problem of healing, housing, and feeding all of the refugees. *If I have my politics right—making Ardis High Bishop might solve some problems here for the Church, in the case of those rogue Priests. The Bishops wouldn't want to give up their authority over their own renegades, but unless the Grand Duke had assurance that the caught Priests would get full and appropriate punishment, well . . .* If *he* had been Duke Arden, he'd have been tempted to hang the bastards from the highest tree and let the Church complain all they liked about it. But by making Ardis High Bishop, everybody would be satisfied—the Duke had assurance that the criminals would get everything they deserved, and the punishment would all come from an instrument of the Church.

She might also know a few inconvenient secrets about the other Bishops herself; most people in power did.

Still, she was a remarkable woman; she would have stood out in any setting, and in this one—

She's amazing. Nothing short of amazing.

Attractive, too. At least, to him. That vixen-grin she'd flashed him, full or humor and what almost looked like mischief; she could charm the boots off a man with that one, if she ever used it as a weapon. Another prejudice; he'd always thought of female Priests as being unattractive, waspish, something like young Kayne, but more so. It was odd to think of a physically attractive woman in a Priest's robes. Very odd, actually.

Why had she become a Priest in the first place? She didn't seem the type to have been pulled in by religion. She just didn't have that glassy-eyed sort of devotion he expected out of someone dedicating their life to religion.

But maybe that's another prejudice on my part. I just don't know that many Priests, I suppose.

Still, she was well connected, probably money or titles or both, attractive, intelligent—why had she become a Priest?

Might have been the traditional thing. I've heard some of the noble families do that—firstborn inherits the estate, second-born goes into the military, third goes to the Church, whether they like it or not.

But he couldn't picture Ardis being coerced into anything, so she must have had some reason to go. A disappointment in love? No, she didn't seem like the type to moon tragically around because someone she wanted didn't want her. More than that—a tragedy? The man she loved had died?

She wouldn't dive into the Church unless she thought she could exorcise the grief in work. But she doesn't seem at all grief-ridden; there's usually a shadow over people who lose a loved one.

Maybe it had something to do with the fact that she was a mage. He didn't know of too many places that could train a person in magic, and most of them wouldn't be the sorts of places that would appeal to someone as well-bred as Ardis. And the rest were all in nonhuman lands.

I certainly can't picture her marching up to an Elf Hill and demanding to be let in. The Elves would drive her mad with their ways.

But he also couldn't picture Ardis ever letting a talent go to waste. Maybe that was the reason; it made more sense than anything else.

Except—*Maybe she went into the Church because the Church was the only place where she would be expected to exercise all of her intellect.*

This was all sheer speculation. He didn't know enough about the Church, the lives of the nobles, or Ardis herself to make a really intelligent guess.

That was part of the trouble; he knew nothing about the High Bishop, except the little that she had told him herself. He had nothing to make judgments on, and that left him at a disadvantage.

I'm going to have to make it my business to learn everything I can about her, he decided. This clearly wasn't going to be the kind of

situation he'd had back in Haldene, where he was just one constable
among many. He was the only Special Inquisitor; he and she were
going to be working closely together. It wasn't even the equivalent
position to the other Abbey Guards.

In a sense, she's going to be both my superior and my partner. Or—
maybe a little more like when I first came into the force, and I was
attached to a senior constable. I had to learn as much about him to
work smoothly with him as I was learning about being a constable.

It was a long time since he'd been in that kind of position; it was
going to take some getting used to. Still—why not? The only trouble
was that it meant he was going to be working on two investigations,
not one. The murder chase, and the investigation of Ardis.

What the hell. I work better under pressure.

And with that thought, his exhaustion finally overcame his nerves,
and he slept.

Chapter Six

Visyr hovered, wings pumping furiously to keep him in place, roughly a hundred wingspans above Archer Lane. Hovering was harder than any other kind of flying, but Visyr was used to it, and his chest- and wing-muscles were stronger and heavier than any of the Haspur who specialized in fancy flying and aerobatics. He kept taking deep breaths of the icy air to bring new fuel to those muscles as he made notes on his pressure-sensitive Deliambren dryboard with the tip of a needle-sharp talon, notes too small for mere human eyes to read. After each entry, he glanced down at the street below and concentrated on the next building on the north side of the street, measuring it by eye and noting its position relative to its neighbors. This was his special talent; any Haspur could hover above a street, and any Haspur could make a rough map that would show the placement of buildings and their sizes relative to one another, but very few could gauge the dimensions so precisely that a physical measurement would be off by no more than a fraction of an inch. It was a peculiarly Haspur talent, this ability to create accurate maps from memory—a useful talent in a race that flew—but Visyr was an artist among the talented.

When he had filled his dryboard—a flat, white board sensitive to pressure, used by the Deliambrens as a note-pad—he would fly back to his drafting room at the Ducal Palace and transform the notes into an actual city block on the new map he was making for the Grand Duke. When he was done, Duke Arden would have a map of Kingsford that showed not only every tiny lane and back-alley, he would have one that showed every structure that existed at the time the map was finished, including sheds and fences. His constables wouldn't have to guess where miscreants might be hiding to ambush the unwary, they would know where every blind-alley, dead-end street, and cul-de-sac lay. This was making Captain Fenris very happy; in fact, the Captain had a page checking on Visyr's maps and making copies of them as Visyr completed each section. *He* could hardly wait for the whole thing to be done. With the rebuilding of Kingsford proceeding rather chaotically in some sections, Fenris's people were at a distinct disadvantage when they had to pursue a footpad into an area that might have changed since the last time they were there.

This, however, was *not* why Visyr had come down out of the mountains. Although the Duke and his people certainly appreciated what the Haspur was doing, and although he was gaining a great deal of support for himself and other nonhumans with this work, this was not what he had intended to do. Eventually, or so Visyr hoped, he would be part of the great Deliambren mapping expedition; that was why he and his beloved, dynamic mate Syri had left their homeland in the first place. But humans were dreadfully short-sighted when it came to permitting nonhumans to do *anything* in their lands, and the Deliambrens didn't want to mount this project until they had iron-clad agreements of cooperation as well as permission from the rulers of all of the Twenty Kingdoms, agreements that no subsequent monarch could overrule.

Not that I blame them, Visyr mused, as he noted down the size of the warehouse below him, and the dimensions of the tiny scrap of yard behind it. *Taking that ship out is going to be an effort worthy of an epic song, and if they ever have to stop it they may not be able to get it started again.* The ship and many of the machines the Deliambrens intended to use were ancient; parts were difficult to duplicate and had to be made one at a time by hand, and the mechanisms themselves were often poorly understood. Intended to be manned by an assortment of races, controls were not always suited to the hands, hooves, or beaks of those who were to operate them. Visyr didn't envy those assigned to tend and use the things. The expedition itself was a massive effort on the part of not only the Deliambrens but of many other nonhuman races, and even of some humans as well. There would be hundreds of people tending and operating the ship and all of its mechanisms, and more working outside it.

His assignment with the ship would be simpler; basically, what he was doing now. He would be one of a few mapping-scouts, making an aerial survey of heavily inhabited areas where the ship couldn't go; other scouts would roam ahead to find a safe route for the behemoth that contained the bulk of the expedition. Once and for all, the Deliambrens hoped to survey *all* of Alanda, or this continent, anyway, to locate mineral resources, underground watercourses, and ancient ruins, as well as mapping the surface accurately.

This wasn't altruistic, although the Deliambrens would provide copies of the general topographical maps to anyone who wanted them. Besides their mechanical wonders, the Deliambrens trafficked in information—in return for permission to cross their land, the rulers of each kingdom would get copies of any of the surface maps they wanted, but if they wished to know the locations of other things the Deliambrens uncovered, they would have to pay.

All of which seemed perfectly reasonable to Visyr, but apparently there were those who were incensed by the idea; they felt that information should be given away, no matter how hard someone had worked to obtain or create it. As a result, the expedition was stalled, and he was taking little jobs like this one to prove just how useful those accurate maps would be. If the Deliambrens could point out that even the basic maps would contribute to generating revenue or solving problems, the various rulers who were causing difficulties might see their way clear to removing their objections. They might also find it easier to accept the very moderate fees that the Deliambrens would charge for other information.

Of course, Visyr thought, noting down the dimensions of another building, *they could always go out and look for their treasures themselves.*

This was no bad way to pass the time while he waited; it was useful and needed work, and the Duke was being quite generous in his wages. The Duke had always wanted absolutely accurate maps of his city—and now that Kingsford was being rebuilt, such maps were more important than ever and not just for the constables. People now had the opportunity to build whatever they pleased, wherever they pleased, and many of them were doing just that. Property owners were taking advantage of the situation to move original property lines, stealing inches and even whole feet of property from their neighbors.

Sadly, there were many who were no longer around to care what their former neighbors did, and their heirs were either children or too wrapped still in grief to realize what was happening. Eventually, though, they might discover what had happened and want some legal redress, and Visyr's maps would give evidence of what had happened.

The trouble with human, ground-pounding surveyors was that they took more time than Visyr did. They had to lay out measuring tapes, and use other equipment, to do what he did by eye. They often stalled traffic while they were working, and they got in the way of pedestrians.

And while they could measure the size of something, they wouldn't necessarily get its placement correct.

Humans do this very well, when they are measuring out open fields. For a job like this, you need someone like me. That was the long and the short of it, so far as Visyr was concerned.

Another problem that surveyors encountered was that people were building things behind walls and fences that they wouldn't let the surveyors pass. Without going and getting an authority who would force the owners to let the surveyors inside, there was no way of telling what was or was not in there, and most surveyors simply didn't want to take the chance of angering home and business owners. Walls and fences didn't hinder Visyr, and there would be a number of folk who would be very unhappy with him when this survey was over, and they got tax-bills for outbuildings, workshops, and secondary dwellings that they hadn't reported.

But by then I'll be gone, so they can be as unhappy as they like. Frankly, I think Arden deserves the extra tax money. If it weren't for the money he *is putting into the city, these people wouldn't have public water, covered sewers, or any of the other more pleasant innovations he's building in.*

Visyr liked Duke Arden; most people did, he suspected. It wasn't difficult to like the Duke, as Arden was personable, persuasive, and really did have the welfare of his people first and foremost in his mind. He had made some very sensible laws about the rebuilding in Kingsford that were being violated every day. There would be some unhappy people when the Duke's men appeared to levy fines or tear down illegal constructions that Visyr had uncovered, but some of those structures were fire hazards and others were clearly not supposed to be where they were. It was one thing to keep pigs and goats in the country, but putting them in a tiny scrap of yard in the middle of a residential district was going to make *someone* sick eventually. Visyr had even spotted a man keeping cows in a shed barely large enough to hold them!

Unfortunately, it will probably not be the fellow who is keeping the livestock who pays the price of their being there. Visyr didn't want to think about what all those little goat- and pig-yards would smell like when summer came. Hopefully by then, the Duke's inspectors would have most of them cleared out. Dove-cots and rabbit-hutches, fine. Those created manageable waste. Not farm stock.

Not to mention the possibility of the damage a large animal could do if it got out. Horses and donkeys were necessary evils, and were properly kept in stables in areas meant for them, but even so, Visyr distrusted such large and unpredictable creatures. He was just glad that he spent the largest part of his time that he was outside the palace in the air.

It might have seemed odd to conduct this survey in the dead of winter, but cold didn't particularly bother Visyr, and he would much rather fly in a snowstorm than in a rainstorm. Besides, in winter no one was doing any exterior construction; any building going on was all interior work. That meant that if he could finish this work before spring (and he certainly should be able to!) he wouldn't have to backtrack to add new buildings.

So far no one but the Duke and a few of his people were aware of what Visyr was up to. Plenty of people knew that the Duke had a Haspur at his Court, but after the great to-do caused by another Haspur at the Court of the High King, the masterful musician and singer T'fyrr, they probably all assumed he was a musician, too. And he was, but not a professional like T'fyrr; all Haspur could sing, and any Haspur would probably impress a human who'd never heard one before, but anyone who had heard T'fyrr would never mistake Visyr for a professional.

I'm not even a really talented amateur, but then, T'fyrr can't make maps either. He'd probably even get lost in the High King's palace.

But as long as people thought he was a musician, no one would wonder why he was hovering over their houses. If they asked, he had a standard—and quite truthful—reply.

Research. A delightful word that covers any number of circumstances. They'll assume I'm making up some epic about the rise of Kingsford from the ashes of the Great Fire, and ignore me. At the worst, they'll want to tell me the story of how they survived the Fire, which might be entertaining.

Actually, very few people seemed to notice him; the humans here in the Twenty Kingdoms were remarkably unobservant creatures, especially when it came to scanning the sky.

Maybe because their eyes are so bad. Humans, poor things, are remarkably deficient in that area.

Hardly anyone ever looked up at him, not even when his large shadow passed over him. Curious, really; a Haspur noted every little floating seed and tiny wren in the sky, and never went more than a few heartbeats without taking a glance upward. The humans who lived in partnership with the Haspur were the same, glancing up at even a hint of a shadow or a moving mote in the sky.

I suppose it's all in what you're used to.

The dryboard was almost full; Visyr made a few more notations about a building with an extension hidden behind a tall fence, cupped his wings a bit and dropped, losing a few dozen feet of height to get some forward momentum. It was a good trade; shortly he was well on the way to the Ducal Palace where it rose above the rest of the city, rivaling even the Kingsford Cathedral. He reveled in the feel of free flight, in the force of the wind through his nares, in the powerful beats of his own wings. It was a lovely day in spite of being overcast; a recent snowfall covered the raw places in the earth that surrounded new construction, hiding signs of dilapidation and shoddy building, and softened the lines of roofs and fences. With clean, white snow everywhere, this really looked like the model city the Duke had dreamed of.

And straight ahead rose the palace, a fine piece of architecture in its own right. He had his own separate entrance into the tower that served him as workroom and private quarters; an aerial entrance, of course. Humans would probably refer to it as a balcony, but the railing was just the right size to land on, the wood sturdy enough to hold up under his talons, and the servants who tended the room had orders to keep the railing and the balcony ice-free. The room had an unparalleled view, too; right over the city and across the river, where the Abbey and Cathedral of the Justiciars presided over Faire Field. He hadn't been there yet; there wasn't much to survey in that direction, so he was leaving it until the last.

At the moment, he was working his way along the Kanar River, at the point farthest from the high, stone bridge that crossed over to Faire Field. He had an idea that the bridge itself was older than Kingsford— it was so tall in the center that virtually any ship that could navigate the river could sail beneath it, and certainly the river barges had no difficulty getting between its massive white piers. The only damage time had done to it was cosmetic, and although it was commonly thought of as being made of stone, the material didn't resemble any stone Visyr was familiar with. The only "improvement" that humans had made to it was a toll booth on the Kingsford side. The road leading to the bridge was unpaved, but that didn't mean anything; the paving could have been pried up by the people who'd built the Abbey and Cathedral to use for construction materials. This sort of destruction drove the Deliambrens crazy. Visyr thought it was rather amusing. It certainly proved the humans were resourceful devils, ant-like in their ingenuity for picking things up and carrying them away.

He pumped his wings through full power-strokes, angling the surfaces to gain altitude rather than speed. Soon, if there was anyone watching him from below, he would be just another dot in the overcast heavens, no different from a crow or a sparrow. He had to go around to the back of the palace in order to reach his balcony from here.

He came around the building and made a wide turn. Sideslipping, he angled in towards his room. The Ducal Palace stood in one of the districts that had been mostly spared by the Great Fire, but if the Church mages hadn't come when they had, it too would have gone up in flames, and the façade still showed the marks of flame and smoke in places. Arden wouldn't have them removed; he wanted those marks as a constant reminder of what the city had endured. The gardens had been destroyed, though, and only steady work by the gardeners for two years had brought them back to their former beauty. Even in winter, under a blanket of snow, they were lovely. Although there were no longer any of the trees and bushes sculpted into fanciful shapes, the gardeners had replaced them with trellises that would be covered from spring to fall with flowering vines, and which in winter formed the basis for snow sculptures.

Visyr was above the palace now, and he folded his wings and dropped in a dive that ended as he backwinged with his taloned feet outstretched to catch the railing of his balcony. It was a pity there was no one in the balcony below to see him; it was a particularly good landing.

Ah, well. They wouldn't appreciate it, anyway.

He balanced for a moment, then hopped down onto the surface of the balcony itself and let himself in through the door. Made of dozens of little square panes of thick and wavering glass set in a wooden frame, it let in welcome sunlight, but a somewhat distorted view. Still, it was better than nothing, and without it, Visyr would have felt rather claustrophobic.

This was his bedroom, with the bed replaced by a peculiar couch shaped to be comfortable for a sleeping avian, and many padded, backless stools. Searching for an alternative to a human bed, he had found the couch in a used-furniture store the first week he had been living here, and had bought it immediately. The servants had all sniggered when they saw it; he wasn't sure why, and he didn't think he really wanted to ask. Whatever it had been used for before, it was comfortable for him, and that was all he cared about, and the odd little stirrups made a nice place to tuck his elbows or knees. Beside the couch was a pile of light but warm down comforters; one of the Duke's people asked him once if it made him feel odd to be sleeping under something made from dead birds, and in answer, he snapped his decidedly raptoral beak. And in case the fellow hadn't gotten the message, he had added, ''Only in that I didn't get to eat any of those birds.''

The only other furniture was a chest that contained the body-wrappings that Haspur used in lieu of clothing. There was no point in wearing clothing with open legs or arms; such garments would get tangled up when a Haspur flew. And the idea of wearing a shirt or a long robe was ludicrous, possibly even dangerous. A Haspur wore as little as possible, something that clung as closely to the body as possible, and was as lightweight as possible. Hence, "clothing" that was essentially wrapped bandages.

He walked through the bedroom without a sidelong glance, and into the second room of his suite, which had been converted into his workroom.

Four large drawing-tables, tables built with surfaces that could be tilted upwards, stood against the walls, with maps in progress on all of them. The first was a general view of the city, river, and surroundings, showing only the major streets and no buildings. The second was a closer view, adding the minor streets, but still showing no buildings. The third was more detailed, with all possible thoroughfares shown, but still with no buildings displayed except for the largest or public structures. The last was the completely detailed map, made in sections, with the current one pinned to the board. That was the table Visyr went to, taking up a set of drafting implements made for taloned Haspur hands, and setting to work translating his notes into deft patterns of streets and structures.

The Duke was often surprised at how unexact those buildings and streets were when drawn out as measured. The streets themselves, even when laid out by the Duke's surveyors and engineers, often meandered a foot or two at a time, so that they were never perfectly straight. The buildings tended to be more trapezoidal than square or rectangular, though the odd angles were more obvious to Visyr than to a human. This was nothing like the Deliambren strongholds, which looked like patterns of crystals from above, so exact were their angles. Then again, these people had none of the advantages the Deliambrens had. No clever machines to give them the advantage of Haspur eyes, no devices to measure without the need for tapes or cords, no machines that flew.

And in a Haspur Aerie, there is scarcely a right angle to be seen. Haspur tended to build curves rather than straight lines, and avoided right angles as much as possible. A Haspur Aerie looked like a patch of strange plants clinging to the cliff-side.

All of which only proves that there's no one way to build a house. He finished the last of his drawings, put down his instruments in their tray, and looked around for a pitcher of water. Although a Haspur beak was a bit more flexible than a bird's, it was still more comfortable for him to drink from a pitcher, with its pouring spout, than from a human cup.

The page had evidently been and gone; the water-pitcher was on a sideboard rather than the table Visyr had left it on. He got a quick drink of water while he stretched his wings as wide as they would go, then put the pitcher down and roused all his feathers with a brisk shake.

He looked back over his shoulder at his progress so far. Had he done enough for the day?

Well, yes—but there's still plenty of daylight, and I'm not particularly tired. I can do another trip easily, then quit flying for the day and add this section to the larger maps.

He picked up the dryboard, took the cleaning-rod out of its pouch on his belt and passed it over the surface of the board, leaving it pristine and white. He stowed the rod back in the pouch and hung the board from his belt, then trotted out to the balcony again.

With no hesitation, he leapt up onto the balcony rail and out onto the back of the wind, returning to the river and the section of taverns, inns, and businesses that catered to river-men whom he had left behind.

It was just about time for the midday meal as he kited to his next position, and it was a pleasant enough day that there were street-musicians setting up all over the city to play for the crowds coming out to find a bite to eat. He was pleased to hear the strains of music drifting up from below, as he approached the next area to be charted, and when he glanced down, he saw that a street-musician had set up on one corner with a stringed instrument that she played with a set of hammers. From the multicolored streamers fluttering from each shoulder, Visyr gathered that she was either one of the humans known as a "Free Bard," or was at least pretending to that status. She was probably the real thing; she was a good enough player to qualify. Visyr relaxed and listened with one ear to her music, habitually filtering out the rushes of wind noise from his own wings, as he went into a hover and took out his dryboard again.

Now that the noon hour had come, the streets were full of people; there was a knot of them around the musician and traffic flowed around them like river-water around a rock. Human surveyors would have had a terrible time with the crowd; Visyr, of course, was unaffected, and felt rather smug about it.

People would be tripping all over a human, all over his equipment— it just goes to show that humans don't have all the answers. Even Deliambrens would be having trouble with people interfering with their measurements! Sometimes there's no substitute for an expert.

This was an interesting block, one with buildings that were all different in style, as if every property-owner on the block had gone to a different builder for his construction. Proportions were all different, and he began to suspect that there were some nonhuman merchants operating here, for some of the buildings had proportions more suited to, say, a Mintak than a human. That made his job even more interesting. As was often the case, he soon became so absorbed in his measuring that he was very like a hunter at hover over prey; he lost sight of everything but the work, ignoring the people and the traffic entirely.

Right up until the moment that movement on the street below snapped him out of his hover-trance and into instant awareness that something was wrong.

Nothing alerts a predator like the movement of another, and in the moment that the young, well-dressed man on the street began his rush towards the musician, that movement broke straight through Visyr's concentration.

What? He glanced down, thinking perhaps it was another purse-snatcher who had caught his attention; he had caught one in the act a week ago, and had pinned the urchin in an alley until the constables could come get him. The child would likely have nightmares for ages of giant scarlet hawks dispensing vengeance.

That's no street-brat— Alert, startled in fact, but not mentally prepared to act, he watched in stunned horror as the man lunged, pulling something from his belt, then plunged a dagger into the woman's back.

One or two of those nearest her screamed, others stared as numbly as Visyr as the man pulled his weapon out of the woman's back, and stabbed her three times more in lightning-fast succession before she fell forward over her instrument and brought it and herself crashing to the ground. Blood spilled out on the snow-pack in a crimson stain beneath her, even more startling against the whiteness.

The sight of blood elicited kill-rage in the Haspur, instinctive and overpowering, as if the man had attacked one of Visyr's own Aerie. Without a second thought, Visyr screamed a challenge, pulled his wings in, and dove straight at the man, foreclaws outstretched to kill. Time dilated for him, and everything around him began to move in slow motion. The man had taken a single step backward. The crowd had just barely begun to react, some trying to escape, one fainting on the spot, one trying to seize the man, most just staring.

The man looked up, eyes blank; Visyr noted in a detached part of his mind that he had never seen a human face look so masklike before. The rest of him was intent on sinking his talons into the masklike face.

Already he had closed the distance between them to half of what it had been a moment ago, and he was still accelerating.

The man reacted faster than Visyr had thought possible for a human, spinning as quickly as a Haspur; he dashed off into the crowd of terrified onlookers, shoving them aside with hands smeared with blood. Those he shoved fell to the ground, tripping his pursuers, further adding to the confusion. Many of the onlookers screamed or cried out and either tried to escape or to catch him; others milled like a flock of frightened herbivores, some trying to get away from the area, some just standing and staring, some confusedly trying to get closer to see what was going on. Inevitably they got in each other's way, some fell to the ground and were trampled, resulting in more confusion and enabling the man to get away from those who were trying to stop him

By now, Visyr was in a flat trajectory above the heads of the crowd. They all got in his way, as the man ducked and writhed through the confusion, and Visyr had been forced to pull up at the last moment, turning the stoop into a tail-chase. That didn't concern him at all. *He'll dive into one of those alleys, thinking I won't be able to follow him, but I will, and since they all turn into dead ends, I'll have him.* The man didn't belong here; he was too well-dressed for this section of town. He couldn't possibly know the area as well as Visyr. Visyr zigged and zagged to follow his erratic movement through the crowd, mindful of his wingspan and taking purposely fast, shallow strokes, still going much faster than a human could run, even though he had to keep changing direction.

But he didn't go the direction Visyr expected.

He dashed down the street to the first intersection, and made an abrupt turn towards the river. Dumbfounded, Visyr was forced to pull up again and do a wing-over to continue the pursuit, losing valuable time. But the man was heading straight for the small-boat docks; he was going to have to stop there! With still and shallow water suitable for the smallest craft, these docks were surrounded by ice. He couldn't possibly get across the river on the ice; there was no ice at all in the middle, it was far too thin except right near the bank, and there were clear channels cut for the barges all along the larger docks.

But he didn't stop; he got to the riverbank, and jumped down onto the ice. Expecting him to stop, Visyr overshot him, talons catching at the air as he shot past, his momentum taking him all the way across the river before he could do another wing-over and start back. Now he had seriously lost speed; he had to pump his wings furiously to get any momentum going at all.

Miraculously, the ice beneath the man held, but he kept going, angling away from Visyr but headed right towards the other side, scrambling and slipping, but still going straight towards the open water.

Visyr clawed his way upwards, intending to make a shallow stoop down on the man, hit him in the head and knock him to the ice.

He didn't make it, of course. Just as Visyr got overhead, the ice broke beneath the man, and he went in. He didn't even make a sound when he did so, either. Visyr stooped, but this time it was to try and seize the man before the current pulled him under.

He grabbed just as the man began to sink, and managed to snag the shoulders of the man's tunic in his talons, pumping his wings with all his might to pull him out of the water. The man suddenly looked up at him, and still his face was utterly expressionless: no terror, no anger, no nothing. Only, as Visyr heaved and pulled, for one brief instant, the eyes of a trapped and horrified animal looked up at him out of that lifeless face.

Then the man suddenly began to writhe and thrash like a mad thing. *Is he trying to get away? Why?* Granted, he *was* in the talons of a giant predator, but he was also about to drown—

No matter; at that moment, the fabric of his tunic tore loose, and before Visyr could snatch another hold on him, he actually *dove* under the water and beneath the ice, and was gone.

Visyr landed on the ice as a group of humans on the docks stared, screamed, and gestured towards him. He stared at the black water in dumbfounded amazement. Had he really seen what he thought? Had the man actually gone under the ice on purpose?

He leapt up into the air, struck by a sudden thought. Maybe the madman had hoped to make open water, swim to firmer ice, and escape! He gained a little height and hovered there for a moment, searching for movement in the water, the flash of a sleeve, the hint of a hand.

Nothing.

He beat up and down the river, from the bridge to the end of the docks and back, and there were still no signs of the man. If he had hoped to escape in any way except into death, he had been cheated of his hope.

Someone beckoned frantically to him from the crowd on the docks; he caught the movement in his side-vision, and turned his head. It was a constable, and he obeyed the summons, flying with wings that felt heavy with more than mere fatigue.

"Are you the bird-man in service to the Duke?" the constable called, as he came within shouting distance. Visyr waited for a moment as it was difficult to speak and concentrate on landing at the same time. He fanned his wings hard, blowing up quite a wind as he powered in to a landing, and the hair and garments of those waiting on the dock whipped wildly about for a moment. He made quite a creditable landing, considering how little room they'd left him, a landing that restored some of the confidence he'd lost in failing to catch the murderer.

"I am," he answered, in his most authoritative and deep voice, flipping his wings to settle them. That voice always surprised humans who'd never heard a Haspur speak and expected a harsh scream or a fluting whistle. "I am profoundly regretful that the miscreant escaped me. Sadly, I cannot swim, so I could not pursue him."

"Escaped? He practically tore himself in half to get away!" one of the spectators said. "And he dove right under the ice when he tore loose!"

The constable looked up at Visyr, a little startled by both the voice and by Visyr's height. "Did you—see any signs of him in the water?"

Visyr shook his head. "None, I am sorry to say," he replied. "I believe he is beneath the ice."

A grizzled old fellow in the garb of a river-man hawked and spat into the river. "He'll be there a while. Current there'll take him in to shore away from the docks. You won't find him till the thaw."

"Or if we get a Justiciar and locate the body, then chop through the ice to get him," the constable said with resignation. "Which is probably what's going to happen. That was a Free Bard he murdered; the Duke won't rest until he knows why." He turned back to Visyr. "I'm afraid I'm going to have to take you to the station to make a statement."

Visyr jerked his beak up in the Haspur equivalent of a shrug. "I expected as much, constable," he replied with equal resignation. "Lead on."

Fortunately, the station wasn't far, because Visyr attracted many stares and a lot of attention as he walked. But it wasn't a single statement that Visyr made, it was several. He was required to repeat his story twice for lower-level constables, then for Captain Fenris himself, then, just as his temper was beginning to wear thin, two new humans were ushered into a room that was beginning to seem far too small. His wings were starting to twitch, and it was harder and harder to get full breaths. He knew why, of course, for what Haspur would ever voluntarily confine himself to a room that wasn't big enough to spread his wings in? Humans didn't know that, though, and he kept reminding himself to be charitable, although it was very difficult. He faced the newcomers with a distinct sense that his patience was at an end.

One, a woman, wore the robes of a Priest, in scarlet, and the other a scarlet and black uniform. It was the latter who peered at him with a slight frown then said, abruptly, "Sirra Visyr, would you care to move to another venue? Are you feeling confined here?"

"Yes!" Visyr replied, with surprise. "And yes! How did you know?"

The man in the uniform glanced at the woman who nodded briefly, thus telling Visyr immediately who was the superior here. "You were twitching, and your eyes were pinning, and since we aren't questioning you at the moment, it had to be because of the room. I have Mintak friends, and they have spoken of Haspur particulars," the man said as he opened the door for Visyr and held it open for the woman.

Visyr nodded; he knew he had been twitching his feathers, but he hadn't been aware that his eyes were pinning—the pupils contracting to mere pinpoints then dilating again rapidly. Many birds as well as Haspur did that in times of acute stress.

And Mintaks, taller than humans, felt uncomfortable in places with low ceilings, so the man would have known how to interpret those signs of stress for what they really represented. Still, it was surprising to find a human in one of the Human Kingdoms who was sensitive to what made nonhumans uncomfortable.

Rather than leading Visyr to another room in the station, the man led them out into the street; as they paused in the doorway, though, it was the woman who spoke. She had a low voice, pleasant, though not particularly musical. "Have you any objections to going across the river with us?" she asked.

"To the Abbey and the Cathedral?" Visyr looked up and down the street, thinking about the last time a Haspur fell into Church hands. "And if I say I do?"

"You can go back to the Ducal Palace, of course," she replied dryly. "We'd rather that we were able to question you while all of this is still fresh in your mind. We aren't barbarians here, no matter what may go on elsewhere. But you should know that no matter how irritated you are with all of this, the Duke will most probably ask you to make a statement for us. He feels very strongly about the Free Bards. Now, with his permission it could be done at the palace, but by then, the incident will be a day or more older in your mind."

They couldn't know just how accurate Haspur memory was, of course; Visyr considered that option, and also considered the fact that he had been curious for some time about the Abbey and the human Church and that this was an excellent chance to ask some questions of his own. The fact that the Duke would definitely want his involvement was another consideration. He could not imagine that the Duke could be coerced by anyone, not even a Church official, after what he'd been told about the Great Fire, so it was unlikely that this Priest was using the statement as a bluff.

"If this is any reassurance to you," the woman said, still in that ironic voice, "I give you my word that you need not fear the kind of 'welcome' that T'fyrr received at the hands of Bishop Padrik."

So she knows about that. "And whose word would I be taking?" he asked boldly, as passersby glanced at them with curiosity, then stared harder, then abruptly looked away. That was an interesting action—they did not act as though they were afraid of attracting attention, but as if they did not want to intrude upon someone they respected. Visyr often saw the same reaction when he walked out with the Duke.

She smiled, as if his question did not offend her in the least, though the man looked a bit irritated. "The word of High Bishop Justiciar Ardis," she replied mildly.

He felt as if he had been hit with a blast of wind shear. The High Bishop? The Duke's cousin? She had come herself to question him?

This must be a more serious situation than I thought.

There could be no doubt of it, now that he looked at her more closely. The family resemblance was not to be mistaken, especially not for someone whose job it was to estimate relative proportions as well as exact measures. She had the same cast of features as her cousin. . . .

"Ah, I beg your pardon, High Bishop," he said, snapping out of his introspection and minute examination of her features. "Of course I have no objections. Do you mind if I fly over, though? I shall be able to shake off the last of my feeling of being confined."

The High Bishop glanced skyward and shook her head. "Not at all. Shall we meet you at the main gate of the Abbey, then? You should have no trouble spotting it from above."

Without waiting for an answer, she and her escort turned and went down into the street, leaving him to do as he pleased. And at the moment, it definitely pleased him to take to the skies and make for the spire of the Cathedral across the river.

He flew slowly, well aware that even with the crowd parting to make way for the scarlet robe, he would beat them to the rendezvous. Unless, of course, they had some of those unreliable four-legged beasts to carry them across.

Just out of curiosity, he landed on one of the bridge-piers and waited for them, perched atop the white monolith like an ornamental carving. Sure enough, he had not waited long enough to feel the chill when he saw two humans in scarlet mounted on a pair of gray beasts, making their way to the bridge. The toll-takers waved them through—no great surprise there—and they moved out onto the span. The one slightly in the lead moved his head constantly, as if he was watching all about them.

Bodyguard, Visyr decided, just as the head pointed in his direction, and the figure raised one hand in a brief but unmistakable salute. Visyr saluted back, pleased to have discovered at least *one* human who was as observant as the ones back home.

Observant, and—dare I say it?—sensitive. And in the uniform of the Church, but in the service *of someone who is supposed to be unusually broad-minded. Very interesting.*

He took wing again, landing before the main gate and startling the gatekeeper there no small amount. "I am to meet High Bishop Ardis," he said shortly, as the gatekeeper, also clad in a scarlet uniform, stammeringly asked his business. The man asked nothing more, probably supposing that if he was here to do some mischief he would not have landed so openly.

A reasonable supposition, that, though not an intelligent one. If he had been prepared to challenge the High Bishop, he would also have landed openly. Sometimes these humans were not very bright, besides being unobservant.

The same could not be said of the High Bishop's guard; as they moved into view, Visyr watched his eyes. Once they had registered the Haspur's presence, they flitted here, there, everywhere someone might be concealed, even in the shadow of Visyr's wings. That did not offend Visyr in the least; it was the man's duty to think of such things.

The two dismounted and left their long-eared creatures in the hands of the gatekeeper. Once again, the man took the lead, escorting them into the building and down a wide, high-ceilinged corridor that led to a huge, elaborately carved wooden door. There he paused with one hand on the handle, sending an inquiring glance towards the High Bishop.

She smiled. "I can think of no more appropriate place," she said in answer to his unspoken question. He opened the door and held it open as Visyr and the High Bishop walked in.

His beak parted in amazement as he looked up—and up—and up.

"We are very proud of our Cathedral," the High Bishop said, behind him, "although it is no match for the one in Gradford. Is this open enough to make you feel comfortable?"

"More than open enough," he replied, taking in the sweep of the building with admiration. *Interesting. That is twice that she has mentioned Gradford, and I believe this is meant to assure me that she knows what went on there.*

Unlike the Cathedral in the heart of the city, which was built all of stone, this one was constructed entirely of wood, many kinds and colors of wood. The vaulted ceiling was of a light, almost white wood, while the curved beams supporting the vaults were of a honey-colored wood. The floor was amber-colored, the walls inlaid with geometric mosaics in every color of wood imaginable.

Figures adorned every pier supporting the vaults of the ceiling, and at first, Visyr thought that they were, impossibly, figures of Haspur. Then he realized that they were humans, but humans with wings and most impractical, flowing robes.

"We're very fond of our angel-vault," the High Bishop said, following his gaze. "There is no Cathedral in any city that has one to match it. Each of the angels is different; I am told that the carvers took as models all of the Priests in this Abbey that they admired."

"That must have caused some hard feelings when some searched the vault for their likenesses and did not find them," Visyr replied, and Bishop Ardis chuckled.

"I would prefer to think that all of the Priests were admired, and that is why there are extra angels tucked up in odd places where you wouldn't expect to find them," she replied. "The choir members sometimes complain that there are so many angels in the choir loft that there is scarcely room for all the singers."

"And speaking of music, the organ loft might be the best place to conduct this interview," the man interjected. "Or the choir loft, depending on whether or not you care if this interview is overheard."

"The organ loft, I think," she replied. This time she led the way to the front of the Cathedral where the enormous pipes of the organ were ranged against the wall in shining splendor. There was a veritable flock of angels here, supporting everything that could be supported, frolicking singly and in pairs, and amid all of this flurry of pinions was hidden the place where the organist sat. They climbed a steep little staircase, more of a ladder, really, and behind a cluster of widespread wings was the alcove holding the keyboard of the instrument, a bench, and two small seats. Visyr hesitated for a moment, but the two humans took the seats, leaving the backless bench for him.

"This area was designed so that sound doesn't escape it," Bishop Ardis explained. "The noise made by turning music pages can be very distracting, I'm told. But more so, if someone is in here between services, meditating or at prayer, is the sound of the musician practicing silently. If the bellows aren't pumped up, there is no sound, and the organist can practice without disturbing anyone, so long as you can't hear the noise of him pounding the keys and the pedals."

"If we keep our voices down, no one will hear us in the sanctuary," the man added. "Are you comfortable enough here?"

Although the alcove was small, the fact that the ceiling was still far above their heads made the situation tolerable. It was very chilly here, but with his insulating feathers, Visyr was comfortable enough— which, interestingly, the humans would *not* be. Sitting here, they would soon get chilled, and they probably knew that. So they were accepting discomfort that he might be comfortable, and that was exceedingly interesting. Visyr nodded.

"We'll try not to keep you too long, then," Bishop Ardis said, then began a series of questions that were far more thorough than anyone had yet asked him, even the redoubtable Captain Fenris. He didn't mind, because neither she nor the man—whose name, he finally learned, was Tal Rufen—ever repeated a question as the others had. They might backtrack and ask something that would elicit more details from him, but they never repeated the same question over and over as if they were trying to trip him up.

In fact, he felt surprisingly comfortable with them; occasionally one would pause for a moment and look thoughtful, and that was when the other would pause in the questioning to make normal conversation and answer any of his questions.

After a little while, the organ loft seemed cozy; the carved wings cupping them could have been the natural sides of a nesting-crevice, and although Haspur were quite beyond nesting in cliffs, they still reacted well to such surroundings. The soft voices did not travel beyond the wall of wings, and they could easily have been at the top of a cliff in the middle of inaccessible mountains.

All of which was infinitely more reassuring to him than a window-less room a few paces across.

He did not learn nearly as much as they did, but he did find out why they were so concerned about this one incident. It was not the first, but the latest of many. They didn't tell him *how* many, and he didn't ask, but he had the feeling that it was a larger number than "a handful."

He didn't think that the local constables were aware of this; their questioning had not tended in the direction that Ardis and Tal Rufen's did. He could not imagine the High Bishop getting personally involved unless this problem extended beyond Kingsford, and he wondered just how far it *did* go.

He was torn between wanting to volunteer his services and wanting to stay out of it all. He really didn't have time to act as a kind of aerial constable. He wasn't trained to do so, he wasn't deputized to do so, and he did have another and very important job to perform.

On the other hand, the more the Bishop and Tal Rufen spoke, the more he admired them. He found himself wanting to help them however he could.

And he could not deny the fact that he was curious, very curious, about what was going on. Never mind that these were not his humans, not of his Aerie, nor allied directly with the Haspur; never mind that he was very busy with his own work. He was intensely curious, alive with curiosity, dying to ask questions he knew would not be answered.

Unless, perhaps, he volunteered his services. Perhaps not even then, but the only chance he would have that they *might* would be if he volunteered. It was altogether disagreeable.

In the end, he couldn't make up his mind, and they finally ran out of questions themselves.

"Thank you, Sirra Visyr," the High Bishop said gravely. "I know that we have, among us all, rather thoroughly disposed of most of your day, and I apologize for that."

"Not at all," he replied graciously, and before he could say anything more, Tal Rufen had escorted him out of the Cathedral and left him in the courtyard behind the main gate. And at that point, there was nothing left for him to do but endure his curiosity and spread his wings to fly across the river in the last scarlet light of sunset.

Chapter Seven

Once they were safely ensconced in her office, Ardis turned to Tal, one eyebrow arched significantly. After a week of spending most of his time in her presence, he knew most of her signals. This one meant, "Well?"

Which in turn meant, "Tell me everything you think about what just happened." When Ardis chose, her expressions could be very eloquent. It was convenient, having a way to convey a broad request with a simple gesture of a single eyebrow. He wished he could do the same thing, but his face didn't seem inclined to oblige him.

He began with the first supposition that the Kingsford constables had come up with. "I never for a moment suspected the Haspur of being involved with this, and I doubt that he deliberately murdered the real killer to keep us from finding out that he was involved."

She tilted her head to one side, which meant, "Oh? Why?"

"For one thing, there weren't any Haspur anywhere near any of the other places where we've had similar murders, and it would be cursed hard to hide a Haspur anywhere around a village of less than a hundred people." He raised his own eyebrow, and she nodded. "For another, I never heard anything about Haspur being able to work magic, and if they could, wouldn't you think that poor bird your friend Padrik tried to turn into the centerpiece of a holiday feast would have worked some magic to get his tail out of that cage?"

"Only a few humans have the powers of magic, so just because *one* Haspur is not a mage does not imply that all of them lack that capacity, but your point is taken," she replied. "Why don't you think he killed the man deliberately?"

"Because he's a predator," Tal said firmly. "You can see it in how he's built—talons and beak like a falcon or a hawk, eyes set in the front of his head rather than the sides like a Mintak's. Predators do their own killing. He'll kill for food, or in the heat of rage, and he'll do it himself, but he won't let the river do it for him. That's what Padrik's captive Haspur did—tore his guard apart in the heat of fear and rage, with his own talons. That's what this Haspur was *going* to do before the killer cheated him and fell through the ice. At that point, the rage ran out, and the Haspur stopped wanting to kill the man."

"As a theory, I would say that is reasonable. In this case—" she paused for a moment. "I would say that in this case, it probably is true. It certainly fits the facts."

"And all the other reports of the witnesses," he pointed out. "They did say that the Haspur grasped the man by his tunic shoulders and tried to pull him out of the water, and the man tore loose and dove under the ice. It was certainly not too far from the docks for them to see clearly, despite the distracting effect of this Haspur's colors."

"All right, all right!" She held up her hands. "I believe that I can trust your reasoning; I am pleased to see that you don't rely on instincts alone."

He flushed; at one point he had waxed eloquent on the subject of "a trained constable's instincts." Perhaps he had been a little too eloquent.

"Never mind," she continued, "I think you are correct and my 'instincts' also agree with yours. I've sent one of the mages to the river to try and find the body, but as we both know, finding it now will probably be of limited use."

"Because it's been in running water." He sighed. "What about the victim?"

She shook her head, sadly. "Useless," she replied. "The poor child was wearing a Gypsy amulet, and the mere presence of that contaminated any slight aura there might have been from her attacker. It would be analogous to looking for a trace of incense smoke in the presence of a smoldering campfire."

"Damn." He bit his lower lip, then hit his fist on his knee, angrily. "We're still reacting after the fact. We have to anticipate him somehow!"

Her face darkened, and she looked away from him for a moment. "I'm sending warnings out, but I can't reach everyone, not even all the Free Bards. Some of them simply won't hear the warnings, especially the ones who are still traveling. Some won't heed them; even if it comes from me, I am still of the Church and they do not trust the Church. And as you yourself discovered, there are many unfortunate women who are not Free Bards who are still street-entertainers, and most of them will never hear anything but the wildest of rumors."

"And most of them can't afford to spend a single day or night off the street, much less weeks or months," he muttered. He thought it was too low to hear, but her ears were better than he thought, and she bowed her head.

"And there, too, the Church has failed." She sighed very, very softly. Her lips moved silently and her eyes remained closed; and he flushed again, feeling as if he was spying on something intensely personal.

She looked up again, her face stony. Evidently God had given her no revelations, not even a hint of what to do.

"We won't be able to prevent him," she said bitterly, her voice steady and calm. "We both know that. And I can't think of any way that we could even catch him in the act, except by accident."

It was unpalatable—but it was truth. He winced, and nodded.

"So we continue to react as quickly as possible, and we pray that he makes a mistake somewhere, sometime."

He nodded again. "I can't think of anything else to do," he replied helplessly. "And he's proven twice that he can act right in the middle of a crowded street at the height of the day and still get away. He doesn't have to wait for the cover of darkness anymore. He has us at a complete disadvantage, because he'll always wear a different face. Witnesses do us no good. I can't think of *anything* that will help except to instruct the constables to keep an eye on female entertainers."

"Unfortunately, neither can I." She bit her lip; it was getting a distinctly chewed-on appearance. "I'll—think on this for some time. Perhaps something will occur to me."

Think? She meant that she was going to pray about it. He knew exactly what she was going to do, she was going to spend half the night on her knees, hoping for some divine advice. Maybe she'd get it, but he wasn't going to hold his breath.

Her eyes were focused on something other than him, and he tried to be as quiet as possible to keep from disturbing her. Abruptly, she shook her head and looked at him again.

"You might as well go," she told him. "You go do whatever it is that lets you think; perhaps you can evolve some plan. If anything happens, or if they find the body, I shall have someone fetch you."

He stood up, gave a brief, stiff nod of a salute, and took his leave.

His own form of meditation was to sit and focus his eyes on something inconsequential while his mind worked. When he got back to his room, that was precisely what he did, leaving the door open so that if Kayne came for him, she would know he was waiting for the summons. He sat down on his bed with his back to the wall, and stared at a chipped place on the opposite wall.

This case was precisely like all the rest, with nothing left to tie the murderer to an actual person. Tal had been studying case-histories in the files of the Justiciars with Kayne's help over the last week, and he had found one other murderer like this one—a man who'd been compelled by some demon inside him to kill, over and over again. "Demon" was the word the Church clerk had used, but Tal and Ardis had both been a bit less melodramatic. "I would say, *need,* rather than 'demon,' " she had commented when he showed her the case. "As you yourself pointed out; domination, manipulation, and control. This man was driven by his own need, not by some other creature's, he was the only director of his actions."

That particular man had taken mementos from each of his victims, some personal trinket from each of them, and once the Justiciar-Mages realized what he was doing it was through those mementos that he was caught. They had done something that allowed them to follow those objects to the place where they were lying—which happened to be the man's apartment, hidden behind a false wall in a closet.

It was obvious to Tal that the missing knife or knives served the same purpose here, but a mage would know better than to leave such a knife uncleansed after the murders, so there was no hope that a trace of the victim's blood would provide the link they needed to find him. Tal was certain—and so was Ardis—that the person they sought was male. The fact that all the people taken over had been male was the telling clue, rather than the fact that all the known victims were female. A woman who hated other women usually felt that way for some other reason than confusion about her gender—in fact, other than women who were of the cutthroat variety of thief, females who murdered other females usually did so out of jealousy or rivalry and considered themselves intensely female. It was Ardis's opinion that in order to control the secondary victims, the murderer would have to identify intensely with them, and it was Tal's opinion that most females, even one with severe mental and emotional warping, would find that distasteful.

They could both be wrong, of course, but again, women who murdered women almost always killed people they knew, and it would simply not have been possible for the murderer to get to know all of the widely disparate victims in the short period of time between murders.

Men kill strangers; women don't, except by accident, or as part of another crime. That was the pattern that had emerged from Tal's study of the records.

As to where their killer got his knowledge of magic—the most logical place to look was the Church itself. This troubled Ardis, and although she faced it unflinchingly, Tal avoided bringing the topic up. But that made it yet more likely that the killer was male, for Ardis knew all of the female Justiciar-Mages in all Twenty Kingdoms personally; none of them had gone missing, was subject to strange or inexplicable trances lately, or indeed ever had been in all of the cities, towns, and villages in question. "I don't think it's possible to do this remotely," Ardis had told him. "I think the killer has to be there, nearby, somewhere. There are just too many things that can go wrong if he can't actually *see* what's happening."

Which meant their killer was hidden somewhere in plain view of the scene. It would have to be somewhere above the level of the street, too, in order for him to have a decent view.

Tal wished that there was some way to conscript that bird-man. If *anyone* had the ability to spot someone watching the murders, it would be him! And no one in the entire city of Kingsford had a better chance of stopping another murder in the act than this Visyr. At least, he would if the murder took place in daylight, in the open street. After this last incident, the murderer was quite likely to go back to murders at night, or even indoors.

We still don't know how he's taking control of his secondary victims. How hard would it be to take a room in a big inn, stand up on the balcony, and take over one of the patrons? Tal thought glumly. *Then, when the constables come to question everyone, the murderer can either be gone completely out the window, or protest that, like everyone else, he was tucked up in his virtuous bed.*

Frustrating.

But if Visyr would just volunteer his services. . . .

Ah, but why should he? He wasn't human, he had no interests here except for his *paid* position in the Duke's household, he probably hadn't the least notion what a Free Bard was. He was a predator; how would he feel about murder?

Well, obviously he felt strongly enough about it to try to kill the presumed murderer. There was that. Tal just wished he could have read the bird-man a little better; obvious things like feather-trembling and eye-pinning were one thing, but what had it meant when the creature went completely *still*? What had some of those head, wing, arm, and talon movements meant?

You can't coerce a flying creature, and I don't know what to say or do that would tempt him or awake whatever sense of justice lives in him. I fear the answer is that there is no answer for this one, unless the Duke lends us his services. That meant that the Duke would have to do without whatever the bird-man was doing for him, and he didn't know just how willing the Duke would be to sacrifice anything he *personally* wanted to this man-hunt. Especially when there was no guarantee that there would be any concrete result from the sacrifice.

Well, he'd mention it to Ardis; she had more channels to the Duke than anyone else he knew of.

If only Visyr had managed to snatch the knife! But once again, it was missing. Visyr definitely recalled that the man had had it in his hand when he bolted from the murder scene, and had *not* had it when he ran out onto the ice. It was a point of pride with the bird-man, how accurate Haspur memory was, and Tal was not inclined to doubt him. So, once again, the telltale knife had vanished into the crowd. Which meant it probably had been *dropped,* deliberately, in a place where the real murderer could find it. The knives were probably serving the same "memento" purpose—or, more accurately, perhaps, serving as trophies—as the small, personal objects had served for that other killer.

One other thing they had learned that they had not known before. It was *not* the same knife, although the blade was the same shape. This one, unlike the one that Tal had seen the knife-grinder use, had boasted a gaudy, jeweled hilt—precisely the kind of toy that a young, well-dressed man might wear as an ornament. So it was reasonable to assume that the murderer had several knives of the same type, each suited to a particular "tool" for murder. For the jeweler it might have been this very piece. For the blacksmith, the plainer blade that Tal had seen, or even a rough, half-finished blade. So the "curse" notion, at least, could be discarded. It wasn't at all likely that there were two or more knives of the same type carrying so powerful a curse!

Well, that's one small spot of progress, anyway. Then again, it could be the same blade, with a different handle.

Movement at his open door caught his eye, and he nodded in greeting to Kayne. "They've brought the body in; Ardis is with it," she said shortly. He nodded again and rose to follow her.

Ardis, assisted by another Justiciar, was already in the process of examining the body with a detachment that Tal found remarkable in someone who was not used to seeing the victims of violence on a regular basis—and certainly someone who was not used to seeing nude young men on a regular basis, either!

The other Justiciar was a much older man; thin, bald, with an oddly proportioned face, very long, as if someone had taken an ordinary man's face and stretched it. His eyes were a colorless gray or faded blue; his hands and fingers as long and nimble as any musician's.

"Well, there's no trace of magic, which is what we expected, but it's more than merely frustrating," she was saying to her assistant as Tal and Kayne entered. Kayne went white, then red at the sight of the nude body, then excused herself. Ardis didn't even notice.

Tal took his place on the other side of the table. The body hadn't been in the water long enough for any real damage to have occurred, but Tal did notice one thing. "He doesn't look drowned," he pointed out. "Look at the expression; he doesn't look as if the last thing he was doing was struggling for air." In fact, the expression on the corpse's face was one of profound relief; if Tal hadn't known better, he would have thought that the man had died in his sleep. It was most unsettling to see *that* expression on *this* body.

"True." Ardis frowned. "Of course, that could be simply because the cold rendered him unconscious first. His lungs are full of water, at any rate, so drowning is definitely what killed him."

But Tal had already moved on to the next thing he was looking for. Again, the fact that the fellow had drowned in very cold water, and soon after committing the murder, had kept the formation of those strange bruises to a minimum—but the bruises were there. Ardis and the other Justiciar bent over them to study them at close range when Tal pointed them out.

"You say you've seen these on the other killers?" Ardis asked, delicately turning the man's arm to avoid further damage as she looked at the bruising on the inside of the upper arm.

"All the ones I was able to examine," Tal replied. "They don't look like the bruises that would come from falling, or from being struck."

"No, they don't," the other Justiciar replied. "There's no central impact point on them; it's more as if the limb was shoved or struck by something large and soft, but shoved or impacted hard enough to leave a bruise." He looked up at Tal from across the table, and nodded. "You must be the Special Inquisitor; I'm Father Nord Hathon, the Infirmarian."

That accounted for his presence here: his medical knowledge. Ardis was calling in anyone she thought might give her a clue. Tal had no doubt of the Priest's competence, for no one who worked closely with Ardis had ever proved less than competent. *I just hope that the same can be said about me.*

"Look on the legs for the bruises, too," Tal told him. "You'll probably find them on the backs of the thighs and the calves."

"Fascinating," Father Hathon murmured, following Tal's suggestion. "I can't account for this; kicks would have been directed towards the shins or the knee, blows to the head or torso, and attempts to seize the hands probably wouldn't have left these bruises on the wrists and hands. Those are particularly odd; they don't look like ligature marks, but they don't look like blows, either. Falls would have left bruises on the outside of the arms, not the inside, and on the shins again. This isn't quite the damage one would see from crushing, but it isn't far off from it."

Tal shook his head. "I don't understand it, either," he confessed. "All I know is, they look just like the ones I saw on the other bodies."

"Fascinating," Father Hathon said again. Ardis straightened up from her own examination and wiped her hands on a towel placed nearby.

"I don't think we'll learn anything more here." She sighed. "There's nothing magical in the clothing, no traces on the body. We might as well turn his corpse over to his relations. We're questioning the relatives, but I'm virtually certain that they're going to say precisely what all the friends and relatives of other secondary victims have said."

"This is a most curious case, Ardis," Father Hathon said, still examining the body. "I fear the only way that you will apprehend this perpetrator is when he makes a mistake."

"So you agree with me?" she asked, turning to look at him. "The man didn't simply go mad and murder a stranger, like the fellow at the Cathedral?"

Father Hathon looked up, and nodded.

"Absolutely," he replied. "This is not behavior that can be rationalized even by a very disturbed soul, and despite what the laity might believe, people do not suddenly run mad and begin killing strangers without giving very powerful signs that all is not right with them long beforehand."

"People don't suddenly run mad and murder *strangers* at all," Tal interjected. "It might look as if they have, but either a person they really wanted to kill was one of the job-lot, or else the people they kill bear some strong connection or similarity to someone they *do* want to kill but don't dare."

When both Ardis and Father Hathon turned to look at him in surprise, he flushed. "I—handled a case like that," he murmured apologetically. "We caught the murderer and I got a chance to question him. Fellow ran mad in the marketplace and killed three older women. Turned out he really wanted to murder his mother. I got curious and looked up other cases of supposed stranger-killings, and indeed they were like his."

Ardis and Hathon exchanged a look; hers was rather proud and proprietary, his was an acknowledgement. Hathon continued, this time including Tal. "I shall question these relatives myself to assure myself about signs of a disturbed mind, but I believe, with you, that I shall find no such signs, for I find no accompanying signs of physical neglect or abuse on this body, and no signs in the belongings that he planned this crime." He shrugged. "I cannot account for these bruises, and they trouble me. I concur with your analysis. If I did not know better, I would argue for demonic possession."

Tal couldn't resist the obvious question. "What do you mean, Father Hathon, that you 'know better'?"

He smiled, thinly—more a stretching of his lips than a real smile. "I have seen nothing in all my years to make me believe in demonic possession. There are spirits, certainly, even ones we humans might term 'evil.' There may even be demons. But I do not believe that such a creature can infest a human soul and make it do its bidding. That a human could *invite* one to infest, I do truly believe, but that is voluntary hosting, and not involuntary possession, and the creature that is hosted is no greater in evil than the one doing the hosting." He lost what was left of that faint smile. "Believe me, Special Inquisitor, the human heart is as capable of evils as any supernatural creature of legend. It is capable of things more terrible than any poor, homeless spirit could engender on its own. In my time, I have seen the worst that man can wreak, and I would prefer to face the worst that a spirit could do than fall into the hands of one of my fellow humans who harbors such a damaged soul."

Ardis drew a sheet over the body, shrouding it from view. "Father Hathon, if you would see to dealing with the relatives, I would be grateful. You can tell them that the Church believes their son was a victim himself, and that he can be buried in hallowed ground with all the appropriate rites."

"And I shall be suitably vague when they ask me what I believe he was a victim *of*." He nodded briskly. "You can trust my discretion."

"I never had any doubts," Ardis replied and, gesturing to Tal to follow her, left the room that evidently served the Justiciars as a morgue.

Once again, they retreated to the haven of Ardis's private office. Once they were in their accustomed seats, Ardis leaned back and watched him under half-closed eyelids. "You surprised me back there," she said slowly. "Pleasantly, I might add. I knew that you were intelligent, but I did not know that you were inclined to supplement that intelligence with research. What other oddities have you studied in the case-books, Tal Rufen? Perhaps we might find some similarities with this case.''

Kayne came in at that moment bearing a tray with the dinner they had both missed, which was just as well, since Tal's stomach was beginning to tell him that it didn't matter what turmoil his head was in, his body needed food. She set mugs of hot tea and plates of bread, cheese, and pickles in front of both of them.

"Rank hath its privileges, including raiding the kitchen-stores, and I borrowed your rank and your keys on your behalf,'' Kayne said crisply. "You two need to eat, or you'll collapse and nothing will get done. May I stay? If you can't find anything for me to do as a secretary, I can take a toasting-fork and make you toasted-bread-and-cheese.''

Ardis seemed more amused than annoyed; Tal was simply grateful for the food. "Certainly,'' Ardis replied, picking up the mug and taking a sip. "At this point, you should be part of our investigation. You may be in my position one day, and have to conduct another like it.''

Kayne made the sign of the flame with her two hands against her chest. "God forbid!'' she exclaimed. "I don't *want* to see any such thing happen!''

Ardis only arched a brow and waited for Tal to begin. *She knows that once a crime has been committed, sooner or later someone will emulate it.* He grimaced.

"Well, the first thing that comes to mind probably doesn't have anything to do with this one,'' he replied, seeing the page before his mind's eye as vividly as if he had a Haspur's memory. "That's the one I call the 'would-be hero.' He's a fellow that does something deliberately to put people's lives in danger so that he can be the first on the scene to rescue them. The fellow in the archives set fires, then rushed in and rescued those who were in peril, but I suppose it would be possible to make holes in boats, set up situations where things could fall on people, lure a boat onto a hidden obstruction—''

"I suppose you find this type out because he's a hero once too often?'' Kayne hazarded. "Or he keeps turning up at the scene, whether or not he gets a chance to rescue anyone?''

"Or as in this case, a Justiciar-Mage found a link between him and the fire. He's lucky no one died, so he was only sold into servitude to pay for the damages.'' Tal personally felt that the man might have gotten off too easily—but then again, it didn't say *who* he'd been sold to. A life of hard labor on a road-crew would certainly have kept him out of any further mischief, though it might not have cured him of wanting to be a hero at the expense of others.

"Another characteristic of people with this nature is that they tend to try and mingle with constables, fire crews, guards—the people they would like to emulate," Ardis noted, and smiled at Tal. "Yes, I am aware of this type, also. Very often you will discover later that they applied to be a constable or something of the sort, and were let go or turned down because they were clearly unsuitable. Go on, please."

Kayne had taken up a tablet of foolscap and was busily making notes, after making good her offer as toasting-cook. Tal continued, taking time as he spoke so that she could keep up with him.

"There was the fellow I mentioned earlier—the one who walked into the marketplace with an ax and cut down three women before he was stopped," he went on. "I had that case—I brained him with an awning-pole and dropped him where he stood. That one was so sensational that the City Council sent for a special Justiciar-Mage from here in Kingsford to examine him and read his thoughts."

Ardis nodded. "I recall—that would be my cousin Arran, the one who can sometimes read what is in a man's mind."

"Well, this Priest discovered that the man hated his mother, who was one of those nagging, selfish women who raise children by telling them what incompetent asses they are, no matter what they do or how well they do it." He shook his head. "She constantly belittled him, then expected him to serve her like a slave all her life. He *wanted* to kill his mother, and had gone after her to the market to do just that. He actually struck *at* her, but she got away, and then he just struck at anyone that looked like her." Once again, he shook his head. "I have to say that I thought and still think that the man deserved hanging, which he got, but once I met the mother, I wished there was a way to hang her alongside him. There was another when I was just beginning in the force, who slaughtered whores—he was inept where women were concerned, never able to handle himself with them. The only women who'd have anything to do with him were the ones he paid. He was punishing all the women who'd mocked him and turned him down by killing the whores."

"And the similar cases you found in the records?" Ardis prompted, looking interested, as Kayne scribbled along as fast as she could.

"There was a young man who'd been denied very unpleasantly by a girl, who went up into a tower and began shooting crossbow bolts into the crowd below—heavy crossbow, too, meant to carry far and kill with a single strike. At first, it was at her and anyone else he imagined had slighted him, but after he'd killed three or four people, he started shooting anything and anyone that moved. His rage and madness fueled his strength, and he fired more quickly than even a professional soldier would with such a hefty weapon.'' Tal closed his eyes a moment and tried to recall the rest of the cases he'd seen. ''A fellow made a practice of murdering wives because the first one was faithless and ran off with a horse-trader, but he didn't do it wholesale, he did it over the course of ten years, and he didn't do it in public.''

''That would come under another heading, I would imagine,'' Ardis agreed, clasping her hands in front of her on her desk. ''In fact, that might be the pattern we are seeing here.''

''Punishment of many for the sins of one who can't be reached?'' He nodded; it made a lot of sense. ''That's what I've been thinking for some time now. Of course, if he ever killed the one person he's obsessed with, that doesn't mean he'd stop.''

''Punishment of many—that would account for the fact that all the women concerned have some connection to music and musicians,'' Kayne put in, looking excited, for she had not been privy to most of the discussions Tal and Ardis had had on the subject.

''If this is true, and we could deduce what kind of person is the source of his anger, we might be able to anticipate him,'' Tal continued for Kayne's benefit. ''The trouble with that is, in order for the deduction to be of any use, we would have to allow that sort of person to walk in danger, and—'' He shook his head. ''It's morally reprehensible. We can't be everywhere, and protect everyone.''

''I agree,'' Ardis said firmly, to his immense relief. ''But let's do what we can for the purpose of *warning* exactly that sort of person.''

This was the first time that they had made a point of delineating all of the similar characteristics of the primary victims. It didn't take long to deduce that the targets that had been attacked with the most ferocity and in the riskiest circumstances were all young, dark-haired or of the Gypsy clans and *real* musicians. Even the half-mad woman Tal's colleague had seen attacked was a real musician in that the source of what little income she had came from her hymn-singing. The trouble was, because of regional tendency, half the young women in Kingsford were dark-haired, and from the way the murderer was behaving, he would probably react to someone simply singing because she was happy.

''This is an awfully broad description,'' Kayne said dubiously, her brows knitted as she studied their too-brief notes.

Tal licked a bit of hot cheese off his finger. ''That's not the only problem. The trouble with this is that even if we get this sort of woman to be careful, he'll either find a way to ambush his chosen victims or he'll switch to something else,'' Tal replied glumly. ''He's done that before, and if he doesn't get the satisfaction of a perfect victim, he's likely to make up in quantity what his kills lack in quality. Look at that list in Derryton—*six* over the course of four evenings!''

Ardis winced, and nodded, and finished her own slice in a few quick, neat bites. ''That would take a mage of considerable power and endurance, unless he was fueled by his determination, like that crossbowman you spoke of. There's another problem, in that we don't have any physical characteristics for him. We certainly can't search door-to-door for every man who feels he's been wronged by a Gypsy musician.''

''Without Arran along to know if they told us the truth, that wouldn't exactly be productive, even if we could confine every man in Kingsford to his own house until we questioned him,'' Kayne pointed out. ''If he knows we're looking for him, he's hardly going to tell us the truth if we find and question him!'' She folded a bit of paper over and over, a nervous habit Tal hadn't noticed until now.

Tal gritted his teeth. ''So, we're back to where we were when we started.''

''Maybe not—'' Ardis said slowly, tapping the desk with her forefinger. ''We actually know a few things about the man himself. He *must* have a source of wealth; he's been moving freely from city to city, and evidently has leisure to seek out victims that match his needs. Conversely, he's unexceptional, unmemorable, because no one has commented a word about seeing strangers lingering conspicuously before the murders.''

''Except for the secondary victims,'' Tal pointed out. ''They're often strangers to the area themselves.''

Ardis nodded, and picked up a slice of cheese, nibbling it delicately. ''If he's doing this within line-of-sight, as I think he must be, he's either in the crowd or above it, which means he's either very good at getting himself into other peoples' homes or businesses and up to a second story, or he's climbing about on roofs.'' She finished the cheese and started as a knot popped in the fire. ''If I were in his place, I'd offer myself as a cheap roof-repair service; after a snowfall followed by a day of sun, roofs are always leaking.''

Tal felt a rising excitement. *Now we're getting somewhere!* ''We could see if there was anyone having his roof repaired at the last site,'' Tal offered.

''That's a start,'' Ardis said, brightening a little. ''We could also check with all the business-owners down by the docks, and find out if there were any strangers working around their buildings at the time.''

Workers; it wouldn't necessarily have to be workers. ''People who claimed they were inspectors, maybe, or surveyors—'' Tal put in, as Kayne scribbled madly. ''Or extra workers they can't account for—''

''Checking inns for strangers—'' Kayne began, catching the excitement, then shook her head. ''Impractical, and besides, an inn isn't the only place a stranger to Kingsford might lodge. Good heavens, he could even *rent* a place, and with all the disrupted neighborhoods, he might not be recognized as a stranger.''

For a moment, there was silence as they ran out of ideas. ''There's another reason why he must have considerable resources,'' Tal put in. ''The daggers. We already know that there was more than one, and the second one was jeweled, decorated well enough that a well-dressed man did not look out of place carrying it. He either had to buy or make them, and I don't expect that sort of blade is the kind of thing you could pick up at an arms shop.'' He gave Ardis a sidelong glance, to see if she admitted that the daggers were what he thought they were.

Ardis's face darkened for a moment at that reminder, and she finally shook her head and put down her tea. ''Perhaps not as rare as one would think, since this is a city recovering from a great fire, and trading an heirloom dagger for a cook-stove or some wood would not be out of place when hunger and cold tap on one's shoulder. I also dislike saying it, after how helpful the Haspur was, but a Haspur's—or most bird's—vision would be good enough that if this killer is seeing the murder scenes from above, perhaps he is also, somehow, seeing through the eyes of birds and is nowhere near the murder site itself.'' Tal nodded grimly, and Kayne looked bewildered despite her best attempts to appear matter-of-fact. Ardis continued. ''I think we are looking for someone who has a grudge against the Church as well,'' she said to Kayne with some reluctance. ''Tal and I have touched on this before. Perhaps even a defrocked Priest. I cannot imagine why anyone else would be using an ecclesiastical dagger.''

''*Probably* a defrocked Priest,'' Kayne snapped, then colored. She must have been thinking the same thing after seeing Visyr's description of the murder-weapon. ''Forgive me, Ardis; I know this is probably the last thing you want to hear, but I'm only a novice and I don't have the—'' she searched for words ''—the emotional investment in the Church that you have. Maybe I can see things more clearly because of that. There just aren't that many lay people who know about ecclesiastical daggers!''

Ardis sighed, and covered her face with one hand for a moment. ''Perhaps you are right,'' she murmured from behind that shelter. ''It must be said, or we won't consider it seriously. Write it down, Kayne, write it down. I don't want to cost people their lives because I don't happen to like the trend the investigation is taking."

"It might not be a Priest at all," Tal pointed out, hoping to spare her some distress by giving her other options to consider. Now that she had made the effort to include this one, she would be honest enough to pursue it to whatever end it led to. "It could be someone who, like those would-be constables, is trying to emulate a Priest in some way. It could simply be someone who wants to make the Church out to be a villain."

Ardis removed her hand and looked up at him. "There is no one who wishes to make the Church out to be a villain so much as someone who has been cast out of the Brotherhood," Ardis said slowly. "And Kayne is right; the number of laymen who know about the ecclesiastical daggers is very low; the ceremonies in which they are used are so seldom performed publicly that it is vanishingly unlikely our particular miscreant could have seen one of them."

An uncomfortable silence reigned, and it was Tal who interrupted it by clearing his throat. "If—*if*—it is a Priest, or a defrocked Priest, it probably isn't anyone you know," he pointed out lamely. "After all, the murders didn't start here; Kingsford is only the last link in a path that goes out past Burdon Heath. I don't actually know where it started; Rinholm was just the last place I got an answer from."

"And it could be that it isn't a defrocked Priest," Kayne admitted after a moment. "I can think of another enemy of the Brotherhood who would know about the daggers. It could be someone who was sentenced to lifelong penal servitude and excommunication by a Justiciar. You *do* have the dagger on view at the sentencing of those you are casting out of the Church, Ardis, and you use it very prominently when you symbolically cut all ties to the community of God and the fellowship of man." She made a few flamboyant and stylized flourishes, as if she was using a blade to cut something in the air. "It's pretty theatrical, and I would imagine it would stick in someone's mind."

"The ceremony of excommunication is performed on those whose acts are so heinous that the Church cannot forgive them, and sometimes they are people we nevertheless have to allow to live," Ardis murmured aside to Tal. "Granted, we don't do that often, but—"

"But when you do, it's on pretty hard cases," Tal pointed out. "*That's* where I saw it! A Justiciar was excommunicating a particularly nasty piece of work—he hadn't killed anyone, but—well, what he'd done to his own daughters was pretty foul. Caught in the act, no less, and the poor child no older than nine! The local sire had him castrated, and the Church excommunicated him, then they both bound him over into penal servitude, and he *still* defied all of us. There's a hard case for you! I thought it was a mock-sacrifice of some kind.''

"Oh, we use the daggers there, too, in another rare ceremony," Kayne said cheerfully. "And it isn't a 'mock' sacrifice. It's a case where—well, never mind; the point is there is no way you would have seen that ceremony unless it was being performed on your behalf, and I don't think you qualify for that degree of urgency. In fact, no one who is the beneficiary of that ceremony is likely to hate the Church; they're more likely to want to spend their lives scrubbing Chapel floors to repay us.''

"Huh.'' He was surprised at her candor. He hadn't expected anyone in the Church to admit that they performed pagan-style sacrifices.

"We also excommunicate heretics—'' Kayne screwed up her face for a moment. "We don't do that often. You have to be doing more than just making a Priest angry or disagreeing with him. Six High Bishops have to agree on it—it's *hard* to be declared a heretic—''

Ardis interrupted. "We haven't excommunicated a heretic since we did it posthumously to Padrik, the original Priest who bound the ghost at Skull Hill, and all those who sent the ghost further victims.''

"The point is, suppose our murderer did something really heinous that warranted excommunication. Maybe a secular punishment too. He'd have seen the dagger, and he'd know it was an important object intimately connected with the Church," Kayne said in triumph.

"Especially if a Justiciar-Mage was the one involved," Ardis added, looking more normal. "We tend to dress the ceremony up quite a bit— invoking ghost-flames on the blade, and auras around the Priest. Well! In that case, we'll need to get access to the Great Archives and find the records on excommunications in the last ten to fifteen years. And, while we're at it, we should get the ones on defrocked Priests. There's no point in ignoring a theory just because we don't like it.''

"I'll go take care of that now," Kayne said, getting quickly to her feet. "I'll send it by a messenger and have him wait for the records. We need this information *now,* not next spring.''

"If there's a Priest-Mage there, have him send it to me directly," Ardis ordered. Kayne nodded and headed for the door.

She was gone before Tal could say anything more, leaving him alone with Ardis.

He tilted his head to one side, watching her, as she subsided into brooding. The crackling of the fire was the only sound in the room. "You've never had a case like this one before, have you?" he asked, softly, so as not to break the silence too harshly.

She shook her head; the dark rings under her eyes bespoke several sleepless nights. The case was making inroads on her peace of mind, as well as Tal's. "Well, I've had difficult cases, but—"

"Not ones that were personally difficult, that involved *your* emotions," he persisted.

She gave him a rueful glance. "True. Never one of those. I've had cases that made me angry, even ones that involved other members of the Brotherhood, but they weren't people I liked. In fact, I must confess now as I did then that it gave me some inappropriate personal satisfaction to put them away where they couldn't hurt anyone else." She looked positively fierce at that moment. "I above all know that the physical Body of the Church is far from perfect, and some blemish can't be helped—but those who misuse their power and authority are *not* to be tolerated."

"But now—now that it looks as if it's a Priest-Mage, it *could* be someone you know, someone you like." He nodded. "It's like knowing there's a bad constable on the force, and knowing it probably is someone you know and like, because otherwise he wouldn't be able to get away with it for long."

She sighed, and rubbed her temple as if her head hurt. "That's it exactly; we overlook things in friends that we are suspicious of in enemies or strangers, and we do it because we just know, in our heart, that the friend couldn't possibly be doing something bad. The trouble is, I've known enough criminals to be aware that they can be very charming, very plausible fellows, and they make very good friends. They use friendship as a cloak and a weapon."

"And someone in the Brotherhood?" he ventured.

"That's doubly hard to face," she said, looking off beyond him somewhere. "We have no families of our own, you see; that makes the ties of friendship within the Priesthood doubly special. And—quite frankly, we're *supposed* to be able to weed bad apples out long before they get out of the Novitiate. We're *supposed* to be able to police our own ranks."

"But if someone entered the Church, intending from the very beginning to conceal his real motives—" Tal shook his head. "You wouldn't be able to catch him until he did something. It's as if someone planned to have a double identity of criminal and constable from the beginning, and kept the false face intact. Until he was actually caught in the act, we'd never know, never guess, and even after being caught, perhaps still never believe."

She glanced at him sharply, then looked away. "This isn't what I anticipated when I joined the Church," was her only answer.

"Why did you join the Church?" he asked, feeling that an insolent question might take her mind off her troubled conscience. "And what did you expect when you got here?"

The fire flared up for a moment, briefly doubling the light in the room and casting moving shadows where no shadows had been a heartbeat before.

She cast him another sharp glance, but an ironic smile softened her expression as the fire died down again. And although she had no reason to answer him, she chose to indulge his curiosity. "Well, I actually joined because I convinced my father that it was more—economical— to send me here. I was sixteen and betrothed to a man who was forty, and not at all looking forward to my coming marriage."

Tal winced. "Not exactly a pleasant prospect for a young woman," he ventured.

"Oh, it *could* have been; there were people in my father's circle— older men—who were quite attractive and clever. I was a precocious child, audacious enough to be amusing, intelligent enough to be worth educating; many of father's friends found me charming and several said outright that if they were not already married, they'd have snatched me up as soon as I was of legal age. Marriage to one of them would have been no hardship—but not the man my father had chosen." She made a little face of distaste. "He wasn't one of my father's intimate circle, rather, he was someone my father had wanted to cultivate. Boring, interested only in his business, and convinced that women were good only for bearing and caring for children and being ornamental at the occasional dinner. He'd already buried two wives, wearing them out with multiple sets of triplets and twins, and I was to be the third. He wouldn't hire a proper overseer for the little ones, and not one of his children was older than twelve."

"You were supposed to shuttle from his bedroom to the nursery and back, I take it?" Tal asked. "Sounds as if he expected you to be a nursemaid as well as an ornamental bed-piece."

"Well, what he *expected* and what he would have gotten were two different things," she replied tartly. "I already had plans—but as it turned out, around the time when the wedding would have been scheduled, the old goat lost his political influence through a series of bad choices. Since political influence was the reason father had arranged the marriage in the first place, it was fairly easy to convince him that he would gain more by sending me to the Church instead. He was skeptical, until I proved to him I had what it took to become a mage. Priest-Mages are *never* without influence in the Church, and it didn't take him a heartbeat to realize how much good it would do him to have one of his own blood saying what *he* would say in closed Church conclaves." She grinned. "So, *he* told the old goat I'd discovered a genuine vocation; the old goat didn't have so much influence now that he was willing to fight the Church for a promised bride. My father told the Justiciars that I had mage-talent, and the Justiciars didn't give a hang if I had a vocation or not, so long as they could make a Justiciar-Mage out of me."

"And you?" Tal asked.

"In the Church I would get things I wanted: education, primarily, and eventual independence. Bless his heart, Father never intended for me to act against my conscience or against the Church itself—what he wanted is essentially what I have been doing, especially with regard to softening the Church's hardening attitude towards nonhumans. It was a good enough bargain to me." She shrugged. "If I didn't have a vocation when I entered, I discovered that there was pleasure in using my abilities to the utmost, pleasure in being of service, and yes, a certain pleasure in piety. Not the kind of piety-for-show that makes up most Church ceremonies, but—well—*belief.* Belief, and living what you believe."

"I see," Tal said, though he didn't really understand that last. Perhaps he just didn't believe enough in anything to know how it felt. "Then what?"

She chuckled. "Then, after several years of fairly pure service, I discovered that my father's talent for politics hadn't skipped my generation. I found myself in the thick of politics, lured in by my own sense of justice—or injustice, perhaps. Eventually that led to a rift in the Kingsford Brotherhood, which led to one faction allying itself with enemies of the Grand Duke, which led in turn to the Great Fire. That essentially hastened a purge that would have been inevitable, though less immediate, costly and dramatic than it was after the Fire." Her smile turned a trifle bitter, a trifle feral. "To be plain-spoken, it was a little war, a war of magic and of physical force. It was a war I didn't intend to lose, not after seeing the Fire raging across the Kanar. In a way, the worst mistake they ever made was in helping to set the Fire. Everyone here knew it had to have been set by magic, and that brought many of the Brotherhood over to my side who might otherwise have remained neutral or helped the opposition. So I won the war, and won it in hours, and I will *never* permit its like here again."

He took in her expression, and decided that he didn't want to be involved with any faction opposing this woman. If she was opposed, and was certain to the depths of her soul that she was right, she would never relent, never admit defeat. "And what happened to the old goat?'' he asked, changing the subject—or rather, returning the conversation to the original subject.

"He found another bride within a month; he still had money, even if he didn't have the influence he'd once possessed. His political star had set, and he knew it, so he found a pretty little kitten with no more brains than a duck. Two more sets of twins, then *he* died, somewhat to everyone's surprise.'' She shook her head. "The girl managed to hold her looks, so now she had beauty *and* money, and needed to answer to no man for what she chose to do. She hired an army of tutors and nursemaids to care for the children, and has been working her way through a series of lovers unencumbered by offspring, scruples, or husband. And there are plenty of my former set who envy her.''

Her gaze wandered off elsewhere, and he thought that perhaps she was wondering what she would have been like, had she tamely allowed the wedding to take place.

She might have been able to prevent having children entirely until he died. She would have had the old man's money, and as a widow, she'd have been able to do whatever she chose. She could have bought that education she craved, helped her father politically, traveled, had freedom she doesn't have now. He wondered if she had thought of that at all.

"Was there anyone you would have rather married?'' he asked curiously. "Your own age, I mean. You were sixteen, that's a pretty romantic age, after all. At sixteen, every pretty girl had *me* ready to pledge my all.''

"But I was never more romantic than I was practical,'' she pointed out to him. "Unfeminine of me, but there it is. In some ways, Tal, you and your peers have far more freedom than me and mine. I knew that the boys my age were all under the same constraints that I was; we had to marry or take positions to suit our families. If we didn't, we'd be cut off, the way my cousin Gwydain was when he passed the Trials and joined the Bardic Guild against his father's wishes. Even when he became a Master Bard and was feted by everyone, his father refused to acknowledge him. Of course,'' she smiled crookedly, "being in the Guild was no great hardship, and being a Master Bard meant he had any luxury he wanted, so he didn't lose anything by his choice. And neither did I, if it came to that, and once I knew I *could* be a mage I'd have gone into the Church whether or not my father consented. He knew it, I think, so—'' She chuckled. "It's a good thing we're a great deal alike. He knew not to push me too far, and I knew not to push him, either.''

"But running off with an inappropriate boy—"

"Would have gotten both of us cut off from family and support, with neither of us suited to or trained for a trade, and I didn't care to live in poverty," she said crisply. "Love in a hovel quickly turns sour for those who aren't mentally and emotionally inclined to sacrifice. Great sacrifice, anyway, all for love and all of that—there was some sacrifice involved in going into the Novitiate, but those who are granted exceptional gifts get exceptional treatment, inside the Church as well as outside of it."

But there was a tinge of regret in her voice, and Tal was suddenly taken with a devilish wish to pursue the subject, but she might have sensed that, and she turned the tables on him.

"And you—there's nothing wrong with your looks, and the constabulary doesn't require celibacy, so why aren't you married?" she asked, a wicked gleam in her eye. "What happened to all those pretty girls you yearned after?"

He flushed in confusion. "I don't know—" he confessed. "For a while, none of those girls was interested in anyone who was earning barely enough in the constabulary to support himself—they'd flirt with me, but they married tradesmen. Then later, when I was a full constable, I didn't ever see anyone *I* wanted to pursue. I suppose it was because I was always in districts that didn't have any decent women. I mean, they had decent women, but the ones who weren't married were brainless. Even most of the ones who *were* married were brainless. And when I saw ones who had a few brains, they spoiled it all by falling in love with some muscle-bound idiot who'd get them with child then leave them with the baby and spend most of every night with a pretty barmaid." He shook his head. "I never understood it."

"Well, maybe they fell in love with muscle-bound idiots because that's what they thought they were supposed to do," Ardis commented sardonically. "It's amazing what sheep women are, sometimes. But it's equally amazing how happy men are to have them that way, so there's plenty of blame on both sides."

"I suppose so," Tal began, and she fixed him with that penetrating stare again.

"You *suppose* so? Did you ever go to one of those women who attracted you and encourage her to think for herself? Did you ever compliment her on making a clever decision? Did you ever show her that you valued brains over looks?" At his shamefaced flush, she nodded. "I thought so. Well, what's a girl to do, when her parents are telling her she has to be a pretty little fluff-head, her peers are rewarding the behavior of a pretty little fluff-head, and the handsome fellows only seem impressed by big, empty eyes and a slender waist? If her parents can't afford to apprentice her, and they don't have a business she can learn or they won't *let* her learn it, what is she to think and do?"

He felt obscurely ashamed. "I suppose—they do what they feel they're supposed to do."

Ardis was clearly relishing her low-key but heartfelt tirade. "If someone ever gave them encouragement to think for themselves, you *might* get a few girls outside of the Novitiate who find pleasure in spending as much time cultivating and nurturing their intelligence as they do their hair," she said crisply. "You know, I tried starting a school down in Kingsford for girls with brains and ambition, and it got nowhere, because there weren't any *men* saying that girls with brains and ambition were attractive. The ones that stuck ended up in the Novitiate, where they'd have gone anyway."

"That was then," he pointed out, rather desperate to get his gender out of trouble. "Maybe now you would be able to make it work. You're a High Bishop, you're a woman, young girls have *your* example. Things have changed in Kingsford, and there are a lot of women who've had to make their own way—"

"Yes, well, maybe now it would work," she admitted, grumbling a little. "Especially now that I could get a Free Bard tutor or three from my cousin, some help and encouragement from Duke Arden and Lady Asher, and I could requisition quite a few folks from this Abbey as teachers. I know Kayne would be perfectly happy to provide her services as example *and* teacher."

"You see?" he said eagerly. "You just took on too much by yourself. All you needed to do was to wait until you had the authority to get more help, and the power yourself to be an example."

She gave him an odd, sideways look. "You can be very persuasive yourself, Tal Rufen," she said. "I shall have to requisition *your* skills for this school; then we'll see what you have to say about it."

"So long as all you ask me to teach is history, I have no particular objection," he said, surprised by the sudden longing that came over him when she made the suggestion. "I am not suited to teaching much of anything else."

Again, she gave him one of those sidelong glances. "Perhaps I shall do just that. But in the meanwhile, we have another sort of work ahead of us." She brooded for a moment. "I want you on the street, Tal. Go make those inquiries we spoke about; get some coin for bribery, and see if anyone knows anything. And warn the women."

"That could let him know we're looking for him," Tal pointed out, "if he's watching for such things."

"We'll have to take that chance." Her face had taken on the look it had when she spoke of the "little war" she'd fought within the Church. "You can defend yourself, Tal; what defenses have those women got?"

He sighed. "None. I'll do everything I can, Ardis—and there is this. We may not be able to catch him—but perhaps we can make it so difficult for him that he becomes desperate. Desperate men make mistakes."

Her face sobered. "We will have to hope for those mistakes. At the moment, that is the only hope we have."

Chapter Eight

Orm Kalend settled into the corner formed by the intersection of the booth-bench he sat on and the wall of this tavern, his eyes discreetly hooded as he toyed with his mug of dark ale. Around him, the muted sounds of conversation and eating provided a soporific background for his thoughts. This was precisely the sort of tavern he most favored, one with such good food that the meals themselves were the attraction for customers, not the liquor nor any form of entertainment. The drink available here was only average in taste, and below average in strength; that fact when combined with the excellent provender assured that there were never any fights in *this* inn.

This was precisely as the proprietor, a famous cook himself, preferred it; in fact, Orm suspected that if he could have managed it, he would have omitted serving wine, beer, and ale altogether and relied entirely on *kaffa* and teas. He was of the pious, Church-going sort that frowned on strong drink and prohibited intoxication. But he probably knew only too well that, if he were to do that, not even the finest food in the world would keep his customers returning. Most self-styled gourmets demanded light wines and passable beer at the least to accompany their meals.

This was a good place for Orm to do business, especially business with some of his more—sensitive—customers. The lighting was low, the clientele incurious, and the atmosphere very soothing to the nerves of gentlemen who might otherwise have second thoughts about working with Orm. Not that Orm appeared to be anything other than a gentleman himself—but if he had insisted on meeting his customers in a place only scoundrels frequented, those customers would naturally assume that Orm belonged among them.

So long as we appear respectable in all ways, the polite fiction of appearance is maintained.

As if that thought had been a magic spell to summon him, one of those gentlemen entered the door of the tavern along with a few flurries from the light snowstorm outside. As the flakes settled to the wooden floor and melted, the gentleman peered around the tavern until he spotted Orm at his usual seat and in his usual posture. He made no sign of recognition, but he did move straight to that corner booth, intercepting a serving wench on the way to place his order. Orm noted with satisfaction that the young man bore a roll of paper in his hand.

Good! One more section of the Duke's maps! Rand will be pleased.

"Greetings, friend," Orm said lazily, paying no outward attention to the rolled-up document. "You're just in time to join me for luncheon."

"Always a pleasure, since you pay," replied the fellow as he slid into place opposite Orm and placed the map on the table against the wall. Ridiculously thin, the young man resembled nothing so much as a normal man who had somehow been stretched an extra few inches lengthwise; even his face had the oddly disconcerting proportions of a normal face that had been elongated. He clearly had difficulty in finding clothing that fit; his sleeves ended above his bony wrists, and his breeches exposed the ankles of his boots. His fingers were stained with ink in the manner of all clerks, and he squinted as if he was a little short-sighted.

Orm chuckled. "The pleasure is mine, both for the sake of your company and the opportunity to reward one of good Duke Arden's hardworking clerks. You gentlemen earn little enough for your efforts that a good citizen should feel obligated to treat you now and again."

The scrawny young man grinned as the wench brought his meal and Orm's. "I wish more of the good citizens of Kingsford felt the way you do," he said, then wasted no more words as he dug into a portion of exquisitely seasoned oysters. Orm never stinted his gentlemen, especially clerks, who were usually perpetually hungry. Every meal was a full one, beginning with appetizers and ending with a fine dessert. Orm knew that men with a good meal in their stomachs were ready to please the person who arranged for that meal to be there.

A full stomach makes for poor bargaining.

The young clerk and Orm continued to exchange pleasantries as their meal progressed, just as the others in this room were doing. At some point during the progress of the meal, several silver coins made up in a paper packet found their way beneath the basket of delectable yeast rolls. At another point, they vanished again—and an intelligent deduction could be made that they vanished into the clerk's capacious pockets, since Orm didn't reclaim them, but no one could actually claim to have seen the coins change hands.

At no time during the meal did either of them refer to the coins, or to the rolled-up map. Nor did Orm ever refer again to the fact that his companion was in the Duke's service. But when the young man stood up after finishing the last morsel of a bowl of bilberry trifle smothered in brandy and whipped cream, and took his leave, he left behind the map, and his belt-pouch bulged a little more than it had when he arrived.

Orm's own meal had been lighter than his companion's, and he lingered over his own dessert and over the mug of black tea that ended his meal. Only when enough time had passed that the tables nearest him held different customers than they had when the young man arrived did he casually pick up the roll of paper and carry it away with him.

Once outside the door of the inn, he waited while his eyes adjusted to the thin, gray light. He stood in the street, out of the way of traffic, as the continuing snowfall dusted the shoulders of his coat with white. To anyone watching, it would look as if he was debating his direction. Then, with no sign of hurry, he tucked his map under his arm and strolled off towards Old Town and the house he had rented.

Old Town was all of Kingsford that had not burned in the Great Fire; the Fire itself had been no respecter of rank, and had eaten as much into the sections housing the wealthy as into the sections housing those of middling fortune. Only the poor had suffered complete devastation, which was hardly surprising, considering that most of the homes of the poor had been, and were again, poorly-built firetraps. But enough time had passed now that there was no longer a shortage of housing; in fact, in some places there was a surplus. There were now segments of Old Town where one could rent modest homes for modest fees, and that was becoming easier all the time. The reason was simple; as more new homes were constructed, the older ones became less desirable.

The owners of those modest—but older—homes had often capitalized on the shortage of living-space by renting out as much of their dwellings as they could spare, with the resultant added wear and tear that was only to be expected when strangers moved into a dwelling they had no vested interest in keeping up. Now the owners of such houses coveted a place with more space, in a better neighborhood, with more of the modern conveniences, and they had the means put by to begin building a new home—renting the entirety of their current abode made the acquisition of such a property much easier. So long as the tenant *looked* respectable and paid down the requisite sum, most such absent landlords saw no reason to be curious.

Orm had counted on this when his employer Rand decreed that it was time for them to move their operations to Kingsford. It had not taken Orm very long to find the perfect house for them.

Orm had further plans for the place; if Rand decided to stay here, it might even be possible to purchase the property outright. It would all depend on what Rand wanted, of course. Rand was the one with the money; Orm merely spent it for him.

That genteel little house looked exactly like its neighbors in the row: tall, narrow houses, made of pale brown stone with gabled, slate-covered roofs, with passages between them too small for most muscular men to squeeze through. Out of habit, Orm did not enter the dwelling from the street-entrance; instead, he went around to the end of the block and slipped into the alley when no one was looking, entering his own house like a thief, through a window at the rear.

It was good to stay in practice; although Orm hadn't stolen anything in years, it was wise to keep the old skills up.

Rand wasn't around, which didn't surprise Orm in the least. He was probably out "celebrating the senses" as he called it; he always did that when his curse left him and he was able to walk the streets unremarked.

Orm was in no hurry for that condition to become permanent. For now, Rand needed him and his skills, and paid well for them. If Rand ever became normal again, he would no longer require Orm. Until Orm amassed enough wealth that *he* no longer needed Rand, Orm would prefer that the curse remain intact.

The two-story, rented house was divided into two suites, each one comprising an entire floor, linked only by a staircase at the front. Orm had the ground floor and Rand the second; Orm seldom entered his employer's domain unless, as now, he had something to leave there. Whistling cheerfully, he stepped into the unheated foyer at the front of the dwelling and climbed the stair leading off the tiny room to the second level.

At the top of the staircase was a door, usually left locked. Unlocking the door, which led directly into the first room of the suite, he stepped just far enough inside to lay the rolled map down on Rand's empty desk. He never went farther than this unless Rand himself was here, and that was not just because he respected Rand's wishes for privacy. Orm's employer was a mage, and mages had very unpleasant means of enforcing their desires.

Besides, there was nothing in Rand's suite that Orm was at all interested in. He already knew everything he needed to know about Rand himself, and Rand had no information Orm was at all interested in. Although Rand had several sources of wealth, Orm was not tempted to steal from him, either. Stealing from Rand would be as unproductive as draining a pond to get the fish; left alone, Rand would be the source of far more wealth to Orm than he would be if Orm was foolish enough to steal and run.

So, leaving the new map in plain sight, Orm descended the stairs to his own cozy den. Rand would return soon enough, and Orm would reap the pleasant results.

Orm built up the fire in the stove he had instead of a fireplace, and settled into a chair at his desk beside it with a pen and a ledger. Although Orm had begun his professional life as a thief, and had in the course of things been forced to injure or even kill, he was now, for the most part, in the less risky business of buying and selling information and expediting (though not carrying out) the plans of others. Rand was not his only client, although all of Orm's other commissions were of strictly limited scope. Rand had been Orm's chief concern since they "met" in a tiny village many leagues and months ago.

Since that day, Orm devoted his time and energy to Rand, and Rand paid him handsomely for information, for personal services, and to ensure Rand's safety and security. Rand needed someone to take care of even the tiniest tasks for him, because Rand was generally not human.

Rand particularly needed Orm now that they were operating in the city; although Orm was not a native of Kingsford, he was quite familiar with both Old Town and New. Rand only knew Kingsford as it had been before the Great Fire, and as a result was frequently disoriented when he went abroad in the streets. This had frustrated him to the point of fury, and Orm had been trying (though with little success) to draw diagrams of the city as it was now. Then when Orm had learned that a bird-man in the service of the Duke was making detailed and highly accurate maps of the city, he had moved heaven and earth to find a clerk who could be bribed to supply him with ongoing copies. To the clerk, he was an enterprising merchant looking for the best spots to place fried-pie stalls; the clerk found nothing amiss in this. A merchant prepared to put money into a large number of fried-pie stalls could stand to make a fortune or lose one, depending on whether he found good locations or poor ones. Vendors of foodstuffs had been operating from barrows since the Great Fire precisely because no one knew yet where the good locations were—but that meant that there was no such thing anymore as a place that people could patronize regularly other than an inn. The first person to capitalize on this situation could find himself a very wealthy man, and it would be more than worth his while to bribe a clerk for advance copies of the new city maps.

Rand had been very pleased when Orm presented him with the first of his new maps; pleased enough to make Orm's reward a golden one, even though the map was of an area that Rand would not be able to use, at least not effectively. The mage rightly considered the reward to be one for initiative rather than immediate services rendered, and had brooded over his acquisition with his strange eyes half-closed in pleasure.

He would not have been nearly so pleased if he'd known that Orm knew why he was going to want those maps—knew why he had wanted to come to Kingsford in the first place—knew what his *real* name was.

It's really very amusing, actually, Orm thought as he finished the last of his little notes and sat back in his chair, listening for the sound of Rand's footsteps on the walk outside. *He's quite, quite naïve. To think that he really believed that since I was not a native of Kingsford I would not have recognized him for what he was!*

Perhaps it was only that it never occurred to him that his employee would turn his considerable skills to ferreting out everything he could about his new employer. Perhaps it was that he completely underestimated the ability of the Free Bards to spread information in the form of songs, and overestimated the ability of the Bardic Guild to suppress it when they tried. Or perhaps it was that he simply had no idea how good a tale the story of the foul deeds and punishment of Priest Revaner was.

Very singable—though that shouldn't be surprising, considering it was composed by the Free Bard they call Master Wren.

Oh, Orm knew all about his employer—more than was in the song, for there were still plenty of people in Kingsford who knew the story in its entirety, and even a handful who had seen the end of it themselves. Those acrobats, for instance. . . .

Once they had reached Kingsford, Orm had made it a part of his business to sniff out those who had actually been witnesses to the tale of Priest Revaner—or, as Master Wren titled it, "The Faithless Priest." Now he knew just about everything there was to know, including a few secrets known only to Revaner's fellow Priests, for even a Priest likes to talk.

Priest-Mage Revaner, of the Kingsford Order of Saint Almon, had often claimed that he never wanted to be a Priest. He had felt himself restricted by the rules of his Order, his vows before God, and the constraints associated with being a Priest in the first place—most notably, celibacy and chastity, but also poverty and humility. Orm personally didn't see where he had anything to complain about—presumably he should have known those rules before he ever took his final vows—but it hardly mattered.

The fact was that Revaner wanted many things. Wealth, for one—and that state was attainable only to those of sufficiently high office. Even then, it was wealth that, in the end, belonged to the Church and not to the Priest, and that wasn't good enough for Revaner. So Priest Revaner had set about using (or misusing) his magics to help him gain wealth and hide it away from the prying eyes of his superiors. So much for that obstacle, and although it chafed him, the virtue of humility was easy enough to feign. Celibacy, while irksome, was constricting only in that it meant he could not attain further wealth and the position he had not been born into through marriage. But chastity—there was a problem.

Revaner craved women, but not just any women. His women had to be subservient to him in every way. Since he did not consider himself to be particularly impeded by his other vows, the vow of chastity made no difference to his desires. Unfortunately, confined to the Abbey Cloister, it was difficult to get away for long to indulge himself, and impossible to bring a woman there.

But when Faire Season came, he saw a possible answer to his problems, for a few weeks, at least. So with a little judicious bribery, a bit of flattery, and cultivation of one of the Masters of the Bardic Guild, he got himself assigned as a Faire Warden, patrolling for unlawful use of magic, for the duration of the Faire.

That much had Orm's admiration. *Clever, that. He had his own tent on the grounds of the Faire, and he knew that on his watch, the only person who would have been checking for magic was himself.*

Revaner saw the Faire as his own private hunting-preserve, a place where he could indulge himself in ways he had only dreamed of before. He had his own private tent and servants whose minds were so controlled by magic that they never saw anything he didn't want them to see. His duty only lasted from the time the Faire opened in the morning until sunset, and mostly consisted of walking about the Faire searching for the signs of magic. And while he was doing that, he was marking women for further attentions, thus combining duty with pleasure. Orm rather fancied that Revaner had assumed that as long as he confined his attentions to those technically outside Church protection—Gypsies, for instance, or other folk who did not consider themselves Churchmen—his victims would never dare report him to Church authorities.

For the most part, he would have been right. There aren't very many pagans or Gypsies who would trust the Church to police its own, and those who had turned from worship of the Sacrificed God to some other deity would be afraid of being taken and punished as heretics. Complaints against a Priest to secular authorities would be turned over to the Church, and where would they be then?

Revaner had used his magic to coerce women who didn't cooperate with him—which was another violation of secular law, twice over; first for using coercion inside the Faire boundaries, and secondly for using magic as the instrument of coercion. Then there was the violation of Church law in using his powers and his position to further his own ends.

Altogether he was a very naughty boy.

Revaner had enjoyed himself to the fullest, with nothing more than merest rumor to alert his superiors to the fact that he was a lawbreaker so many times over that he would be doing penance until he died if he was caught.

The blatant misuse of everything the Church gave him would have had even the most corrupt of them livid. Not to mention the amount of keep-quiet money they would have had to pay to his victims.

They did not even know *who* the cause of the rumor was; he had managed to keep his identity secret. But he had already made one fatal error, and that had been when he had checked to see who the Prior of the Abbey of the Justiciars at Kingsford was without also making the effort to discover who his underlings were. The Prior was lazy and subject to a venial sin now and then of his own—but immediately beneath him in rank was Justiciar-Mage Ardis, already known for dispensing the purest justice without regard for rank, privilege, or station, and it was Ardis who was truly in charge of the Faire Judiciary. Then, after three weeks of enjoyment, Revaner had made his second fatal error.

He had approached a Gypsy Free Bard named Robin and was rebuffed, publicly, vehemently, and in such a way as led to a great deal of humiliation on his part and amusement on that of the witnesses. But his success had bred overconfidence and inflated his pride, and his pride would not tolerate such a blow. Obsessed with the girl and angered at her contemptuous refusal, he had conspired with a Guild Bard named Beltren, one of his cronies, to kidnap her.

Even that might only have earned him exile to some distant, ascetic Abbey in a harsh and unforgiving climate, constant penance and prayer, and perpetual confinement to his cell if he had been caught—but his pride was too high to merely use her and discard her. No, he had to triumph over her and keep her as a private trophy. He had used his magic to transform her into a man-sized bird of gaudy plumage, placed her in a cage, and compelled her with further spells to sing for his pleasure. Then he displayed her for all the Faire to see.

Pride and folly went hand in hand, and he was bound to fall over such a blatantly stupid action; Revaner was found out, of course, and he was condemned by the Justiciars to the same condition he had forced upon the Gypsy girl. Transformed into a black bird of amazing ugliness, he was displayed in a cage above the gate of the Abbey as an example to others. And since he was a bird, without access to his wealth, his connections, or his persuasive tongue, no one was tempted to try to defend him.

When fall came that year, he was taken down and lodged in a cell in the Abbey until the warmer weather arrived, in larger, if not more luxurious quarters. But when spring came, it was easier to keep him there instead of putting him back on display. Eventually, he became a fixture in the Abbey gaol.

Then came the Great Fire, and the revolt within the Abbey itself. And, presumably, during the confusion or perhaps out of misguided compassion, someone left the cage door open and the bird escaped.

The Gypsy transformed into a bird had not been able to fly, but even as a bird, Revaner was still a mage, and he could use his magic to aid his wings. He had put as much distance between himself and Kingsford as possible, ending up at last in Sandast, a trade-city situated below a cliff riddled with caves. There Revaner had made a home, stole food, and attempted to work out how to change himself back.

That much Orm had managed to reason out for himself. What he didn't know was how Revaner had learned that the key to transforming himself back to a man was the death of someone else, and it was the one thing that he was not likely to ever find out. There were only two people who had ever known that, and Revaner's first victim was the second. Short of bringing back the dead spirit to speak, Orm was unlikely to discover what the circumstance had been.

Orm had recently removed himself to Sandast from the vicinity of Kingsford until a certain party returned to his homeland. A business deal had gone awry, and it wasn't particularly healthy for Orm to linger in the vicinity of Duke Arden's city. Although his original customer was no longer available, it had occurred to Orm that the information he possessed could easily be sold elsewhere. Sandast, for instance. And it was in the course of trying to find a buyer for that information that he had come upon Revaner in the moment of his third attempt at transformation.

Now, there had been rumors of a madman stalking the streets at night and murdering unwary victims by driving an enormous spike or spear through their chests, but Orm had dismissed it. After all, such a person would hardly be inconspicuous, loping about with a spike the size of a small tree trunk over his shoulder! So when his search for a client took him out into the dense fog of a typical Sandast evening, he wasn't particularly worried about coming across anything worse than a pickpocket or back-alley assaultist, either of which he could handle easily.

Not until he rounded a corner and found himself in a dimly lit cul-de-sac, facing a scene out of a nightmare.

Filtered light fell down from windows above onto the murderer and his latest victim, and the murderer was a great deal *more* conspicuous than a madman with a spike. A huge black bird, with the body of a street-singer impaled on its lancelike beak, glared at Orm out of angry red eyes. Blood was everywhere, turning the dust of the street into red mud, plastering the feathers of the bird in sticky tufts, splattered against the peeling walls of the buildings surrounding the cul-de-sac. Orm had been so startled, and so *fascinated,* that instead of running, he had simply stood and stared.

And so he had the unique experience of watching the bird transform into a black-robed man.

Or rather—try to watch it do so, for there was something about the transformation that made his eyes hurt and his stomach churn, as if whatever was going on was not meant to be *watched.* He looked away for a moment, and when he looked back, there was a man in the black robes of a Priest standing over the body of the girl. The man was unarmed, but Orm did not for a moment assume that he was helpless. The very opposite, in fact.

So he did the only thing logical under the circumstances.

"Well, you seem to have a situation on your hands. I believe you can use my help," he had said, as calmly as if the man had just walked into an inn looking for him. "Would you care to come with me to my quarters where we can discuss it?"

Whether it was due to Revaner's own desperation, or Orm's glib tongue, Revaner engaged his services on the spot.

Revaner still had most of his money, and a great deal of it, all deposited with the Goldsmith's Guild, and thus accessible to him any time he cared to write out the proper papers to get it. But when it took seven days to get the money, and he was able to remain in human form for considerably less than that—

Well, he had a problem to say the least.

In the first few days of their partnership, Orm's role had been a simple one; he got a suite of rooms with windows overlooking a bare courtyard used for storage, so that Revaner—or "Rand," as he now called himself—could come and go at his leisure when he was a bird. Orm made certain that all of Rand's physical needs were cared for, both as a bird and as a man. But Rand's period as a human did not last more than three days, and when he transformed, he was nearly beside himself with rage.

Orm let him rage, for there was nothing much in his room he could damage, and waited for him to calm—or at least, to exhaust himself.

Rand-as-bird had learned how to speak, although his Gypsy captive had not had the time to master that art, so when he finally stopped stabbing holes in the bed-linens, Orm ventured a few words.

"This is hardly a surprise," he had pointed out. "You knew you were going to revert eventually."

The bird's voice was a harsh croak, unpleasant but understandable. "Not so *soon*," Rand protested, and made another stab at a pillow. White feathers flew out of the hole, and Orm shook his head.

"But it held for longer this time than the last," Orm replied. "You told me the last time it only held for two days. Things are improving."

Rand tossed the pillow aside with a savage twist of his head, scattering more feathers across the floor as it landed. "It should have been longer," he muttered. "It should have been *permanent*."

Orm shrugged, and spread his hands. "I'm no mage," he replied, "but this is the most powerful piece of magic that I have ever *heard* of outside an Elf Hill—and cast by a—a mage that powerful, I can't imagine how three paltry deaths could negate anything like *this*."

He had caught himself for a moment, realizing that he had been about to say something about a spell cast by a Justiciar-Mage, and even though he hadn't actually said anything incriminating, he caught Rand giving him a suspicious look out of those ruby-red eyes.

It occurred to him that Rand might well consider him expendable at that moment, and he hastened to deal with that contingency.

"It's obvious to me that if each death lengthens the time you are—" he chose his word delicately "—*cured,* you simply have to find more victims. The trouble with that is obvious: already people in this little town are beginning to talk, and it's only a matter of time before someone has the bright idea of starting a house-to-house search. Granted, you *could* fly away during the search, but you wouldn't be able to pick your moment to fly, and what if someone saw you and made the obvious conclusion? You clearly need more sacrifices, but you simply cannot stay here and keep killing people.''

"So what am I to do?" rasped Rand. "Move somewhere else and kill people?"

"Why not?" Orm countered. "*I* can move you comfortably—well, more comfortably than flying all that distance. I can find you safe quarters, I can stand watch for you—I can even find potential victims for you. But I think you ought to find a safer way of doing your killings, a way in which you're less likely to be caught in the act. It's already happened once, and you were just lucky that it was me and not a constable who discovered you. Think about life in the long term—we don't have to stay in once place, we can move on when things become risky. Think about what you need to accomplish, instead of frantically slaughtering in the hopes that this time something will work!''

Never before or since had he seen such a transformation come over a creature. Rand went from a creature dangerously enraged and making no effort to hide that fact, to one suddenly locked in thought. Literally locked in thought—Rand went rigid, and his eyes unfocused. Silence prevailed for some time, but Orm was in no hurry to leave, so he waited the creature out. He had, he thought, just proved to Rand that his services were indispensable. Rand had a great deal of ready cash, and Orm wanted as much of that money transferred to himself as possible. He also wanted to continue living, and he was under no illusions about his continued existence if Rand decided to get rid of him.

This, of course, was not the first time he had found himself in that position. A man who sells information often comes into possession of knowledge that others would rather he didn't know, and sometimes those others are willing to take drastic steps to ensure that the information is lost again. Orm had always saved himself in the past by proving that it was more expensive to eliminate him than to purchase his cooperation, and he was fairly certain he could do the same thing this time.

Finally, Rand shook all of his shabby drab feathers and fastened his gaze on his would-be partner. "You are right," the bird croaked. "And I want to think about this for a while. I have been very shortsighted until this moment."

"In that case," Orm had said, rising and making a little bow, "I shall leave you in peace to think." He knew then that he was safe, for

Rand had spoken the key word: *shortsighted.* Rand had just made the jump from thinking only about the immediate need of becoming and staying human, and had moved on to other desires as well. And a man who looked as Rand did probably had a major desire driving him.

Revenge. Orm loved that motive; it was one of his most profitable. Revenge was complicated and expensive; it involved elaborate plots and a great deal of planning. And given that Rand would probably want revenge on at least one person moderately difficult to find—well, the possibilities for profit were staggering.

Rand made several requests of Orm over the next couple of weeks, with the most difficult being the acquisition of an ecclesiastical dagger. Rand had probably intended for Orm to steal one, but Orm had no intentions of leaving that kind of trail for the Church to follow. It wouldn't be too difficult for Church mages to put the theft of a piece of regalia of that sort together with a murder by means of that kind of weapon—and Orm had the suspicion they might be able to tell who had taken it and what had been done with it. Instead, he broke into a Chapel all right, but when he found one of the daggers, he only studied it. The next day he purchased a triangular file of approximately the correct dimensions, broke into a smithy whose owner was out of town, and ground it into a similar knife-blade himself. Since the new "knife" already had a wooden hilt of sorts, Orm had judged that it would do.

When he brought it to Rand, the creature studied the offering closely, then clacked his beak in a way that Orm had come to learn signified his approval. "Very clever, and usable for the first attempt, anyway," the bird croaked. "We may have to do something else next time, but this will do. Now—I want you to find me two people."

Rand outlined the kind of victim Orm had already assumed he would want: female, a musician—a Gypsy or a Free Bard by preference, but any musician or dancer would do, so long as she was female. But he also wanted a *man,* someone who might plausibly pick up the clumsy knife that Orm had constructed, at least for a moment.

Orm already had a few candidates for the first position, but the second was something of a puzzle for him. In the end, he chose a petty tough with a penchant for knives; the man couldn't resist a blade, no matter how clumsy or poorly made, and once he had one, he could be counted upon to carry it with him. If the man ever fell into the river, he'd sink to the bottom from the weight of steel he carried.

Rand made the final selection of the girl, and gleefully chose a wench who at least wore the ribbons of a Free Bard, though Orm privately suspected that if any real musician heard her sing, they'd demand the ribbons back. Too much drinking and other abuses of her own body had taken a heavy toll of her voice, mind, and musical talents. All of her songs sounded alike, and all of them were similar in theme as well. She fancied the company of people precisely like that young street-tough, perhaps for the thrill of association, although she claimed that they gave her ideas for more of her songs. Bitter, uncertain of temper, aggressive and yet cowardly, she made trouble just for the sake of seeing what happened. Orm privately considered that he would be doing the world a favor in helping to rid it of the ill-natured creature.

Orm got the blade into the hands of the street-tough as Rand requested. Only then did he hear the rest of the plan.

"We'll be using the knife for the killing, rather than this beak I've been cursed with. For the moment, don't worry about *how*; I'll explain that in a moment. You seem to know enough about magic to know that mages can read where objects have been and you were probably wondering how I intended to deal with the traces of *your* personality that you left on that knife, as well as the magic that I shall imbue it with," Rand-the-bird rasped smugly as he cocked his oil-sheened head to the side to gauge Orm's reactions. "It's simple, really. After the woman is dead, *you* move in and steal the knife before anyone else can touch it."

Rand had probably expected Orm to put up a strenuous objection to this; Orm just waited for the details. Rand wouldn't have tried to shock him with this if he didn't have a damned clever plan to avoid the two of them getting caught.

Orm had been correct in his assumption. Rand did have a damned clever plan, and the more he outlined, the more at ease Orm became. Rand knew what a Justiciar-Mage could and could not do (as well he should), and he had planned for everything.

"I use the knife to gain control of the street-thug's body," Rand explained carefully. "Once I have done that, I use him to murder the woman. Then I have him throw the knife away, which is when you will look for it and carry it off, bringing it back to me. When that is done, I have the man throw himself into the river as a suicide. The very few traces of magic contamination will be washed off in running water. This will look like a simple crime of passion or a robbery gone awry, and no one will think that this is anything out of the ordinary. People are murdered all the time in an area like the one these two frequent."

"You take control of him?" Orm had asked, fascinated in spite of himself. "How?"

If Rand had possessed such a thing as an eyebrow, he might have raised it sardonically. "It is a great deal more simple that you would think," Rand had replied, assuming the manner of a vulture. The wicked bird chuckled harshly, an odd sort of crow, and fluffed his feathers.

Orm had laughed softly with delight; this was the kind of clever scheme he enjoyed the most, and when Rand detailed just how he would control the bodies, he gave the mage credit for even more cleverness than before. The only unanswered question was why Rand didn't suggest that after Orm stole the knife, he get rid of it elsewhere; Orm had a suspicion that Rand wanted it for personal reasons. That was perfectly acceptable to Orm, and Orm planned from the beginning to see that the knives Rand used were clean of even the slightest trace of blood before he ever turned them over to his employer. Blood could also be used to mark a trail for a mage hunting a murderer, but if there was no blood, there would be no way to follow the path of the knife.

It had all followed just as Rand had wished, from the first killing to the last. Orm would find several possible victims and Rand would watch them, stalking them in either human or avian form. When he had chosen who he wanted, if he had not already reverted to birdshape, he would wait until he had done so while Orm made a note of every movement of their days, finding places and times where it would be easy to ambush them. Orm would construct the knife, then find a way to get the knife into the hands of the man, often commissioning a hilt to suit the victim, but always making the blade from a triangular file so that there would be no trace of where it came from. He was no fool; sooner or later someone would begin to notice that there were strange murder-suicides committed with a very odd weapon, and he didn't want any smiths recalling the fellow who had asked for triangular blades.

When everything was in place, Rand would follow the first victim and take him over, then make his kill. When their activities began to draw the attention of constables or other people in positions of authority, they moved on before the civil authorities could begin a real investigation. In small towns and villages, they would move after only a single death; in larger, they might take four or five victims before judging it prudent to move to the next venue. Occasionally, circumstances would permit Rand to enjoy a lingering and elaborate ritual of mutilation of his primary victim—this, of course, increased the anguish of his secondary victim almost as much. Rand relished these opportunities, although they were few, and looked forward with anticipation to opportunities for more such. Rand kept with him a growing collection of knives, and he would take them out to gloat over them as soon as they were established in their new home.

Orm had a secret of his own which he had no intention of sharing with the mage. He enjoyed watching the murders; it gave him all of the pleasure with none of the risk. And the moment he got his hands on the blades that did the deed, he experienced a thrill that was almost as good as being with a woman. He wondered sometimes if Rand felt the same.

Well, whether he did or not, each successive victim allowed him to spend time as a human being again, although how much time varied from victim to victim. The best had been the jeweler and the Gypsy, both for Orm and for Rand. Once the girl had been pegged down to the worktable, Rand had made the jeweler let them in, and they had both watched every step of the proceedings. When the girl was dead and the man had drunk every drop of caustic chemicals in his workshop, it had been Orm who dragged the body beneath the water-barrel and let the water flow over him, erasing the taint of magic that was on him. The beautifully jeweled knife had been sold to him by a thief who had in his turn "stolen" it from Orm—careful study had shown that at least half the jeweler's income had come from the purchase of stolen property and the sale of the component parts. Orm himself had directed the Gypsy to that jeweler on the fatal night, after seeing to it that the clasp of her belt of copper coins was broken past amateur repair. Rand had stayed human for an entire week after that.

Some of the murders had gone slightly awry, which was inevitable considering the neighborhoods in which they were operating. Twice the knife was stolen by someone else before it could be used on its intended victim, and a new victim of opportunity had to be found—Rand had hated that, but there was nothing to be done about it if he wanted to take on human form again. But on the whole things were going entirely to plan, or to the plan as Orm knew it.

He suspected that Rand had some specific goal in mind, which was likely to be the murder of the Justiciar-Mage who had put him in the form he now wore. A few wenches more or less wouldn't cause an authority to issue an all-out manhunt, but the murder of a High Bishop would bring out every Hound of God, every constable, and every private guard until the killer was caught. Too risky, far too risky. If that was the case, Orm had plans of his own. Once the deed was done, the knife would *not* be stolen and carried away, because Orm would not be there.

Rand was so busy controlling his victims that he had no time to watch for Orm, and on this final occasion, Orm would be elsewhere, possibly even on a horse on his way out of Kingsford. This would neatly circumvent the problems that would arise when his employer no longer needed his services. Once Rand was caught and punished, Orm would be free to return and take up his old profession again. The very construction of this house would make it possible for Orm to claim that he had no idea that the other tenant of the place had been up to no good, no matter what claims Rand made—for although the suites did share the common entrance, that was *all* that they shared. Orm would be shocked and appalled, professing horror and relief that he himself had escaped the fate of so many. He would express the opinion that a man mad enough to murder so many people was mad enough to claim anything, including the idea that his innocent fellow tenant had a hand in the evil deeds. And as for how many victims the madman had claimed—well, the collection of blades in Rand's bedroom would serve as mute testimony so powerful that the Justiciars would need to look no further for their killer.

A light tap on his door alerted him to the fact that Rand was home again, and he went to answer it. No one but Rand ever knocked on his door; none of his other clients knew where he lived.

As he expected, Rand was standing at his door, impatiently tapping a foot. "Did you get it?" Rand asked, in lieu of a greeting. He was probably a handsome man in his human form, though Orm's taste more mundanely ran to women. His body was kept in perfect physical shape by the exertion of flying in his avian form; his features were regular and almost aggressively masculine. Although he no longer wore the black robes of a Priest, he continued to favor black clothing. It seemed that when he transformed, whatever he was wearing became his feathers, and a black bird was less conspicuous than any other color.

"It's in your room," Orm replied, and Rand smiled in a way that had very little to do with good humor.

At least he transformed immediately this time. Rand's bird-form made Orm feel a little queasy, although he managed to hide his reactions, and he was always very well aware of the deadly potential of those claws and that spearlike beak.

"Well, how did it go? Did anyone see you?" Rand continued, without bothering to thank Orm for what Orm considered to be a very neat little bit of theft. He had plucked the knife literally out of the gutter, with at least a dozen people around him looking for it as well.

"No one saw me," he said, restraining his irritation. "The birdman set off after your man, and everyone was watching the bird-man. They never even noticed I was there, much less saw me taking the blade."

"Good." With an abrupt nod, Rand turned on his heel and went up the steps to his own rooms, leaving Orm standing in his own doorway like a dismissed servant, his breath steaming out into the icy foyer.

Orm repressed more irritation and simply closed his door. He reminded himself that Rand had been a high-ranking Priest and a wealthy man, with servants who were accustomed to being ordered about like Deliambren automata. Rand would never change, and that was that.

Still, he grumbled a little as he threw the latch on the door, it *would be nice to be appreciated for good work once in a while.* It annoyed and sometimes angered him to be treated like a scullery-maid.

But then again, if he suspected how clever I am, he might be more wary of me, and more inclined to get rid of me. I am a convenience, he reminded himself. *He is used to having me around to do his work for him, but now he* could *be rid of me without harm if he chose. All he needs me for is to steal the daggers, and he could hire a petty pickpocket to do that for him.* Given that—perhaps it wasn't so bad to be dismissed.

Orm went back to his chair before the fire, settled in with his feet near the grate, and considered his actions for the rest of the day and evening. *I should go down to the Purple Eel,* he decided. *By sunset every constable not on duty will have heard what happened, and all of the ones in that district will be there to flap their mouths over it.* This was an easy way to discover what the constables knew and what they didn't, and Orm had used it in every city they'd worked so far.

Orm had been a constable himself for about a year, in between being a thief and becoming a broker of information. He had come very near to being caught after a theft that had resulted in the death of his victim, and had decided to learn how the constables themselves thought and reasoned so that he would know what they were likely to do in a given situation and assess the risks of a given action in an instant. As a result, he was able to pretty well anticipate every move that the constables made so long as he knew how much information they had.

It did bother him that the murder victims were always women of a particular type; that was a pattern, and patterns made them vulnerable. If the particular women Rand insisted on ever took this seriously enough to start staying off the streets altogether, Rand would either have to pursue them inside—which was very, very dangerous—or choose another type of victim. Knowing Rand, it wouldn't be the latter. He was brilliant, but obsessed, and quite insane.

More than that, although it hadn't yet occurred to them, the constables *could* set up a trap for them by using a seemingly ideal victim as bait. Of course, that would mean setting her up in such a way that neither Rand nor Orm detected the trap, which would mean that her behavior would have to be perfectly consistent for several days. And that in turn would mean either that the constables were able to deduce that these were *not* victims of opportunity, or that the constables planned to set up a trap around a street-girl who was unaware that she was being used as bait.

The former wasn't likely, he decided. For the most part, he had been very careful to select potential victims that no one cared about. The closest they had ever come to getting caught was that obsessive fellow a few towns back—and he had been working alone, without the co-operation of the constabulary officials. As for the latter—well, there were hundreds, if not thousands, of potential choices in Kingsford, and the chance that the constables would select exactly the same one as Orm and Rand was minimal.

But I should listen for such a plan, he decided. *The Purple Eel is definitely the place to go tonight.*

But he was loathe to leave his chair just now. He'd gotten horribly cold out there, waiting for Rand to make his move. Before he went out again, he wanted to be warmed down to the bone.

He thought back once again over the last set of murders and could see no flaws in them. Most murders not committed for gain were committed by people who knew the victims, often very well—most often, relatives. Orm made very certain that no one ever connected him with the recipients of the knives, generally finding ways of getting the blades into the chosen hands indirectly, as he had with the jeweler. The only pattern was in the women, and none of them were *ever* seen near, much less with, Orm.

Rand would be unbearable this evening, exulting in his stolen power and his new form, but by tomorrow he would be pleasant enough, if overbearing. That was the pattern, and Orm was used to it. There *would* be a generous reward for a successful "hunt," as Rand termed the murders, and as soon as Rand calmed down from the intoxication of success, he would want to know who Orm had singled out for the next prey. Orm, of course, would have his list, and Rand would be very pleased, which would make him generous.

It's too bad he's so obsessed, Orm thought idly. *If he didn't mind spending time in that bird-form, he would make a good thief. As soon as it got warm, and people in the fine houses began opening their windows at night for fresh air, he could nip in, snatch up jewelry-cases, and fly out without anyone ever knowing he'd been there.*

Well, that was not likely to happen. Rand wanted to break his spell entirely.

Which is probably a very good reason why he would like to choose High Bishop Ardis as a victim. Not only is she female, not only is she the direct cause of him being the way he is, but she cast the spell in the first place. Not only would he gain revenge, but since she's the mage involved, the only way to break the spell might be to kill the caster. I hope he doesn't think of that.

He sighed. It was a pity that Rand couldn't be more content with life as it was. *He* wouldn't mind spending about half his time as a bird! Think of all the things he could overhear, perched in the shadow of chimneys or lurking in the branches of trees in private gardens— listening outside windows, or on balconies!

Too bad, but things aren't going to change, and I need to start for the Purple Eel, he decided, getting reluctantly up from his armchair. *All of his brilliance and my cleverness aren't going to help if someone's got an unexpected card up his sleeve.*

You couldn't plan for the unexpected, but you could prepare your mind to deal with it. That was Orm's motto, and he went out into the dusk to make good on it.

Chapter Nine

Ardis, Tal, and Kayne sat in Ardis's office with the door locked and a guard posted to ensure that no one disturbed them unless it was a life-or-death emergency. Ardis had finally gotten the last of her information. Some came from the farthest town with murders that matched the pattern, and more detailed information arrived from Master Wren, her cousin. She also had something that Tal would never have access to: the records from the Confessional for all of the victims—or at least, all of those that attended Confession. Rather surprisingly, a majority of them had, and she now possessed detailed glimpses into their personalities.

"I'm going to try something different this time," she said to the other two. "Instead of trying to deduce anything more directly about the murderer, I want to look at his victims and come up with more information about him based on what they were like. And I want to start from the negative—what those victims *aren't*."

Kayne looked alert and thoughtful, but it was Tal who spoke first. "Rich," Tal said promptly. "Or even moderately well-off. I'm talking about the women, of course, but only one of the men was what you would call rich, and that was the last one—the first one we know about in Kingsford. The rest were never better off monetarily than working tradesmen."

"They aren't whores, either; in fact, most of them would have been insulted if you suggested they were," Kayne put in, as Ardis noted that the word "whore" slid off her tongue without eliciting so much as a blush, which was in itself an interesting development. "There are more whores in any town or city than there are street musicians, so he's really having to make an effort to find them."

Ardis nodded, for that agreed with the information she had; when she had been able to find the female victims in the Confessional records, they had been honest musicians who left paid love to the professionals. "What about the men?" she asked.

Tal scratched his head. "There you have me," he admitted. "They don't match a pattern, not even close. They're all kinds."

Now was the time to spring her surprise. "Until you look in here." She tapped the folder of records. "I have access to certain confidential records; I can't let *you* look at them, but what I see shows at least one pattern, which is that our murderer worked very cautiously, at first."

"Oh?" Tal said skeptically. "He doesn't seem all that cautious to me."

"The men who attacked women in the open, in daylight, in front of witnesses are all recent. I think he's gotten bolder with success." She placed her palm on top of the folder. "Now, the others, the ones that occurred in the street at night under cover, or even under the protection of a roof—that's where I'm seeing a pattern. The men all confessed to sins of the flesh and preferred lights-of-love who at least pretended to be musicians. If at all possible, they wanted a mistress, even for an hour, who was more than just a whore. It made them feel as if they had discernment and taste, according to what I read here."

"Interesting." Tal chewed his lower lip. "So what we have is a man who is likely to be out in the street in the first place, and equally likely to accost women who are acting like musicians to see if they might have other—ah—talents." *He* blushed, which was interesting; it was unlikely he felt embarrassment on his own behalf, so it was probably because he was in Kayne's presence—or hers. "So, the question is, why go to all this trouble to pick that kind of victim?"

"So that he wouldn't break a pattern of behavior and alert the neighbors or the family that there was something wrong," Kayne declared, her head up.

But Tal shook his head. "Not logical; most of the murders took place too quickly. It wouldn't matter if the neighbors saw something just before that made them think there was something wrong with the man. I still don't think there was a pattern there, or a reason—unless—" He paused, as if struck by a thought.

"Unless what?" Ardis asked.

He frowned and rubbed one closed eye before replying. "Unless it was a peculiar sort of revenge. We've got one theory that he's taking revenge on the girls for being scorned by a female musician, but what if he's also taking revenge on the men they *are* willing to sleep with?"

"That's not a bad thought," Ardis replied after a moment. "It has a certain twisted symmetry." She considered it for a moment. "But what about the others, where there was no previous contact with street-women? There was at least one man who had no interest in women whatsoever as I recall.''

Tal shrugged. ''I agree with you that there is a pattern of increasing complication and risk-taking. At first, he takes men who have a reason to be alone with women who make their living in the street, and women who have a reason to go along with these men. This, of course, keeps him from breaking the established patterns of his male victims, which keeps anyone from noticing that there is something wrong.''

''There were some cases early on where that isn't true,'' Kayne protested.

Tal nodded agreement. ''But those could have been cases where something went wrong—either he couldn't get the kind of victims he wanted, or something else interfered. And remember, all of *those* took place under cover of night and four walls, in neighborhoods where no one ever looks to see what's going on if there are cries or screaming in the night.''

Ardis couldn't find anything to disagree with yet. ''Go on,'' she said. ''What next?''

''Next is more risk,'' Tal told them, as Kayne frantically scribbled notes. ''He takes longer with the victims, mutilating them as well as killing them. Next, he goes out into the street, into the open, and takes men who are strangers to the women he kills, and women who wouldn't normally go off with a stranger unless they thought his purpose completely honest. He breaks the patterns of the lives of his male victims, but he's moving quickly enough that even if anyone notices there's something wrong with the man, they don't have time to do more than wonder about it. Then—we have things like the killing here, in broad daylight, with a male victim who *never* set foot in that part of town, who might well have been stopped by a family member or retainer before he had a chance to act on behalf of the murderer. A thousand things could have gone wrong for him at that last killing. They didn't, which only means that either his luck is phenomenal, or he's studying his victims with more attention to detail than we've guessed.''

''And the jeweler?'' Kayne asked.

Ardis shook her head. ''I don't know. The jeweler often had women in his home, but that doesn't mean that the Gypsy girl didn't go there with legitimate business in mind.''

''If he's clever, he could have manufactured that business,'' Tal pointed out. ''Gypsies often wear their fortune; she could have come to the man with coins to be made into a belt or necklace. All he'd have to do would be to drop a good handful of silver into her hat, and she'd be off to the nearest jeweler to have the coins bored and strung before she lost them.''

"A good point,'' Ardis said with a little surprise, since it wasn't a possibility she'd have thought of. "But what else do the victims *all* have in common?''

Tal made a sour face. "They *are* people no one will miss. The fact is, all of his male victims were such that even if they did things that were out of character, no one would care enough to stop them until it was too late. Even their relatives don't pay any attention to them until they're dead and the way of their death is a disgrace to the family. Even then, they seem relieved that the man himself is no longer around to make further trouble for them.''

Ardis smiled sardonically. "You caught that, did you?'' she asked, referring to the behavior of the young dandy's parents when she had questioned them.

Tal nodded, and so did Kayne.

"So we can assume that these men, the secondary victims, are people who would not question the origin of a stray knife that came into their hands, especially if they had any reason to believe that it was stolen.'' She raised an eyebrow, inviting comment, and once again the other two nodded. "They would simply take the object, especially if it appeared valuable. They would most probably keep it on their persons.''

Tal held up a finger and, at her nod, added a correction. "All but one or two—I think the knife-grinder I saw had been given the knife to sharpen. And it's possible the jeweler was brought the knife to repair some damage to the hilt. In both those cases, the men were perfectly innocent of everything. But I'd say it was more than possible in a couple of cases that the men who had the knife actually stole it themselves,'' Tal told her. "And that may account for a couple of the victims where the connection with music is so tenuous it might as well not be there.''

"He took what he could get in those cases, in other words.'' Ardis made a note of that on the side of a couple of the dubious cases. "That argues for a couple of things. Either there is only one knife—''

"That isn't right, unless he's changing the hilt,'' Tal interrupted. "The one I saw didn't look anything like the one Visyr saw.''

"Then in that case, it is a very powerful and complicated spell, and he can't have it active on more than one weapon at a time.'' Ardis made another note to herself, suggesting a line of magical research. "To a mage, that is very interesting, because it implies a high degree of concentration and skill, and one begins to wonder why so powerful a mage isn't in Duke Arden's Court.''

"Maybe he is—" Kayne began, but Ardis shook her head.

"There's only one mage in his Court, and she's one of my fellow Justiciars. Furthermore, she hasn't detected anyone casting a spell that requires so much power anywhere in the Ducal Palace." Ardis sighed, for it seemed to her that the answer was, more and more, likely to involve a Church mage. "There simply aren't that many powerful mages in the Human Kingdoms outside the Church.''

Tal grimaced, and Kayne shook her head. "It certainly seems to be the direction the hunt is tending." She sighed philosophically.

Ardis closed her eyes and told her stomach to calm itself. "I would much prefer to be able to point a finger at an Elf, since there are plenty of Elves who would gleefully slaughter as many mortals as they could get their hands on, but I have been assured that no Elf would be able to cast magic on anything made of iron or steel. So, that's the end of that idea."

"What about other nonhumans?" Tal asked. "*I* don't think it's likely, mind you, but what about them?"

"I don't think it's likely either," she told both of them. "Any nonhuman is going to be very obvious, and a nonhuman mage even more so. Even if a nonhuman mage didn't practice magic openly, he'd be conspicuous, because he would have to be wealthy. He simply wouldn't be able to purchase the privacy he would need to work magic without being wealthy.''

"If this Justiciar-Mage can detect the casting of spells in the palace, why can't we have mages watching for the casting of magic out in the city?" Tal wanted to know.

"You can see the smoke from a fire in the forest quite clearly, but can you pinpoint the smoke from an individual fire in the city?" Ardis countered. "There's too much else going on out in a large population of humans; with as much disruption as there is in Kingsford, a mage would have to be in the same city block as the caster in order to detect the casting of even a powerful spell.''

"Have we enough mages in Kingsford to try that?" Kayne asked. "Couldn't we station mages around to catch him in the act?"

A reasonable idea, but not very practical, considering that the priestly mages of Kingsford had more demands on their time than they had hours in the day. "I think we would have better luck trying to find where the knives themselves are coming from," Ardis said tactfully. "If he's using more than one, someone has to be making them for him. There just aren't that many missing ecclesiastical knives.''

Tal went very quiet at that. "I didn't know that," he said finally. "I'd just assumed that he'd stolen or found ritual knives—maybe in secondhand shops or something of the sort. But if he's making them— that almost means there has to be more than one person involved."

Ardis felt her stomach turn over again. One murderer was bad enough—but *two*? "I've had people looking for a maker in Kingsford, and I can't find any smith who'll admit to making triangular-bladed knives."

"Oh, I wouldn't worry about that too much," Kayne said with a wave of her hand. "They don't have to come from Kingsford, or this kingdom, or even a Human Kingdom. Any little village smith would do, and I bet there are plenty who would be happy to get a job in the winter when people don't need farm equipment mended. All he needs to do would be to get a smith somewhere else to take a commission for the finished blades, and he can put whatever hilt he wants to on them. For that matter, he could be rehilting the same knife, over and over. That would solve the question of why you saw one kind of knife, Tal, and why Visyr saw another."

Tal shook his head. "I don't think so," he said firmly. "I think I've figured out why they're disappearing when all he'd need to do would be to drop them into the river to destroy our ability to trace him from them. What he's doing is taking them as his mementos."

"His what?" Kayne asked.

"Mementos." Tal offered an apologetic smile. "Trophies. Killers like this like to have things to remember their victims by. A lock of hair, an item of clothing, even jewelry. It lets them experience the thrill of the murder all over again. I know of one man who gave his wife a present of the jewelry he'd taken from the woman he killed; made a point of asking her to wear it, and he said later it was so he could relive the murder. I think that's why the knives are disappearing; I think our man is collecting them, cleaning them, and keeping them as trophies. He probably has them all mounted on a wall somewhere, or done up in a little display case."

Kayne looked a little green. "That's sick," she said in disgust.

"And murdering twenty or thirty women isn't?" Ardis countered, feeling certain that Tal had uncovered another piece of the puzzle. "I think Tal's right. I also think that the mage in question is smart enough to wipe not only every vestige of blood off the blade but cleanse it of every glimmer of magic, so we can't trace it. He may even have shielded the room the knives are in against a trace. We could search till we die of old age and never find the daggers."

Kayne gritted her teeth in frustration, showing openly what Ardis was keeping hidden beneath a veneer of calm. "You do realize what you're saying? We have a murderer who knows as much about the way crimes are traced by way of magic as the constables and Justiciar-Mages do! How can we even *try* to catch him?"

Tal reached out and patted her hand in a very fatherly fashion—which relieved Ardis. She'd been hoping those blushes weren't on Kayne's behalf. Not that Tal and Kayne would make a bad couple, but . . .

She lost the thought, and didn't care to pursue it.

"We catch him the way constables have always caught clever criminals," Tal said, his calm and even tones belying the tension Ardis sensed beneath his stoic surface. "Firstly, there are more of us than there are of him. Secondly, he *will* make a mistake. He may already have done so, but we just didn't catch it at the time. Once he makes one mistake, he'll make more, and the consequences will begin to pile up."

"How can you be so sure of that?" Kayne demanded.

He rubbed his forehead and shut his eyes while replying. "It's the oddest thing, you know," he continued, in a matter-of-fact voice, as if he was talking about one of his fellow Guardsmen rather than a multiple murderer. "But I've never seen it to fail. A clever thief can and will continue to steal all his life—a clever sharpster continue to extract money from the unwary until he's in his grave. But a murderer—he may show no signs of remorse at all, may even claim that his victims deserved what came to them—but sooner or later he starts to make mistakes that get him caught."

"Remorse?" Kayne suggested. "Even if he doesn't realize it? Could his conscience be manipulating him so that he *does* get caught and pays for what he did?"

Tal shook his head. "I don't think so. Maybe it's contempt—when he keeps escaping the net, he starts to think he doesn't need to work so hard to avoid it. Maybe it's a feeling of invulnerability, that we can't catch him however careless he gets. After all, every bit of evidence that *he* gets shows him that we simply can't find him."

"And maybe it's God," Ardis put in quietly. Tal looked at her with a brief flash of startlement. "God doesn't often act directly in our lives, but when He knows that we are doing all that we are able and are still out of our depth, He may choose to give us a little help." She felt that; she truly did. She only hoped that He would see that they were at the end of their resources and grant that help before any more women died.

I am not going to tell myself that He has reasons for letting those

others die, however. God is not cruel; He is not some Eternal Tor-
mentor and Tester. They died because they were unlucky or careless,
and not because God had a purpose for their deaths.

Her Special Inquisitor looked for a moment as if he was about to
challenge her to a theological discussion, then his lips twitched a little.
"I'm not about to argue the point with you, High Bishop," Tal said
finally. He looked for just a moment as if he was going to say something more, then just shook his head and remained silent.

I had better change the subject—or rather, get it back where it was
supposed to be. "The way this man treats the tools he takes over is
interesting," Ardis pointed out. "Once he's done with them, he discards them immediately—within moments of the murder, in fact."

"He doesn't have much choice!" Kayne replied.

"Oh, but he does," Tal responded instantly. "At least, he does in
the cases where he's killed in private. I assume he could walk around
with that body for as long as he likes, but he doesn't—he kills his
chosen victim, then discards the man he's taken." He suddenly looked
startled. "I don't suppose we could be dealing with a ghost, could we?
Or something like a demon? Something that can come in and possess
the killer?"

"Ghosts can't place orders for knives," Ardis pointed out dryly.
"And although I'm a Priest, I have to say I truly doubt the existence
of demons that can move in and possess someone's body." She
thought about the few cases of so-called possession that had been
brought before her—until people likely to claim possession realized
that she was entirely unsympathetic to the idea. *"I've* never seen an
authentic possession, nor do I know anyone who has. Sometimes it's
a simple case of someone being struck with an illness that affects the
mind; at other times, it is all fakery. All the accounts of what are
supposed to be genuine possessions are at third or fourth hand—or
else the symptoms of possession as described are such that they are
clearly hysteria or the clever counterfeit of someone with an agenda
of her own to pursue."

"Her?" Tal asked wryly.

Ardis shrugged. "Most people claiming to be possessed are female
and more often than not young. You can read what you like into that."

Kayne snorted with contempt. "I'll read it as fools for pretending
and idiots who believe them. Back to the knives. You've said it before,
and I'll repeat it. I don't think the shape is an accident, but we need
to discuss that in depth for a moment."

"There could be a number of reasons for picking that shape," Tal mused. "The most logical is that this fellow wants to give the Church and its mages a powerful reason not to pursue him too closely."

"There is no doubt that is why the authorities tried to prevent you from investigating back in your city, Tal," Ardis told him, pleased that her investigation had proved his own suspicions were correct. "No one wanted to be the one to uncover a killer inside the robes of a Priest."

"He could be hoping that a faction of the Brotherhood will take him for a vigilante," Kayne observed. "After all, he's getting rid of people the Church doesn't approve of. Truth to tell, Ardis, if *you* weren't the High Bishop here, I don't know if the Justiciars would even consider trying to catch him." She pinched the bridge of her nose a moment. "It makes me wonder if he might not be in the pay of someone."

"Who?" Tal asked, surprised.

"I don't know; the Bardic Guild, maybe?" Kayne hazarded, a little wildly. "They'd just as soon be rid of *every* kind of entertainer that isn't a member of the Guild."

Ardis grimaced. "A madman acting on behalf of the Bardic Guild? I'm afraid you're reaching a bit too far for that one."

"Or being too redundant," Kayne retorted.

"We don't have sufficient evidence that the killer has a collaborator," Tal pointed out gently. "And I don't think I've ever heard of a murderer of this type who had someone working with them."

Kayne made a disparaging face. "It was a thought. Things *would* be much easier for him if he had a partner in this."

"These murderers tend to be loners," Tal replied. "What you *do* hear from the neighbors when it's all over is, 'He kept to himself a lot,' and 'He was always very quiet.' My feeling is, people like this man are too obsessed with their own desires, needs, and rituals to want to share them with anyone else."

"Frankly," Ardis said, rubbing her thumb and fingers together restlessly, "I think he has several reasons for what he does—we don't need to limit him to just one. He's obviously intelligent enough to have complex motives." As the other two acknowledged that she was probably right, she continued. "I think he's trying to throw confusion into the ranks of Church officials, and he would get many benefits from doing so. He certainly wants to delay pursuit, and this is one good way to make sure that cooperation with Priest-Mages will be somewhat less than perfect. If he doesn't realize that using a ritual dagger as a murder weapon is likely to cause *severe* conflict within the Church itself, I'd be very surprised, and as Kayne pointed out, there is a substantial minority among the Brotherhood that would applaud what he's doing—in private, if not in public."

Tal looked as if his stomach was giving him as much trouble as Ardis's was giving her. "Once word gets around that there are murders being done with a piece of priestly equipment—" Tal said very slowly. "God help us. People in the street will be only too willing to believe in some bizarre secret society, sponsored by the Church, dedicated to murder. There is no love lost between the Church and Gypsies, the Church and street-women, or the Church and Free Bards. All three of those groups have good reason to think of themselves as persecuted by the Church. The very people we need to protect most will flee from us in fear."

"And start more rumors," Kayne added.

"And I can't argue with either of you." Ardis couldn't just sit anymore; she got up and paced back and forth in front of the fireplace, keeping a restraining hold on her temper. "I have worked and sacrificed to make the Justiciars *respected* rather than feared, and trusted to give absolutely impartial justice to those who were loyal Churchmen and those who weren't," she said fiercely. "Now—this! It feels like a personal attack!"

"It can't possibly be, Ardis," Kayne soothed, swiveling her head to watch Ardis pace. "How could anyone connect you with these murders?"

"Perhaps they wouldn't directly connect me—but what if the Justiciars can't find the murderer?" Ardis asked. "Won't people say that we just weren't trying very hard because we knew that the murderer came from our own ranks? Everything I've built up with the people of Kingsford is in jeopardy!"

Since neither of the other two could refute that, they remained silent.

But Ardis realized that she was being a bad example to both of them. She stopped pacing and returned to her chair, willing herself to the appearance of calm if not the actual state.

"We considered the least pleasant possibility about the identity of the murderer; now let's make it a priority," she said grimly. "We have to do more than allow that this man could be a Priest, we have to actively pursue the idea. Tal, there is nothing you can do to help us with this, so simply continue your investigations as you have been; perhaps you will come up with more information that will help us. Kayne—"

The secretary waited, alert as a greyhound waiting to be loosed.

"I want you to undertake another search among Church records," she said, with a tightening of her throat. "Look for Priest-Mages who have been disciplined in the last ten years. I can't believe this man has just sprung up out of nowhere; I feel certain that he must have been caught at least once."

Kayne grimaced, but made the note. "You are right," she agreed. "A Priest who's been disciplined is the one most likely to have a grudge against the Church—or at least, the Church Superiors."

"The other thing you might look for is Priests who've gone overboard in their chastisement; assigning really dreadful penances or the like." Ardis put the tips of her fingers to both temples and massaged.

"Good idea; a Priest like that won't necessarily get Discipline, but he'll show up in the right records—and that might point us to someone likely to turn vigilante." Kayne looked preoccupied, as if some of these suggestions were turning up uncomfortable thoughts.

"I've got a third request," Ardis finished. "While you're at it, you might ask for the records of those who had a history of sexual crimes or violence against women *before* they entered the Priesthood. Just because we think he's reformed, that doesn't mean he has."

Kayne nodded, noting all of that down.

"You're probably right in this, Ardis," Tal said slowly. "The signature traits of these crimes—I've been thinking about the things he *has* to have, the ones that always appear, without exception. Death by stabbing—"

He flushed so scarlet, that Ardis was distracted for a moment with amusement. "Go on," she told him.

"This is—rather indelicate," Tal choked. "You're a—"

"I'm a Priest, dear man, and I've taken my turn in the Confessional with condemned criminals," she reminded him. "There isn't much you can tell me that I haven't already heard in one form or another. You mentioned stabbing—which is, after all, a form of penetration. I assume you think this is his form of rape *in absentia*?"

Tal was so red she was afraid he would never be able to speak, but he nodded. "I think so; that makes these sexual crimes. The knife is the primary part of his signature, and the shape may be part of that—fantasy. Either he hates the Church or he views himself as an arm of the Church's vengeance. There's nothing in between, and in either case, a Priest would be more—frustrated. More likely to choose a knife as the instrument of death."

"And for either, we have to look at the Brotherhood itself." She sighed, and felt a headache closing down over her scalp like a tootight cap.

"The second signature element is the sex of the victim, which, if I'm right about this, goes along with the sexual nature of the murders.

I have to think that the third element is that the victim preferentially is a musician," Tal continued, his red face slowly fading. "I know I've said all this before, but it was more in the light of speculation than certainty. I would stake my life on the fact that no matter *how* this man kills people, he has to have those three signature elements to be satisfied. I wish I'd seen more of the crime scenes myself, or I would know more."

"So look particularly for Priests who have had problems with musicians," Ardis directed her secretary. "Either while in Orders or before taking them." A thought struck her, and she voiced it. "I wonder if he's a failed musician himself?"

Tal nodded, now completely back to normal. "Could be. Particularly if he was obsessed with the idea of being considered a Master. Love and hate—add obsession, and you have a nasty little soup. If he tried getting into the Bardic Guild and failed, he might be able to forgive men for making a living at music, but never inferior females."

"He could even consider that the female musicians were somehow polluting music itself," Kayne offered, which drew an approving glance from both Ardis and Tal. "Music being supposedly pure, you wouldn't want an unclean female mucking about with it."

"That's a good thing to add to the list of possibilities," Tal told her. "Once again—love and hate, love and worship of music, hate for those who are desecrating it. But that certainly doesn't preclude it being a Priest."

"Far from it," Ardis admitted. "There are plenty who came into the Priesthood after failing at their first choice of vocation. He might even have discovered his ability at magic after he failed at music. Don't forget, we *are* looking for mages. He can't do this without magic."

But that seemed to exhaust their inventiveness for the moment, and after they had thrashed the subject around a bit more, they all went back to their respective tasks. Kayne went off to her office to draft more orders for records, and Tal went—wherever Tal went, when he wasn't specifically to meet with someone or go off on one of Ardis's errands. She suspected he had gone back into the city, chasing down elusive leads.

When they were gone and the door to her office closed and locked, the room felt strangely quiet and empty. It was difficult to tell what time of day it was in here, since the room had no windows. The previous occupants had all been old and subject to rheumatism; this office shared a wall with the huge kitchen ovens, and as a consequence was nicely warm all winter, even without a fire in the fireplace. There might have been problems in the summer, but as soon as the weather was warm enough, all baking was done in ovens in the kitchen court.

Usually the lack of windows didn't bother her, but this afternoon it occurred to her that she was curiously isolated from the world outside because of that lack. Was this good, or bad? As a Priest, perhaps she should cultivate that isolation, since it theoretically would enable her to get closer to God. But as a Justiciar, she needed to remain within the secular world so that she could understand and dispense justice to its inhabitants. As with so many things in her life, it seemed this required striking a delicate balance, too.

Ardis removed a fat, brown folder from the locked drawer of her desk: the record of the Priests and Priest-Mages who had vanished from the Kingsford Abbey during the Great Fire. Coincidentally, she had not had enough time to devote to unraveling the mysteries the stiff pasteboard contained before all this fell upon her, and now the very records she would have requested from the Archivist for her own Abbey were already on her desk.

But these were only the records of those who had been severely disciplined by the Order over the past ten years, and it could be that this simply wasn't long enough.

Should I go back twenty? she wondered. *Or perhaps just fifteen? Where should I place the cutoff? I'll have to look at more than severe penance, that much I know. The first clues to trouble may lie in seemingly minor infractions.*

Kayne was already planning on bringing the full record for the last ten years, and that would be a fair pile to go through, even if she eliminated all those who weren't mages. Well, perhaps if she looked at these records in the light of this new trouble, something would spring out at her.

But nothing came immediately to mind as she skimmed over the records again. Those who were missing simply did not fit the pattern, unless something had occurred to them between the Fire and now that set them off. Mostly, they were undergoing penance for the sins of lust and greed—quite common expressions of both, with no indication of the kind of cruelty exhibited by the murderer. Her headache worsened as she held the records concerning Priest Revaner.

This—this is so frustrating! The only obvious possibilities are dead, or just as good as dead, and he's at that top of that list.

The one thing working against Revaner—aside from the fact that he was probably dead, and the fact that he was a giant bird—was that the murders began so far away from Kingsford. He would have had to travel an enormous distance to get there.

How would he travel as a bird? He couldn't fly—he was too heavy. I very much doubt that he could have walked the distance, and he would have been incredibly conspicuous if he had. Even if he somehow found someone to take him that far away, why would he bother to come back here? There was nothing for him here; even if I wanted to take the spell off, since it was a backlash of his own magic, I'm not sure that I could. He probably ended up in Kingsford and was burned to a crisp—or was killed by some farmer thinking he was after chickens. Or he's in a freak-show as one of the star attractions, which would be nothing more than poetic justice.

No, it couldn't be Revaner, but she wished she could find some sign that it might be one of the lesser Priest-Mages who'd escaped. Any of them had a perfectly good reason to return to a place they would find familiar. Any of them would be perfectly happy to take revenge on the Free Bards who had foiled the attempt to kill Duke Arden in his own theater.

The trouble was, none of *them* were powerful enough to work this kind of magic.

But would it take power? That's something I still don't know. It might be a brilliant spell, difficult to execute, but actually requiring very little power. This certainly didn't act like the variations on coercive magic she knew; every one of those left the victim still able to fight for his freedom, and the more heinous the act he was forced to do, the more successful he was likely to be at breaking free. Perhaps the mage executing this magic was not powerful, merely brilliant.

Or it might be someone still in the Brotherhood. She couldn't evade that possibility. There was no use in saying that an active Priest couldn't possibly be doing such things when she knew very well that there were those who could, and with a smiling face. Men with a profound hatred of women often went into the Church because they knew that there would be fewer women there, and that most, if not all of them, would be in subordinate positions to males. The killings themselves demonstrated such hatred of women that even Kayne had commented on it. The garb of a Priest only meant that a man had mastered the book-learning and study required to become a Priest—it didn't mean that the man had automatically acquired anything like compassion on the way to taking Holy Orders. Every person who took vows had a different reason for doing so, and not all of those reasons were admirable.

She made a little face at that thought, for it came very close to home. *Even my reasons were not exactly pure. They could be boiled down to the fact that I took vows, "because I didn't have a better offer."*

Her head throbbed. She buried her face in her hands, wondering if this was the punishment she had earned for her cavalier decision of years ago. Was this God's way of chastising her for not coming to Him with a wholly devoted heart?

No. No! I can't believe that. God does not punish the innocent in order to also punish the guilty—

But were those people who had already died so very innocent? By the strict standards of the Church, they were all apostate and in a state of sin. The Gypsies were pagans, and the Free Bards were hardly model citizens or good sons and daughters of the Church. Was God punishing Ardis for her pride and the victims for their sins at the same time?

She dropped her hands and shook her head stubbornly, as if to rid it of those thoughts. *No! Nothing I have ever seen can make me believe God is so arbitrary. It makes no sense!*

She could not, would not, believe in the petty-minded God so many of the Brotherhood worshiped—the God who demanded obedience rather than asking for worship, who punished like a petulant and autocratic patriarch.

Besides—I may not have had a strong vocation when I entered the Church, but neither have hundreds of others. I have served God and the Church faithfully; I have never swerved from that path, never questioned why I was in the Brotherhood.

Until now, perhaps.

A twinge of guilt assaulted her, as she recalled how, less than an hour ago, she had been admiring the strong line of Tal Rufen's jaw. Something was threatening to come between her and her service.

If there was ever something she would have named as a test of her fidelity, it had come in the person of Tal Rufen—intellectually her equal and willing to acknowledge it, resourceful, creative. Precisely the sort of person she would have been willing to spend a lifetime with.

Unwedded. And, if I'm any judge of human nature, attracted to me.

Ardis had never been particularly impressed by rank, not when so many of her own set were absolute idiots. That Tal was a commoner would not have bothered her before she entered the Church, and it certainly didn't now that she'd spent years in the company of other commoners who were her equals or superiors in intelligence *and* rank within the Church. She was pleased to have him as a subordinate, would be even more pleased if the relationship became one of friendship. But she would have been lying to herself if she denied that, from time to time, she didn't wonder how her life would have turned out if she had met someone like him before taking her final vows.

Now, with Tal on the scene, she was doing more than wonder about it.

Give me the motivation and opportunity to break my vows—oh, yes. I can see that. The God *she* pictured had a finely-honed sense of humor as well as curiosity, and she could readily see Him giving her great temptation just to see if she could resist it—

Or see if she could find another solution to her problem.

Like leaving the priesthood.

There was no great stigma attached to a Priest who resigned her position, left the Church, and took up a secular life. There were always those who discovered that something inside them had changed, and with that change had come the need to leave the Church. Of course, if she did leave the Church, she would no longer have any more status than any other commoner. She had formally given up all secular bonds with her family when she took vows, and if they took her back, they would probably do so grudgingly, since in her tenure as High Bishop she had made as many enemies as friends. Those enemies would happily take advantage of the fact that the Church no longer sheltered her, and the friends were not always exactly in high places.

In short, she would have nothing more to rely on than her own personal resources and abilities. She would come back into the secular world with rather less than when she had left it.

And that is why Priests break their vows rather than taking the step of renouncing them. They want to have their pleasure and keep their position.

She was no more suited to the secular world of trade and business than Kayne was, and she had never really thought about earning her place in the world. Now, she found herself making plans. Perhaps she could use her abilities as a mage to solve thefts, find missing persons— perhaps she could get permission from the Church to act as a physician. She would still sacrifice status and comfort, but neither meant *that* much to her.

Given the right set of circumstances—it might be worth it. Physical comfort wasn't everything. Status didn't mean a great deal except as protection from current enemies and to make the way a bit smoother. The loss of status could be compensated for with cleverness and charm.

With myself using magic and the skills I've learned as an administrator, and Tal using his wits and experience, we could do a great deal of good. The mental image that accompanied the thought was attractive. Very attractive. There were always crimes that the constables had difficulty solving. There were also the occasions when a solution was found, but it was difficult to bring a burden of proof before the Justiciars. Justiciar-Mages were not necessarily supposed to *solve* crimes, and more often than not, Ardis had been forced to sit back and grit her teeth while constables bumbled through a case or let the real criminal get away for lack of evidence. But if she left the Church—she could take on anything she chose. Granted, the people she would probably want to help most often wouldn't be able to pay her much, but there would be so much satisfaction in seeing *real* justice done!

You know, I imagine my cousin the Duke could see clear to hiring us. . . .

She shook her head suddenly. What was she thinking of? How could she even contemplate renouncing the Church?

Her stomach knotted, and her hands clenched. This was insanity; what was Tal Rufen that she should throw out everything that had come to give her life meaning? Where were her senses?

Dear and Blessed God—what's putting this into my mind? The stress? Am I under such pressure that my mind is conjuring these fantasies just to give me something else to think about?

Surely, surely that was the explanation. Now was not the time to even consider such things; she did not want to continue this case with anything less than the full authority that her status as High Bishop gave her. That would be a betrayal of herself and all those victims as well as of the spirit of her vows. If this murderer really was an active Priest, nothing less would serve to catch and convict him.

She fiercely recited one of her favorite meditations to drive all thoughts of Tal Rufen as anything other than a subordinate and a colleague out of her mind—for the moment, anyway. She *must* concentrate. Her own feelings meant nothing in the face of this threat.

She returned her rebellious mind to the proper path, but at least in its wanderings something else had occurred to her, based on the fact that as a commoner, she would be treated very differently from the deference her current status afforded her. There was another characteristic of the murders that made her think the murderer was either a Priest or a noble—or both. The sheer contempt with which the man used and discarded his "tools" argued for someone who regarded the common man as completely disposable and not worth a second thought. So many Priests in her experience held commoners in scarcely concealed contempt, a contempt she thought she saw operating now.

There didn't seem to be any point in pursuing another hare—all the information they had fit the idea that this mage was or had been a Priest-Mage. If he was a former Priest, well, he had earned himself double punishment, both secular and sacred, and neither the secular nor the sacred Judges would be inclined to grant him any mercy. *But what do I do if it is an active Priest? How can I handle this to do the least amount of damage to the trust that people have in the Church?* The disaster in Gradford had shaken the trust of many to the core. Ardis and many others had barely averted a worse disaster involving the High King. There were many nonhumans who feared the Church and its representatives so much that they would probably do anything in their power to avoid even casual contact with it. If this was an active Priest—

I have to hope it's an apostate, someone who has been ejected from the Church for previous crimes. Otherwise—no matter how well we handle it, the situation is going to result in an enormous setback. It will take decades to recover from it.

Her hands and feet were cold; her ankles ached. Her stomach was a mass of knots. She left her chair behind her desk to take her place beside the fire.

For a moment she felt completely overwhelmed by the situation; felt that it was more than she could handle. She wanted, desperately, to give it all up, put it in the hands of someone else, and run away. Oh, if only she could do that! If only she could retreat somewhere, to some place where she could concentrate on minutiae and forget this dreadful burden of responsibility, the torment of a wayward heart! She clenched her hands on the arms of her chair and forced back tears of exhaustion.

But when the Sacrificed God faced the Flames, He *didn't run away. He entered them bravely, without looking back. And I don't care what the cynics say that the fact that He knew He was immortal made him fearless; the Flames weren't any less agonizing as they burned away His mortal flesh and permitted His immortal soul to escape. He had every reason to fear the Flames, yet to save the world, He stepped into them. If He could face His own death, how can I not face my own life?*

She wanted faith, wanted to believe. The problem was that she was at heart an intellectual creature, not an emotional one. Belief didn't come easily for her; she wanted empirical evidence. She envied those whose belief simply *was,* who believed as matter-of-factly as they breathed, or dreamed.

And the only evidence I have is that evil has a freer hand in this world than good.

All her life she had waited in vain for that tiny whisper in the depths of her soul to *give* her an answer. She didn't really care what question the answer addressed—she just wanted to hear the whisper, once.

Maybe she was unworthy. If that was true, then maybe she ought to renounce her vows and run off with Tal Rufen. There would certainly be no loss to the world if she did. She was no Priest if she could not believe herself in what she preached. If she was unworthy, she should give over her place to someone who *was* worthy of it.

But maybe the reason she had never heard that whisper was only because she had *always* had the capability to find her own answers, if she just worked hard enough at it. And if that was the case, then running off with Tal would be a terrible betrayal of everything she was, everything she hoped to be, and most importantly, everything God had placed her here to do. Would a person with more faith and fewer wits be making a better job of this problem, or a worse one? She had to think that it would be the latter. Faith would only sustain a person through this situation; only intelligence and reasoning would bring an end to it.

The murderer will make a mistake, she told herself. *That's the pattern with crimes like these, too. He'll get overconfident and make a mistake. He'll choose a target who has protection—or one of our people will get the knife before he does. I have to believe that. If we just work hard enough, we'll find him.*

She wasn't altogether sure she *wanted* to face the troubles that would erupt when they did find and catch him, but failure was not an option here.

Perhaps I can have the Free Bards in Kingsford spreading the word to be wary among the women of the streets. If I can keep them all within walls, I'll have an easier chance of finding him.

Of course, the only Free Bard likely to believe her was that disreputable rascal, Raven—and Raven was off somewhere else this season with that saucy young bride of his. But maybe he'd returned by now—

I can certainly find out. And just maybe the letters from Talaysen will convince his friends that I'm trustworthy.

Action. Doing something. *That* made her feel better, less helpless, more effective.

Maybe a little more discreet pressure on the bird-man. I could remind him that some of the people dying are friends of his friends. How important are kin and friends to one of his kind? I should find that out if I can.

Now that would be a coup; if she could get Visyr to cooperate, *he* might be able to get his talons on a knife before the killer stole it back. If they just had a knife, their job would be enormously easier.

I'll concentrate our efforts on stopping the murders by getting women under cover, she decided. *And once they're under cover, I'll concentrate on getting hold of a knife.*

She sighed, and felt a little of the tension ease. With clearly formed tasks of her own to concentrate on, it would be easier to keep other, more troubling thoughts at bay.

She got up and returned to her desk, prepared now to open the complicated channels of communication between the Church and the people of the streets. There was, after all, only so much time before the murderer struck again, and she was determined to give him as few opportunities as possible.

Chapter Ten

Tal was not altogether certain that Ardis would be happy about the course he was pursuing today, but he had decided to take advantage of his status as a Special Inquisitor to pry into a number of records he probably should not see under ordinary circumstances. He'd tell Ardis when he made his report; it was always easier to apologize for overstepping one's bounds than to get permission aforehand, though careers and friendships would always suffer from that policy's overuse.

He'd had Kayne get him copies of the Abbey records of Priests, all of whom had been associated with the Kingsford Abbeys, who'd been dismissed or resigned from the Church over the past twenty years. He wasn't confining himself to Priests who were also mages; although he had never seen or heard of such a killer working with someone else, it had occurred to him that the stakes were too high for him to ignore the possibility. The murderer *could* be a Priest in league with a mage, and they didn't even have to have identical obsessions for the partnership to work. If the Priest in such a partnering, for instance, had been expelled from the Church for misappropriation of funds, well then, there might certainly be substantial enough money to just hire a mage. Alternately, a mage might be in conspiracy just for the side benefits. It was easy enough to guess what the mage would get out of such an association; everyone knew that there was power to be had from death, and the more violent the death, the more power could be obtained. For someone with no morals and a great deal of ambition, this would be a situation too tempting to refuse. Often magical prowess was directly linked to the power available to be used, in much the way that a glass-blower could only become adept at creating huge ceremonial bowls by having enough raw glass and fuel for his furnace to practice with.

So, against the occasional grumblings of his old, walk-the-streets-and-listen constable reflexes, he spent more time in papers and tablets. There were six Priest-Mages who fulfilled those qualifications, and another nine Priests. Written at the end of the records of four of the Priest-Mages was the disappointing word, "Deceased," followed by a date, but at the end of two were the more cryptic words, "Missing, presumed dead." Since the dates on these records were clearly the time of the Great Fire, he could only assume that the two Priest-Mages had somehow gotten misplaced in the confusion. Where they were missing *from,* the records gave no clue, although he suspected very strongly that there were other records associated with these that only Ardis had access to.

The causes for dismissal were enlightening, but not particularly surprising. Tal had been a street-constable for too long not to know that Priests could be as fallible as ordinary folk, and as weak. It often appeared to him that the real sin was in getting caught sinning rather than the act itself.

Fraud, embezzlement, fornication, abuse of privilege—those were the most common, though there were one or two other references that might have puzzled someone with less experience than Tal. "Inappropriate behavior with children," for instance, followed by a very heavy punishment, made him very glad that this was a file on a Priest who was demonstrably *dead,* or Tal might have been tempted to pay an extra-legal visit to the man.

In the end, he had only five names out of the possible fifteen who might still be living in Kingsford. To track them down quickly, he would need help. It was time for a visit to Captain Fenris.

He'd already made one visit, as formal as one ever got with that energetic man, presenting himself and his credentials to Fenris during one of his instructional rounds for new constables. Fenris had been skeptical of Tal's abilities—not that he'd been so ill-mannered as to show that he was, but Tal could read volumes into his little pauses and silences. But as it happened, an altercation over a game of chance had broken out not far from where he met up with the Captain, and Tal had gotten caught up in quelling the small riot and sorting out the claims and counterclaims afterwards. After that, Fenris treated him with the respect his own superiors never had, leaving word with his own men that Tal was to get full cooperation, no questions asked.

Tal tucked his list of names and descriptions into his belt-pouch, bundled himself against the cold, and headed for the stable. His old nag of a horse was patient and easy to handle; it was a matter of a few moments to get him saddled and bridled, and he was through the Abbey gate and heading across the bridge into Kingsford.

Captain Fenris worked out of a common-looking, three-storied building just outside the walls of the Ducal Palace; though it had no stable of its own, a servant took Tal's horse and led it through a postern-gate to the Duke's stables. As Tal dusted the snow from his shoulders and approached the front door, he had to chuckle a little at the thought of his stocky, common-as-dirt gelding being housed side-by-side with the Duke's matched carriage-horses and fine saddle-breds.

As soon as he entered the front door, he was greeted by a Desk-Sergeant stationed just inside. He presented his identification, and the man's attitude changed from civil to positively submissive.

"Sir!" the man said, all but rising to salute. "The Captain is not in, but I can send a runner after him, or send a runner with you to guide you—"

"I don't precisely need to see Captain Fenris in person," Tal replied, interrupting the man, but as politely as he could. "What I need is access to city records. I have the names of five men who were once associated with the Abbey who might still be living in Kingsford, that I would like to track down. If that's possible."

The Sergeant nodded, his lips thinning a little. "I'm sure I don't have to point out that these men might have changed their names—" he began.

Tal didn't quite chuckle. "And I'm sure I don't have to point out that if they've been up to any more—mischief—the constabulary records will have noted those name changes."

The Desk-Sergeant smirked. "Third floor, fourth door on the right. Show the guard your credentials; the Captain has already left standing orders about you."

As Tal climbed the stairs, he wondered just what those "standing orders" were, since he had stressed that Ardis did not want it known that he was a Special Inquisitor. Evidently the Captain had his own way of establishing someone's authorization without resorting to the actual titles.

A guard on a records-room, though—that's interesting. I suspect there's a great deal of delicate information in there. Dear God—Fenris must trust me more than I thought! Or he trusts Ardis to know that I'm trustworthy, which amounts to the same thing. With a sensation of unsettled emotion, he wasn't quite sure how he should react to that revelation. Should he feel flattered? Perhaps a little, but he suspected that situation was due more to Ardis's competence than his own. He was embarrassed, certainly; it was embarrassing to be accorded so much respect when he didn't really feel he'd earned it.

Still it was helping him get his job done, and for that alone he was grateful. When he presented his papers to the guard at the end of the corridor (who was evidently guarding *all* of the rooms at that end, not just the single records-room) he got another smart salute, and was able to return it with grave equanimity.

The room in question was small, but lit quite adequately by means of a clearly often-patched skylight. Folios of papers filled all four walls, and if it had ever boasted a window, the window had long since been boarded up. Tal would have been at a complete loss as to where to start had there not been an indexing-book on the table in the center of the room.

It still took hours before he found three of his five men. He resolved to take what he had and come back later; as it was, he would only be able to investigate one before he was due back at the Abbey.

He picked the easiest of the lot, a former Priest who had resigned with no reason given. That, to his mind, was the most mysterious of them all; there had been no disciplinary actions taken, no marks against him, yet out of nowhere, he resigned and left the Church altogether. There was nothing about him in the constabulary records either, except his name and address.

Tal saluted both the guard and the Desk-Sergeant on his way out; both seemed gratified by his courtesy, which reawoke that faint sense of embarrassment. He could only chase it away by telling himself that it was not *himself* they were reacting to, but to the fact that he served Ardis. She was the one they really respected, not him. He was a walking Title, rather than a respected person, and the humility of the realization was an odd but real comfort.

Snow fell steadily now, and it had accumulated to ankle-depth since he'd entered the building. He waved away an offer to get his horse; the address he was in search of was not in that far away, and he would be less conspicuous on foot.

He pulled the hood of his cloak up over his head; the Church Guards were assigned plain black wool cloaks to cover their resplendent uniforms, wonderfully inconspicuous garments unless you happened to be going through a neighborhood in which garments without patches and holes were oddities. The place he sought now was not that shabby an area, although it could best be described as "modest" rather than "prosperous."

This was a street of small shops and tradesmen, many of whom were now lighting lanterns and candles against the sudden gloom of the late afternoon snowstorm. As snowflakes fell thickly all about him, Tal paused to check his address against the shop to his left.

This is the place, he decided, a little surprised to find that it *was* a shop and not the address of a place that had rooms to let. "BERTRAM— CHANDLER" said the sign above the door, with a picture of a lighted candle to make the meaning clear to the illiterate. *I hope this isn't just an address where letters are left to be picked up.* If that happened to be the case, the shopkeeper could in all honesty claim that he didn't know Dasel Torney, and had no notion where the letters left there in that name were going.

Tal brushed snow from his shoulders, shook it off his hood, and opened the door. A bell jingled cheerfully as he did so, and he entered a shop that was no wider across than his outstretched arms, but was a warm and cheerful place nonetheless, brilliantly lit, and softly fragrant.

On shelves to the right and left were displayed bottles of lamp-oil. On the bottom-most shelf were common pottery jugs that contained equally common rendered animal oil; in the middle were large casks of distilled ground-oil, which the customer would use to fill his own container; on the top, delicate glass flagons of clear, scented oils distilled with rare gums and berries. A solid wooden counter stretched across the middle of the room; on shelves behind it were barrels of tallow-dips bundled in dozens and wrapped in paper, cakes of raw waxes, and candles. There were hundreds of candles, from simple tapers to elaborately colored, carved, and molded sculptural pieces. The warm air was gently scented with barberry, presumably from the candles burning in glass-and-brass lanterns in the four corners of the room.

Behind the counter stood a woman neither old nor young—a woman with such a cheerful, vital countenance that Tal could not for the life of him put an age to her. Cheeks of a flushed pink, no sign of wrinkles around the smiling lips or blue eyes—her hair was hidden beneath a sensible scarf, so he couldn't see if there was any gray in it. She could not possibly be as youthful as he thought, yet he had never before seen a middle-aged woman who was so entirely happy. Her dress was modest, blue-and-white linen, impeccably clean but nothing like luxurious; she was clearly not a wealthy person, yet he had the impression that she was completely content with her life in every way.

"Can I help you, sir?" she asked, beaming at him, her eyes sparkling in the candlelight.

"I don't know," he said, hesitantly. "I really—I'm looking for a man named Torney?" Her very cheer and confidence rattled him; he would almost have preferred some surly old man to this charming woman, and he dreaded seeing her face fall when he mentioned the name of his quarry.

But if anything, she glowed at the mention of the name, as if one of her own candles had suddenly come alight within her. "That would be my husband," she said immediately, her face softening at the final word.

If I had a wife like this one—is she why he left the Church?

"But the sign says Bertram—"

"Is my father," she replied promptly. "Dasel is my husband. I never had a knack for the chandlery and he does, oh, most certainly does! My father could never have made lovely things such as this," she gestured at one of the carved candles, "and he'll be the first to tell you that. He's mostly retired, but he comes in now and again to help me or Dasel." Now she tilted her head to one side; her eyes grew keener, though no less friendly, and a look of recognition came over her, though she lost none of the glow. "You're with the Church, I take it?"

He didn't start, but he was surprised. "How did you know?"

"The cloak. I saw a few of those before Dasel's troubles were over." She did not lose a flicker of her cheer or her composure, but her next words startled him all over again. "You've come about the girls, haven't you? The poor things that were stabbed. I don't know that Dasel can help you, but he'll tell you anything he knows."

He didn't say anything, but his face must have given him away, for she raised her eyebrows and continued. "How do I know what you've come about? Oh, the wife of a *former* Priest-Mage is going to know what it means that there are women dead and a three-sided blade has done the deed. We knew, we both did, and we've been expecting someone like you to come. The High Bishop ordered everything taken out of Dasel's record when he was allowed to leave—which only makes it look the more suspicious when something out of the common happens, I know."

Now she picked up a section of the counter and let it fall, then opened a door in the partition beneath it. "Please come into the shop, sir—your name, or shall I call you Master Church Constable?"

Her cheerful smile was irresistible, and he didn't try to evade her charm. "Tal Rufen, dear lady. Would you care to be more specific about why you were expecting someone like me to call on you?"

"Because," she dimpled as he entered the area behind the counter and waited for her to open the door into the shop, "we knew that the records *you* would be allowed to see wouldn't disclose the reason why Dasel resigned, as I said. The High Bishop is the only one who has those, and she would keep them under her own lock and key. With those girls done to death by ecclesiastical dagger, the first suspect *has* to be a Priest or a Priest-Mage, and you would be trying to find every Priest that had left the Church that you could. *You'd* rather it was someone that wasn't in the Brotherhood anymore, and the Church would, too, so that's the first place you'd look. We've already talked about it, Dasel and I. Dasel—" she called through the open door "—Tal Rufen from the Justiciars for you." She turned back to him, still smiling. "I have to mind the shop, so go on through."

He did so, and she shut the door behind him. He had never been in a chandlery before, and looked about him with interest, as a muffled voice said from the rear of the room, "Just a moment, I'm in the middle of a muddle. I'll be with you as soon as I get myself out of it. Don't fret, there's no back entrance to this place, it butts up against the rear wall of the building on the next street over."

The workroom was considerably wider than the shop; Tal guessed that it extended behind the shops on either side of this one. To his left was an ingenious clockwork contraption that dipped rows of cheap tallow candles in a vat, one after the other, so that as soon as a layer had hardened enough that it could be dipped again, it had reached the vat for another go. There was another such contraption doing the same with more expensive colored beeswax, and another with a scented wax. There were rows of metal molds to his right filled with hardening candles, an entire section full of things that he simply couldn't identify, and a workbench in the middle of it all with several candles being carved that were in various stages of completion. At the rear of the workshop was another door, leading to a storeroom, by the boxes he saw through the open door.

Again the air was scented with barberry, and Tal surmised that this room was the source of the scent, which was probably coming from the warm wax in the dipping area. As he concluded that, the man he had heard speaking from the rear emerged from the storeroom with a box in his hands. He was considerably older than the woman in the front of the shop; gray haired, with a thick, gray mustache and a face just beginning to wrinkle. He was, however, a vigorous and healthy man, and one who appeared to be just as content with his life as his wife was.

"Well, there is one thing that a bit of magic is good for, and that is as an aid to someone too scatter-brained to remember to label his boxes," said Dasel Torney as he set the box down. "Fortunately for one such as myself, there is the Law of Identity, which allows me to take a chip of Kaerlyvale beeswax and locate and remove a box of identical wax. Unfortunately, if that box happens to be in the middle of a stack, I can find myself with an incipient avalanche on my hands!''

Dasel Torney would not look to the ordinary lay-person like a man who could kill dozens of women in cold blood—but looks could be deceiving. Such men, as Tal knew, could be very charming if they chose.

But they were seldom *happy,* not as completely, innocently happy as Dasel was. Once again, except for the gray hair, Tal could not have put an accurate age on Torney if he had not already known what it was from the records. His sheer joy in living made him look twenty years less than his actual age, which was sixty-two.

"Well!" Torney said, dusting his hands off. "Welcome, Tal Rufen! You'll find a stool over there, somewhere, please take it and sit down.''

Looking around near the workbench, Tal did find a tall stool, and took a seat while Dasel Torney did the same on his side of the bench. "Your wife is a very remarkable woman, sir," he ventured.

For the first time since he entered the shop, Tal saw an expression that was not completely cheerful. There was a faint shadow there, followed by a softer emotion that Tal could not identify. "My wife is the reason I was dismissed from the Church, Sirra Rufen," Torney told him candidly. "Or rather—I was permitted to resign. The permission did not come without a struggle.''

Tal felt very awkward, but the questions still had to be asked. "I know that you may find this painful, but your wife did say you'd discussed the fact that someone like me would be coming to talk to you—''

Torney shrugged. "And I know it will be my job to convince you that I had nothing to do with the murders—which, by the way, *I* think were done with the help of magic, speaking as a mage. Mages—Priest-Mages, at least—are expected to study the darker uses of magic so that they will recognize such things and know how to counteract them. I doubt I have to tell you that, though; I can't imagine that as learned and intelligent as High Bishop Ardis is, she hasn't already come to that conclusion.''

Tal hesitated, then said what he'd been thinking. "There was only one murder in Kingsford, sir—''

"That you know of. There's stories in the street of another two beggar-girls with triangular stab-wounds here, and I know of a dozen or more down the river," Torney interrupted him. "I'm in trade, sir Rufen; I deal with people who sell me scents, oils, and waxes from all over the Human Kingdoms and beyond. The one thing that tradesmen do is talk—and there hasn't been anything more sensational to

talk about in the last six months than murder—especially the murder
of that poor Gypsy girl by the jeweler. Stabbed with a file, indeed! I
knew then it was an ecclesiastical dagger, and when another girl was
killed in the same way here, I knew it was only a matter of time before
Ardis sent a Hound of God out on trail.''

Tal sighed. "And you, of course, never leave the city."

Torney nodded. "I could bring witnesses to that, obviously, and it
is just as obvious that they could be lying for me. Take it as given
that I have the witnesses; what can I do that will convince you I could
not have anything to do with these horrible crimes?''

"Tell me why you left the Church," Tal replied instantly.

Dasel Torney nodded as if he had expected that very answer. "I
will give you the shortest possible version—I was a Priest-Mage,
trained by the Justiciars, but not of the Order myself. I was out of the
Teaching Order of Saint Basyl, and at forty years of age, I was given
the assignment of acting as tutor to the daughter of a wealthy and
extremely influential merchant of Kingsford—the head of the Chandler's Guild, in fact. I had the bad judgment, although the exquisite
taste, to fall in love with her, and she had the poor taste to fall equally
in love with me. The inevitable occurred, and we were discovered
together. At that point, neither of us would give the other up, not even
after ten years of separations and penances, nor under the threat of far
worse punishments than we had already undergone.''

"Worse?" Tal asked, curiously.

Torney chuckled. "There were those who thought I ought to pay
for my sin by having the organ in question removed—and I don't mean
my heart!''

Tal blanched; he couldn't imagine how Torney could joke about it.

"Fortunately," Dasel continued, "cooler heads prevailed, and both
my fellow teachers and the Justiciars prevailed upon both the High
Bishop and my darling's father to soften their wrath. In the case of
the former, they prevailed upon him to simply allow me to resign
provided I never used magic directly to make a profit—and in the case
of the latter, they prevailed upon the Guildmaster to accept me as a
son-in-law.'' He quirked a smile. "It did help that I have a talent with
wax and scent, and that my ability as a mage was never better than
minimal. It was very uncomfortable for all of us, however; he acted
to both of us as if we were strangers. I thought he would never really
forgive us. We never spoke outside of the shop until the Great Fire.''

Tal could well imagine what the Fire must have done to a candle
and oil shop. "Was there anything left?''

Torney shook his head. "Not a thing. Nothing but ashes, and by the time we got back to where the shop had been, scavengers even had sifted those and carried away any bits of metal they'd found.''

All this had the ring of truth about it—furthermore, it would probably be very easy to verify all these facts. "What happened then?" Tal asked.

"Well, the Great Fire destroyed Loren Bertram's fortune and business—but—" He smiled. "I suppose it's my training as a Priest that makes me value things of the spirit and heart more than of the material world. My minimal ability in magic saved our lives, and when Bertram was deepest in despair, I was ready to fight. He gave up, but I was just beginning, and determined to prove that I could be his friend and restore what he'd lost. Between Loyse and myself, we scraped together enough for a tiny slice of a shop. The good will we had built among the traders got us raw goods on credit. My considerable talent in the business has brought us back to where we are now. We have a level of comfort, if not luxury. It's been a difficult time, but the results of our efforts have been well worth it. But best of all, Bertram saw how I stood by him as well as Loyse, and now he *is* my friend, not my enemy."

A very short version of what must have been a difficult twenty years, but all of it was verifiable now that Tal knew the facts behind the simple resignation. And if Torney had been trying to rebuild a business out of the ashes of the Fire, there was no way he could have been out of Kingsford to commit the earlier murders.

And there must be a world of things that had been left out of that simple story—Tal could only wonder at a love that was powerful enough to defy Church and parent, and still emerge radiating joy.

"I knew when I saw her that your wife was a remarkable woman," Tal said. "She must be far more than that—"

"I wish I were a poet or a musician," Torney replied softly, turning a half-carved candle in his hands. "I cannot begin to tell you what she means to me. I would have given up everything simply to be in her presence—and if they had locked me away in a solitary cell for a lifetime of penance, I would never have repented a moment of the time I spent with her. And she feels exactly the same towards me." He looked up. "I suppose that's remarkable. To us, though, it is as natural as breathing, and as necessary."

If a man's soul could be said to shine from his eyes, Tal saw Torney's at that moment—and felt a little in awe.

Of all of the things that he could have uncovered in the course of this investigation, this was the most unexpected.

"Have *you* any idea who this might be?" he asked after a moment.

"Is there anyone among the Priests or the Priest-Mages that you knew who could be doing these things?"

"That's what has me troubled and puzzled," Torney replied, picking up a knife and gently carving petals of wax out of the side of the candle in his hands. "I'm older than Ardis—she wasn't the High Bishop at the time I was dismissed, she was nothing more than the most promising of the young Justiciar-Mages. There is one man who *could* very easily be doing these things, but the last time I saw him, he wasn't a man anymore."

Well *that* certainly made Tal sit up straight. Torney didn't chuckle, but it was clear that he was amused—he'd obviously intended that his statement would startle Tal, perhaps as a gentle sort of revenge. Without any prompting, he told Tal the tale of Priest-Mage Revaner, Guild Bard Beltren, and the Gypsy Free Bard called Robin.

"I've heard something like this before—" Tal said, uncertainly, when Torney was through.

"Likely enough; the Free Bards made a ballad out of it, though they changed the names to protect their own hides," Torney replied. "Now, the part that didn't make it into the ballad was that Ardis doesn't know how to reverse that particular effect, since it was all tangled up with Revaner's original dark sorcery, the Bards' magics, and her own. As far as any Priest-Mage I ever spoke to knew, Revaner was going to be a bird for the rest of his life. And the part that no more than a handful of people know is that during the Great Fire, the Black Bird disappeared."

"Could he have changed back, somehow?" Tal asked eagerly. "I've heard that there was a lot of magic going on during the Fire—could he have gotten caught in some of it and changed back?"

Torney spread his hands wide. "If you're asking could more tangled and confused magic undo what tangled and confused magic did to him in the first place?—well, I can't tell you. I was never that good, and the theory up at that level of things just goes clean over my head. But if there was ever a man likely to want revenge on the Church, it was Revaner. And if there was ever a man convinced that the world should run to his pleasure, it was Revaner. *Could* he have escaped? Could he have survived on his own? Does that make him a man evil enough to do these horrible deeds?" He looked helpless. "I don't know. I couldn't judge my own heart, how can I presume to judge my fellow man's?"

"You're a charitable fellow, Dasel Torney," Tal said at last.

But Torney shook his head. "Not as charitable as I should be. It's easy enough for me to say that I can't judge Revaner, or the man who's done these things—but I haven't suffered harm from either one of them, either. If it had been Loyse who'd been seduced and left by Revaner—or slain, like that poor girl—'' He dropped his eyes, and put the candle and the knife carefully down. "Let me just say that I might *repent* what I did to the man, but I wouldn't hesitate to do it.''

"If you had seen what I have," Tal said softly, "you wouldn't repent of it, either.''

Torney looked up sharply; their eyes met, and the wordless exchange that followed left both of them with deep understanding and respect.

"The fact remains, though, that the last time anyone saw Revaner, he wasn't capable of doing anything more than any other bird could do—rather less, as a matter of fact, since he was too heavy to fly. That's the problem with *that* particular suspect.'' Torney shrugged. "How he could get from here to down-river without being seen, I couldn't tell you—unless someone netted him to use in a menagerie and he escaped his cage later.''

"Well," Tal said, tucking that thought away for consideration. "I have a little more to go on; I'll see about tracking down some of the others on my list.''

"You'll find Gebbast Hardysty somewhere along the docks," Torney told him. "If he's not cadging drinks, he's in one of the dosshouses sleeping off a drunk. I doubt he could muster up enough moments of sobriety to work a simple spell, but you had better be the judge of that. Ofram Kellam has changed his name to Oskar Koob, and he's set himself up as a fortune-teller—the constables probably have an address for him under that name, though I doubt they know who he really is. The only reason *I* know is that I ran into him on the street and called him by his right name—and he blurted out that I was mistaken, he was Oskar Koob, not the other fellow. I know what he could do when he was dismissed—for embezzling Church funds, if you don't already know—and I don't think he has the ability to work magic this powerful.''

"Do you keep track of your fellow sinners?" Tal asked lightly.

Torney raised his eyebrow. "Actually, yes, I do," he admitted. "When I can. A little self-prescribed penance, but there are only three here in the city that I know of. I heard that Petor Lambert was still in Kingsford, but I haven't been able to find him, so he may be on the far side of the city. If he is, I suspect he's up to some old tricks of using magic to create 'miracles' to fleece the credulous. If I find him first, I'll get word to you, but you have more chance of tracking him down than I do.''

"And I will leave you to enjoy the evening with your charming wife, as I hope you will," Tal told him, rising. "I can promise you that there won't be any more calls like this one."

Torney came around the bench to shake his hand. "I am just pleased that Ardis has found worthy men to help her," he said warmly as he opened the door for Tal. "She is a fine Priest, a hard worker, and an estimable woman. Not—" he added mischievously "—as estimable as my Loyse, but estimable nevertheless."

"Oh—as if I ever had a hope of being as wise or as intelligent as High Bishop Ardis!" Loyse said playfully as she held the counter-door open for Tal. "Here," she continued, holding out a package wrapped in brown paper to him, "take these with you. They're something new in the way of strikers that Dasel is trying. They might come in useful, and if you like them, perhaps you can get Captain Fenris and the constables to try them."

Torney looked proud but sheepish. "Kindling-sticks with chemicals on the tip, dipped in wax," he explained. "Watch—"

He took out a small bit of wood with a blob of odd bluish stuff on the end, and scraped it against the countertop. Tal started as a flame flared up on the end of the stick with an odd hissing sound.

"People are afraid of them," Torney explained. "They either think it's bad magic, or they think the things might suddenly go off in their pockets. But if the Church Guards and the constables started carrying and using them—"

"Obviously. I'll give them a try—though I warn you, if they *do* suddenly go off in my pocket, I'll be very annoyed!" Tal grinned a little.

Torney chuckled. "No fear of that—unless you're being dragged by a horse and the pocket you've got them in gets ripped open. It needs a hard, rough surface—preferably stone—and you have to scrape with some force to get through the wax coating. But the wax makes them waterproof, which is why I use it."

Tal put the packet in his breeches-pocket, and thanked them both, then went out into the evening shadows and the thickly falling snow.

Two of the three men that Dasel Torney had mentioned were the ones missing from his list, and he decided to track down the easiest one first. With the help of a fat purse of coppers to buy beer and the cheap, strong liquor served in the dockside taverns, Tal went in search of Gebbast Hardysty. He hoped he wouldn't have to drink any of the rot-gut himself, but he was resigned to the fact that he would probably pay for this excursion with a throbbing skull and a queasy stomach in the morning.

At first, given that Hardysty haunted the dockside area, he thought he might have found his murderer. After all, a man who haunted the docks might be getting jobs as day-labor on barges, and that could put him in any city up and down the river with relative ease. As a casual laborer, no one would pay much attention to him. Hardysty was another of the mages on the list. Altogether, things seemed to add up properly—but after tracing him to a particularly noisome cellar-hole of a sailor's bar, Tal was having second thoughts.

By now it was fully dark, and Tal made sure of his long knife as he paused for a moment outside the tavern entrance—if that wasn't too grand a name to put on a gap in the cellar-wall of a warehouse, framed by three rough-hewn beams, with the only "door" being a square of patched sail. There wasn't even a sign outside the door, just a board with a battered tankard nailed to it. They couldn't even afford a lantern at the door; the only illumination came from the street-lamp two doors down, and a dim, yellowish light that seeped around the curtain at the door.

Tal had been in and out of many similar places in his career as a constable, and he wasn't afraid, merely cautious. In the winter there wasn't as much traffic on the river, which meant that sailors and rivermen had less money to spend. It wasn't a festival night, the weather wasn't very cooperative, and most men would chose to stay where they bunked if they had a bed or a room. On a night like tonight, the men in this place wouldn't be looking for trouble—but they wouldn't try to avoid it, either. As long as he watched his step, he should be all right.

He trudged down the five steps made of uncut rock, and pulled the curtain aside to enter.

The reek of unwashed bodies, stale beer, cheap tallow-lights, and other scents best left unnamed hit him in the face like a blow. He almost turned around and walked back out, but his sense of duty prevailed and he stalked across the dirt floor to the bar, avoiding the tables, chairs, and a staggering drunk more by instinct than by sight. What light there was didn't help much in navigating the room. There were only four thick tallow-dips to light the entire room, and two of them were over the bar. They gave off a murky, smokeladen light that didn't cross much distance.

Then again, I'm probably better off not being able to see. The closer he got to the bar, the more his eyes stung from the smoke. *If I knew how much filth was caked on the tables and the floor, I'd probably be sick.*

Behind the bar was a huge man, running to fat, with the last two fingers of his right hand missing, and a scar across the top of his bald head. The man grunted as Tal approached, which Tal took as an inquiry. "Beer," he said shortly, slapping down a couple of copper pieces on the unpolished slab of wood that passed for a bar-top.

The bartender poured flat beer out of a pitcher into a cheap earthenware mug. The stuff looked like horse-piss, and probably tasted the same. Tal took it, but didn't drink. "Hardysty here?" he asked, and without waiting for an answer, shoved a handful of coppers across the bar. "This's for him. Split on a bet. Said I could leave it here."

With that, he turned and took his beer off to a corner table, where he sat and pretended to drink. In reality, he poured the beer onto the floor, where it soaked in without adding measurably to the stink or the filth.

His eyes were adjusting to the gloom; now he could make out the rest of the room, the scattering of tables made of scavenged lumber, the few men who sat at them, slumped over the table or drinking steadily, with a stony disregard for the wretched quality of the stuff they were pouring down their throats.

The bartender scooped up the money, pocketed part of it, then poured another beer and took it over to a man half-lying on another table nearby, as if he had passed out. He grabbed the man's shoulder and shook it until the fellow showed some signs of life, batting his hand away and blinking at him blearily.

"Wha?" he slurred. The bartender slapped both the beer and the remainder of the money down on the rough wooden table in front of him.

"Yours," he grunted. "Ya made a bet. Part paid off the tab, this's what's left."

Hardysty stared at him a moment, as Tal pretended to nurse his beer. "Ah," he slurred. "Bet. Yah." Clearly he didn't *expect* to remember the apocryphal "bet" that had been made on his behalf. All he knew was that money had somehow appeared that supposedly belonged to him, and he wasn't about to question the source.

He drank the beer down to the dregs in a single swallow—Tal winced inside at the mere idea of actually *drinking* the stuff. He knew what it was; the dregs out of the barrels of beer emptied at more prosperous taverns, and the dregs of brewing, mixed together and sold so cheaply that it often went as pig-slop. There was not a viler beverage on the face of the earth. A man that drank the stuff on a regular basis cared only for the fact that it would get him drunk for pennies.

Whatever Hardysty had been, the fact was that he was too far gone in drink to have had any connection to the murders. If he remembered who he was and where he was supposed to go from one day to the next, he would be doing well.

When Torney said he was cadging drinks, he meant it. He's probably a street-beggar for just long enough to get the money to drink.

Whatever had gotten him dismissed from the Church? Tal thought he remembered something about theft of Church property. Had the disgrace broken him, or had the drinking started first? Perhaps the thefts had gone to pay for drink.

This was one vice gone to excess that Tal never could understand; intellectually, he could sympathize with a man who had lost his head over a woman, and he could understand how the thrill of risk could make a man gamble away all he had in the heat of a moment—but he never could understand this rush to oblivion, be it by drink or by a drug. Why do something that made you feel *less* alive, rather than more? Why would anyone willfully seek to remove ability?

Hardysty dropped the mug down onto the table, stared at the pile of coppers for a moment, then shoved them back across the table to the bartender. "More," he said—which was probably what the bartender had expected him to say. Before Tal could blink, the coppers were gone.

Tal pretended to drink two more mugs of the awful stuff before staggering out into the darkness. At no time did the bartender ask him about his connection to Hardysty; at no time did Hardysty make any attempt to find out where the money had come from. That was typical behavior in a place like this one. No one asked questions, and information was seldom volunteered, though it could be bought.

At this point it was too late to look for any of the other former Priests, but he felt he had made enough progress for one night. He could definitely scratch Torney and Hardysty off his list. The practice of magic—especially magic as powerful and tricky as this one must be—required a sharp mind. Even sober, Hardysty wouldn't be capable of that much concentration. Dreg-beer came contaminated with all sorts of unpleasant things, and the people who sold it often adulterated it further. There was no telling how badly Hardysty was poisoned; the only thing that was certain was that he had no more than half the mind he'd started out this slide to oblivion with. He might just as well have taken two rocks and hammered his own head with them on a daily basis for the last few years.

Tal was grateful for the heavy snowfall; it kept footpads off the street. This was not a neighborhood he wanted to have to visit again by night. He was immeasurably glad when he got into a better area without an incident, and even happier when he reached the constabulary headquarters and was able to get his horse from the Ducal stables. The ride across town and over the bridge to the Abbey was quite some distance, but in contrast to his walk away from the docks, it seemed to take no time at all.

A person could draw quite a parable from those two, Torney and Hardysty, if he knew everything that brought them to where they are now. Torney was driven by love to give up everything in order to have it, but what drove Hardysty to oblivion? Greed? Fear?

That was the end of the puzzle for every really good constable that Tal had ever met. Once you knew who'd done the crime, you'd caught him, and you had him safely disposed of, you always wondered why he'd done what he'd done. Even things that seemed obvious were sometimes only obvious on the surface. Why did some people, born into poverty, go out and try to make their lives better honestly instead of turning to crime? Why did one child, beaten and abused, grow up to vow never to inflict that kind of treatment on his own children, while others treated their offspring as they'd been treated?

Tal didn't know, and neither did anyone else, but he sometimes had the feeling that the answer *was* there, if only he knew where to look for it, and was brave enough to search.

The next day, in absence of any other orders, he crossed the bridge again to resume his hunt for former Priests. Following Torney's information that one of them had changed his name to "Oskar Koob" and had set himself up as a fortune-teller, Tal went to the office in charge of collecting taxes on small businesses. "Koob" would not call himself a "fortune-teller," of course—fortune-telling was illegal, and possibly heretical. No, he would call himself a "Counselor" or "Advisor," and that was the listing where Tal found his name and address.

He had come prepared this time, dressed in civilian clothing, with a pouch full of letters and a few business papers that referred to him as a trader in semiprecious gemstones. There was nothing about him to reveal his true identity, although the papers all called him by his real name. There were so few people in Kingsford who knew what Tal Rufen really was that he felt perfectly safe in using a name he *knew* he would respond automatically to. In taking an assumed name, there was always the chance that you would forget who you were supposed to be for a moment, and give yourself away.

I just hope that this man hasn't got the ability to read thoughts.

Yesterday's snow had been shoveled off the streets and packed in piles against the walls of the shops and houses; today, although the sky was overcast, it didn't feel to him as if it was going to snow again. *So odd, to think that a few weeks ago I was wishing I lived somewhere where it snowed in the winter instead of raining, and now here I am. I think this is an improvement.* Somehow he'd gotten the impression that snow just didn't bring the numbing cold that winter rains did, because rain brought dampness that penetrated even the thickest clothing. Too bad *that* impression was wrong! And the thought that his feet wouldn't get soaking wet was wrong, too; it just took snow a little longer to melt and soak into your boots, but it happened all the same.

So much for theory. But then again, he wasn't out walking a patrol anymore; he was in and out of buildings most of the time, not in the street. It could be the contrast that made him feel the cold more.

As he walked, he began mentally constructing the way he would think and react by the time he reached the right address. In his persona as a small merchant, it was natural for him to consult a fortune-teller; anyone making a precarious livelihood could be forgiven for being superstitious. *I operate on a very small margin, and anything I can find out to help me is going to make a big difference. I want to know the way that fashion is going to run—like that fashion for gem-cut steel baubles a while back. If I can anticipate a fashion, I can make a fortune. I want to know where I can buy stones cheaply, and I want to know if someone's going to make a strike so rich it will run the prices down and make my stock worthless. I want to know if there are going to be bandits, and which Faires are going to prosper this year.*

All these things would make a difference to a small merchant operating in a risky venture. When Tal had them all firmly in mind, he cultivated just the right amount of nervousness mixed with eagerness. When he arrived at the door of "Oskar Koob" he was ready.

There was nothing in the plain house-front to suggest what Koob really was; the man was clever enough to run a very discreet service. *Too bad it isn't an honest one.*

This was just one in a row of identical middle-class homes, all thrown up shortly after the Fire to accommodate people who still had money and the means to continue to make a living. Each was tall, narrow, with a set of stairs leading up to a front door, a window on either side of the door, and three windows in each of the remaining two stories. The buildings ended in attics that had a single window just beneath the gabled roof, and had identical tall wooden fences around the sides and back, dividing the yard from the neighbors' yards.

This one was painted beige, and had a very modest little sign beside the door that read, "OSKAR KOOB, COUNSELOR."

Tal lifted the polished brass knocker and knocked at the door; it was opened by an attractive young dark-haired woman dressed in a slightly exotic robe of brown embroidered with intricate geometric designs. She regarded Tal with a vacant gaze that suggested she'd been hired for her looks and not her intelligence. "I'd like to see Oskar Koob, please," Tal told her.

"You got an appointment?" she asked, without opening the door enough for him to see past her to the room inside.

"No," he replied doubtfully, wringing his hands for emphasis. "Do I need one? My friend didn't tell me I needed an appointment."

The girl assessed him and his clothing for a moment. "I'll see if the Master is free," she said, and shut the door, leaving him standing on the front step.

But not for long—the "Master" had probably been lurking nearby, perhaps at a window so that he could make his own assessment of the prospective client. Tal had made certain to dress as if he could afford Koob's fees.

The girl opened the door—completely, this time, so that Tal could enter. The foyer was nothing impressive, just four plain walls with doors in them. The girl disappeared through the left-hand one, and reappeared before he had time to have second thoughts and take his money elsewhere. "The Master's powers have told him that his usual morning client is ill," the girl announced grandly. "As soon as the Master has sent a messenger with the medicines he will concoct, the Master will be with you."

The Master never had a client to begin with, Tal mentally chuckled to himself, as he followed the girl into the right-hand room. *The Master was wondering how long the current goose could be induced to lay magic eggs. The Master is thanking God or his own powers for bringing in a fresh goose to cultivate.*

The room was precisely what he had expected—dark brown draperies concealed all four walls and covered the window; light came from an oil lamp hanging over the table in the center of the room. Draperies were fairly standard for "Consultants" like Oskar Koob—it was easy to hide confederates and props behind draped fabric. The floor was covered with a worn and faded carpet—and again, this was standard, for it was easier to hide trapdoors under carpet than in a plain wooden floor. There was a small table in the middle of the room, with a globe of smoky crystal in the center of it. There was a chair on the far side, and a slightly shorter chair on Tal's side. Without prompting, he took the smaller chair, and waited.

After an interval calculated to impress the person waiting with the importance of the one he was waiting for, Oskar Koob made his Entrance, sweeping aside the draperies which concealed a shabby door behind his chair.

Oskar Koob was ill-equipped for the part of a mysterious and powerful fortune-teller. He looked like nothing so much as a peasant straight out of the farm—complete with the innocent and boyish face that makes people want to trust such an individual.

Well, his face is his fortune, I can see that.

As for the rest, he was dressed in a sober black tunic and breeches, with a most impressive gold medallion around his neck. The fabric was excellent, the tailoring superb. Evidently the "Consultation" business was going well for Oskar Koob.

Tal rose immediately, and held out his hand. "Sir! I'm—" he began, but Koob hushed him with an imperiously raised hand.

"Silence," he commanded. "Take your seat again, my brother. *I* will consult with the spirits and they will tell me who you are and what your business with me is."

Tal did as he was told, and Koob seated himself behind the crystal sphere. He made several elaborate hand-movements above the sphere, muttering things under his breath as he did so, while Tal simply watched and waited.

"Your name is Tal Rufen," Koob announced, squinting into the ball. "You are a gem-merchant, and you wish to consult me concerning the best investments in stock for you to make."

Tal contrived to look and act astonished—never mind that the way Koob had probably learned all this so far was by means of a scrying-spell to read the papers in Tal's pocket. Koob continued to give him details about his supposed life, all of them lifted from the letters and other articles he had with him. It was an interesting variation on the same game Tal had seen run elsewhere—the difference being that there was no pickpocket accomplice to lift a pouch, learn who the client was by opening it and examining it, and replacing it without the client ever being aware that it was gone in the first place.

"Now," Koob said, deepening his voice, "I must call upon other spirits in the matter of your business. These are very powerful spirits, powerful, and sometimes dangerous. The spirits who know the future are far more risky to call upon than those who know the past and the present."

The light in the lantern dimmed, and an eerie glow came up from the crystal sphere in the middle of the table. As the lantern-light dimmed to next to nothing, strange sounds filled the room, the sounds of people whispering, the distant rattle of a tamborine, a few notes on a flute, a drumbeat echoing his heart. Then, as Tal looked away from the crystal globe, he saw things floating in midair—the face of a young woman, disembodied hands, the very tamborine he'd just heard.

So just what is it about the tamborine that makes it so attractive to spirits? Tal had never been to one of these little "Consultations" without "the spirits" floating a tamborine around the room and beating an occasional solo on it.

You'd think that, since they're in the afterlife, they'd have enough talent to play more than just a tamborine! If they're Blessed Spirits, shouldn't they have at least the talent of a minstrel? If they've been dead a while, wouldn't they have the time to practice, oh, a gittern at least, or a floor-harp, if not a pipe-organ of the sort from a Cathedral?

Furthermore, as a constable, Tal had trained himself to remember faces. He was not particularly surprised to see that the young woman levitating above the floor was the same one who'd met him at the door. Now she had unusual lighting and some fresh powder makeup and quickly-painted brows, but it was the same woman.

The young woman proceeded to give him advice about his various plans and investments—the ones mentioned in the papers in his pouch, that is. When he asked for further advice—should he undertake new projects?—she was curiously silent. And when she spoke, her lips didn't move.

This was the first time Tal had gone to a fortune-teller who was also a real mage, but he had a good idea which effect was produced by fakery, and which by applied magic. *The girl's face and veil glowing— that's foxfire, I've seen that before. The levitation is either magic or a platform lowered down from the room above us. Probably the platform, it's easier. He's reading the documents I have with me by magic; he probably sees them in that crystal ball of his. Then he's the one speaking in a female voice, not the girl; that's ordinary voice-throwing, pitched high. Once in a while his lips twitch.*

Just as he came to those conclusions, the Master "collapsed," the "spirit" vanished, and Tal, professing concern, went to the Master's side. This, of course, gave the girl time to shed her veils, foxfire and makeup; he kept careful track, and she appeared in about the time it should take for her to get rid of the costume, wipe off powder and greasepaint, and come down from the second floor. She assisted the Master out, and returned a moment later.

"The Master must rest; it has been a difficult morning," she said stiffly, as if making a rehearsed speech. "The usual fee is five ducal florins for each consultation."

Five florins! That was steep, even by the standards of the best! Then again, Oskar Koob's show was a bit more impressive, so perhaps he was worth it. Tal paid without protesting, and left, after he made an appointment for a second consultation—one which, of course, he would not attend.

Of course by that time, Oskar Koob would no longer be in residence here; he would be taking up space in either the Ducal Gaol or the Church Gaol, depending on which authority got to him first.

Unless, of course, Tal thought with some amusement, as he made his way back towards the bridge, *the spirits warn him first!*

Chapter Eleven

Despite diligent searching and enough bribes to equal his old wages as a constable, Tal was able to contact only a single one of the rest of the men on his list. He got to find one, and that was the extent of his luck. One had actually set up his own Chapel in one of the poor neighborhoods and was acting as a Priest in spite of the fact that he had been specifically forbidden to do any such thing. But by incredible but genuine coincidence, before Tal located him, the people of the neighborhood discovered what he was doing with their daughters during his "special religious instruction" sessions, and he'd fled from an angry mob that chased him outside the city limits. A quick interview with the fellow from horseback, as he relentlessly stomped away from the city, convinced Tal that this one was in no way able to muster so much as the concentration or resourcefulness to *plan* a killing, much less follow through on one. Tal felt no sympathy at all in seeing that sad excuse for a man shamble off in his tattered Priest-clothes with just one small pouch of money—and a by-now-shriveled manhood—to his name.

The other suspects had simply vanished shortly after they'd been dismissed from the Church, and no one knew, or would admit to knowing, where they were.

Time was running out; it would not be long before the killer struck again, and Tal was getting desperate. He had yet to find even a tentative candidate for his killer.

So when his last lead ran out and he found that his path back to the bridge led him towards the Ducal Palace, he acted on an impulse.

I need something more than the resources I have, he told himself, gazing around at the darkening city streets and up into the overcast sky. The sun had set a little while ago and dusk was descending swiftly; surely that bird-man Visyr couldn't fly at night. If there was any way to persuade the creature to help in watching for suspicious persons, he'd be worth more than twenty constables. If, as they thought, the magician was directing his "tools" from some vantage point above the city streets, Visyr might be the only person able to spot him.

He had had an almost instant sense of trust for the Haspur. Perhaps it was due to some early-childhood fascination with the raptors that the Haspur resembled, or a mental echo of the hawks and eagles of command banners and insignia which called forth thoughts of loyalty and respect, or perhaps it was the personal manner of this Visyr, but the constable's instincts did not call for him to be suspicious beyond the norm. That in itself was remarkable, since he reflexively made himself even more thorough in his self-questioning when dealing with any nonhuman, since their expressions were so often harder to read. But Visyr was possessed of such an intense, open presence and his mannerisms were so plain to read that Tal believed that dealing with him as a colleague would not be difficult, and his impression of Visyr's ethics indicated he would likely want to help the side of right.

Now, if ever, was the time to use his special privileges, because it was going to take those privileges just to get into the palace without an invitation.

He went first to the constabulary headquarters, and for a wonder, Captain Fenris was actually there; a constable-in-training showed him to the Captain's office without any delay, and once there, he explained what it was that he wanted.

Fenris, a tall, dark man with a full beard and mustache, stroked that beard thoughtfully. "That's a good idea," he said when Tal was finished. "I suppose the question is whether or not acting as a lookout for us is going to interfere with Visyr's duties for Arden. Getting the Duke to agree if it does interfere might be problematical."

"Oh, it's going to," Tal admitted. "There's no question of that. If he's going to do us any good, he's going to have to stay over the common sections of Kingsford, even after he's already mapped them, and that means he's not going to be getting much of the Duke's work done."

"In a way, he gets some of that work done by just being seen. People look up and see him, working for the Duke, they're reminded of the Duke. The bird-man is a reassurance these days to people who are afraid the Duke might start to forget them. But he's not going to be doing that scouting on a steady basis," Fenris replied. "When the killer strikes again, you're going to have a week or more before he has to make another kill, and during that time Visyr can go back to his map-making. If we point that out to him, he might be more co-operative; certainly the Duke will."

Tal winced inwardly at the casual way that Fenris had said "*when* the killer strikes," not "*if*," but he knew that Fenris was right. Only the most extraordinary luck would stop this monster before he had another victim, luck amounting to a miracle, and so far miracles were in short supply.

But Fenris had already taken paper, pen, and seal out of his desk, and was writing a pass to get Tal past the first few guards who would not know what a Special Inquisitor was and into the palace. Once Tal got as far as the Duke's Seneschal or Major-Domo, those officials would be *quite* well aware of the power that he represented, and would get him the interview he wanted without a lot of tedious protocol.

"Here," Fenris said, handing him the folded paper, and winked at him. "Now you can walk into the palace and see whoever you damned well want to, including Arden himself, if you're so inclined. Did it ever occur to you that you've come one hell of a long way from a simple constable?"

When hasn't it? "Every waking moment," Tal told him soberly. "A year ago, if anyone had told me I was going to walk into a palace on the strength of my own authority, I'd have asked what he was drinking and ordered the same for myself." He licked his lips, and shook his head. "Sometimes I think I'm having a particularly vivid dream and that I'll wake up at any moment; the rest of the time, I'm sure it's not a dream, it's a nightmare. I don't mind telling you that this so-called power is making me nervous."

"Good," Fenris replied. "It should. Every morning I get out of bed and ask myself what the hell I think I'm doing, and I hope you're doing the same. As long as you never take it for granted, you'll do all right, Tal Rufen."

Fenris gave him a nonprotocol salute, nodded, and stalked out snapping orders at a trainee, and thus the meeting was concluded.

With his papers in his hand, Tal left the building and crossed to the official entrance to the Ducal Palace, presenting his pass from Captain Fenris to the guard at the gate. From there, he was taken to the guard at the palace door, from there to the Captain of the Watch, and from there to the Major-Domo. The wizened little Major-Domo examined his papers, turned white, and sent a page to the Duke while Tal waited in the Major-Domo's office. They were both horribly uncomfortable; the Major-Domo kept watching Tal while his hands twitched nervously. There were stacks of papers on his desk which were probably very important, but the Major-Domo looked as if he was afraid to take his eyes off his visitor. Tal would have been happy to make small talk, but the poor man acted as if Tal's every word might have the potential to send himself or his master to the Church Gaol, and Tal finally gave up.

Finally the page arrived, and Tal thankfully left the Major-Domo's office in the young boy's wake. The page was too young to be intimidated by a mere Church official, and Tal was happy to listen to the child chatter as they passed along the hallways brightly lit with the best wax candles and oil-lamps in sconces on the wall. But when the page brought him to the door of what were clearly the Duke's private chambers, Tal was taken aback.

He didn't have time to act on his surprise, though; the boy walked past the guard at the door, pushed the door itself open, and announced, "Tal Rufen, milord," waving him through. At that point, Tal could only go through into the Duke's private suite as the boy closed the door behind him.

The first room, something of a cross between a sitting-room and an audience chamber, was empty and lit only by two of the wall-mounted oil-lamps and a low fire in the fireplace. "In here, Rufen," called a voice from beyond the next door. "Come along through."

He ventured into the next room, which was lit as brightly as the hallways, and furnished with a few chairs, several wardrobes which were standing open, and a floor-length pier-glass. There he found the Duke surrounded by three servants and a perfectly stunning woman. The Duke was a handsome man, his hair thinning a little, but otherwise showing no sign of his age. Still athletic and fit, the form-fitting blue velvet coat that his servants were helping him into only did him justice rather than making him look ridiculous as might have been the case with a man who was losing his figure. The woman held a scarlet satin sash with a jeweled decoration or order of some sort on it, and watched him with her lovely head to one side and a faintly critical look on her face.

When the coat was on, the sash in place over it, and every last wrinkle smoothed away from the coat, the white silk shirt, and the matching blue-satin breeches, the critical frown vanished to be replaced by an approving smile. "I wasn't at all sure of that cut, my love," the woman said, "but you were right after all."

"Perhaps now you'll admit that I know what I'm doing when it comes to clothing," he admonished playfully, turning and craning his neck so he could see his back in the mirror, as the servants discreetly swept up the clothing that he had discarded. "I think this old thing of my grandfather's is likely to set a new fashion." He turned to Tal. "What do you think, Rufen?"

Caught off-guard, Tal could only stammer incoherently, "Uniforms are more my suit than fine clothing."

The beautiful woman laughed and pretended to cuff the Duke. "That is *not* fair, nor is it kind," she chided, and turned to Tal. "Inquisitor Rufen, I hope you will forgive my Duke. He enjoys discomfiting people, and one of these days the habit will get him in trouble."

The woman, Tal realized now, was Lady Asher, the Duke's wife. He'd been told she was lovely; he didn't realize that she was so beautiful that she could leave a man dazed just by speaking to him. She had him so dazzled that he really couldn't have said what it was that *she* was wearing; something claret-colored, that left a flawless expanse of white shoulders and milky neck exposed. He mustered what was left of his wits, and answered, as gallantly as he could, "For your sake, my lady, I would forgive anything short of tossing me in his personal dungeon."

"Well, it's a good thing I don't have a personal dungeon, or I might see if that was true!" the Duke laughed. "You've done it again, my love; you've charmed even an impervious Church Inquisitor. Do you care to stay and hear what he has to say, or am I keeping you from other business?"

"You aren't keeping me, but I do have other business of yours to see to—that wretched little Count Lacey, for one," Lady Asher replied. "I'll run along and charm him so that he forgets to pry." She bestowed a kiss on his cheek; he returned one to her hand, and she floated out of the room with the servants in attendance.

The Duke watched her go with a possessive and pleased expression on his face. "Well?" he asked, when the two of them were alone. "And what do you think of my lady wife?"

"She's—amazing," Tal responded, still feeling a little dazed. He shook his head. "You ought to use her to interrogate people, my Lord Duke; they'd never be able to stand against her. She's astonishing."

"She is, isn't she?" The Duke chuckled. "Well, Rufen, what is it that you want? Since you're my cousin's own special Hound of God, I know at least that it isn't to throw *me* in a gaol. And since I believe you're in charge of finding the fellow who's slaughtering musicians, I assume it has something to do with that?"

"You've got a bird-man doing mapping for you," Tal began, and as the Duke's face darkened a little, he continued hastily, "It's not about *him,* not directly, anyway. I'd like permission to ask him for some help, but it's going to be at the expense of his mapping duties."

The Duke motioned to him to take a seat; the Duke himself remained standing, though, so Tal did the same. The Duke did not pace or otherwise show any signs of impatience; he remained standing, with his arms crossed over his chest and his eyes fixed on Tal's face. It was obvious from Lady Asher's comments that Tal was keeping the Duke from some official function, so he hurried through what he'd planned to say. Quickly he outlined what he had in mind for Visyr; the Duke listened carefully, nodding a little now and again.

"You can see for yourself how he'd be worth a dozen times more than a constable on the ground," Tal concluded. "And I know that you could order him to help us—but this is one of those cases where you can't order cooperation—"

"Hmph." The Duke nodded again. "Wise of you to realize that. He's a Haspur. Willful and principled, and he is already taking less pay than he deserves just out of an ethical desire to help the people of Kingsford." Tal made another mental note of that, and the Duke's nod showed him that it hadn't gone unnoticed. "There is another problem here; I've promised not to hold him past a certain date, and if he spends too much time helping you, I may not get my maps done before that date arrives." He held up his hand to forestall Tal's protests. "On the other hand, I'll be the first to tell you that no map is worth a human life. *I'm* certainly eager for you to bring this monster to justice, and if you can persuade Visyr, then by all means, go ahead with this plan of yours."

He gestured to Tal to follow him into the antechamber; once there, the Duke went over to a small desk took out pen and paper and scrawled a brief note. "Here," he said, handing it to Tal. "If he tells you that he's willing if *I* agree, just hand him this, so he doesn't think he has to wait for an audience with me in order to ask me."

"But I thought he was working only for you, directly—" Tal began.

"He is, but Haspur are—painfully polite. Or at least Visyr is." Arden grimaced. "I detest all this protocol nonsense, but Visyr is so intent on not offending me that if I didn't cut through the etiquette, he'd be wasting far too much time going through channels for ridiculously simple requests. Now, I have to go rescue my lady from that odious little Count; you just follow the page to Visyr's quarters."

In that moment, Tal saw the resemblance between Arden and his cousin, the High Bishop. There was more than a mere family resemblance; there was a resemblance in the way they thought. The biggest difference showed only when Arden was with the Lady Asher; at that point, there was a relaxation and a softening that never showed on High Bishop Ardis's face.

As Tal followed the page to the upper-level area where Visyr's rooms lay, he wondered what Ardis might have been like if she had followed the Duke's path. Would she have been happier, unhappier, or much the same?

He couldn't picture her dressed in an ornate gown like Lady Asher, trailing about the seemingly endless corridors of this palace. He couldn't imagine what she'd do with her time; what *did* women like Lady Asher do all day? Ardis would go mad with boredom in a fortnight.

And he recalled Torney, that former Priest who had given up everything he had and was for the sake of his true love. There were many who would call him a fool for the decision he'd made; would Ardis say the same? Would Ardis have made the same choice he had, given the same set of circumstances?

Tal just couldn't picture it. Ardis was so much a creature of intellect that he couldn't even imagine her making a decision that was so clearly an emotional one.

And yet, if she *had* made such a decision, he couldn't picture her ever looking back on it with regret. No matter what she decided, she would stand by her decision, just as Dasel Torney had, and find a way to make the best of her situation.

But for a moment he envied Dasel Torney and his wife, and not just because of their happiness, but for the ease with which they had made their own choices. He suspected that for them, there had never really been a matter of "choice"; it had all been a foregone conclusion that they would stand by each other. There *were* no questions, only certainties. Perhaps that much certainty was a form of insanity.

He only wished that he could be that certain of anything. It sometimes seemed that he spent all of his life second-guessing himself. Perhaps, if *he* had spent less time in analyzing things, he wouldn't be here; he'd be an ordinary constable with a wife and children.

Certainly the Duke was another one of these happily-wedded fellows, and he certainly would not have made any other choice but the one he had; no man who saw Lady Asher would ever think he could have done otherwise. But of course, he was the Duke of Kingsford, and he could do whatever he chose to and with whoever he wished; if he'd wanted to marry a common street-entertainer, he could have, and the cheers from his people would probably have been just as loud. As she herself had told Tal, Ardis had been blessed with fewer options than her cousin by simple virtue of her gender.

But now—what about now? Doesn't she have more options now than she did when she was subject to the will of her father?

Now the page stopped beside another door—this one with no guards outside it—and tapped on it. It was answered, not by a servant, but by the Haspur himself.

He looked larger here than he had in the station, or even in the Abbey. Perhaps it was because of the way he was holding his wings; arched above his body and held slightly away from it, instead of closed tightly in along his back. The page didn't seem the least intimidated by the bird-man, but then the boy probably saw him several times every day.

"This gentleman wishes to speak with you, Sirra Visyr," the boy said in his high, piping voice. The bird-man turned that huge, sharp beak and looked down it at his visitor. Tal became the focus of a pair of enormous, golden eyes that regarded him out of a face that had little in common, at first impression, with human features. It bore no expression that Tal could recognize, and no real sign of recognition.

That, however, did not mean that the creature didn't remember him. A Haspur, it seemed, could project a flawless raptoral expression of indifference when he so desired.

"This has nothing to do with the incident you were involved with, sir," Tal said hastily, trying not to appear uneasy beneath that direct, raptoral gaze. "Or rather, it does, but not directly. I have the Duke's permission to speak with you, if you would be so kind."

Visyr continued to examine him, unwinking. Finally the beak opened. "Perhaps you had better come in," he said, in his deeply resonant voice. Then, as he held the door open for Tal to enter, he looked back down at the page. "You may go, Joffrey," he said to the boy, his voice a bit softer and kinder. "I'll ring if I need someone."

"Thank you, Sirra," the boy replied, as Tal entered Visyr's suite and the bird-man closed the door behind him.

Well. So the Church has come to me in my own aerie. Interesting. I wonder why? Visyr regarded his visitor with a somewhat skeptical air. He felt much more at his ease here, in the Duke's Palace, than he had back in the city. This was *his* ground, his place, and the Duke had assured him personally that no one was going to be able to coerce Visyr into anything while he was under the Duke's protection.

Visyr busied himself for the moment in lighting his Deliambren lamps so he could see his visitor more clearly. Visyr was not particularly comfortable around open flame; no Haspur was. Feathers were terribly flammable. He would put up with lamps and fires if he had to, but he didn't have to. The Deliambrens had supplied him with his own lamps, and his own heating-unit that sat inside the fireplace. Both were supplied with power from plates that sat on his balcony all day to collect sunlight.

The human sighed as he took a seat at Visyr's direction; the Haspur wasn't all that well-versed in reading human expressions, but he thought the man looked tired. He finished lighting his lamps and turned around; the slump of the man's shoulders told him that if the human wasn't tired, he was certainly dispirited. There was nothing of the interrogator about him; in fact, he hadn't asked a single question yet. So, it was fairly obvious that the human hadn't come here to make further inquiries, so the next likeliest reason was that he had come as a supplicant.

I might as well come straight to the point. I am tired, and I need my sleep. "And what brings you here this cold night, Tal Rufen?" he asked. "Am I correct in assuming that you wish to ask my help?"

The man did not look at all surprised that Visyr had divined the reason he had come, which at least showed that he respected Visyr's intelligence. He nodded. "I wish we had been able to find even a suspect by ordinary means, Sirra Visyr," he replied, and there was no mistaking the weariness in his voice. Visyr read nuances of expression in the voice far more readily than he read them in the body, and this man was frustrated, tired beyond his strength, and near his breaking-point. Visyr wondered just *how* near he was. Did he himself know, or was he simply concentrating so intently on the moments in front of him that he was unaware of his own weaknesses?

This is more difficult than he or anyone else had anticipated. I wonder just what is going on here? Visyr felt sorry for him—and ever since he had seen that dreadful murder, he had spent much of every day thinking about the situation. More than once he had been on the verge of going to the Duke himself to ask permission to help. That he had not was only because his own work was proving to be so all-consuming, and after all it was his commanded task. Flying in the cold was grueling work, especially the kind of flying and hovering he was doing in order to make his maps. A Haspur expended a great deal of energy in this kind of weather just keeping the body warm; feathers were a good insulator, but a Haspur couldn't keep adding more layers of clothing the way a human could as the temperature dropped. For one thing, he wouldn't be able to fly with that kind of burden. He spent most of the daylight hours in the air, a good part of the evening hours bent over the drawing-table, and the rest in eating and sleeping. He seldom saw anyone but the Duke and his own personal helpers, and when he did, it was never for more than a moment. The time he'd spent being interviewed by High Bishop Ardis and this man was very nearly the most he'd spent unconnected with his work since he'd arrived here.

So how could he, in all good conscience, volunteer his services to the law-people? He had his own duty to attend to, a duty he had promised before he ever met these other humans.

And how can you not*?* whispered his conscience. *How can you not do all in your power to help them stop this murderer?*

"The Duke—" he began.

The man coughed diffidently, and handed a piece of paper to him. "The Duke said that I was to tell you that he deems this of equal importance with his maps, and that if the maps are not finished by the date that you must return, then he will do without them."

Oh so? Visyr opened the folded paper and read it, but had really had no doubt that it said just what Tal Rufen claimed. For one thing, it would have been very foolish of him to put false words in the Duke's mouth when they were bound to be found out eventually. For another, Tal Rufen did not strike Visyr as the sort of man who was given to telling falsehoods.

Well, that put the situation in another light, altogether.

"If the Duke places this search of yours in equal importance with his maps, then of course I am at your disposal," he said evenly, not yet disposed to make any display of how he felt in the matter. But the case was that he was relieved, deeply and profoundly relieved. Now his conscience would no longer trouble him when he flew over the city streets and heard the street-musicians playing below him. Now he would no longer be troubled at night with dreams of that poor girl. At last he would be doing something to prevent such a slaughter from happening again.

Tal Rufen was not so shy about showing his feelings in the matter; his face displayed every bit of the relief that Visyr felt.

But Visyr was not expecting the depth and complication of the situation that Tal Rufen proceeded to reveal to him. Magic, the possibility of a renegade Priest, the sheer *number* of the dead so far quite took Visyr's breath away. "I thank you, sir, for myself and for the High Bishop," Tal Rufen finished, his voice telling Visyr that he was grateful out of all proportion for what Visyr had offered.

Visyr waved a talon to prevent him from becoming effusive. "I cannot promise that I will be of any great help to you," he warned. "I am only a single Haspur, not a legion of winged Guardians. I might not be in the right place, next time, and this city is not small." Inside, he quailed at the idea that he was taking on the role of one of the Guardians—that select group of Haspur who were warriors and worked side-by-side with the warrior humans of the land to patrol the borders and deal with trouble-makers. *I am a map-maker, not a warrior!* he thought, now that the words were out of his mouth. *What am I volunteering for?*

"We know that," Tal Rufen replied. "And I didn't intend for you to think that I was asking you to stand guard in the air. No, what we would like you to do is to be a pair of eyes, not a pair of talons!"

"Ah," Visyr said, feeling relieved, and guilty for feeling relief. "What is it that you wish me to look for, and when, and where?"

The heating-unit hummed to itself in the fireplace and blew warm air in a steady stream while the human thought the question over. Visyr spread his wings to absorb the heat. *I have not been properly warm except in bed for months now. I fear I shall not until spring arrives again, and with it some of the better effects of spring—ah, Syri. I miss you.*

"The last is the easiest—we would like for you to spend the most time over the areas where street-musicians are most likely to play," Tal Rufen told him. "You would probably know where those places are better than I would. When—well, obviously you can't fly at night, so it would be during the daylight hours. But *what* you are to look for—that's the problem." He shrugged. "We think that the murderer is controlling the people who are actually committing the murders, as I *think* I told you. We believe that he is using magic to do this, but what kind, we don't know. All that we do know is that in order to be able to see what his tools are doing and what is happening to them, every kind of magic or spell that the Justiciar-Mages know of dictates that he has to be somewhere that he can actually, physically see them. Our best guess is that this means he's going to be up above the street, somewhere."

"As in—on a rooftop?" Visyr hazarded. *That would be easy enough to manage to spot; there are not too many folk scrambling about on their roofs in the dead of winter.*

"Possibly; we just don't know anything for certain," Tal Rufen admitted. "I wish we did, fervently, but we don't. All I can say is, we want you to look for anything unusual."

"Unusual? On the rooftops?" Visyr chuckled dryly. "Well, at least you ask this of me in the winter; it will be much easier to determine what is unusual when there are not people coming out to frolic by twos where they think they will not be seen, or to sit where they can see sun and sky and open air." He chuckled again, recalling some of the gyrations that humans had been up to during the milder months.

"I have seen many things on the rooftops of the Duke's city, and a goodly share of them could be considered 'unusual,' Tal Rufen."

"Yes, well, I have seen more than you in the streets of cities, Sirra Visyr," Tal Rufen replied with a laugh as dry as Visyr's. "I think I can guess." He proved that, with a rather mordantly and morbidly humorous anecdote that ended with the line, "Lady, I think your sign just fell down."

Perhaps a gentler creature than Visyr might not have found it amusing, but he did, and he felt a little more kinship with Tal Rufen in that moment. Haspur could be more bawdy, in their way, than any non-Haspur would suspect. "Well, and what if I don't find anything?" he asked.

"If the worst should happen, and this madman kills before either of us catch him, I will send word to you if you have not already reported to me." The human looked pained. "Then you may go back to your maps for about a week or so before you need begin watching again. He's obviously planning these killings carefully, and while he's planning them, he probably won't be doing anything where you can see it."

Visyr nodded soberly. "I understand." He thought for a moment, and volunteered something else. "Before you go, let me tell you what I can that I have already observed."

He was pleased to see that the human had come prepared with a notebook and a scriber. He spent the better part of an hour relating as many of the incidents that he had witnessed that could be considered "unusual" that he could recall—and since he was a Haspur and his memory was exceptional, there were a great many of them. Most of them struck him as odd largely because he wasn't familiar with the humans of this land—and some made Tal Rufen laugh out loud when he related them. He was pleased enough to hear the human laugh, for each time it occurred, the man lost some of his tension and came a bit farther away from the edge of breaking. And every time Visyr did describe such an incident, the human very courteously explained *why* it had made him laugh, which gave Visyr a little more insight into the ways and habits of the odd people who dwelled here.

Finally, when he had come to the end of his tales, something else occurred to him. He sat for a moment, clicking his beak as he thought about it. Was *that* "unusual" enough for the human? On the surface, it wasn't, but—

I shall err on the side of too much information, he decided.

"There is one final thing, Church Constable," he said at last. "In the past few weeks I have seen a very strange new bird in this city. It is as large as I am, quite remarkably ugly, and black—and I have never seen more than the one. It is a bird of no species that I know, and quite frankly, it should not be able to fly.''

"Neither should a bee, or a Blue Parrot," Tal Rufen observed. "But go on, please.''

Visyr roused his feathers with a shake, and yawned. "I have seen it watching what goes on below it for hours. And even when there was noise and activity that frightened away every other bird, it remained. It seems to place itself where it cannot easily be seen from below— but so do many birds. I *did* see it watching the square where the murder occurred at the time of the murder, but it didn't do anything, and I didn't see it again that day or the next. In fact, I haven't seen it for several days now." He shrugged. "That is all I can tell you. I have never seen it do anything other than watch, but it could be watching for prey, for opportunities to steal human food, or just because it is curious. There are strange species crossing borders all the time, and for flyers it is doubly easy. It could simply be migrating lazily.''

"Well, you've told me quite a bit," Rufen replied, making a few more notes, then closing the notebook and stowing it in a capacious pocket inside his cloak. "Believe me, it is appreciated.''

"And I am glad to help you, Tal Rufen. Truly I am. But—'' He yawned again, hugely, feeling exhaustion of his own overtake him. The human gazed at him, apparently slightly astonished at the width and depth of a Haspur gape. "But I had just finished eating, and flying in the cold takes much out of one. I was just going to sleep.''

The human glanced over at the Haspur's unusual bed and blushed a bit. "Then I will not keep you awake a moment longer," Tal murmured, and echoed Visyr's yawn, which set Visyr off again with another. "Hunting scraps of information is almost as tiring, I promise you, and I would like to see my own bed." He extended his hand, and Visyr took it, gingerly, keeping his talons from scratching the delicate human skin. "Thank you again. Would it be too much to ask you to send a report to the Abbey once a day?''

"I shall do better than that; I shall fly one there myself at day's end," Visyr promised him. "Tell your guard at the gate that I will drop it to him, tied in ribbons of Duke Arden's colors, unless I have something I believe you must hear in person. Will that do?''

"It will more than *do*, and again, I thank you." Now the human stood up, and Visyr did likewise, towering over him. "I told Captain Fenris and the Duke that you would be worth any twenty constables, and I don't believe I was exaggerating. I will be looking forward to seeing your reports.''

"And I will be pleased to make them." Visyr held open the door, and the human went out into the hallway. "Travel safely to the Abbey, Tal Rufen," he finished, by way of a pleasant farewell.

"And you fly safely in the morning," the other replied, and gave a brief wave of his hand before turning and walking towards the staircase down.

Visyr closed the door behind him and retired to his sleeping room and his comfortable couch. It was going to be a cold night tonight, and he was very glad for his down comforter to keep him warm. He disliked having a fire in the same room with him as he slept, and even his Deliambren heater had the potential to be hazardous.

He extinguished his lights, wrapped himself up in his coverings, and settled himself over his bed for sleep. He had not lied when he told the human that he was about to retire for the night; the fact was that he had barely been able to keep his eyes open when the page knocked on his door.

But sleep was now a reluctant quarry, for Visyr had plenty of leisure to think about what the human had said and ponder the possible consequences of what he had agreed to.

If the killer *was* using magic, did it not follow that he could use that magic against Visyr if he suspected he had been seen? The Haspur themselves used very little magic, with but a few exceptions, but the humans who shared their mountain kingdom with them often did make use of that power. The idea that he might be struck out of the sky by a bolt of lightning was not one likely to summon sleep; the remaining pieces of a lightning-struck Haspur could be very small indeed.

On the other hand—no one had struck him down out of the sky yet, and the killer had probably seen him a dozen times by now. As long as he didn't change his own patterns, he ought to be safe enough.

As if I haven't already changed my patterns by chasing that first killer—or "tool," rather, since that is what Tal Rufen called him.

Never mind. In that, he was no different from a dozen other witnesses who gave chase. The mage could hardly target everyone! And perhaps, since he was so visible in the sky, a secretive mage might prefer *not* to strike at him.

With that comforting realization, sleep finally came, and Visyr drifted upwards on its dark wings.

Tal Rufen left the palace, reclaiming his horse on the way out, and allowed the horse to pick its own way back through the darkened and snow-covered city streets. As always, knowing that it would be going back to its own stall and a good meal, the horse walked briskly along the shortest path.

For once, he was glad of the time that the trip would take, even by the shortest route. Something had occurred to him, back at the palace, and he wanted to face his realization down before he got inside the Abbey walls again. It filled his mind so thoroughly that he thought on it rather than reviewing his talk with the Haspur, as he normally would have.

He was no longer appropriately dispassionate about his position. Over the course of this investigation, he had become increasingly attracted to the High Bishop, and not just intellectually, either. The fact that he had compared her to Lady Asher told him that he wasn't just interested in her mind or her friendship.

And that, frankly, was a dangerous situation.

It wasn't something that could have come up in the course of his former job. There were no such things as female constables, nor was there any possibility that a woman might assume the position of Captain. He was perfectly free to admire any female that came within his purview, and perfectly free to do more than admire them if the situation was appropriate. When he'd sought an audience with the High Bishop of Kingsford, it had never occurred to him that said official might be a woman. Then, when he'd discovered her sex, it hadn't occurred to him that in working closely with an attractive lady of a similar age, he might get himself into difficulties.

But then, it obviously hadn't occurred to her, either. He didn't think he was misreading the occasional sidelong glances, or the way her gaze lingered when she thought he wasn't aware of it. Just at the moment, things were still at the stage of speculation, at least on her part, but if there hadn't been admiration there wouldn't be anything to speculate about.

He was troubled by this, more troubled than he had been by any emotional situation in his life.

I'm not particularly devout, but then, few constables are. It was difficult to be devout in the face of some of the blatant corruption within the Church that constables uncovered from time to time. The Church might successfully engineer ways to hide such scandals from the eyes of the public, but the constables always knew the truth. Still, he had always considered himself to be an upright man, a man of morals and integrity if nothing else.

So how could he even begin to permit himself to be attracted by a Priest? And, at that, a co-worker, a peer, and his commander?

Yet she was the ideal companion for him in so many ways.

We share common interests and goals, she is intelligent and clever, and our skills are perfect complements. Never once had he encountered a woman with even half the qualities he admired in Ardis. He frankly doubted that he ever would again.

But she is a Priest, vowed to both chastity and celibacy, and there is no getting around that.

He tried not to squirm in his saddle, but this entire train of thought was making him dreadfully uncomfortable, as if he had swallowed something too large and it was stuck halfway down his throat. This was a new thing for him; he was anything but young, and he had thought with some complacency that he was well seasoned and past the age when he might be enflamed by a momentary passion or infatuation.

So much for complacency. I ought to know by now that it's a dangerous feeling to harbor.

He certainly had never subscribed to the ridiculous notion that people are destined to find a soul-mate. *Soul-mates! What nonsense! Searching for the perfect soul-mate is never going to get you anything but heartache at best. At worst, you find yourself all alone in your declining years, having turned down people who loved you just because they weren't perfect.*

But what did Dasel Torney have in his wife *but* a soul-mate?

And just how many perfect matings are there likely to be in the world? Just because I have seen one, that makes it all the less likely that I'm likely to find one myself!

But in seeing Torney with his wife, he had felt an envy he had never expected to experience. He had never even considered marriage in the past; his career simply wouldn't allow it. And yet now—he wondered if the career would have been worth sacrificing, under the right circumstances.

So, what exactly did he intend to do about the situation? As complex as it already was, adding in *this* would only make it worse all the way around.

My first option is to do nothing, of course, he told himself, as the horse picked his way gingerly across icy cobbles. *If I don't make any overtures, she isn't going to know how I feel. Then, if I'm misreading all this, things will be fine. Certainly no one has ever died of an unrequited passion—it's usually the ones that* are *requited that get people in trouble.*

It wouldn't be a comfortable situation for him, but it was certainly better than having a superior officer who couldn't stand him.

Ah, but what if she makes overtures? What then? He already knew what happened to priests who became involved in an affair. *I'm not going to put a pretty name to it; what we'd be involved in would be a clandestine affair, in violation of her vows.* The horse skidded and scrambled for a foothold in an odd counterpoint to his thoughts. *It would be bad if we were caught, and almost as bad if we weren't. When the passion blew out, we would be angry and bitter with each other. It would cost both of us a great deal in the way of self-respect if nothing else.*

Unless this was all something more than simple passion. Would he be willing to give up everything for the sake of love, as Dasel Torney had? Would she?

But there was one factor overriding every other concern right now, and that was the simple fact that none of them had any right to consider *anything* other than the case at hand. It was too important; literally a life-and-death situation. If he were to waste time and resources in pursuing an emotional goal, he would never be able to look at himself in the mirror again.

He came to that conclusion as the horse left the city and took to the road leading to the bridge at a brisk trot. With the Abbey looming up at the other end of the span, he felt a certain comfort in that thought. This job came first; anything else would have to wait until it was concluded, and in a way it was a relief to have to put off a decision. Although it was the last thing he wanted, it was possible that they would not be able to bring a killer to justice for months or even years. Perhaps, when this was over, there would no longer be a decision to make.

There is nothing that Rand hates worse than being told "no," Orm thought cynically. *What is it about this man that he has never learned how to accept anything other than his way?* "If you really want a musician of any kind this time, it's going to be difficult," Orm told his employer as they sat across the table from one another in Orm's apartment. The map of the section Orm thought most promising was spread out between them. "They've gotten wary here in Kingsford a great deal sooner than I would have thought. None of them are going out at night at all, and a great many of the lone women of the Free Bards have left the city altogether."

Rand frowned, and Orm noticed that he was no longer as handsome as he had been. His features had coarsened, his forehead seemed lower, and his resemblance to the Black Bird was more pronounced. "One would think that they had gotten word from some of the other places we've been," he said, his tone accusing.

Interesting. Does he think I *warned them? If that is the case, he may be losing intelligence along with his looks each time he transforms.* Orm held back a smirk. "Well, I did point out to you that the Duke has an interest in these Free Bards. Evidently, he's given orders that his constables are to warn street-musicians here. They might not have believed the constables at first, but they certainly do after your rather spectacular killing on the riverfront."

Rand didn't snarl, but Orm got the impression that he would have liked to. He glowered instead, and it was clear that he would really have preferred to find someone to punish for these checks to his plan. "Damn the Duke! Can't the Bardic Guild hold him in check?"

"Not after the Great Fire they can't," Orm replied, feeling rather smug. "Their credit is not very high with anyone in Kingsford, not when there are still persistent rumors that they had a part in trying to kill Duke Arden and in starting the Fire. Hadn't you noticed that you never see a Guild Bard on the street? When they have to travel, they do so in closed carriages, and not for warmth or ostentation. If they show their faces in *some* parts of the city, they're likely to get pelted with refuse." He warmed to his subject, since it was so obviously annoying Rand. "And meanwhile, since the Free Bards were the ones who actually foiled the plot, their credit is at an all-time high. Now if it was Guild Bards you wanted to murder, I'd have no shortage of them for you, and very few would mourn their passing."

Perversely, Orm found that he enjoyed annoying Rand. Perhaps it was the man's superior manner; perhaps it was just that he tried so hard to establish control over everything he came into contact with. Orm had never cared for being "under control," and any attempt to put him there only ended in resentment. So often in "conferences" like this one, the more annoyed Rand became, the more Orm's own humor improved.

Right now Rand was frowning so fiercely that his eyebrows formed a solid bar across his forehead. He looked curiously primitive, as if he might slam a club or gnawed thigh-bone down on the table at any moment.

"There are no women in the Guild," Rand replied sullenly, stating the obvious. "If you haven't got any Free Bards, what *do* you have for me?"

"Oh, the usual," Orm told him. That made Rand look blacker than before, if possible, for "the usual" was a mix of whores and street-entertainers, and such victims rarely yielded the amount of energy that kept Rand in his proper form for as long as he wished.

Then again, nothing ever kept Rand in his proper form for as long as he wished, so what was the difference?

Instead of answering that frown, Orm ignored it, bending over the map. "There's a good little prospect who lives here," he said, indicating a building with the feather-end of his quill-pen. "She's the closest thing to a musician that we're likely to get for now. Makes her living as half of a pickpocket team; she chants bawdy ballads to collect a crowd while he picks the pockets, he juggles objects thrown to him by the crowd while she picks pockets. It wouldn't be at all difficult to get your knife into his hands, and it could be a fairly plain one. He's often tossed knives to juggle, and if no one claimed this one at the end of his turn, he wouldn't go looking for the owner."

Rand nodded, still frowning, but listening now. "What else?" he asked.

"Unlicensed whore living here—" He touched another spot. "Calls herself a courtesan on the strength of reading poetry to her clients, and the fact that she doesn't charge a set fee. Of course, if you don't pay her what she thinks she's worth, you'll find your pockets lighter after you're home again. She's trained her brat to lift purses while the client's busy. We've done her type before." He tapped another spot on the map. "Now, if you don't mind going for a target who works under a roof, you might want this one. Girl here who thinks she's a musician; ran away from home on the strength of it. Can't make a copper on the street, so she's a tavern-wench until somebody notices what a genius she is." Orm chuckled heartlessly, for the girl was unattractive, sullen, and rebellious, and was probably going to get herself fired before too long. "She'd be all right if she just played other people's songs. But she's a genius, so she's got to do her own. Problem is, she's got two tunes, no voice, and a knack for lyrics that insult her audience. She's as easy as the pickpocket."

Now Rand's face cleared a little. "We'll look at her and the pickpocket, and I suspect we'll take both of them. Probably the pickpocket first, unless you find an opportunity to get the tavern-wench. I don't like working under a roof, but—"

Orm shrugged. "Suit yourself; unless the constables get her, the pickpocket is always there for the taking. I'll see if the other girl has a boyfriend or something; if she does, then we have a solid prospect for your knife-holder."

Orm watched Rand's brows furrow as he thought the situation over. "Does the girl lodge in the tavern?" he asked.

Orm shook his head. "I don't think so; the other girls have said something about her being 'too good' to sleep on the floor with them when the tavern closes. And once in a while she'll try a street-corner. For that matter, maybe there's a way to lure her somewhere of your choosing by making her think someone's taken an interest in her as a singer."

And those should be obvious solutions, Orm thought with disgust. *He ought to be able to reason that out for himself.* Orm had his own reasons for steering the selection towards Shensi, the tavern-wench. *He* would much rather study a potential target indoors.

"All right," Rand said at last. "Get me more on this tavern-girl. Maybe it wouldn't be such a bad thing to try for her."

Rand got up from the table without another word, and stalked off to the front door. A moment later, Orm heard his footsteps on the staircase.

"Well, thank you for the audience, Your Majesty," he muttered, resentfully. Rand must be about to turn bird again; he was always unreasonable and rude, but he got worse just before he was about to turn.

With nothing better to do, Orm rose, shrugged on a coat, and went out into the dusk. Other folk scurried by, probably in a hurry to get home before full dark. Far down the street, Orm saw warm beads of light blossoming, as if someone was lighting up a string of pearls. The public lamplighters were out; an advantage to living in this neighborhood. Where Orm was going, there were no public lamps, which made the going occasionally hazardous, and made easy work for footpads. Not that Orm had to worry about footpads; when he entered areas with no lanterns, he moved as if he was one of the footpads himself. In lean times, it often amused him to fell one of *them* after they had taken a target, and help himself to their ill-gotten gains. It made him think of an old illustration he had once seen, of a big fish, about to swallow a small fish, who was in turn about to be swallowed by a bigger fish.

It was snowing again, which was going to keep some people home tonight. Thinning the crowd in a tavern wasn't a bad thing; it would enable Orm to see who the regulars were. Even if one of them had nothing whatsoever to do with the girl except order food and drink, the fact that he was a regular would bring him into contact with her on a regular basis. With the knife in his hands, perhaps he could be forced to wait for her outside the tavern door. Then, a note might lure her outside. You never knew.

For once, this wasn't the sort of tavern that Orm avoided at all costs—the kind where you risked poisoning if you ate or drank anything. One of his other prospects—one he hadn't bothered to mention—worked at one of *those,* and Orm would really rather not have had to go in there. Mostly drovers and butchers ate at the Golden Sheaf; it was near enough to the stockyards to get a fairly steady stream of customers.

Orm didn't look like either, but he could pass for an animal broker, and that would do. He knew the right language, and he kept rough track of what was coming into the stockyards. Depending on who he had to talk to, he could either have already sold "his" beasts, or be looking for a buyer.

The windows were alight, but there didn't seem to be a lot of people coming and going; Orm pushed the doors open and let them fall closed behind him. The place smelled of wet wool, mutton stew, and beer, with a faint undertone of manure. The men tried to clean their boots before they came in here, but it just wasn't possible to get all of the smell out.

The ceiling here was unusually high for a place that did not have a set of rooms on an upper floor. This might once have been a tavern of that sort, with a staircase up to a balcony, and six or eight rooms where the customer could take one of the serving girls. That sort of establishment had been outlawed on the recommendation of the Whore's Guild when Arden began the rebuilding of the city. The licensed whores didn't like such places; there was no way to control who worked "upstairs" and who didn't. A girl could *claim* she was only a serving wench, and actually be taking on customers. There was no sign of such a staircase or such rooms, but they could have been closed off or given back to the building next door, which *was* a Licensed House now.

Beneath the light of a half dozen lanterns hanging on chains from the ceiling, the Golden Sheaf was a pretty ordinary place. The floor, walls, and ceiling were all of dark wood, aged to that color by a great deal of greasy smoke. The tables had been polished only by years and use, and the benches beneath them were of the same dark color as the walls and floor. At the back of the room was a hatch where the wenches picked up food and drink; pitchers of beer stood ready on a table beside the hatch for quick refills. There were two fireplaces, one on the wall to the right, and one on the wall to the left; after working all day in the stockyards, drovers and butchers were always cold, and a warm fire would keep them here and drinking even though there was no entertainment.

Orm looked around at the tables and saw that the place was about half empty; he chose a seat in a corner, though not in his target's section, and waited for one of the other wenches to serve him.

You didn't get any choice in a place like this; mutton stew, bread, and beer was what was on the menu, and that was what you got. The girl brought him a bowl, plate, and mug without his asking, and held out her hand for the fee of two coppers. He dropped it in her hand and she went away. There was a minimum of interaction with the customers here, and that apparently was the way that Shensi liked things.

Shensi was the name of his target; Orm had already learned by listening to her and to the other wenches that she was the child of a pair of common shopkeepers who probably had no idea where she was now. Skeletally thin, pale as a ghost, with black hair the texture of straw, a nose like a ship's prow, owl-like eyes, and a grating, nasal voice, she had run away from home when they refused to allow her to join the Free Bards. Winding up in Kingsford, she found that no one was going to give her food or lodging, no one really wanted to hear her music, and she had the choice of working or starving. She chose the former, but she was making as bad a business of it as she could. If it had not been that labor was scarce in Kingsford—especially menial labor like tending tables in a tavern—Shensi would not have had this position for more than a week.

As it was, the tavern-keeper put up with her sullen disposition and her acerbic comments to the customers, because the customers themselves, who were mostly brutes a bare step above the cattle and sheep they drove to market or slaughtered, hadn't the least idea what she meant by the things that she said to them. She wasn't pretty enough or friendly enough for any of them to want to bed her, but as long as she kept their plates and mugs full, they didn't particularly care what she said or did around them.

What Orm hadn't bothered to tell Rand was that Shensi was one of a small band of malcontents intriguing to overthrow Duke Arden. The constables knew all about them, of course, and left them alone because they were so totally ineffectual. Orm had taken the relatively bold step of reporting them to the constables just to see what they would say, and the results had been laughable. According to the constabulary records, they spent all their time arguing about the structure of their group and not a great deal in anything else. They had no fixed addresses, because the members of the group, disdaining such plebeian pursuits as employment, usually squatted in the ruins of buildings until they were evicted, lived with relatives, or left their lodgings when the rent came due. Shensi wrote what *she* thought were stirring songs about Arden's tyranny; what she didn't know was that most people who heard them thought they were comic-songs, and bad ones at that.

Orm hadn't bothered to tell Rand about this, because he was afraid that Rand would consider it too dangerous to target a member of a rebellious political group. Not that anyone was going to miss Shensi, or even consider her a martyr to the cause—her death wouldn't even make the constables heave a sigh of relief, except for those few who were music-lovers. But it was a possibility that Orm could find the knife-wielder in that group, and he was hoping to see some of them here tonight.

As he ate his tasteless stew and equally tasteless bread, he looked over the occupants of Shensi's tables.

Two were drovers, who shoveled in their food with stolid obliviousness to their surroundings. There was a butcher at a second table; evidently he had been working past his normal quitting time, for he hadn't even bothered to remove his leather apron before coming here to eat. But at the third table was a group of four, clearly some of Shensi's coconspirators.

There were three men and a woman. All four wore shabby, ill-fitting black clothing, all four had identically sullen, furtive expressions, all four sported the pale complexions of people who seldom came out during daylight hours. They huddled over their food and spoke in hushed voices, casting suspicious glances at the drovers and the butcher. The former ignored them with indifference, the latter with amusement.

They might have resembled footpads, except that they were armed with ostentatious knives instead of sensible saps and cudgels, and they all wore great clumping boots instead of soft, waterproof shoes.

From time to time, Shensi came over on the pretext of renewing their drinks, but she spent longer than she needed to, and she whispered to them while she filled mugs. Orm also noted that she didn't take any money from them; evidently they were meeting here more for the free beer than because it was a good place to meet.

He watched them closely, although they had no idea he was doing so. Any of them would make a good tool, even the woman, who watched Shensi with the worshipful eyes of a puppy. In fact, that would be a very amusing combination, now that Orm came to think about it. He wondered how Rand would react to that idea.

Probably poorly, he decided. *He has to identify to some extent with his tool, and the last thing he would want to identify with is a woman. Or maybe by now for him the term is "sow."*

When his plate was empty, he signaled to his wench that he wanted a refill; the portions here weren't particularly generous, and it wasn't difficult to find room for another round. As he finished that second helping, the conspirators at the table got ready to leave; he left what remained and followed them out into the darkness.

The snowfall had eased to mere flurries, but the snow still covering the street reflected all the available light and made it quite easy to follow the group. They stood out against the white snow quite remarkably well. He didn't stay close enough to them to hear what they were talking about; what he wanted to know was where they lived, not what they were saying. They were completely oblivious to the fact that he was trailing them, in spite of the fact that he was not being particularly subtle about it. His presence actually protected them, ironically enough; he saw more than one footpad assess them and give them up as not being worth the trouble when he came into view.

Interestingly enough, they led him to a cheap storefront which displayed a few badly-printed books in its window. This was evidently their headquarters and their sole source of income—unless more of them had finally stooped to take on jobs, as Shensi did. This must be where she slept at night. He wondered which of them she shared her bed with—or was it with all of them in turn? That would have suited the stated philosophy of the group, as Orm understood it—share and share alike in everything, with everyone equal to everyone else, and nothing held in private, not even personal secrets.

Well, that was all the information he needed. He turned and headed back to his own cozy dwelling, with a rudimentary plan already in mind. He could go into the store by day and buy one of their silly books. He could leave the dagger behind, dropping it on the floor in a corner where it probably wouldn't be noticed for a while. When it was, obviously *someone* would pick it up and put it on; he'd watch them to see which it was, then inform Rand. Rand could do the rest, forcing the tool to wait outside the storefront for Shensi.

Easy, simple, neat. Everyone would assume it was a lovers' quarrel, or had something to do with the power-struggle within the group. Or both. There would be nothing to connect *this* killing to the others.

From here, it was no great distance to the stockyards, which stood beside the river. The tool could go right down the blood-sluice into the river itself. He might even get eaten by the fish that lived there, which fed on minnows that fed on the tiny creatures that in turn fed on the blood.

It was as nearly perfect a plan as possible, which was probably why Rand wouldn't like it. He hadn't thought of it himself.

So now came Orm's second-hardest job; convincing Rand that he *had* thought of it.

But that could wait for tomorrow. Tonight, he intended to enjoy himself, with Rand's money, in places that Rand could never go. And just possibly, he would see if there was anyone out there who might be willing to pay for information about the mysterious killer of musicians. Who knew? The price might be high enough to risk betrayal. There was, after all, a price for anything and anyone, if only you could find out what it was. Especially in cities.

Chapter Twelve

Shensi was going to be an ideal kill, so far as Orm was concerned; as he had it laid out, everything would be accomplished quietly, with an absolute minimum of fuss.

The day of the kill, Orm went into the shabby little bookstore as he had planned and purchased a book—the only title for sale, which might account for the scarcity of customers—explaining the philosophy and goals of Shensi's group. Orm wondered where they got the things printed, and how they managed to afford the printing costs. But the poor quality of the work made him think that they might be printing the things up themselves in the back; certainly the binding was incredibly crude, reminiscent of the little chapbooks children made up to draw in or to use as journals. The sullen boy who sold him the book sneered at him as he made incorrect change; Orm didn't challenge him on the sneer or on being shortchanged, but dropped the dagger in a corner as he had intended. He lurked about in a doorway, waiting to see who would pick the blade up. It pleased him no end to see that same dark-haired, lanky boy leave the place wearing it not more than a quarter hour after Orm had left the shop.

By now, of course, Rand was in the form of the Black Bird, and was lurking up among the chimneys. Except for Orm and the boy, there was no one else on the street. When the boy's back was turned, Orm gave Rand the signal to tell him that the boy was wearing the dagger, and began looking for a place to spend the day—and night, if need be.

He found a place, somewhat to his surprise, directly across the street from the bookshop. It was some indication of the poverty of this group that they were all crowded into a single room at the back of the shop when the building across from them had plenty of real living-spaces.

There were several sparsely-furnished rooms to let by the week; he hired one for a week that had a window overlooking the street and moved in immediately. The proprietor was incurious; evidently this was a place where transients moved in before moving on. Then again, there wasn't much that could be damaged in Orm's room, and nothing that could be stolen, so perhaps the proprietor's indifference didn't matter. The bed was a shelf bolted to the wall and furnished with a straw mattress, the chair was too large to fit through the narrow door-way or the window, the wardrobe was also bolted to the wall. The tiny stove, meant for heating and cooking, was of cast-iron, and burned coal provided in a pile beside it. This was supposedly a week's worth of fuel; the stone-faced proprietor informed Orm that if he burned it all, he'd have to provide more at his own expense. Probably the owner didn't care what happened here as long as the resulting stains could be scrubbed off or painted over.

The room was icy, and Orm started a fire as soon as the landlord left. The fuel would barely last the night, by his current standards, but he could remember when it had been otherwise in his life. *And I can remember when this would have been a haven of luxury.*

As soon as the sun set, Orm opened the window, and the Black Bird flapped clumsily down to the sill.

"I'll be just above," Rand croaked, then pushed off from the sill and flapped up to perch somewhere on the roof. Orm already knew the plan; Rand would have the boy waiting when Shensi appeared just after midnight. There probably wouldn't be any witnesses, since the group couldn't afford candles or much in the way of fuel, and generally went to bed right after returning from their free meal at the tavern. It would be a long wait, but Orm was prepared for it; he amused himself with a little pocket-puzzle he'd purchased from a street-vendor. That, and keeping the stove stoked and the ashes shaken out kept him busy. These tiny stoves needed a lot of tending, but he managed to get the room tolerably warm.

Night fell, the group across the street went out by fours and returned the same way, until everyone had been fed at the expense of Shensi's employers. When the last one returned, the dim light visible through the shop window went out. The midnight bell struck in a nearby Chapel, and Rand's tool walked stiffly out of the front door of the shop. A few moments later, Shensi appeared at the end of the street, walking towards the shop with a careless swagger.

A few moments after that, it was over. In a way, Orm was disap-pointed; he had thought that the girl, after all her posturing, would have at least sensed that she was in danger soon enough to put up a struggle. But Rand wasn't taking any chances; he waited for the girl to pass his tool, then, with a single blow to the back, dispatched her. Shensi lay face-down in the street, with a spreading puddle of blood staining the snow, the knife-hilt protruding from the middle of her back. The tool moved down the street in a jerky, uncoordinated fashion that suggested that Rand was having difficulty controlling him, but he was headed in the direction of the nearest slaughterhouse. Orm trotted silently down the stairs and out the front door; he plucked the knife out of Shensi's back and kept going in the opposite direction, keeping the knife well away from him to avoid getting any blood on his clothing. Not that he intended to do anything other than burn this outfit as soon as he got home. Blood could be traced, and Orm never left anything to chance.

He stopped just long enough to clean the blade in a stream of water from the public pump at the corner, and went on. He took care to go by way of major streets so that his tracks were muddled in the midst of hundreds of others. By the time he reached home again, Rand was already waiting for him in the foyer shared by their apartments, in human form again.

The light from the entry-way lamp cast a sickly yellow glow over his features; the mage held out his hand wordlessly, and just as silently, Orm dropped the dagger into it. Rand turned on his heel and climbed the stairs, and Orm knew by his silence and glower that the kill had not given him the power that he had hoped for. His current tenure as a human would be short-lived.

Well, that was too bad, and it was hardly Orm's fault. At least they had another couple of easy prospects with the pickpockets; long before Rand transformed again, they'd have the next kill set up.

But the next day, when he went out to check on the pickpocket pair, he got some bad news. While he and Rand had been setting up Shensi, the pickpockets had been caught in the act by a private bodyguard and taken off to gaol. And on looking into the third prospect, he learned that one of her clients had set her up as his private mistress, which was evidently the goal she'd had in mind all along. She was no longer to be found in her old neighborhood, and even if he could find her again, she would no longer be accessible to strangers. It would take longer to find her and her patron than it would to locate a new set of targets—and even if he did find them, they were now dangerous to use. If a man of wealth suddenly slew his mistress and killed himself, *someone* would investigate. They'd gotten off lucky with the young fop; they couldn't count on that kind of luck a second time.

He had hardly anticipated *this*!

Is it Rand's luck that's gone bad, he wondered, as he returned home, *or mine?*

Whichever it was, Rand took the news badly, and Orm found himself the victim of a torrent of verbal abuse as well as physical intimidation that strained even his patience.

As Rand heaped abuses on him, and towered over him, brandishing his fists and stopping just short of actually landing a blow, Orm seethed. *If this goes on much longer,* he thought, his stomach a hot knot of resentment and suppressed anger, *I am walking out of here and going straight to the constables.*

From there, he could go to the room he'd hired, change his appearance, collect the money he had hidden elsewhere, and escape the city. By the time they collected Rand, Orm would be long gone, and Rand could implicate him as an accessory as much as he liked. Another kingdom, another identity, and it would be business as usual.

But Rand stopped just short of that point, and suddenly sat down in his chair.

"You'll have to find someone else," he said stiffly. "Your choices haven't been good lately; I think it's time you started obeying my orders. While I was—flying—I did some of my own scouting." He stabbed a finger down stiffly at the map on his desk, and an area circled in red. "You will go look there," he ordered. "There must be a dozen prospects, or more, available there. The quality is much higher."

Orm moved warily towards the desk and looked down at the map. He saw to his dismay that the area Rand wanted him to investigate was not one *he* would have chosen. This was a quarter of the city that contained mostly middle-class shops and businesses, along with a few genteel boardinghouses and inns, and working there was going to be very difficult. Such places had a regular set of customers; people knew each other by name. There were few transients, and people asked a lot of questions. Strangers there would be obvious.

But he also knew better than to argue with Rand in this mood. He simply nodded subserviently and started to leave.

But Rand stopped him.

"Don't think you can go to the constables, Orm," he said as silkily as his voice would let him. "You're as much a part of this as I am. I've taken steps to ensure that they'll know this, even if I'm dead, and I've left them the means to find you even if you leave the city in disguise. Until I have the ability to stay human, the only way you leave my employ is dead."

Orm didn't answer, although his heart froze. He just continued his path towards the door as if he hadn't heard what Rand had said. There was no point in protesting that he hadn't even thought of going to the constables; Rand wouldn't believe a protest. But that certainly put a damper on his notions of escape.

He walked down the stairs and out of the building altogether, wondering just what it was that Rand had done. If it was something magical, there wasn't a great deal that *he* could do to counteract it—but if it was something merely physical, such as a journal or letter, or a set of notes, he might be able to find such an object and destroy it. *If* it wasn't guarded or protected, that is.

But in the meanwhile, he was as tied to Rand as a slave was to a master. The one thing that he was sure of was that he didn't dare abandon Rand; even if the item Rand referred to was a physical one and he destroyed it, the mage would have to be in Church custody or dead before he would feel safe. There were too many things that Rand could do magically to find him, no matter where he tried to hide.

With no definite destination in mind, Orm wandered until he found a small eating-house, half-empty at this hour, with tables in quiet corners. He went in, gave the serving-girl his order, and took his place at a one-person table in an odd little nook. The owner was evidently a frugal soul, for there wasn't a candle or a lantern lit in the entire place; what daylight came in was filtered and dim, which precisely suited Orm's current mood.

Well, now what do I do? he wondered. This was not the first time he'd been caught off-guard since going to work for Rand, but from his point of view, it was the most unpleasant.

The first time he'd had plans go awry, it had been when the wrong person had gotten one of the daggers; a pickpocket had taken it from the intended target. That hadn't worked out too badly, though—the pickpocket had a woman who'd been singing to herself at the time, and Rand had gotten a decent kill out of the situation. The second time, though, *had* been a disaster from start to finish; the dagger had been intended for a pawnbroker, but had been picked up by the pawnbroker's apprentice, a scrawny, undersized preadolescent who wasn't strong enough to threaten anything, with or without a knife. The magic that caused a tool to pick up the dagger had been a little too strong; once the boy had it, he wouldn't let the blade out of his possession. In the end, Rand just gave up, and forced the boy to jump into the river and drown himself.

That kill had been most unsatisfactory on all accounts, but it had been early enough in their partnership that Rand had not gone off on a tirade. He'd been human for less than a day, and he'd been so anxious to get a real kill in that he hadn't done anything but urge Orm out to find a second target as quickly as possible.

Every time he transforms, he's a little more brutish, and not just in looks. He never was a personable fellow, but he could *be charming enough when he exerted himself. He doesn't bother to try anymore. Is this what he really was, all along? It could be.*

Orm's meat pie and tea arrived, and he began to eat in an absent-minded fashion. No one bothered him here; even the serving-girl left him alone, which suited his mood perfectly.

I should have seen this coming, he realized. *Not just that Rand was taking steps to make sure that I couldn't escape him, but that he was going to make our work dangerous.* Since arriving in Kingsford, Rand had been steadily working his way up the social ladder in regard to his victims; he had not been pleased with Shensi, and only the fact that she *was* a musician, even if it was only in a small fashion, had made him agree to settle for her. He obviously hadn't liked the fact that Orm continued to work the poorer districts; he'd wanted choicer prey, in spite of the increased risk.

I have the feeling he is working his way up to something he has been planning for a very long time.

That would explain why he had insisted on coming back to Kingsford—which should have been the very last place he'd want to go. He stood a better chance of being caught here than anywhere else in this kingdom, and more to the point, if he ever *was* caught, the Church Justiciars would know exactly who and what he was. Secular constables would only kill Rand; the Church could arrange for a much more prolonged punishment. There were rumors about some of their "penances" for erring Priests. Orm wondered how Rand would enjoy being locked back in the body of the Black Bird, then imprisoned in a cell with no door or window, and fed seed and water for the rest of his life.

The higher up on the social scale our target is, the more likely we are to get caught. That was bad enough, but what if the ultimate target that Rand had in mind was someone *really* important?

He had the sinking feeling that he knew just who that target might be. He already knew that there were three women Rand *could* have in mind, all of whom were responsible in some way for him being the way he was now.

There are the two Free Bards, one called "Robin" and the other called "Lark." "Lark" is well out of the way, in Birnam, another Kingdom entirely. As the wife of the Laurel Bard of Birnam, she is well protected, but she might be accessible since she would not antic-

ipate being a target. Nothing is impossible if you are really determined. The question is, could Rand be that determined?

But if that was to be the case, why stay in Kingsford? They should be traveling now, not lingering in a city already warned against them. That went entirely against logic, and it wasn't likely that Rand wanted to stay here to build up more targets. There were just as many possibilities on the road, if not more.

And if Rand has this woman in mind, he'd better be prepared to pay me quite a tidy fortune, both for having to leave my own Kingdom and for targeting an important woman. I know Rand has money, but I don't think Rand has that much.

The woman called "Robin" was the one responsible for Rand getting into trouble in the first place; she vanished altogether some time ago, shortly after that debacle in Gradford involving High Bishop Padrik. Given the outcome of that particular incident, it was not too surprising that she had disappeared. *It's going to take a while to find her, and if she's gone out of the Human Kingdoms, we may never find her.*

But the third woman in question was the one who had actually tried, judged, and punished Rand, setting the bird-spell on him—and given that she, too, was a Priest, that made her the likeliest target of Rand's anger.

She is quite well within reach at the moment—provided that you are obsessed and not particularly sane.

Orm could not for the life of him imagine how Rand thought he would be able to pull off killing *her*, for she was better protected than Lady Lark. Justiciar-Mage Ardis, High Bishop of Kingsford, not only had the protection of the Church, she was a powerful magician in her own right. How could Rand expect to get a dagger anywhere near her? And whose hands did he think he was going to put it into?

I don't suppose he thinks to slip the knife into the priestly regalia and wait for the Justiciars to excommunicate someone, does he? We might be here for years, if that's his plan!

He finished his meal and told himself not to panic. It could be that Rand already knew where Robin was. He might be building up resources for a kingdom change.

It could be that he's working his way up to going after Lark alone, which would not displease me. I would be quite happy to part company with him.

The only problem was that Rand would probably "part company" with Orm only if the latter was dead. That was hardly in Orm's plans.

I will grant that part of this has been enjoyable. I have found watching the kills to be quite . . . pleasurable. There's a distinct thrill to watching a death, and knowing that you were the one who had the power to bring that particular death to that particular person. Nevertheless . . . this is one set of thrills that I can manage without, given the increasing risk. He could get a great deal of excitement from other experiences just as easily, including a little discreet hunting in the gutters on his own.

I've learned a lot from working with Rand, and the lessons haven't been wasted.

Unfortunately, Rand had not learned reciprocal lessons. One lesson that Orm never, ever forgot was "never pick someone important enough to warrant revenge."

If Rand wants to change the hunts, he can go do it by himself. He's still dependent on me to pick the initial targets, and if I can't find anything suitable that doesn't include risks I find acceptable, well, maybe he ought to try hunting on his own again. He had to remember that the only real hold Rand had over him was to implicate him in the murders. Rand could threaten and rage as much as he wanted, but the moment that Orm was outside his own door and into the street, there was nothing that Rand could do to control him. Rand might or might not realize that, but in the long run, it didn't matter. Words and threats meant nothing; if Rand wanted his victims, he had to leave Orm free to find them and set them up, for he couldn't do it all himself.

With that resolution firmly in mind, Orm paid for his food and left the eating-house. He would go ahead and scout the district that Rand wanted him to work, so that he could honestly say he'd been there. But if there was no good prospect—and by that, he meant a *safe* prospect—well, he'd just have to look elsewhere, wouldn't he?

He passed a group of children playing in the snow and chanting rhymes; one of them caught his attention for a moment.

"Four and twenty black birds?" Well Rand hasn't gotten four-and-twenty victims quite yet, but it's very nearly that, and they aren't exactly baked in a pie—but they aren't likely to sing anymore, either.

Orm kept one ear attuned to the music of a hammered dulcimer as he strolled up to the door of his chosen shop; there wasn't much traffic on this side of the street. Most of the pedestrians were over across the way, listening to the street-musician who had set herself up next to a food-seller's stall. And there wasn't anyone who looked interested in the shop Orm was heading for. With the sign of a rusty ax out front, there was no doubt that the merchant within dealt in used weapons.

By going just outside the district that Rand had specified, Orm had found a target that suited both of them. By sheer luck, a rather homely

Free Bard wench named Curlew had a regular stand right across from this particular shop; either she hadn't heard the warnings, or was disregarding them. It really didn't matter; the fact that she was a Free Bard made her irresistible to Rand, and that was what made it possible for Orm to insist on a district that was a step lower than the one Rand had wanted to work.

Ashdon, the merchant, saw Curlew at least once every day; she went to him to sell him the pins she accumulated in her collection hat from those who couldn't afford to give her even the smallest of copper coins. Ashdon was terribly touchy about status and normally would never lower himself to so much as take notice of a guttersnipe Free Bard except that she had something marketable to sell him. It was easy for him to clean and straighten pins, and when women came into this shop accompanying their lovers or husbands, they generally bought all the pins he had, assuming from their shiny condition that they were new. So he gave Curlew just enough attention to exchange a couple of coppers for her handful of pins every day, and otherwise ignored her.

Orm strolled into Ashdon's shop, and before the balding, stringy fellow could break into his sales-speech, he laid a flannel bundle on the counter and opened it. Inside was a lot of a dozen mixed knives, including the all-important one. It had just enough ornamentation on it in the way of twisted gold wire on the hilt to make Ashdon's greed kick in.

"Ten silver," Orm demanded. This was about six more than the collection was worth, if you left out the important knife. With it, the collection was easily worth nine. If he got seven, he could pretend to be pleased, and Ashdon would be gleefully certain that he'd gotten a bargain.

Ashdon hawked and spit to the side. "For those?" He picked one up—the cheapest of the lot. "Look at this—" he demanded, holding the rusty blade up. "Look at the state of these things! *If* I can get them clean, they'll never sell! Five silver, take it or leave it."

"Nine, or I walk out of here." Orm retorted. "I can take these anywhere and get nine."

"So why aren't you somewhere else?" Ashdon replied with contempt. "You've already been elsewhere, and you got told what I just told you. Six, and I'm doing you a favor."

"Eight, and *I'm* doing *you* one," Orm said, with spirit, and picked up the special blade—carefully. With luck, Ashdon wouldn't notice that he hadn't removed his gloves. "Look at this! That's real gold! I've had a touchstone to it!"

"It's probably gold-washed brass, and you're probably a thief trying to sell me your gleanings. Seven. That's my last offer." The flat finality of his voice told Orm that it was time to close the bargain.

Orm whined and moaned, but in the end, he pocketed the seven silver pieces and left the bundle, feeling quite cheerful. Rand's spell and his own greed virtually ensured that Ashdon would decide to put the dagger on his person or have it at hand rather than putting it away with the rest.

That left the first stage over and done with. Orm slipped back after dark, at closing time, to see what Ashdon had done with the blade. He watched as Ashdon closed and double-locked his shop door, and walked off to his home nearby. As Orm had hoped, the weapons-dealer had improvised a sheath and had the dagger on his own belt, where it would stay until Rand was ready. Once he touched it with bare flesh, he wouldn't have been able to leave it anywhere.

Orm walked off under the cover of the night, feeling well pleased. They would not strike tonight nor tomorrow, nor even the following day, despite Rand's impatience. They would wait for two whole days to eliminate the chance that anyone would remember Orm going into that shop with a load of weapons to sell. That left Orm free to scout another part of the city for the next target, while they waited for memories to fade.

Two days later, Orm lingered over a hot meat pie at the stall of a food vendor near Curlew's stand. He would have to slip in and get the dagger quickly once the girl was dead, since this was going to be another daylight kill. He didn't like that. He would have much preferred a nighttime kill like Shensi, but there wasn't much choice in the matter; Curlew respected the warnings enough that she packed up and left just before sunset every night, and spent the hours of the night playing at the tavern where she slept. They would have no chance of taking her after dark, for she could not be persuaded to leave the company of others after nightfall for any amount of money.

While he waited, he watched Ashdon putter about in his shop, making a concerted effort not to show his tension. In order for Rand to take the man over, Ashdon would have to put his hand right on the hilt of the dagger. Normally that happened several times in a day as Ashdon made certain he still had the weapon with him, but timing could be critical in this case. They wanted a *lot* of people in the street when the kill took place—the more people there were, the more confusion there would be.

Rand was up on the roof above Orm's head, near a chimney. No one would pay any attention to him; he was only a bird on the roof.

Granted, he was a man-sized bird, but no one would believe that; they'd sooner think that the chimney was unusually small, or that there was something wrong with their eyes.

Finally, as Orm's meat pie cooled, the watched-for contact took place.

Rand sensed the contact, and took over; now Orm's tension was for what was to come. Ashdon walked stiffly across the street and waited for a moment, until a break came in the crowd. Then he made a sudden lunge through the gap, and knifed the girl with one of those violent upward thrusts that Rand seemed so fond of, lifting her right off the ground for a moment on his closed fist. It seemed incredible that the scrawny little man had that much strength, but that was partly Rand's doing.

The girl's mouth and eyes widened in shock and pain, but nothing came out of her but a grunt. As usual, the crowd didn't realize what had just happened at first; it was only when Ashdon shoved the body away and it flopped down into the street, with blood pouring out over the snow, that they woke to what he'd done.

It was a particularly nasty butcher-job; the knife-thrust had practically disemboweled the girl. Orm sensed that Rand had just vented a great deal of frustration and anger in that single thrust of his blade; this was convenient for both of them, because the sight of the corpse had the effect of scattering most of the onlookers and sending the rest into useless hysterics.

Now real chaos erupted, as people ran screaming away, afraid that they were going to be the next victims, fainted, or froze in place with terror. This time there were no would-be heroes trying to catch and hold Ashdon; the crowd was composed mostly of women, ordinary merchants or laborers, and youngsters, not of burly longshoremen or bargemen.

Rand forced Ashdon into the peculiar, staggering run of his tools that looked so awkward and was actually so efficient. Orm felt sealed inside a strange little bubble of calm, while all about him, onlookers were screaming and running in every direction. Still, no one did anything *but* try to escape, even though merchants, craftsmen, and their customers were coming out of the shops to see what had happened; no one tried to stop Ashdon, or even moved to block his escape. The ones in the street were all trying too hard to put as much distance as they could between themselves and the knife-wielding madman, and the ones coming out of the buildings didn't know what had happened yet.

Ashdon sprinted past Orm, dropping the dagger, which was no

longer needed for the spell by which he was being controlled. Now it was Orm's turn. Orm darted out into the street to pick it up—

Then came the unexpected. Something dove down out of the sky, headed straight for him, like a feathered bolt of lightning.

For one crazy moment, he thought it was Rand—but the flash of color, scarlet and blue, told him he was wrong. At the same time, he was already reacting; he had not been in this business for as along as he had without developing excellent reactions. When things happened, his body moved without his mind being involved.

He ducked and rolled, snatching up the dagger at the same time, and continued to roll onto his feet as his pursuer shot over his head. He took advantage of the fact that his attacker had to get height for another dive, and dashed into a narrow alley, too narrow for the creature to fly or even land in. His heart was in his throat; what in Heaven's name was after him?

He looked back briefly over his shoulder and saw it hovering at the alley entrance. The winged thing was a bird-man, and there was only one bird-man in Kingsford; it could only be Visyr, the bird-man who worked for the Duke, who had nearly caught another of Rand's tools during a kill.

But *how* had he known to go after the dagger rather than the tool?

No matter; he'd worry about that later. Now he had to get away, as quickly as possible!

The alley was protected from above by overhanging eaves, as Orm very well knew from his study of the area and of Visyr's own maps. The bird-man couldn't track him from above, or follow him into the alley without landing and coming in on foot, losing his advantage. Evidently he came to that conclusion himself, and disappeared for a moment.

But Orm had already gone to ground in a shallow doorway; from the bird-man's vantage at the head of the alley it should look as if he vanished into the alley and got away. And Orm doubted that a bird would care to penetrate into a place barely large enough to allow his folded wings to pass; cut off from the sky as it was, this alley was a claustrophobe's worst nightmare.

With a thunder of wings, the bird-man slammed into the snow at the entrance and peered into the alley. His eyes could not possibly adjust to the darkness in here well enough to make Orm out; Orm could see him as he peered carefully around the edge of the doorway, but he couldn't possibly see Orm.

Could he?

Orm waited with his heart pounding. Could the bird-man hear that? If he did, would he know that it was his intended quarry?

For a moment that stretched into eternity, Orm waited, but the bird-man lost patience before Orm did. With a scream of frustration, the bird-man turned and launched himself back into the air, on the trail of the controlled killer. He would be too late, of course. Ashdon was long dead by now; Rand had certainly forced him into an enormous vat of acid used to clean and etch metal.

Orm waited just long enough to be certain that the bird-man was gone, then cleaned the dagger in the snow, and slipped down the alley. He followed it for several blocks, crossing streets with care in case the bird-man was watching for him from above.

From there, he threaded his way through back streets, stopping once to buy a coat of faded blue and exchange it for his brown one, stopping again to get a cap and pull it down over his forehead. By hunching himself up inside the oversized coat, he managed to look much smaller than he actually was. From above, there was no way to tell he was the same man that Visyr had seen taking the dagger—he hoped. Finally, when he was absolutely certain that there was no one watching, either on the ground or in the air, he washed the dagger in the water from a pump in someone's backyard.

Only then did he head homewards, shaking inside with reaction at his narrow escape.

Something was going to have to be done, if the bird-man had gotten involved. Orm could not spend his time watching for attacks from above as well as trying to snatch the daggers!

He stopped once to buy a new meat-pie to replace the one he'd dropped, and got himself a particularly strong beer to wash it down with. As he ate, he listened to the gossip around him for word of the latest kill.

There wasn't much; people weren't talking about it in this neighborhood yet. That was encouraging at least, since it indicated that people still weren't paying a lot of attention to the kills of street-folk like Curlew. Ducal edict or not, people simply didn't think such murders warranted much attention.

Good. Excellent. Let's hope we can keep it that way. Rand should be content for a while; he had a female Free Bard in a daylight kill and that should keep him human for a good while.

Orm hoped that this would be enough to make him very, very content because somehow he was going to have to persuade Rand to accept lesser creatures and work at night for a while. If they did that, there was always the possibility that the constables would think that the kills were over, or that the cause was a disease or a poison that had run its course in the population. With luck, no one would look any further than that for a cause. Above all, they *had* to get the bird-man looking elsewhere; Orm still didn't know why he'd gone after the person with the dagger and not the man who'd done the kill, and he didn't like it. What if someone among the constables had figured out that the *cause* of the kills was the dagger? That could be very bad. If word began to spread among the people of Kingsford that these peculiar daggers were dangerous, anyone trying to pass one would be in serious trouble. And Rand was going to insist on that one shape; Orm just knew it. It was part of Rand's obsession and nothing was going to make him give it up.

Orm sighed, pulled his hat farther down on his head, and trudged homewards in a dispirited slouch. This was all getting very difficult, and very dangerous. It was more than time to start exploring some options.

Ardis was torn by feelings of mingled grief and elation, a mix that made her so physically sick she doubted she'd be eating anything for a while. The Priest in her grieved for the dead, mourned over the useless, senseless act of murder that had ended the lives of two more innocents, but the side of her that was a Justiciar was overjoyed by the break in the situation. At long last they had a face to go with the knife.

Patrolling in the air as Tal had asked him to, the bird-man Visyr had witnessed the murder of a Free Bard called Curlew. As he had the first time, he reacted instantly, and with speed that no human could have matched. Even though he was a quarter mile away at the time, he was literally at the scene in an eyeblink. But this time he had not followed the apparent murderer as the culprit ran off; this time, under Tal's orders, he had kept his eye on the knife, and dove for it to try and retrieve it.

Then had come the moment when the break occurred. Only the Haspur's superior peripheral vision had enabled him to catch what happened next. As the murderer tossed the knife away, Visyr had seen a man drop a meat-pie he'd been holding and sprint across the street, running towards the murderer and the knife. It was obvious when the murderer ran off that this man intended to snatch up the knife and try to carry it off. Visyr had gotten an excellent look at the man's face as he turned his dive into an attack, and barely missed catching him. He'd pursued the man, but the culprit had gotten into a narrow, covered alley and Visyr had not been able to follow him in there. Once he'd gotten into that protective cover, Visyr had lost him.

Ardis felt very sorry for the Haspur. Visyr sat—or rather, was in a position between sitting, mantled and perched—on a stool across from her now, drooping; frustration and depression shaded every word he spoke. He felt terrible guilt over his inability to force himself to enter the alley, despite the fact that it was a place where he would have been helpless against anyone who attacked him.

"I am sorry, High Bishop," he said again for the fourth time. "I am truly sorry. I *tried* to follow him, but the alley, it was so small, like a rat-hole—"

"Visyr, you're a Haspur, your kind get claustrophobia even in small rooms, outside your homes!" she said patiently, as she had said before. "It would have been like asking a man who couldn't swim to pursue someone who went underwater. I know that, and I do believe you, I promise you. No one blames you for anything; on the contrary, you did very, very well."

Visyr shook his head, still brooding over his failure. "I know where that alley goes, and I tried to find him where it crossed into the open, but somehow I missed him. Either he stayed in it longer than I thought he would, or he escaped out of one of the buildings. I should have—I ought to have—" He stopped, and sighed. "I don't know what I should have done. I only know that it should have been something other than what I did."

It was Tal's turn to bolster Visyr's sagging self-esteem, and he did so. "You did just fine, Visyr," he said emphatically. "If you hadn't flown straight back to the palace and hunted down Master Rudi, we wouldn't have this." He tapped the sketch on Ardis's desk, a copy of the one Visyr had carried post-haste to the Abbey. The Haspur had really made some incredibly creative and intelligent moves; when he realized that the quarry had escaped, he flew at top speed to the Ducal Palace and sent pages scurrying in every direction to bring him Duke Arden's best portrait-artist. Within an hour, Master Rudi had produced a pencil sketch that Visyr approved, and the Haspur then repeated his speeding flight, this time heading for the Abbey. With the best of the Abbey artists working on it, they now had a half dozen of the sketches to give to the constables patrolling the areas where street-entertainers performed.

"I doubt that this is the mage," Ardis continued, picking up the sketch and examining it critically. It was not an ordinary face, although it was not one that would stand out in a crowd, either. "And not just because no one here in the Abbey recognizes him. You distracted the man pretty severely, Visyr. If he'd been trying to control the murderer—or rather, the tool, as Tal calls them—he'd have lost that control at that point, and—'' She frowned. "I'm not sure what would have happened at that point, but the man certainly wouldn't have thrown himself into a vat of acid.''

"So you think this is an accomplice?'' Visyr asked.

Both Ardis and Tal nodded. "We discussed this before; the murderer might have an accomplice, but we always thought that it might be a Priest and a mage working together. From the way you described this fellow acting, though, he seems to be an accomplished thief, and that possibility hadn't occurred to us. It does explain a lot, though.''

"And we can speculate on who he is and why he's doing this when we've caught him.'' Ardis narrowed her eyes. "In a way, this is going to simplify our task. When we catch him, I very much doubt that he's going to care to protect the real killer.''

"Why wouldn't he claim to be a simple thief?'' Visyr asked. "And why wouldn't you believe him if he did?''

"It is unlikely that a real thief would try to steal a murder-weapon with fresh blood still on it,'' Tal said rather sardonically. "He might try that particular ploy with us, but it would take a great deal to convince me.''

Ardis sniffed. "A little creative application of magic as the Justiciars practice it would certainly induce him to tell us the truth,'' she said, just as sardonically. "Magic is *so* useful in these cases—we're forbidden to torture to derive the truth, but the definition of 'torture' includes damage to the physical body, and what I intend to use on him wouldn't harm a single hair.''

"No, he'd only think he was being torn limb from limb,'' Tal said sardonically.

"Oh no, nothing so simple as pain,'' Ardis assured him. "No, he'll have a foretaste of the Hell that awaits him. There are very few men that have been able to withstand that experience, and all of them are—were—quite mad.'' She studied the sketch again. "If you can imagine everything you most fear descending on you at once—and your terror multiplied far beyond anything you have ever felt before—that's a pale shadow of what he'll feel. And it won't stop until he tells us everything he knows. That is why, on the rare occasions that Justiciars use this form of interrogation, we always learn the truth.''

"Harsh. Not that he doesn't deserve it.'' Tal's face could have been carved from stone. "So far as I can see, he's as directly responsible for the murders as if he held the knife.''

There was a strangled, very soft moan from Visyr.

Oh, Ardis. You stupid woman, you. Look at what you and Tal have done to Visyr.

The Haspur's wingtips were shivering and he'd drawn himself in. It was obvious that his mind had still been on his fear of going into that confined space, when she and Tal had inconsiderately gone into detail about the terror-spells and punishments. Now Visyr was probably experiencing not only the fear he had felt at the alley, but the feelings he had suffered any number of other times in his life, all the while speculating what it would be like under one of those interrogation spells.

"But Visyr," Ardis said gently, trying to correct the situation, "you don't have anything to fear from us. In fact we owe you our gratitude."

Tal echoed the sentiment, and added, "You have been as brave as any of us, Visyr. None of this is your calling, yet you've taken to dangerous pursuits twice now. You are helping tremendously."

Visyr sighed heavily. "Do you really think this will help?" he asked.

Ardis exchanged a look with Tal, and Tal answered him. "I have no doubt of it," he told the bird-man. "You can probably go back to mapping for the next few days, and with any luck, before this monster can kill again, we'll either have him or we'll have his accomplice and be on the way to catching him."

Visyr gave the Inquisitor a penetrating look, and Ardis wondered if he'd heard anything in Tal's voice to make him doubt the human's sincerity. Tal looked straight back into his eyes, and Visyr finally shrugged and rose to his feet.

"I do not fly well after dark," he said, by way of apology, "and I would rather not trust myself afoot then, either. I must go."

"I can't begin to thank you enough, Visyr," Ardis told him, as Tal also rose to let him out. "You have gone far beyond anything we would dare to ask of you."

But when Tal returned to his chair, Ardis gave him the same kind of penetrating look that Visyr had graced him with. "Well?" she asked. "Just how useful is this sketch?"

"For now—quite useful," Tal replied, "but its usefulness is going to degrade very rapidly. The moment that this fellow gets word—and he will—that there's a picture of him circulating with the constables, he's going to change his appearance. Hair dye, a wig, a beard, those are the easiest ways for him to look like another person, and if he's really clever, he knows the other tricks, too." He closed his eyes for a moment, calculating. "I'd say the longest this will do us any good is a week; the shortest, two days."

She nodded, accepting the situation. "Maybe we'll be lucky."

Tal snorted. "So far, luck's all been with the killer. Think of it! Visyr actually had the accomplice cornered, if only for a short while, and the man got away because he went to ground like a rat down a hole!"

She tried not to grind her teeth with frustration; it only made her jaw ache. If only she could get her hands on one of those daggers!

"I wish Visyr could have gotten the dagger, or even a scrap of the man's clothing or a piece of his hair," Tal said, sighing, echoing her thoughts. "Well, he didn't. We'll have to make the best use of what he *did* get us."

"He's getting bolder," Ardis said, thinking aloud. "This is another daylight killing, and in a crowd. Maybe someone in the crowd saw something."

"The tool this time was the used-weapons dealer across the street, so he probably got the dagger in a load of other things," Tal noted. "I don't suppose anything could—well—rub off from the dagger with the magic on it?"

Ardis pursed her lips and nodded. "Contagion. That's not a bad thought to pursue; it certainly is going to give us as much as we've been getting off the bodies of the victims. If we can at least identify what other weapons were in the lot, maybe we can trace one of *them* back to where it came from."

They continued to trade thoughts on the subject, but eventually they found themselves wandering the same, well-worn paths of speculation as they had so many times before this. Ardis noticed this before Tal— and she also noticed something else.

She was deliberately prolonging the session and he wasn't fighting to get away, either.

We're both tired, she told herself, knowing at the same time that it was only a half truth. *We both hate idleness, and sleeping feels idle. We need rest, and sitting here and talking is the only way we get it aside from sleeping.* But there was something more going on, and she wasn't going to face it until she was alone.

"You'd better go off and get some real rest," she said, with great reluctance. "I know this is something of a rest, but it isn't sleep, and that's what you need. If you can't get to sleep, ask the Infirmarian for something. I know I will."

He made a sour face, but agreed to do so, and with equal reluctance, left the office.

That set off alarms in her conscience.

Instead of going to bed, she went to her private chapel to meditate.

On her knees, with her hands clasped firmly in front of her, she prepared to examine herself as ruthlessly as she would any criminal.

It wasn't difficult to see what her symptoms meant, when she came to the task with a determination to be completely honest with herself. And this was a road she had already gone down before. The simple fact was that she was very attracted to this man Tal Rufen, but the longer she knew him, the more attracted she became. She knew now that if she had met him before she went into the Church she might not be sitting in the High Bishop's chair.

The bitter part is that the attraction is not merely or even mostly carnal, it's emotional and cerebral, too. That was another inescapable conclusion. He was her intellectual equal, and what was more, he *knew* that she was his. He showed no disposition to resent the fact that she, a woman, was the person in charge, his temporal superior.

And I had no real vocation when I entered the Church. I took vows as a novice in a state of pique and not for any noble reason. Perhaps that was why she examined the novices herself when they came to take their final vows; she wanted to be sure none of them had come here under similar circumstances, and might one day come to regret their choice.

Later she had surprised herself with the level of her devotion, once she got past the rote of the liturgy and into the realms of pure faith, but her original intent had been to find a place where she would be accepted, judged, and promoted on her merit. She knew that; she'd admitted it in Confession. She had thought that she was happy. Now—now she wasn't sure anymore.

If the man I'd been promised to had been like Tal I would have been perfectly happy as the Honorable Lady Ardis, probably with as many children as cousin Talaysen. I certainly do not seem to have lost the capacity for carnal desire and attraction.

Drat.

This was disturbing, troubling; did this mean a lack of faith on her part? Had her entire life been based on a lie?

What am I supposed to do now? she asked the flame on the altar. *What am I supposed to think?*

But the flame had no answers, and eventually, her knees began to ache. Giving it up, she went to bed, but sleep eluded her. Finally she resorted to one of the Infirmarian's potions, but even though it brought sleep, it also brought confused dreams in which a winged Tal pursued a murderous mage who had her former betrothed's face.

The next day brought more work, of course; just because she was pursuing a murderer, that did not mean that other judgments could wait on the conclusion of this case. All morning long she sat in sentencing on criminals who had already been caught and convicted, and in judgment on other miscreants, hearing evidence presented by junior Justiciar-Mages. In the afternoon, she read the latest round of case-records brought from other Abbeys of the Justiciars.

She hoped that a little time and work and the realization of the direction her emotions were taking would enable her to put some perspective on things. Tal did not appear to give his report until after dinner; but she discovered to her concealed dismay that nothing had changed.

She listened to his litany of what had been done and the usual lack of progress, and wondered what was going on in his mind. She *thought* he had given some evidence of being attracted to her in turn, which would have been another complication to an already complicated situation, but she was so out of the habit of looking for such things that she could have been mistaken.

I feel like a foolish adolescent, she thought, with no little sense of irritation. *Look at me! Watching him to see if he is looking at me a little too long, trying to second-guess what some fragment of conversation means! The next thing you know, I'll be giggling in the corner with Kayne!*

"We need a more organized effort, I think," she said at last. "We're going to need more than the tacit cooperation of the Kingsford constables. I think we're going to need active effort on their part. Do you think Fenris would object to that, or resent it?"

"Not really," he replied after a moment of thought. "He's a professional, and he doesn't like these killings in his streets. I think the only reason he's held back from offering to put on more men to help is that he's afraid *you* might resent his trying to get involved. After all, this is a Justiciar case."

"Well, it ought to be more than just a Justiciar case," she replied. "Get us a meeting with him tomorrow, if you can—"

She broke off as he frowned; he had been trying to take notes with a pen that kept sputtering, and his efforts at trimming the nib only made it worse.

"Only scribes ever learn how to do that right," she said after the third attempt to remedy the situation failed. "Here. Take this; keep it. I can always get another, but to be brutally frank, it isn't something you would be able to find easily."

She handed him a refillable Deliambren "reservoir" pen, the only gift her fiancé gave her that she ever kept. He accepted it with a quizzical look, took the cap off at her direction, and tried it out. His eyebrows rose as he recopied the set of notes he'd ruined.

"Impressive," he said quietly. "Deliambren?"

She nodded. "One of those things that you have to have connections for. I can get another from Arden, and considering who gave me that, I really ought to." She smiled crookedly. "We *are* supposed to discard everything from our past when we take final vows; I should have gotten rid of it long ago."

And was that reminder of what I am meant for him or for myself?

He finished his notes and went away, intending to go across the river and try to catch Fenris in his office to set up that conference for the next day. She played with the quill pen that he'd ruined for several minutes, caught herself caressing the feather, and threw it angrily into the wastebasket.

She was having a serious crisis of conscience, there was no doubt of that. But second-guessing her life-decisions was not going to solve anything.

The cure for all of this is work, she decided, and went back to that old file of defrocked Priest-Mages. There was something there, she *knew* it had to be there, if only she could figure out what it was. Thanks to Tal's investigative work, there were some she could remove from the file altogether—although she left the drunk in. The drunkard-act could have been just that, an act, intended for the benefit of Tal alone. No, she would not dismiss him just yet.

But if I'm going to keep him, perhaps I ought to reconsider some of the others I'd dismissed.

She came to the file of Revaner Byless; she remembered him with extraordinary clarity, and every time she reread his file, she became more convinced that he fit the profile of their killer perfectly. But although the Black Bird had escaped, it was surely dead by now—

And how could he be doing all this as a bird, anyway? How could he possibly work magic?

But—maybe he wasn't a bird anymore.

A sudden thought struck her with the force of a blow—the recollection of an incidental comment that Tal had made.

Dear and Blessed God—didn't Tal say that Visyr had seen some sort of odd bird around during the first murder?

She scrambled frantically through her notes, but couldn't find any mention of it. She drummed her fingers on the table, wanting to leap up and take a horse across to Arden's Palace, rouse the poor Haspur from sleep, and interrogate him then and there!

I can't do that. It can wait until the morning. I can talk to him in the morning. The killer has already taken his victim, and he isn't going to take another for a while. It can wait until the poor creature is alert and able to actually remember things. What's more, there are other things I have to put into motion now, if it's him, and those can't wait at all. She wrote out a note to Visyr and had Kayne find her a messenger to take it over immediately.

If Revaner is alive and this is his work, then Robin and Talaysen's wife are in danger, terrible danger! She'd tried to send oblique warnings once, but now she *had* to be more direct. She hastily wrote a letter to Talaysen and another to the Gypsy named Raven in the Duke's household who might know where Robin was or how to reach her to warn her—then wrote a third to Arden asking him to send the first letter to Talaysen by special courier. As she finished her letters, the messenger Kayne had gotten out of the Guard-room presented himself, and she gave him all four missives.

Her work wasn't over for the night, and she knew it. Revaner! This would certainly explain the pattern of victims.

When we caught the blackguard, he was working with a Guild Bard named Beltren. I think we should have a little interview with Beltren, she decided, and reached for pen and paper again. She addressed the letter to the Guildmaster, and phrased it in such a way as to make them believe that she had a commission in mind for Bard Beltren. *And I do have a commission for him,* she thought sardonically, as she signed and sealed it, *I do want to hear him "sing," as the thieves cant has it. I want to hear every note he can "sing" about Revaner.*

Now she had a last set of letters to write, all of them brief and to the point. It might be that Revaner was already gone on his way after Lark or Robin, and in that case, she had to warn anyone who would listen about the danger he represented. That meant any and every Free Bard and Gypsy she had ever come into contact with, for there was no telling what direction he might take, or where he might go. From the Free Bards resident in Kingsford to the Gypsy called Nightingale who was the High King's own special musician; all must have every scrap of information *she* possessed. Above all, they must watch for the Black Bird. . . .

She still did not know *how* he was doing the killings and there was no telling when or where he might strike. This, too, she told them. Admitting that she, and by extension the Church, was powerless in this situation was galling—but better a little loss of pride than another life lost.

This took precedence over any personal matters. She continued to work in a frenzy, long into the night, writing and dispatching letters to anyone she thought might be able to warn those at risk.

When it was all done, and every letter written, she sat for a moment with empty hands—weary, but still unable to sleep.

There has to be something more I can do. . . .

Just as she thought that, a restless movement at her altar caught her eye, and she turned to see the flame flaring and falling like a beating heart.

There is something that I can do.

She rose, deliberately emptying her mind and heart of any personal feelings, and retired to her private chapel to pray.

It was the one thing she could do for all those potential victims that no one else could.

With hands clasped before her and her jaw set stubbornly, she stared at the flame on the altar. Lay-people often made promises to God in the mistaken supposition that one could bargain with Him. She knew better; God did not make bargains. He seldom moved to act directly in the world, for He had given His creations free will, and to act directly would take those glorious or inglorious choices from them.

But she did *ask* for one, small thing. *Let the killing end,* she begged. *And if there is a cost to ending it, let me be the one to pay it. As I am the servant of the Sacrificed God, let me be permitted to offer myself as a lesser sacrifice. Let no more innocents die; let the deaths end, if need be, with mine.*

Chapter Thirteen

Perhaps others might have stayed discouraged by the failure to either stop the murder or capture the murderer's accomplice, but Visyr was now more determined than ever to help. Bad enough to have one poor creature slaughtered right under his beak, but to have two? It was not *fair*! Whoever was doing this was not only a murderer, but a cheat who hid himself and did his evil work only through others! Other cultures had a right to their ways, and theories of honor were different place to place, but this was patently, universally *not acceptable.*

He spent a restless night, not tossing and turning as a human would, but staring into the darkness, reviewing his memories, trying to think of any other information to be gleaned from his brief encounter with the knife-thief.

But he couldn't think of anything. Or to be more accurate, he *could* think of one thing, but it made him very uneasy and was discouraging, not encouraging.

If he had gotten a good look at the dagger-thief, the man in turn also got just as good a look at him. There was only one Haspur in Kingsford, and the fellow was probably quite aware of how much Visyr could see in a limited amount of time. Or, in other words, he had to know that Visyr could identify him in a moment, now.

He has surely discovered that our vision is hundreds of times better than a human's. And he must have deduced how accurate my memory is. After all, how else could I be making these maps for the Duke? Even if he didn't know it already, that fact is easy to find out. It was possible that Visyr was in danger himself now, and it wasn't going to be all that difficult to find him. As T'fyrr's experience showed, a Haspur made a good target, especially aloft. He would be safe enough in the Duke's palace, but nowhere else.

This is not a good thing. Not at all a good thing. The only way to make myself less of a target—besides being totally absent—is to somehow foster the idea that my interference has only been a matter of accident, not intent. Would Ardis and Tal Rufen agree to that, I wonder?

Well, why shouldn't they? They had nothing to lose by it. The murderer might become more cautious if he thought that Visyr was spying from above, watching for him; they needed him to become careless, not more wary than he already was. They needed him to start taking risks, not go into hiding. *Perhaps I ought to even stop flying altogether for a while.* If the killer assumed that Visyr was only acting as any right-minded bystander would have, he should take only minor precautions. Perhaps he would simply make certain that he was not acting in the same area where Visyr was aloft.

Wouldn't he? Visyr wasn't entirely certain how a mad human would think, and the fellow must be mad to be doing this. Was it possible that a mad human would react to this situation by attempting to lure Visyr into an ambush so as to be rid of him?

But if he made himself less of a target, he not only would not be doing his job for the Duke, he'd be avoiding his responsibilities to the Justiciar.

He ground his beak; this was a most uncomfortable position to be in! Not only that, but it was one that went right against his nature. He *could* stick to safe and expensive areas of Kingsford and just go on with his mapping until the murderer was caught, but that wouldn't help find the killer, and although he had been reluctant at first to involve himself, now that he was in, he didn't want to give up.

It feels too much like failure, that's what it is. It feels as if I, personally, have failed. And I hate *giving up!*

Besides, I'm not sure they can continue without me. Maybe that's false pride, but the only breakthrough they've had was because I was able to see the murder in progress and act on it. I have been involved in this mystery in a key way twice now, so obviously the Destiny Winds wish to push me in this direction. Defying those Winds can kill, or worse, leave me with the knowledge of my failure. Flying with those Winds could raise me up, and save the lives of innocents. Or kill me just as surely, but at least it would be in doing something right!

He wrestled with his conscience and his concerns for half the night, or so it seemed. On the one hand, he wasn't a warrior; he never had been, and all of his reactions and attempts at combat thus far had been purely instinctual. Instinct wasn't a good quality to keep counting on in this case. On the other, how could he abandon these people?

He finally decided that the responsibility was great enough that the risk to his hide was worth it.

Well, it seems to me that the place for me *to start is in looking for that black bird. It was at the first murder, and it was at the second. I don't know* what *it is, but it has to be involved somehow.* The few people he'd spoken to about it, including Tal, had been mystified by his description, and absolutely adamant in their assertion that there was no such bird native to these parts. If it wasn't native, then what was it doing here? Its presence at one murder might have been coincidence, but not at two. And it had behaved in a way that made him certain that it did not want to be seen.

He felt himself relaxing enough to sleep once he'd made that decision, satisfied that he was going to take the right course. It would be easier to track another winged creature without exposing himself; after all, it couldn't fly as well as he, and he knew from his own experience how difficult it was for something his size to hide. And in the meantime, *he* had the probable advantage of much superior eyesight; he could fly at a considerable height and see it, where it likely wouldn't be able to see him. Even if it could, it was difficult to judge distance in the sky; it might assume he was a smaller bird, rather than a large one farther away.

He wondered what on earth this bird could possibly be. Maybe it was some sort of messenger to the accomplice; maybe it was the "eyes" that the mage used to view the scene. Whatever it was, it would probably lead him to the accomplice, if not to the mage himself.

The next morning, as soon as he was "publicly" awake, a message came for him from the High Bishop. It had evidently arrived in the middle of the night; in an uncanny reflection of his own thoughts, Ardis asked most urgently if he had seen a large black bird lurking about the two murder sites. And before he could form a reply, right after the arrival of the message came the High Bishop herself.

She didn't even return his greeting as she followed her escorting page into Visyr's rooms. "The bird—" she said, with intense urgency, looking as if she would have liked to seize his arm and hold him while she spoke to him, even though her hands stayed tensely clenched at her sides. "Tal said you saw a strange black bird at the first murder— did you see it yesterday as well? Was it big? Human sized? And incredibly ugly, with ragged feathers and a thin, slender beak?"

His eyes widened with startlement and he stared at her with his beak gaping open. "It did! It was!" he exclaimed. "How did you know? Did you see it? Did you know I was going to look for it today? How did you know what it looks like? I haven't described it that closely to anyone!''

"I know what it looks like because it isn't just a bird," she replied grimly. He waved her to a seat, and she took it, sitting down abruptly and gripping the arm of the chair as a substitute for whatever else it was she wanted to catch hold of. "It's a man—or it was. If the bird you saw and the one I'm thinking of are the same creature, it was a human—and a mage—and a Priest, before it ever was a bird.''

Quickly she outlined what seemed to Visyr to be a most incredible story. If it hadn't been Ardis who'd been telling it to him, he would never have believed it, not under any circumstances. Oh, he'd *heard* of all the things that magic was supposed to be able to do, but it all seemed rather exaggerated to him. The only "magic" he had any personal experience of was not the sort of thing that could turn a human being into a bird! The kinds of magic he was used to could influence people and events, sometimes predict the future or read the past, or create impressive illusions. He'd heard of things that the Elves could do, of course, but he'd never seen anything of the sort—perhaps he had been among the Deliambrens too long, but he had a difficult time believing in things he'd never seen for himself, or seen sufficient proof of.

Still, it *was* Ardis who was telling him this, and she said that *she'd* been the one who'd done it, turned the man into the bird. What was more, she'd done it more than once, so it wasn't a fluke.

His beak gaped in surprise, and he had to snap it shut before he looked like a stupid nestling.

"I transformed another couple of excommunicates into donkeys," she continued. "Ones who were indirectly responsible for the Great Fire and were directly responsible for keeping those of us who could have quelled it from doing so. As such, as my fellow Justiciars and I saw it, they were accessories to hundreds of murders. It seemed to us that turning them into beasts of burden was actually a very light punishment—and it gave them the opportunity for repentance.''

Visyr shook his head, unable to understand why she should have been concerned that these people repent. Like most Haspurs, he was somewhat incredulous at the concept of omniscience and deities at all, but allowed as how they might be possible, and it was certainly impolite to say nay around anyone who believed in them. Believing that human criminals turned into donkeys would want to repent to an omniscient deity went far past the high clouds of logic, to him, and into very thin air. *Well, that doesn't matter,* he thought. *She's a human; who can understand a human completely? Not even other humans can, and Ardis is a Church power atop that.* "But you can't turn them back into humans?" he asked.

"With time—I might be able to," she said, cautiously. "It would be a bit more difficult than the first transformation, because it would be layering one spell on top of another, but I think I could. The spell as I learned it was never intended to be reversed, even by the death of the mage who cast it, but I think I could work a reversal out. But Revaner—no. No, I couldn't. The circumstances that created him were so complicated and so unpredictable that I doubt I could reverse them. It wasn't just *our* magic that was involved, it was the snapping of the spell that he had cast, and the involvement of Bardic magic from two Bards who were acting on sheer instinct, and Gypsy magic from Revaner's victim. The chances of deducing just what happened are fairly low."

"And you still aren't certain that the bird I've seen and this Revaner fellow are the same." He ground his beak a little. "Still—whatever this creature *is*, I can't see how it could fail to have something to do with the killings. You don't suppose that someone else entirely found out how to change himself into a bird, do you?"

Ardis looked as if she would have ground her beak, if she'd had one. "I can't give you any reason why it *shouldn't* be the case," she admitted. "My main reason for thinking that it's Revaner is that the pattern of the murder-victims matches the kind of women that Revaner would be most likely to want to kill. On the other hand—"

"On the other hand, when you changed him into a bird, he wasn't a murderer." Visyr couldn't help pointing that out.

"No, he wasn't. He was unscrupulous, immoral, utterly self-centered, egotistical, a liar, a thief, and ruthless, but he wasn't a murderer." She wrinkled her brow as if her head pained her. "On the other hand, there is one way to overcome just about any magic, and that is to overpower it. And one sure way to obtain a great deal of power is to kill someone. Now, when you combine *that* fact with the motive of revenge—" She tilted her head in his direction, and he nodded.

"I can see that. Well, I was already going to make a point of looking for that bird, and now you have given me more reasons to do so," he told her. "And you have also given me plenty of reasons to make certain that it doesn't see me!"

Now Ardis rose, full of dignity. "I will not ask you to place yourself in further jeopardy, Visyr," she said solemnly. "If this is Revaner, he is very dangerous. If it is not—well, he may be even more dangerous. Please be careful."

In answer, Visyr flexed his talons, a little surprised at how angry and aggressive he felt. "I am more than a little dangerous myself," he said to her. "And I am also forewarned."

She looked him directly in the eyes for a long moment, then nodded. "Good," was all she said, but it made him feel better than he had since he lost the dagger-thief.

She left him then, and he took his mapping implements and went out to resume his dual duties.

Only to discover that now he couldn't find the damned bird!

He spent several days criss-crossing the city on every possible excuse. He thought perhaps that the Black Bird might have decided to lurk in places he had already mapped in order to avoid him—then he thought it might be in places he *hadn't* mapped yet. But no matter where he looked for it, there was not so much as an oversized black feather. It was as if the creature knew he was trying to find it and had gone into hiding. On the other hand, if all of their suppositions were true, and it was in league with the knife-thief, perhaps it had the suspicion that he was hunting it. At the very least, it now knew that there was danger in being spotted from above, and might be taking steps to avoid that eventuality.

Frustrated, he spent all of one evening trying to reason the way *he* thought a crazed human in bird form might.

It made him a little less queasy to think of it as a hunter as he tried to ignore the type of quarry it was taking; he came from a race of hunters himself, and it wasn't all that difficult to put himself in that mindset.

When one hunts a prey that is clever, particularly if one is hunting a specific individual, one studies that individual, of course. He'd done that himself, actually; the trophy-ringhorn that he'd wanted to take to Syri as a courting-gift had been a very canny creature, wily and practiced in avoiding Haspur hunters. It knew all of the usual tricks of an airborne hunter, and it would race into cover at the hint of a shadow on the ground. He'd had to spend time each day for months tracking it down, in learning all of its usual haunts and patterns, and in finding the times and places where it was most vulnerable.

Now, the Black Bird was probably not that clever a hunter itself. This creature was hunting prey that was not aware it was being hunted, nor were humans as versed as that ringhorn in avoiding a hunter, but the Black Bird still needed to find the moment that its prey was most vulnerable. It couldn't hunt inside buildings, and if it was going to hunt again but didn't want to be seen, it had to come out on the rooftops eventually. There was no other possible hunting ground for it.

That was how a Haspur would hunt in the same situation. But unlike a Haspur, the Black Bird might well have decided that there was another hunter that might be stalking *it*. So it was torn between two courses of action: don't hunt at all, or find another way to hunt.

It still has to find prey. It still has to find the prey's most vulnerable moments. But somehow it is managing to do so when I won't see it.

That would be very difficult to do, unless—

Unless it is hunting at night.

It *was* black, and perfectly well camouflaged by darkness. And if the records were to be trusted, there had been plenty of killings at night, including at least one possible killing here in Kingsford, between the first one he'd witnessed and the second. That meant it had hunted by night before, which meant it could probably see just fine at night.

Which, unfortunately, I cannot. But I am not limited to my own unaided eyes, which is something that I doubt it has thought of.

He *could* fly at night, he just didn't like doing so, because unlike T'fyrr, his own night-vision was rather inferior by Haspur standards. Once night fell, all of his advantage of superior vision vanished; he couldn't even see as well as some humans he knew. That was why he always got back to the palace before dusk, and never went out at night if he could help it. It was a weakness he had never liked about himself, so when the opportunity had arisen for him to compensate for it, he had. He had something in his possession that he hadn't had occasion to use yet, something that would render the best of camouflage irrelevant at night.

He chuckled to himself as he thought of it. There hadn't been any need to use it in Duke Arden's service, because it wasn't at all suited for his mapping duties. No one here knew he had it. And he rather doubted that anyone in all of this Kingdom had ever even *seen* this particular device.

He reached immediately for a bell-pull and summoned one of his little attendant pages. Talons were not particularly well suited to unpacking, but clever little human hands were.

At his direction, the boy who answered his summons dug into the stack of packing-boxes put away in a storage closet attached to his suite. The boxes were neither large nor heavy; the few that were beyond the boy's strength, Visyr was able to help with. In less than an hour, the page emerged from the back of the closet with an oddly-shaped, hard, shiny black carrying-case.

The page looked at it quizzically as he turned it in his hands. "What is this?'' he asked, looking up into Visyr's face. ''What is it made of? It's not leather, it's not pottery, it's not stone or fabric—what is it?''

Visyr didn't blame the boy for being puzzled; the material of the case resembled nothing so much as the shiny carapace of a beetle, and the case itself was not shaped like anything the boy would ever have seen in his life. ''I'll show you what it is,'' he said to the youngster, taking the case from him and inserting a talon-tip into the lock-release. ''Or rather, I'll show you what's inside it. The outside is a Deliambren carry-case for delicate equipment; what I wanted is inside. But you have to promise that you won't laugh at me when I put it on. It looks very silly.''

''I won't,'' the boy pledged, and watched with curiosity as Visyr took out his prize. Indeed, prize it was, for arguing with the Deliambrens for its design and manufacture had fallen upon Visyr himself, and it was with no small amount of pride that he knew these very same devices would be in use by Guardians and rescuers, thanks to him.

A pair of bulging lenses with horizontal lines, made of something much like glass but very dark, formed the front of the apparatus. The device itself had been formed to fit the peculiar head-shape of a Haspur, and the hard leathery helmetlike structure that held it in place had been added in place of the straps that Deliambrens used so that no feathers would be broken or mussed when he wore it. That ''helmet'' was based on a very old and successful design, and the page recognized it immediately.

''It looks like a falcon's hood!'' the boy exclaimed, and so it did, except that where the hood was ''eyeless,'' this was not meant to restrict vision, but rather the opposite. With its special lenses in the front and the mechanism that made them work built in a strip across the top curve of the head, rather like one of those center-strip, crestlike hairstyles some Deliambrens wore, it almost looked fashionable, and certainly sleek.

That was so that Visyr would be able to fly with the thing properly balanced; in the Deliambren version, the mechanisms were all arranged around the front of the head, which would have made him beak-heavy. It would be very hard to fly that way.

''These are Deliambren heat-lenses,'' Visyr explained to the boy. ''They let me see at night. If you'd like, I'll show you how.''

The boy needed no second invitation; Visyr lowered the ''hood'' over his head and turned the device on, then turned the lights of the suite off one by one.

The page held the hood steady with both hands, as it was much too large for his head, and looked around curiously. "Everything's green," he said, dubiously, then exclaimed when he turned the lenses in Visyr's direction. "Sir! You're glowing!"

"No, it's just that you only see what is warm," Visyr told him. "It is a different way of seeing. The warmer something is, the brighter it seems to be through the lenses. I am very warm, and it looks as if I am glowing. Come to the balcony and look down."

The boy did so, picking his way unerringly across the pitch-dark room. He passed through the second room, came out on the balcony with Visyr, and spent some time exclaiming over what he saw through the lenses of the device. Even though it was broad daylight, the lenses worked extremely well, for things that were warm stood out beautifully against the cold and snowy background. The boy chattered on as he picked out a sun-warmed stone, courtiers strolling in the gardens, birds in the trees near him, and even a sly cat slinking along under the cover of evergreen bushes.

Finally, though, the cold became too much for him. They went back into the room, and Visyr took the "hood" from him and turned the lights back on.

He satisfied the page's curiosity then by donning the device himself. The youngster looked at him quizzically for a moment as Visyr adjusted the device for the sharpest images. "I wouldn't have laughed," the page said finally. "You just look like a hooded falcon."

"Well, fortunately, I can see *much* better than a hooded falcon," Visyr said. "And now that I've found this, you can go. Thank you."

The page was nothing if not discreet. Although he might be very curious why Visyr wanted this particular device brought out, he knew better than to ask, just as he knew better than to tell anyone about it.

Deliambren heat-vision goggles, Visyr thought with satisfaction. *Not even the cleverest of hunters can avoid being seen when I have these on—not even if he decides to take to the ground and walk. The only way he can avoid me is to stay inside buildings. And a man-sized black bird strolling through the inns and taverns of Kingsford, even at night, is going to be noticed!*

The Deliambrens had included this device in his equipment for the Overflight mapping, and he had simply brought all of his equipment with him when he'd taken the Duke's commission. It was easier than trying to unpack and repack again, or trust it to be sent from another location. Now he was glad that he had hauled it all with him. The goggles were so good, he could see things the size of a mouse on a summer day, and on a winter day, he could do better than that.

But—I think perhaps I won't tell Ardis and Tal Rufen about these, he decided. *I think this will be my little secret.*

If the Black Bird was out there at night now, with these, he was on an equal footing with it. Maybe better. It might have the night-vision of an owl, but with these, he had night-vision that an owl would envy.

He could hardly wait for nightfall.

When night came, he made sure that the power-cells were fresh, donned his "hood," and went out onto his balcony.

He perched on the rail of the balcony for a while, getting used to the way he saw things through the lenses. It wasn't quite the same as real, daylight vision; his depth-perception seemed flattened, and it was more difficult to tell distances accurately. He actually had to judge how far something was from him by the size it was. He'd never actually flown with these things before, and as he leapt off onto the wind, he realized that he was going to have to allow for some practice time after all.

His peripheral vision was quite restricted, which meant that he couldn't see as much of the ground below him at a time as he could unencumbered. As clever as they were, the Deliambrens could not give him lenses that gave him the same field of vision. That, in turn, meant that he had to take his time—not hovering, but not using what he would call "patrolling speed."

And although the hood and the lenses were relatively light, any weight was considerable to a flying creature. In a few short hours, he was quite tired and ready to quit for the night. He returned to the palace with a new respect for the night-patrols, who now quartered the borders of his homeland wearing these things every night of the year. They were truly great athletes to be able to take dusk-to-dawn patrols without any significant rest.

This is going to take time, he thought, a little dispiritedly, as he fanned his wings for a cautious landing on his balcony-rail. *Not just one night, but several. And each patrol is going to take four times as long to fly at night as it does by day. And I still have to sleep some time.*

He took off the device as he entered the balcony door, and removed the power-cells, putting them into the device that renewed them by day. He set the hood on a peg meant to hold a human's hat, and turned off the lights as he entered his sleeping chamber.

But as he readied himself for sleep, another thought occurred to him. Perhaps this wasn't going to be as difficult as he had thought, after all.

There are fewer places where humans are abroad after darkness falls, he realized. *The Black Bird won't be in places where there aren't any humans. So my search can be much narrower.* He could avoid the docks entirely, for one thing; there were absolutely *no* women there at night. Residential districts were quiet after dark as well. The Black Bird had to go where its prey was, and that narrowed the area of search.

It won't be as easy as I first thought, he concluded, *but it won't be as difficult as it seemed tonight.*

And with that comforting thought, sleep stooped on him and carried him away.

Orm spent the next week or so in a state of blissful calm. It was a wonderful time, and he finally recalled what it was like to serve clients rather than employers. He made a vow that he would never again put himself in this position; from this moment on, he would never have anything to do with people who wanted more than information. He had not realized how Rand's mere presence grated on his nerves until that moment.

But during that pleasant interval, Rand gave him no special orders, issued no edicts, made no outrageous demands, uttered no threats. Part of the reason for that might have been that a reasonably accurate copy of a sketch of Orm's face was circulating among the constables, and even Rand realized that if Orm ventured out before his disguise was complete, Rand would lose his all-important envoy to the outside world. Even Rand would have difficulty in paying the rent or acquiring food in the shape of the Black Bird, and he could not count on being able to find and kill prey to keep him human for very long on his own.

So Orm grew facial hair and altered his appearance. Meanwhile, taking advantage of his temporary human form, Rand spent most of his time away from their lodgings, giving Orm even more peace and quiet. It was wonderful; Orm put on weight by cooking and eating luxurious meals, secure in the knowledge that he could drop the weight as easily as he put it on. The most he heard out of Rand was the sound of footsteps through his ceiling, or ascending and descending the staircase.

Out of curiosity, once his disguise had been perfected, Orm followed Rand to see what he was doing—without his knowledge of course, and it was gratifying to see that the disguise worked so well that Rand didn't recognize him, at least at a moderate distance. Orm now had a jaunty little beard, a mustache trained so that he always appeared to be smiling, and darker, much shorter, hair. He was also some twenty pounds heavier, and he'd darkened his skin to make it look as if he'd been outdoors most of his life. He walked with a slouch and a slight limp, and wore clothing just slightly too big.

In this guise, he followed Rand out into the city, staying about twenty feet behind him. Rand went only two places: one, a tavern, and the other, an ale-house that served only drink, no food. He seemed to be spending most of his time plying off-duty constables with drink and talking to them at length. Now that was actually a very reasonable way to acquire information, and one that Orm had made liberal use of in the past, but was no longer going to be able to pursue. His disguise was a good one, but there were constables with a sharp enough eye to see past the beard, mustache, and other alterations to the things that didn't change. There wasn't much that someone could do about his eye-color or bone-structure, and although Orm had done a few things to make himself look slightly more muscular, anyone grabbing his arm would know that those muscles were made of wadding. He couldn't change his height significantly, and he couldn't do anything about his hairline, receding as it was. Orm would no longer dare to get within conversational distance of any constables unless he was able to ascertain in advance that they were particularly dim ones. And unfortunately, Captain Fenris hadn't hired very many dim constables; he valued intelligence in his men, and rewarded it.

So, while Rand pursued whatever hare *he* had started, Orm took the opportunity of his absence to begin protecting himself from his employer. He hadn't forgotten that threat of exposure, not for a moment, and if there was anything he *could* do about it, he would.

He still had no idea what it was that Rand had arranged to implicate him in the murders. Most probably it was something as simple as a written confession. He spent most of one day in Rand's apartment, looking at everything he could without touching it, and was unable to come to any conclusions.

He couldn't see anyplace where such a confession might be concealed, and Rand would want it to be found quickly after his death, so he wouldn't conceal it all that well. He would probably count on the fact that he had protected such a confession magically to keep Orm from touching it—

Perhaps, Orm thought, as he looked for what, to him, were the obvious signs of secret drawers or other such devices. *Then again, once he was taken, he could count on the constables to tear his apartment apart and render the furniture down to toothpicks in an effort to get as much evidence as possible. So he could have decided not to waste precious magic, and hidden the confession without magic.*

Rand might not be a thief or have ever fabricated places where small objects could be concealed, but he had money enough to pay those who *could* hide things so well that the only way to get them out was to know the trick or smash the offending object to pieces. Could a mage tell if something was hidden inside another object?

Does it matter? I think not. It would be easier to smash things and see if there was anything hidden inside. Quicker, too. He had to chuckle a little. *Ah, the advantage of being on that side of the law!*

He couldn't see any place where possible papers lay out in the open, and he really didn't want to open any drawers and search them.

The message could be magical in nature, but would Rand waste magical energy that could keep him human in creating a message that could be created in an ordinary fashion? That was a good question. *Once again—it is what I would do, but would Rand?* Rand hoarded his energies like a miser with coins, but would he spend them on safeguarding himself in this way? It was difficult to tell, but vengeance played a major part in his life, so perhaps he would spend that power to make certain of his revenge if Orm betrayed him.

But would he sacrifice a single day of being human? He's crazed enough to decide that he wouldn't.

It might simply be that Rand was counting on other factors to implicate Orm, though it was doubtful that he knew how much Orm had learned about magic from him. Rand could not help talking, boasting about his powers and his plans, especially in the euphoria that followed his transformation back into a human. Orm had picked up quite a bit about the way that magic worked, and he could be implicated simply by the fact that his magical "scent" would be all over this place. And even though he tried to cleanse the murder weapons, they would also carry his traces. But what Rand would not anticipate was that Orm could solve that little problem easily enough—and possibly render any written or magical confession suspect as well.

He took hair from his own brush, put it in a little silk bag, and left it among dozens of identical little silk bags holding other bits of flotsam among Rand's magical implements. He had not stolen anything, so he took the chance that the guard-spells Rand surely had on his equipment would not betray him. Evidently, they didn't; Rand never said anything, and Orm now had a piece of evidence that would bolster his own protestation of innocence. Why else, after all, would the mage have some of his hair, except to implicate an otherwise blameless man?

The hair could be used to do almost anything, including to create an illusion of Orm at the scene of one of the crimes—and that might take care of that incriminating sketch. After all, he'd "disappeared" after he went into the alley—and that could have been the illusion vanishing.

And why would Rand want to implicate an innocent man in his crimes? Orm had reasons, if anyone asked. They might not bother to ask; Rand was so clearly mad that they might assume this was another of his mad acts. But Orm intended to claim he'd had conflicts with his fellow tenant, and that Rand had threatened to seek revenge after one of them. The assumption then would probably be that Rand intended to escape, leaving Orm to take all of the blame for the murders. That was how constables tended to reason, and that interpretation suited Orm perfectly.

He also began establishing his own alibis and an unshakable persona as a solid citizen who couldn't possibly have anything to do with Rand and his kills. First, he obtained the registration records from a respectable (if common) inn that was within a short walking distance of his current neighborhood. It didn't take a great deal of work to alter the records so that they showed that he had arrived in Kingsford and taken up residence there in early fall, had stayed there until early winter, then removed himself to the apartment he now lived in. He slipped the records-book back into the inn the same night he obtained it. No one would notice the alteration; it was very likely that the people whose names he had removed were there under false identities in the first place. This gave him an arrival date that was much earlier than his actual arrival in Kingsford, and this was a date that conflicted with some of the other murders Rand had done outside of Kingsford. With the Church involved, there was every reason to expect that at least some of the killings in other cities would be tied to Rand.

That done, he began reaffirming his acquaintance with all of his neighbors. He already knew them, of course, and they knew him, but now he went out of his way to cultivate them. By dint of careful conversations, he was able to establish himself in their minds as having been in the general vicinity since that early autumn date listed in the inn records. All he had to do was to mention events in the neighborhood that had taken place during that time period as if he'd witnessed them, and agree with the version the person he was talking to related. And how did he learn of those events? By asking leading questions of a different neighbor, of course. It was an amusing game; he'd find out about event A from neighbor One. He'd then establish himself with neighbor Two by relating event A, then solicit event B from neighbor Two. He would take his tale of event B to neighbor Three, and so on, until he came back to neighbor One with the story of event G, and solicit the tale of Event H to take on to neighbor Two, beginning the chain again. Within a few days, at least a dozen people were not only convinced he'd been in the neighborhood, but that they'd actually seen him there at the times he spoke of.

It was amazingly easy to convince people of trivial things of that nature; he'd done it before when he'd needed to establish an alternate identity. As long as your version of what you wanted them to remember fitted with their real memories, you could insert yourself into almost anyone's recollections.

He also established himself in their minds as a very fine, affable fellow—and his fellow tenant as a rather odd duck, surly, unpleasant, possibly something of a troublemaker. That, too, was easy enough to do, since Rand didn't go out of his way to be polite when he was in his human form.

Now Orm needed a reason to be in Kingsford, which he established when his neighbors "knew" enough about him to want to know what he did for a living. His profession? Oh, he was a small spice-trader, a very convenient profession that required no apprenticeship and not a great deal of capital, merely a willingness to take personal risks and a taste for exotic places and danger. It was also one that required a great deal of travel, at least at first, as a young man would build his contacts with spice-growers or collectors in more exotic lands. It was also a highly seasonal profession; most trading took place in the spring and fall, with summer being the time for a small trader to set up at Faires, and winter being the time to rest and get ready for spring, which would account for his apparent idleness.

Now that he was of middle years, he presumably had his spice-sources in hand, and he should be ready to settle and operate from the secure venue of a shop. He needed a city where there was a great deal of trade, he told his neighbors, and Kingsford seemed like a fine choice of a home. Duke Arden was a great leader, the city was clearly thriving, the people here honest and hardworking—with the nearness of the Faire and the river, who could ask for more? He was looking for a place for a shop, trying to make sure he would have no rivals in the immediate neighborhood, hoping to find a suitable place that was already built, since he could only afford to lease the place at first.

This was a simple and understandable explanation for money with no obvious source of income, and irregular hours. It passed muster with all of his neighbors; the only danger was that one or more of them might ask him if he could sell them some exotic spice or perfume oil. Fortunately none of them did, so he didn't have to make an excursion out to obtain what he *should* have had at hand.

And having had their curiosity satisfied about *him*, that left Rand open to inquiry. The fellow upstairs—well, he really couldn't say what that man did. Never seemed to be at home very much, but never seemed to do anything that you could count as *work*, either. He added a touch of scorn to that last, as would be expected from a hard-working fellow who'd made his own way in the world without any help from anyone else.

And finally, he managed to get himself an alibi for at least one of the murders, the latest. He began playing daily games of fox-and-hounds with an old man living three doors down; by the time the week was over, thanks to Orm's gentle persuasion, the old fellow would honestly believe and claim that they had been playing fox-and-hounds every afternoon for the past month. Since a game of fox-and-hounds generally lasted all afternoon, any questioners would discover that he'd been with his neighbor at the time that Rand's accomplice was trying to make off with a murder-weapon.

Now he had his identity established as an honest small trader looking for a home to settle down in, and any claims that Rand made to the contrary would have witnesses with stories that directly contradicted the mage's claims.

Of course, given a choice, if Rand were caught, Orm would much rather be far away from Kingsford. He had running-money in a belt he wore constantly, and knew how to get out of the city quickly by means of routes that were not easily blocked. But in case he couldn't run far or fast enough, well, he had a secondary line of protection.

He completed his precautions with no time to spare; it wasn't long afterwards that Rand transformed back into the Black Bird.

But even then, in a pronounced change from his usual habits, the mage didn't stop going out—he simply did so by night, and for the first three days, he didn't summon Orm or attempt to give him any orders. This was definitely odd, and it was obvious that Rand was up to something new.

By now, Orm had found another four possible targets, so he had something to show for all the time that Rand had left him to his own devices. But this sudden interest in something besides the usual pattern made Orm very nervous. What was Rand planning? Given his habits of the past, it *had* to be dangerous.

It had better not be revenge on the High Bishop, Orm thought, more than once. *If it is—I don't care what his plan is, I want no part of it. That's not dangerous, it's suicidal, and I am not ready to throw my life away.*

Maybe he was planning how to leave the city; perhaps he had gotten information of his own on the whereabouts of the Gypsy called Robin.

If Rand was going to pursue any of his three "worst enemies," Robin would be the safest.

But if he is going outside this Kingdom, unless it's to a place I already know, he can do it without me. Orm had no intentions of trying to learn his way around a new city with new laws and new customs—and coming into inevitable conflict with residents who were already in the same line of work that he was.

Or perhaps he was planning to leave in pursuit of his vendetta with Lady Lark.

I'm having no part of that. It would be as suicidal as going after the High Bishop! It would be worse! At least here I am operating in my own city—if Rand went off after Lark, we'd be in a Kingdom and a city I know nothing about. Go after someone who's in the King's Household and *is allied with Elves? No thank you!*

Finally the expected summons came, and Orm went up the stairs to Rand's apartment trying not to feel as if he was climbing the steps of a gallows. He opened the door to find the Black Bird waiting for him, perched on a stool, and watching him with its cold, black eye.

"I've got some possible targets for you," Orm offered, but the Bird cut him off with a shake of its head.

"I have an assignment for you," the Bird croaked. "I want you to follow a man called Tal Rufen. He's probably a Church Guard, since he lives at the Abbey of the Justiciars, even though he very seldom wears the uniform. I don't know what his rank is, other than that of Church Guard and not Guard Captain, but he's involved in trying to find us, and you can thank him for that sketch of you that's being handed around to all the constables."

Rand did not bother to tell him how he was to follow this "Tal Rufen" fellow; Rand at least gave him credit for expertise in his own area. Picking up a subject who came and went from a place as isolated as the Justiciar's Abbey would be a challenge, but it wasn't insurmountable.

"I want you to learn all you can about him, and every time he leaves the Abbey, I want you to watch his every move. I want to know the slightest of details about him; what he wears, what he carries, even what he eats and drinks." The Bird cocked its head to one side, but it wasn't a gesture calculated to make Orm feel amused. "No matter how trivial it is, I want to know it. I want to know this man better than his best friend. Do you understand all that?"

Orm shrugged and nodded. "Not easy, but not all that difficult," he acknowledged. "How long do you want me to follow him? Do you want me to try and obtain something of his?"

"Two days, at least, and no, I don't want you to get that close."
The Bird gave a croak of what was probably supposed to be amusement. "I have reason to believe that he is the High Bishop's personal guard and assistant, and if he thought that something was missing, Ardis might try to trace it back to whoever took it."

Why is Rand so interested in this man? And why follow him? It didn't make a lot of sense, unless—

No one really made any attempt to pursue us until we came here. I wonder if this fellow has something to do with that. If that's the case, he may be the only reason why the High Bishop is interested. If Rand can eliminate him, pursuit may die for lack of interest, especially if we can be rid of him by somehow discrediting him. He nodded, and waited for the Bird to give him more orders. But Rand only yawned and said, "You may go. Come back up here when you have your first report for me."

Orm stood up and left, now very curious. But the only way he was going to satisfy that curiosity would be to follow Rand's orders and trail this Tal Rufen fellow.

The more I learn, the more I'll know—or be able to deduce. Whatever pie Rand has got his claw into, this Tal Rufen fellow is somehow involved.

His first difficulty was to discover what his quarry looked like; that was easily solved. He made up a parcel of unused blank books—blank books being the most innocuous and inexpensive objects he could think of—and paid a boy from his neighborhood to take them to the Abbey. He didn't want to send real books on the chance that Rufen might open the parcel and examine what was in it—and if by some horrible chance Orm managed to send books that interested him, Rufen might well try to find the rightful owner to buy them himself. That would be a recipe for trouble. These were inexpensive blank books of the kind that young girls used for journals and artists liked to sketch in. They would hardly be of any use to someone from the Abbey, who could get better quality versions of the same things simply by presenting himself at the Scriptorium, where they made hand-lettered and illuminated copies of books to add to the Abbey income.

"Someone left these at my table at lunch," he told the boy, "but I'm not sure who it was; it was crowded, and there were a number of people I didn't know sharing my table. A fellow called Tal Rufen from the Abbey was one of the people there, and I would think that someone from the Abbey would be the likeliest to have a parcel of books; go and see if it was him. I'll be here doing my inventory."

No boy would ever question an adult about a paid errand; for one thing, no boy ever turned down the opportunity to run an errand for pay, and for another, any boy would automatically assume that the business of an adult was too important to be interrupted for a simple errand.

He had paid the boy just enough to make it worth the trouble to go across the bridge in the cold and blowing snow; he waited until the boy was gone, then followed in his wake. Once the boy had started out on the bridge, Orm took up a position in a clump of bushes on the bank, watching the gate with a distance-glass until the boy arrived.

When the boy reached the Abbey, he was made to wait outside; rude treatment, that was just what Orm had hoped for. After a bit of time, a fellow in the uniform of the Church Guards came out and listened to the boy's story. He didn't even bother to look at the parcel; he shook his head, gave the boy another small coin, and sent him back across the river. Orm got a very good look at the man, and was satisfied that he would recognize him again; before the boy reached the bridge, Orm was hurrying back to his apartment, where the boy found him.

"It wasn't that Tal Rufen fellow, sir," he said, when Orm answered his door. The boy handed over the parcel—which was, remarkably, still unopened. "He says he isn't missing anything."

Orm made a noise of mingled vexation and worry. "Well, I'll just take it back to the inn and leave it there with the proprietor," he said at last, waving his hands helplessly. "I really don't know what else to do. What a pity! I'm sure someone is missing these. Well, you did your best, and I'm sorry you had to go out in all that snow."

He gave the boy another small coin, thus ensuring his gratitude, and sent him off.

Well, now I have a face. Let's see what that face does.

He bundled himself up to his nose with a knitted hat pulled down to his eyes, and took a fishing-pole and bucket of bait out to the bridge. There was reasonably good fishing in the clear water under the bridge, and he wouldn't be the only citizen of Kingsford who paid the toll to perch out on the span and attempt to add to his larder, especially not in winter, when a job at casual labor was hard to find and no one was building anything, only doing interior work. This would be the best place to intercept his target, and even though his target might well know what Orm looked like from the sketch circulating among the constables, not even Rand would be able to pick Orm out from the rest of the hopeful fishermen out on the bridge in the cold.

Nevertheless, it was a miserable place to have to be. The wind rushed right up the river and cut through his clothing; he soon picked up the peculiar little dance of the other fishermen as he stamped his feet and swayed back and forth to try and increase his circulation. By the time Tal Rufen finally appeared, mounted on a sturdy old gelding, Orm was more than ready to leave the bridge. He hauled in his line and followed in Tal's wake; the bridge guard looked at his empty string, gave him a grimace of sympathy, and didn't charge him the toll. Orm gave him shivering, teeth-chattering thanks, and followed in Tal Rufen's wake.

Orm's disguise was quite enough to permit him to follow Tal unnoticed through the city, but it wouldn't have gotten him into the Ducal Palace, and as Tal presented himself at the postern-gate, Orm went on with his head down and his shoulders hunched.

Now what? If he'd had several weeks to follow Tal Rufen, he might have been able to get himself into the palace by obtaining or creating a suit of livery and slipping over a wall or in the servants' gate. But with no notice, no idea that the man was allowed inside the gates, and no time to obtain livery without risk—it wasn't going to be possible.

His best bet at this point was to abandon the pole and bucket somewhere, and come back to watch the gate. There were plenty of places where he could loiter without attracting attention to himself. The palace was surrounded by the homes of the wealthy and powerful, like hens clustered around a rooster. But unlike the Ducal Palace, they did not have extensive grounds and gardens, only little patches of garden behind sheltering walls—which meant that the area around the palace was a maze of streets and alleys. In the summer and at night those would be patrolled by guards to discourage ne'er-do-wells and would-be thieves, but in the middle of winter no one would bother to patrol by day. The hard part would be to find a place where he could leave a fishing pole and a bucket without someone noticing and wondering where they had come from.

In the end, he had to wait for a rubbish-collector to come by, collecting rags and bones from the refuse of the mighty, and throw the items onto his cart when he wasn't looking. The rag-and-bone man would not question his good luck when he found those items; the poor never questioned windfalls, lest those windfalls be taken from them.

Now freed of his burdens, he hurried back to the palace and watched the gate.

Eventually Tal Rufen emerged, but without the horse—and no longer wearing his Church Guard livery. That probably meant that the man was planning on going about within the city.

I just hope he isn't planning on visiting any other places where I can't go, Orm thought glumly, anticipating more hanging about on freezingly cold street corners while the constable did whatever he was doing out of Orm's sight.

But luck was with him, for Tal Rufen headed straight into neighborhoods where Orm felt most at home. And then, to Orm's great pleasure, he went into a tavern. Orm followed him in, got a seat at a table near him, and warmed his hands on a mug of hot ale while the constable began interviewing people, who arrived punctually, one with each half hour, as if by previous appointment. It wasn't too difficult to overhear what he was talking about; Orm wasn't overly surprised to learn that Tal Rufen was looking for information about Rand—or rather, about the person or persons who had killed the girl called Curlew. Through some miracle of organization, he had managed to find many of the witnesses to the kill; by a further miracle, he'd arranged consecutive appointments with all of them. Why he was interviewing them here instead of in a constabulary, though, Orm couldn't hazard a guess.

Unless, of course, there were constables *also* interviewing witnesses, and there was no room to put all of the interviewers and interviewees. That idea rather amused Orm, the thought of the chaos such a situation would cause. Why, they might not have the room to actually interview criminals! It indicated to him, at least, that the authorities were grasping at straws, which was a comforting thought, given the inconvenience and worry that the sketch of his face had given him.

Needless to say, no one had much to tell Rufen, other than their obvious eyewitness accounts, many of which conflicted with each other. One witness swore that the killer had been snarling and swearing at the girl before he killed her, for instance; another claimed that the killer had slipped through the crowd unnoticed, dressed in the black costume of a professional assassin. What Rufen made of those accounts was questionable, though if he was a trained constable, he would already know that "eyewitness" accounts were seldom as accurate as their tellers thought. People would change their memories to suit what they thought *should* have happened—so for twenty people who saw something happen, there would be at least three who would make things up that fell in line with their own pet conspiracy theories. Orm had already taken advantage of that in manipulating the memories of his neighbors to suit his own purposes.

Orm had to admire Rufen's persistence, though; he gave no indication that any of what he was told bored or disappointed him. He merely listened and took notes with a rather ingenious little pen that never needed dipping in an inkwell. Deliambren, Orm guessed; most clever mechanisms were Deliambren.

That gave Orm another idea; he went out and purchased a change of outer clothing—this time something less threadbare, but all in black, like one of Shensi's artistic friends—a graphite-stick, and one of those inexpensive blank books. He returned to the inn, got another table near Tal Rufen, and ordered a hot drink.

When the drink arrived, he took turns sipping it, staring into space, and scribbling frantically in the book. After one amused look, the serving-wench left him alone. It would have been obvious to any dolt that Orm was—supposedly—composing something, probably poetry, and probably *bad* poetry. In actuality, he was writing down everything Tal Rufen wore, ate, drank, used, and said, in something that looked very like blank verse. Orm knew from experience that between his abbreviations and his tiny, crabbed, slantwise letters, no one could read his handwriting except himself, so he had no fears that one of the serving-girls might get curious and read something she shouldn't.

He'd used this particular ruse more than once in his career, but never had it been more useful than now. So long as a place wasn't jammed with people, and so long as he kept paying for frequent refills of his cup, no one minded a mad poet taking up a little table-space. He was clean, moderately attractive, and he gave the serving-wenches something to giggle about. None of them would make overtures towards him, of course—as a class, serving-girls were sturdily practical little things, and had no time in their lives for a—probably impoverished—poet. Any flirting they did would be saved for someone with a steady job and enough money in his pocket to buy more than an endless round of tea.

He continued the pretense of being a writer for as long as Tal Rufen interviewed people who had been present at the kill; pretended fits of thought gave him the opportunity to stare at the Church constable or anyone else for as long as he liked without anyone taking offense, because it *looked* as if he was staring blankly into space, and not actually at anyone. The serving-girls found it amusing or touching, according to their natures. Tal Rufen noticed, then ignored him, precisely as Orm had hoped. The last thing that a constable of any kind would expect would be that a man he was trying to track down would come following *him*, so Rufen paid no further attention to the "poet" at the corner table.

Orm was neither impressed nor amused by Rufen; he was adequate, certainly, and thorough, but hardly brilliant. In his opinion, there was nothing really to fear from this man except his persistence.

Orm took care to leave first, when he sensed that Tal was about to wind up his interviews. He thanked his latest serving-girl shyly, picked up the bag that held his other clothing and stuffed his writing para-phernalia into it, and left. He ducked into the shelter of an alley and changed his coat back to that of the fisherman, pulled a different wool cap down over his head, and waited, bent over and tying a bootlace, for Tal to emerge from the tavern.

When the constable appeared, Orm gave him a little bit of a lead, then followed him. From the inn, Tal went back to the palace, got his horse, and returned to the Abbey without making a single stop along the way. By this time, it was late in the afternoon, and Orm doubted that Tal would be doing anything more until the morrow. It would, however, be an early day for him; most of the people associated with the Abbey rose before dawn, and he suspected that Tal Rufen would be no exception.

Orm took his time, getting himself a fine dinner, and only returning to his apartment after dark. Coming in through the back, he listened for sounds of Rand, but complete silence ruled the place. Rand could not walk up there in his current form without making scratching noises on the floor; either he was asleep, or out, and in neither case would he be aware that Orm was back. Orm grinned; let him assume that his employee was out keeping an eye on Tal Rufen all night; it would avoid an argument. Besides, the heavy meal made him sleepy, as he had hoped it would. *He* was going to have to get up with the dawn if he expected to catch Rufen on his way out tomorrow, and that meant he really ought to go to bed now if he expected to get a decent night's sleep.

The following day, at dawn, Orm was back on the bridge with a new fishing-line and bucket, and while he was waiting for Rufen to put in an appearance, he actually caught two fish! Both were river-salmon, large and fat, and he gave one to the toll-guard who'd passed him through the day before. Let the man think that it was out of gratitude; Orm wanted to have a reason for the man to think well of him and let him out on the bridge without question if he had to come back here anymore. He and the guard exchanged a few words—Orm sighed over the difficulties of finding work in the winter, complained about showing up where there was supposed to be some work this morning, only to find a dozen men there before him. The guard made sympathetic noises, and promised that Orm could fish without toll whenever he was out of work. This pleased Orm twice over—once that the guard would not be surprised if he didn't show up for a while, or indeed, ever again; and twice because he wasn't going to have to pay out toll-fees for the privilege of spying on that damned Tal Rufen.

This time when Rufen appeared, it was at the side of a woman that

Orm assumed was High Bishop Ardis. He recognized Rufen at a distance just by recognizing the old gelding, and there was someone else there with him—someone obviously of very high position within the Justiciars. It was a woman, dressed in a fine cloak and robes of Justiciar red, and although she was not wearing the miter of the bishopric, she was wearing a scarlet skull-cap edged with gold under the hood of her scarlet cloak. She was also mounted on a fine white mule, and most of the Justiciars rode very ordinary-looking beasts when they left the Abbey. Given all of those factors, it would have been more surprising if the woman *hadn't* been Ardis.

Orm followed them discreetly, but they went straight to the headquarters of the Kingsford constables, and from there to the Ducal Palace again. Both were places he couldn't go, so he loitered in the freezing cold until they came out again. They went straight back to the Abbey, and did not emerge again that day.

Uneventful—except that by seeing them together, Orm had actually established that Tal Rufen was acting for the High Bishop and as her assistant as well as her personal guard. If she'd had any other assistant, there would have been three or four people going across the bridge to Kingsford. That was useful information, and Rand would be pleased to have it.

The Black Bird was waiting for him this time, and from the look of him, was a bit impatient. Orm heard him scrabbling about upstairs as he paced, and went straight to his room as soon as he changed, with his notebook tucked under one arm. Rand's eyes grew alert at the sight of it. With talons instead of hands, of course the Black Bird was unable to read these things for himself, so Orm read to him from his own notes. The Bird's eyes grew very bright, and when Orm was done, he gave a cawing laugh.

"Good!" he said. "Very good! Excellent, in fact. You don't need to follow Tal Rufen for the present, Orm. I might ask you to resume later, but for now, the next couple of days, we can concentrate on other things. For one thing, there are some odd articles I'd like for you to get for me. One or two of those Deliambren pens, for instance; I'm aware that they'll be difficult to obtain, so make a concerted effort to get them."

Baffled, Orm nodded. *I suppose that Rand is trying to find a way to take Rufen out of this equation. That makes sense; by now it certainly seems that Ardis is the main force behind investigating the kills. Without her pursuit of the case, it won't get very far. Without Rufen, Ardis will be effectively without hands and feet. The Bishop can't move around the streets unobtrusively, and she certainly can't interview the kinds of people I saw Rufen talking to today.*

He wondered about the pens, though—unless—

A lot of spells have written components—with one of those pens, even the Bird might be able to manage writing.

Or perhaps he wanted to try writing letters.

It's Rand; he's crazed. He might just want a pen because Rufen has one.

That made about as much sense as anything.

The important thing was that it looked as if Rand was concentrating on getting Rufen disposed of; and for once, Orm was in agreement with the madman's ideas. If Rand decided to take the direct approach, perhaps even by eliminating the constable forever, well, Rufen wasn't going to be guarding his own back, he was going to be watching out for Ardis. And if he decided to take the indirect approach, there were any number of ways that Orm could think of that would tie Tal Rufen up in complications and even scandal until he was unable to do anything about the murders.

And meanwhile, he isn't *going after anyone dangerous and he isn't ranting at me.* That in itself was enough to keep Orm contented—

For now, anyway. It might be a warm day in Kingsford before he felt completely content again.

Chapter Fourteen

Obtaining the Deliambren pen was not as difficult as Rand apparently assumed it would be; Orm had information about who might have such items within a day. He'd been quite confident that he would have word within a week at the latest, although Rand obviously was under the impression that such an exotic item would have to be imported at tremendous expense. But a small Deliambren contrivance, while a luxury, was also useful—and it was something that a wealthy person would want to be able to show off. That meant that the wealthy would not leave such an object safely at home, they would take their pens with them. When they removed their little prizes from the secure area of their home, eventually, the pens would be lost—or stolen.

It was the latter that Orm was most interested in. Such things turned up now and again in the goods that pickpockets disposed of to fences. There was one minor problem, at least as Orm foresaw. Because they were the expensive toys of the very rich, they should be relatively rare, but Orm's information led him to believe that there were more of them here in Kingsford than in many cities Orm had been in. This might have been because a good many of them were gifts from Duke Arden to people he particularly wanted to reward, and Arden had strong Deliambren alliances. This was especially evidenced in the presence of the crimson-winged map-maker, who was, word had it in some circles, helping Arden and Kingsford as a token of Deliambren concern. Pens, however, were more tangible, and likely cheaper than even a day's work from the Haspur.

The fence that Orm was sent to had three of the things, all three of them identical to Rufen's. The case was of black enameled metal, with a close-fitting cap and a lever on the side that somehow enabled the contrivance to drink up the ink it was dipped into. The fence demonstrated one of the devices for Orm with considerable casualness that suggested he must have had these three for some time.

"How much?" Orm asked.

The fence laughed. "What would you say to fifteen silver for the lot?"

Orm was extremely surprised at the low price for a Deliambren rarity, and allowed his surprise to show. "I would tell you I would buy the lot," he said, certain that the fence could not be serious. "And you, of course, would laugh at me and tell me that of course, you meant to say gold and not silver."

The fence acknowledged his surprise, and grimaced.

"I haven't had anyone that wanted one of these for a year. I would gladly sell you all three for fifteen silver, and think myself pleased with the bargain."

Fifteen silver! Orm thought. *Why, that's a fraction of their real value—*

"Now, don't think to go making a profit," the fence admonished, "Don't think to take 'em out on the street and peddle 'em. Fact is, a constable that notices you've got one of 'em had better know you're a High Muckety Muck yourself, or you'll get clapped in gaol faster'n you can think. That's the trouble; they're easy t'lift but hard t'get rid of. Lots 'o people look at 'em and want 'em bad, but what's the point if you're gonna get arrested if you show one?"

"Then why did you take them if you know you can't be rid of them?" Orm asked.

"I got them in a lot of other stuff," the fence told him. "If I'd known they were in there, I might not have bought it. Maybe you could take 'em out of the city and sell 'em, but not here—and you'd have to get a good piece away just to be safe."

"The things just are not like jewelry, are they?" Orm observed, and the fence nodded his round head vigorously.

"Pree-cisely!" His head bobbed like a child's toy as he waxed enthusiastic. "You get a bit'o jewelry that's hard to dispose of, you can break it down—not these! You even try to open one to see how it's put together, you got a big mess and a lot'o little useless bits."

He speaks as if he had experience with that situation, Orm thought with amusement. *I wonder if he meant to try and have the things duplicated? He could make a lively business of them if he could—but I suppose he didn't know that the Deliambrens have a habit of making sure no one can actually take any of their devices apart for precisely that reason.*

"And if I don't show them in public?" he asked.

Again, the fence shook his head. "If you figger on keeping these in the house, like, you'll be all right. But don't forget and carry one out with you. I won't be responsible if you do."

Orm chuckled, and promised he'd be careful, then bought all three pens for half the price he thought he'd have to pay for one.

He tucked them into a hidden pocket inside his coat, making sure they were secure from pickpockets. It would be supremely ironic to have bought them from a fence only to have a pickpocket steal them back.

He decided to keep one for himself, and give the other two to Rand; he rather liked the look of the things himself, and was already thinking of ways to disguise his so that he could use it in public. He always had enjoyed a challenge, and this was one worth pursuing as an exercise for his cleverness.

Rand was so pleased that Orm had gotten, not just one, but two pens, and quickly, that he actually produced a monetary bonus for his employee. The bonus was a sizable one, large enough that Orm was taken aback by it. Rand hadn't given him a bonus since the earliest days of their association, and never one this big.

Rand also gave him the evening off—officially—and leave to go spend it however he cared to. "Go on," the Bird croaked. "Enjoy yourself however best pleases you. Do not return until dawn, if that is your wish."

"Thank you," he said flatly. Such "permission" was as galling as the bonus was pleasurable, although Rand probably was not aware that it was.

There wasn't much else that the Bird cared to say, so Orm stood up to leave the apartment with mixed feelings. *Arrogant bastard. I can damned well take any night I please any time I please, and without his leave.* Orm was half tempted to stay at home—but then another thought occurred to him.

He might want me out of the house because he's planning on trying something magical, and he doesn't want me around when he does. So he thanked Rand solemnly without showing his anger and went down to his own apartment to consider his actions for the evening.

Curiosity ate at him; if Rand was going to try something while he was in the Black Bird form, Orm might very well want to watch. *It could be amusing to watch him trying to work magic with no hands.* Orm didn't know much about how actual magic was worked, but he had some vague notions culled from tales and common songs. This could be quite hilarious, if Rand had to draw diagrams or mix potions. How would he do it? With his feet?

But another notion was not so amusing. This might very well have something to do with that earlier threat Rand had made. If that was the case, Orm had a vested interest in keeping an eye on the proceedings.

On the other hand, if things went badly, did Orm really want to be there? *If he is going to work magic, and he makes a mistake because of his form—it could be very dangerous. I have heard of such things; it would be better if I was far away at the time the mistake is made.*

And if Rand was doing something that involved Orm's future, would he have been so blatant about wanting Orm out of the way? *No, he's mad, but he isn't stupid. And—I have only silly tales to base my concerns on. He is the last creature in the world to risk himself.*

Rand had been too cautious for too long. *No, he probably wants me out of the way because whatever he's about to do is going to be noisy, and he doesn't want me trying to burst in on him in the middle of it, thinking he's gotten himself into trouble.*

Not that Orm was likely to try to burst in to rescue Rand from his own magical folly; far from it! But too much noise of an odd variety, and even Orm might be tempted to go knock a door down to stop it.

Or too many stinks coming down from above. Orm actually grimaced a little at that thought; Rand had once perpetrated something that caused the worst odor Orm had ever had the misfortune to encounter, an effluvia so rank that it burned the eyes and made the nose water, made him cough for two days, and forced them to get rid of every scrap of food in the house. He wasn't certain what had caused that particularly horrid stench; it might have been Rand trying magic, or it might have been Rand bringing home something his bizarre bird body craved. If something that was going to cause a reek like *that* was what Rand was up to, Orm would very happily leave for the evening.

So he did, and for the first time in months, enjoyed an evening at one of the city's better Houses. Why not? He certainly had the money for it. He chose the *Fragrant Orchard,* a House which accommodated discriminating but not exotic tastes—and which had *no* entertainment other than good food and the ladies themselves.

He entered wearing a suit of clothing he had kept back to use for blending in at just such an establishment; clearly expensive, but in an understated fashion and somber colors. Even though he had not made an appointment, he was ushered to a fine table, and the Madame herself came to ask him his preferences. She sent over a server immediately, and his evening commenced, beginning with an excellent meal, proceeding on to the services of a very talented and supple lady who believed in taking time to appreciate the finer things, and ending with a steam-bath and a massage. He even took a hired carriage home, although he took the precaution of having it leave him on the corner, and he walked the rest of the way. It lacked a few hours until dawn; there was a certain damp quality to the air that promised more snow, though none was falling now. Could the Black Bird fly in snow? Probably, most birds could. There was no one on the street, and not a light to be seen in the windows. Except for the street-lamps at each corner, the only light came from the stars.

He sniffed the air gingerly as he entered, and thought he detected something dubious; he went back into his kitchen and made a similar trial of the food, but couldn't taste anything wrong there. Well, maybe Rand had learned something the last time; the hint of bitter aroma was stronger in the kitchen and bedroom than in the sitting-room, but opening the windows cleared it out, and once the fires were built up again, the rooms warmed quickly. Orm thought once during the process about checking on Rand, but there was no sound from above, and he decided not to bother. Rand had indicated that he didn't want to be bothered; very well, Orm wouldn't bother him. If he was awake and aware, he certainly knew that Orm was home, for Orm hadn't made any attempt to be quiet. When neither sound nor summons came from above as the rooms warmed up to a reasonable temperature, Orm decided to complete his night of freedom with a good rest.

In the morning, however, the expected summons came in the form of three hard raps on the ceiling of his bedroom. Orm answered it with a calm he had not expected to feel. No matter what Rand came up with, he was confident that he had everything he needed in place to deal with the consequences.

But Rand's new plan was a considerable surprise. "We're going back to the old ways," the Black Bird announced, before Orm could even say anything. "I don't need Free Bards, I don't need Gypsies, I don't even need musicians. Just women—but I'm going to need a lot of them; frankly, Orm, the kind of kills we were taking when we first started just don't supply nearly as much power, so what we will lack in quality we must make up in quantity."

"But they're easier to get, and you can get a lot of them," Orm pointed out, feeling a little light-headed from such a pleasant surprise. "For that matter, you could do a few more of the long kills, the indoor ones, like the jeweler-kill—that was how you got more power out of the poorer quality women back when we started."

The Bird's beak bobbed as Rand nodded agreement. "You're right. And we can do that. There's just going to be a slight difficulty for you, though."

Orm's shoulders tensed. *A slight difficulty. Now it comes! Now he tells me something outrageous.* "What would that be?" he asked.

"I'm going to want you to hide the bodies for a while," Rand told him. "Not forever! Not even for more than a few weeks. I want them found, but I don't want them found immediately—I want them found in a time and place of my choosing."

Oho! There's a complicated plan going on here, and he has no intention of telling me what it is until it's too late for me to do anything about it. Should I be pleased or alarmed?

Pleased, he decided. At least the kills would be easier, safer—"In certain cases, you might not want to use a tool," he said cautiously. "I could take care of the situation myself."

"Oh?" If the Bird had possessed a brow, Rand would have arched it. "I thought you didn't do that sort of thing."

"I can make an exception in the case of expediency, if it's too difficult to find a tool," Orm replied. *And I'll be wearing silk gloves so you can't take me over,* he added silently. *I have no intention of following in the footsteps of the tools.*

But Rand only gave a strange, gurgling sound that was his equivalent of a chuckle. "That won't be necessary. I've picked out the women already. The first one is going to be another of that crowd that lives in the bookstore—in fact, I'd like to dispose of all three of the women living there now. We could take all of them in a single night if we planned it right. The women always come back to the shop long before the men do."

"Oh, really?" Orm laughed. Ordinarily, he wouldn't have wanted the exposure that came from repeating a pattern, but if the bodies were going to be hidden, it wouldn't matter. "Fine. Let me find a place to put them. I'll go looking now; when I have a place, I'll come back and tell you."

He wanted to go out immediately, because the idea that immediately occurred to him was to use one of the boathouses or small warehouses out on the riverbank. Pleasure-boats were all in drydock at repair houses for the winter and wouldn't go into the boathouses until spring; if he could find a sufficiently dilapidated place, he might be able to rent it for a bit of next to nothing.

And if Rand doesn't care how and where the bodies are found, only when, *we could dump them all into the river unseen from the boathouse, and let the current carry them away.* If nothing else, the bodies could be left amid chunks of ice to preserve them as long as winter lasted. There was no reason for customs officials or constables to search boathouses in the winter; there was no smuggling in winter worth mentioning.

Failing a boathouse, a warehouse would certainly do, if it was small enough—but there would not be the option of a quick and "invisible" means of disposal of the bodies.

Perhaps it wouldn't be a bad thing to take some initiative before he delivers orders. "I'll go out and find a—storage facility," he said, standing up. "Unless you have something else in mind?"

Rand was still in a fine mood, and perfectly ready to allow Orm to make his own choice, apparently. "Good. Get something today, if you can. I'd like to begin immediately with this little project; we don't have any time to spare."

We don't have any time to spare? Suddenly, it seems, we have a schedule to meet.

But Orm was not loathe to take the hint, and by nightfall, Orm the spice-merchant had acquired a strongly built but shabby little boat-house, *and* a small warehouse a mere block away from it, convenient to the districts in which Orm proposed to find most of their kills.

After all, it didn't hurt to be *really* prepared.

Five kills in one night, and Rand was human again.

In fact, he'd been human after the first kill, a standard scenario for them. One girl was alone in the shop; the young man who'd taken their blade entered the bookshop, knifed the lone girl, dropped the knife beside the body, then threw himself into the river. That left the shop empty as they waited for the arrival of the other two girls. But it was Rand who took up the blade and ambushed the other two as they came in, first rendering them unconscious, then disposing of them at his leisure. He had not personally made a kill since the last woman he'd taken as the Black Bird, several months ago.

Orm watched with utter fascination as Rand made the second two kills; the fierce, cold pleasure the man took in the act, the surgical precision with which he first disabled them, then vivisected them.

Very enlightening. He hadn't known Rand was capable of that much concentration. But then again, Rand had a great deal to gain from these exercises, and the women themselves were limited in use and power unless he drew out their experience as long as he could.

In the end, they were interrupted by the unexpected arrival of one of the men. The fellow entered the shop without either of them hearing him, and blundered right into what must have seemed like a scene out of the Church's tales of Hellfire.

He didn't have long to appreciate it, however. As he stood there, mouth stupidly agape, Rand leapt for him, both blood-smeared hands outstretched and reaching for his throat.

A moment later, the man was on his knees at Rand's feet, making gurgling noises as Rand throttled the life out of him. The mage's hands were locked about the fellow's throat so tightly that although his victim clawed frantically at the fingers, there wasn't a chance of budging him.

Orm watched in detached fascination. Rand didn't let up until the man's face was black, his tongue protruding from his mouth, and his eyes bulging, froglike, out of their sockets. Then the mage released his grip, knuckles crackling, and the body dropped to the floor with an audible *thud*.

Orm coughed, and Rand turned; he hardly recognized the mage, his face was so distorted with a rage and hunger far beyond anything Orm could even imagine. For one moment, Orm was actually shocked. He had never dreamed that there was this kind of emotion locked within the mage.

He is far more dangerous than I thought.

Then Rand's expression changed, all in a moment, and it was so bland and smooth that Orm wondered if what he had seen had been a trick of the light.

No. I don't think so. I saw it, and that's my warning. But I'd better pretend I didn't see it.

"Why didn't you use the knife on him?" Orm asked, mildly.

Rand sneered. "He wasn't worth it," the mage said. "Now, let's get these husks into hiding, before any of the rest come back unexpectedly."

Orm had already made provision for this night's work; in the alley behind the shop was a handcart, the kind the rag-and-bone men used to hold their gleanings. He and Rand wrapped the bodies in sheets of rags, then carried the bodies out to the cart, which easily held four with room for a pile of rags atop them. The alley might have been in a city of the dead; there was no sound other than their heavy breathing, their grunts of effort, the *thuds* as they heaved the bodies into the cart, and the squeaking and rattling of the cart itself. When they finished loading the cart, they went back into the shop and spent a few moments throwing all the books, paper, and printing supplies to the floor, then dumping out the cans of ink on top of it all. When the rest of the group returned, it would look as if some enemy had come in and ransacked the shop. They might assume it was Duke Arden's people, or the constables. If they did, they would probably flee without ever reporting anything to anyone. No one would ever know what had gone on here, which made Orm perfectly happy.

By the time they were done, the place not only looked as if it had been ransacked, it looked as if several people had worked with great malice to destroy everything here. They glanced around for a moment, and Rand nodded with satisfaction at the extent of the damage. Then, throwing shabby, patched cloaks over their own clothing, they each took a handle of the cart and trundled it openly out into the street. There, they were completely ignored even by a passing constable, for who would ever look at a refuse-collector? The cart was well balanced and light, but it was still dreadfully difficult to pull when fully loaded. As it rumbled and squeaked, Orm laid aside his concern with being stopped, and just concentrated on getting the cart back to the boat-house.

Orm was thoroughly fatigued by the time they reached the haven of the boathouse, though Rand seemed perfectly capable of hauling the cart halfway to Birnam if need be. Orm wondered about that; wondered if the last kill didn't have something to do with this unusual energy.

Or perhaps it was simply because Rand got so much exercise in the form of the Black Bird that he was far stronger than Orm would have supposed.

With the cart inside the boathouse doors and the doors themselves closed, Orm took up the second stage of the night's work. Not too surprisingly, Rand now abdicated in the further work to be done, leaving it all to Orm. Orm suspected that the only reason he had helped in loading and pulling the cart was to get the bodies cleared out before anyone else came back—he was able to handle one intruder, but a pack of them would have been too much even for a mage. But now that they were safely in hiding—well, it would all be on Orm's shoulders.

And if Orm *didn't* take certain precautions, he could be tied to the kills as easily as Rand. The bodies needed to be immersed in running water for at least an hour to cleanse them of all of the magical traces of Rand's power—and, incidentally, of Orm's touch. That was the easy part; Orm tied ropes around them and lowered them into a hole he'd chopped in the ice. There they would remain for the requisite time, and in the meantime, he and Rand changed their clothing, cleaned up, and threw the clothing, weighted by an old stone anchor, into the hole.

When the hour was up, they both hauled the bodies out of the water and stacked the now-rigid corpses in a corner, throwing an aged tarpaulin over them, just in case. They'd be frozen stiff by morning, and easier to handle. By then, false-dawn lightened the eastern horizon, and Orm was so weary he would have been perfectly prepared to share the boathouse with their four "guests." He and Rand made their way back home together, like a pair of late-night carousers; Orm was too tired to even think and too numbly cold to care. He fell straight into bed and slept around the clock.

They made a kill every two nights for two weeks. Rand remained in human form the entire time, and their kills were mostly by simple ambush out on the street. There were two more that were under roofs, but Orm didn't see those; instead of using a tool, Rand handled the kill personally. Rand was alone with the women, and Orm stood lookout for several hours. Afterwards, the condition of the bodies suggested that Rand had found leisure to be even more inventive than he had been with the bookshop girls, and much more like the jeweler-kill in grisly details.

Other than those two, however, the kills were quick; the longest part of the proceedings was bringing the bodies back to the boathouse and cleansing them. Rand picked out the kills, Rand made the kills, usually with a tool, and Orm cleaned up afterwards. With only one body to pick up in the handcart and take to the boathouse, cleanup wasn't all that difficult and it didn't take a great deal of time. Orm became quite confident as he casually wheeled his rag-cart past constables, though the constabulary appeared more tense day by day. During the days, he continued to pursue his safeguards, as Rand spent most of the rest of the days and part of each night engaged in something in the room of his apartment that Orm associated with magic. Orm could hear him walking about up there, and wondered what he was doing. It was more than idle curiosity; after seeing the mage's "other face"—and one that Orm was more and more convinced was the true one—Orm was very concerned about his own safety. When Rand went down, he wouldn't go without taking Orm with him if he could. And if Rand thought he could arrange for Orm to take the whole blame, he certainly would.

The street-kills were, in some ways, riskier than the ones Rand performed through a tool, and the power-payoffs were nowhere near as high. Orm figured that Rand must need the extra power to stay human, in order to work on something special. He was certainly keeping at his work with amazing diligence, the like of which he had not demonstrated before.

Finally, after three days without a kill, Rand emerged from his apartment and came down the stairs to enter Orm's sanctum, wearing that peculiar nervousness that warned Orm he was about to change back into the Black Bird. He had a small package wrapped in old silk (probably cut from a secondhand garment) in his hand, and gave it to Orm.

Orm unwrapped it; he expected another knife, but it was one of the pens, lying on the yellowed silk in his hand like a sleek, slim black fish.

"I want you to find a way to substitute this for the same object Tal Rufen carries," Rand said, clasping his hands behind him, a gesture that Orm already knew was to hide the fact that they were trembling uncontrollably. "When you've done that, it will be time to move the bodies. Pile them up in the dead-end alley behind the bookshop—no one ever comes there at night. Try to do it artistically if you can."

Orm nodded. "What then?" he asked, taking care not to show the slightest trace of dismay. But he knew—he knew. There was only one reason why Rand would want him to plant an object on High Bishop Ardis's personal bodyguard and assistant.

I can't believe it. He's going to do what I was most afraid of. He's going after the High Bishop. He's beyond insane.

Rand smiled, the corner of his left eye twitching. "Tal Rufen and Ardis will certainly go inspect the site, and that is when—" He broke off. "Never mind. Just go out now; take care of it."

With that, he turned on his heel and left, moving very quickly, though not at all steadily. He was about to turn back into the Black Bird, and he wasn't going to do it in front of Orm.

Meanwhile, Orm was holding himself to this room only by force of will. He *wanted* to bolt, now, before he got caught up any further in this madness. *Steady on,* Orm told himself. *I saw this coming; I'm prepared for it. The only question is, when do I jump? I have to pick the time and place when Rand won't expect me to abandon him, and when he'll be the most vulnerable.*

After due consideration, he decided to wait until the last possible moment at this "special Kill" itself.

I'll get the pen into Rufen's pocket, dump the bodies the way Rand wants me to, and wait around for Rand to make his move. When he does, I'll get out of here. I won't wait around to watch and see what he does. Maybe all he plans is to get Rufen to give the High Bishop the pen and then take over her, but I'm not counting on it. Even if he kills her, he's never going to get away with it; every Church mage in the Human Kingdoms is going to descend on Kingsford to catch the murderer. And when they do, I am not going to be here to see it.

The first order of business was to find Tal Rufen, who could well have been anywhere, and many of the places he might be were those where Orm could not go. The simplest course of action—sending him the pen as if he'd left it somewhere—would just not do. It was likeliest that he would check, discover that he still had his pen, then try to send it back or find its rightful owner. The knives had all had magic on them intended to make the person who touched them *want* the knife, and feel uncomfortable when it wasn't on their person, but Orm doubted that the same was true for the pen. A spell of that nature wouldn't do for an object that was to enter a place that was the home to dozens of mages, who would likely sense something wrong. The magic on this pen would have to be invisible, undetectable, right up to the point when Rand invoked it.

Find Rufen. That was his first order of business. So, with a hearty sigh, he donned his fisherman-gear, and plodded out into the freezing cold to wait on the bridge. Sooner or later, Tal Rufen would have to pass him here, no matter where he went in the city.

But as the day dragged on, Orm thought for certain that his luck had deserted him; he had gone out onto the bridge before noon, and never saw the least sight of Tal Rufen all day. Even his fishing-luck left him: his bait was stolen a dozen times without ever getting a solid bite; Orm suspected that there was a single, clever fish down there that kept taking the bait and passing it out to his friends. He could picture the miserable thing now, thumbing its nose at him—if fish had noses—and telling an admiring crowd just how poor a fisherman Orm really was.

He was just about frozen all the way through, his feet numb, his fingers aching, as the sun hovered redly just above the western horizon. *Rand is just going to have to wait a day,* he told himself, wanting to shout aloud with frustration. *Maybe two. Maybe more! After all, it's not as if I could somehow call Rufen out into Kingsford—it's not my fault that he hasn't been stupid enough to leave a perfectly comfort-able, warm building and traipse across a bridge in a frigid wind.*

He looked up to gauge the amount of time left until dark, and for a change looked back at the city instead of the Abbey.

That was the moment that he saw Tal Rufen being carried along in a knot of congestion towards the bridge, heading for the Abbey.

He didn't stop to think, but he didn't move quickly, either. He al-ready knew what he had to do, but he had to make it look genuine.

I'm a discouraged fisherman after a day of catching nothing, and when I go home, I can look forward to no supper. I'm numb with cold, and I'm too wrapped up in my own troubles to pay attention to where I'm going.

He bent in a weary, stiff stoop to pick up his bait-bucket, draped his pole over his hunched shoulders, and began to make his way towards the Kingsford side of the bridge, nearing that tangled clot of pedestrians, small carts, and riders with every step. Rufen was afoot rather than on horseback, and there would never be a better time than this to make the substitution.

I can't feel my fingers; what if they won't work right? What if he realizes I've gotten into his document-pouch? What if—

As his mind ran over all the worst prognostications, his body was acting as he had told it to act. He limped towards Rufen with the gait and posture of a man twice his age. At just the right moment, he stumbled and fell against the constable.

And even as Rufen was apologizing, asking if he was all right, and handing him back his fishing rod, Orm was continuing to "stumble" against him, accepting his support and using it to cover his real actions. Rufen had dropped his document-pouch; Orm picked it up, dropped it, picked it up again, and dropped it a second time, then allowing Rufen to pick it up himself. In the blink of an eye, as Orm picked the pouch up the first time, the pen was gone, lifted neatly out of the document-pouch. In another blink, as Orm picked it up the second time, Rand's pen was in the pouch with the rest of Tal Rufen's papers—and Rufen never knew his "pocket" had been picked twice, once to extract the first pen and once to replace the pen.

Orm "shyly" accepted Rufen's apologies, stumbled through a clumsy apology of his own, then hurried on to the city as Rufen headed back to the Abbey. Orm's job wasn't complete yet. He still had a baker's-dozen bodies to put out before daybreak.

Captain Fenris was an actual veteran of combat, a survivor of one of the feuds that had erupted among the nobility until the High King came back to his senses and put a stop to them. The Captain was no stranger to mass slaughter, but most of his constables were not ready to see bodies heaped up in a waist-high pile. The callousness of the scene unnerved them completely; even the hardiest of his constables was unable to remain in the vicinity of the cul-de-sac. Only Fenris waited there, as Tal and Ardis answered the early-morning summons. The rest of the constables guarded the scene from the safe distance of the entrances to the alleyway.

"It's not as bad as it could be," Fenris said, quite calmly, as he led the two Church officials down the alley. "No blood and the bodies are all frozen. If this had been high summer, it would have been bad."

It was quite bad enough. Tal had learned after many hours spent in morgues how to detach himself from his surroundings, but the number of dead in itself was enough to stun. Fenris's warning about what they would find made it possible for him to face the pile of about a dozen bodies with exterior calm, at least.

The corpses were all fully clothed, in straight positions as if they had already been laid out for burial. That made the way they were neatly stacked all the more disturbing; just like a pile of logs, only the "logs" had been living human beings before they were so callously piled. Three of them had been severely mutilated, with patterns carved into their flesh; patterns resembling, in a bizarre way, ornamentation. These three were on the top of the pile, their garments open to the waist, to best display their condition.

Of all the many scenes where crimes had occurred that Tal had seen over the years, this was the most surreal. The alley was deep in shadow, the sky overcast, the area so completely silent that the few sounds that passing traffic made never even got as far as this cul-de-sac. This could have been the Hell of the Lustful, the damned frozen in eternal immobility, denied even the comfort of their senses.

Inside, while part of him analyzed what was in front of him, the rest of him was trying to cope with the idea of someone capable of such a slaughter. *And someone capable of making a display like this, afterwards. That's what's the most unnerving.* He strove to take himself out of the scene, to view it as if it was a play on a stage, but it was difficult not to imagine himself as one of those victims.

"I sent a runner to tell Arden's people. What do you think?" Fenris asked as he edged his way around the pile.

"Have them laid out, would you?" Tal asked, instead of answering him. The bodies were all coated in ice, which was interesting, for it suggested that they had all been in the water at one time. Even their garments were stiff with ice.

And that would make sense, if he's using the water to remove magic we could trace. That would be why there was no blood, and no obvious bloodstains; they had been underwater long enough for the blood to wash out of their clothing.

And isn't that what all the advice-givers say? Rinse out blood with cold water to keep it from staining? He fought a hysterical urge to laugh.

Fenris nodded at the two silent figures waiting to one side; robed and hooded, these must be two of the Priests who collected the dead in Kingsford. They said nothing, but simply went to work; handling their charges respectfully, carefully and gently, as if the corpses they moved were of the highly-born, or were sleeping, not dead. Tal, watching them with surprise and admiration, found himself wishing that all those who cared for the dead were as compassionate as these two.

When they were finished, Tal walked along the row, carefully examining each one. Interestingly, one was male, and strangled, but the rest were all women, and had been stabbed. With a third of them, the mutilated ones, it was difficult to be certain, but he thought that the final, fatal wound was the knife-blow to the heart that was so characteristic of "their" killer. In the case of the rest, except for the man, that was certainly so.

These victims were not musicians, but there were enough similarities in how they had died that Tal was certain that they tied in with their murderer, and he told Fenris so.

"You think perhaps that one was someone who walked in at the wrong time?" Fenris hazarded, pointing to the lone male.

Tal nodded. "And those, the ones that were cut up—he's done this before, that Gypsy I told you about."

"That was at the hands of a jeweler," Fenris noted.

"As it always has been at the hands of a tool," Tal agreed. "But this time it does look as if he's done the work with his own hands, and I have to wonder why."

Fenris leaned over one of the bodies to take a closer look. "Interesting. I think you may be right. Maybe he didn't want to expend the magic he needed to use tools? But I can see something else here—these are all—well, human flotsam. They're not musicians. Is he getting desperate? Could that be why he didn't take tools?"

Tal considered that for a moment. "He might be. We've made a fairly good job of warning real musicians off the street. But do remember—just because we haven't found tools, that doesn't mean he didn't use them—they may simply be under the ice downstream, and we won't find them until spring."

"He may need power, and a great deal of it." That was Ardis, her face so white and still it could have been a marble likeness. "That would make him desperate enough to do the work himself, and to murder so many in so short a period of time."

"Or he's taunting us," Tal suggested. That was his private opinion. "He's piled up all these victims to say—'Look at me! See what I can do, and you can't stop me!' He knows we're after him, and he knows we haven't got a single idea of who he is or where to find him. This is his way of thumbing his nose at us."

Ardis shook her head dubiously. "I don't know about that. I've never heard of a murderer flaunting himself—"

"People like this are different," Tal reminded her. "They have something to prove. They want to show that they're better, smarter than anyone else; it enables them to think of the rest of us as inferior.

But at the same time, they have to have *someone* to impress. So—you get displays—'' he gestured at the line of corpses ''—though I'll admit the displays aren't usually this lavish.''

Ardis shuddered visibly. "With this many victims—one person couldn't have moved all of them here in a single night. It would take at least two people; that means that he *had* to help his accomplice. This may be the mistake we were looking for. I think that there will be traces of both of them here—maybe a less-practiced mage wouldn't be able to find those traces, but if they're there, *I* will. And once I have the 'scent,' I'll be able to find the men.''

Fenris blinked at her, at the fierce tone of her voice and stepped to one side. "Your site, High Bishop," he replied, in the most respectful of voices.

Tal stepped to the side as well, and watched her as she knelt down by the side of the first in line. He fingered the pen in his pocket as he wondered what she intended to do.

The pen—odd, he didn't usually carry it there, but this morning, he felt as if he wanted it there, like a luck-piece. The smooth surface was oddly soothing beneath his fingers, like the surface of the prayer-beads so many of the Priests carried—

Suddenly, with no warning at all, something seized complete control of him.

It felt as if his clothing—or the air surrounding him—had hardened around him like a shell. And the shell had a mind of its own. His throat was paralyzed, and the air over his face had hardened like a mask, keeping his features from moving. He watched, his heart beating in a panic, as his hand slowly came out of his pocket holding the pen exactly like a fighting-knife.

His hand rose with the pen in it, and held it in front of his eyes, mocking him. He knew, with dreadful certainty, just what this strange and powerful force meant him to do, and that the pen had been the means by which it had taken him over. How had the spell been put on the pen? When and where? Never mind—the killer now had *him* as a puppet; this entire scene had been a trap, a way to put *him* where the killer could get at him. Somewhere above them, he was laughing, and about to use Tal just as he had used every other tool he had taken. Tal knew what his expression was—he'd seen it before, on other killers. A blank, dead mask, with only his eyes giving a glimpse of the struggle going on within him. Only his mind was free—and that was meant to be a torture, that he should know what he was doing, and be unable to stop it.

No! he thought at it, anger blazing up in him. *Not this time!* Red-hot rage flared inside him, consuming him, mind and soul. He would not let the killer do this again!

He fiercely fought the magic that encased him, and within a few moments he knew exactly why the tools all had strange compression-bruises on their limbs. They, too, had struggled against this shell, this second skin of force, and their struggle had left bruises where the force crushed their flesh. There was nothing for him that he could fight with his *mind*—this was no mental compulsion, it was a greater power than his forcing his limbs to do what *it* willed, as an adult would force a child's clumsy and unwilling limbs to walk. He could as well try to force a river in flood to reverse its course; nothing he could do would make it release him.

He wanted to shout, to scream, but he could not even move his lips. His hands removed the cap of the pen and dropped it; he advanced on the unsuspecting Ardis, who still knelt with her back to him, the sharp-pointed pen in his hand held ready to stab her at the base of her skull, killing her with a single blow.

Fenris, completely oblivious to what was going on, had gone to the end of the alley to speak to his men. Tal heard his voice echoing along the brickwork, in a murmur too soft to be properly understood. Ardis was wrapped up in her magics, and wouldn't move until it was too late.

Horror twisted his stomach and throat, and sent chills of fear up his backbone. Anger reddened his vision and put a fire in his belly. Neither helped. He was still a prisoner to the crazed killer, and in another few steps, Ardis would be dead.

Abruptly, he gave up trying to fight in all areas but one—his voice. He *had* to shout, to scream, to get out something to warn her!

His body reduced the interval between them to six steps—five—

"Rrdsss!" He managed to make a strangled noise and Ardis looked up, and saw him poised to strike, hand upraised.

She was bewildered for a moment, probably by his expression, or lack of it. It would never occur to her that he was a danger to her! As he continued to lumber forward, he labored to get something more out of his throat. Despair gave him another burst of strength. She didn't understand; he *had* to make her understand!

"Rrrdisss!" he gurgled through clenched teeth. *"Rrrnn!"*

Then, she blinked, and bewilderment gave way to startlement; then startlement gave way to astonishment. He saw her tense, and start to move. She knew!

As he made his first lunge at her, she managed to get out of the way. But that put her into the cul-de-sac, out of sight of Fenris and help, and well within his reach. As he pursued her, chasing her in the filthy, slippery alley, he was astonished and appalled to realize that she *wasn't* trying to escape him!

Instead, she kept edging backwards as she frowned with concentration and focused her intent gaze on his face. He saw her lips moving; saw her fingers weaving odd patterns in the air—

Then he knew what she was trying to do, and if he could have screamed with anguish, he would have.

My God—my God—she's trying to break this thing to save me— she'll get herself killed trying to break this thing—

Visyr had gone out at dawn, brought by the summons of a messenger from the Abbey sent by Ardis. An odd message, he had not been entirely certain what to make of it.

We have victims, it had read. *Please meet us at this address, but stay up above. I want to see who—or what—is watching us.*

That had him a little puzzled. Why would anything be watching them? It was *during* the time of a murder that the Black Bird appeared, not afterwards.

Nevertheless, he obeyed the summons, launching himself out onto a damp, chill wind into an ugly gray morning. This was not a day he would have chosen to fly in; the air was heavy, and the dampness clung to his feathers.

I'm going to be late, he realized, as he thought about how long it would have taken the messenger to come from the Abbey, then for one of the pages to bring the message to him. *It would be just my luck to get there after they've all finished and gone away.*

He pumped his wings a little harder, wishing that the cloud-cover wasn't so low. He wouldn't be able to get any altitude to speak of in this muck.

As he neared the area Ardis had directed him to, he started to scan the rooftops for possible landing-spots. The address the messenger had specified was in an alley, not in the street; he couldn't hover there indefinitely. Sooner or later he would have to land and rest.

It was then, with a startled jolt, that he finally spotted the Black Bird he'd been looking for all this time.

It was dancing around on a rooftop overlooking the alley; it probably thought it was hidden from view by an elaborate arrangement of cornices, chimney-pots, and other architectural outcroppings, but it wasn't, not from directly above. And there was something about the way it was moving that was the very opposite of comical. In fact, the moment he saw it, he had the same feeling that vipers, adders, spiders and poisonous insects gave him—a sick, shivery feeling in the pit of his stomach and the instinctive urge to smash the cause flat.

Without a moment of hesitation, he plunged down after it. As he neared the halfway point of his dive, it saw him. Letting out a harsh, startled, and unmusical set of squawks, it fled, half flying, half scrambling along the roofs, like no bird he had ever seen before.

The very sound of its voice made him feel sick; he pumped his wings hard and pursued it with all of his strength. Whatever it was, whatever it had been doing—well, it was *wrong,* evil. There was nothing Visyr wanted at that moment more than to feel his talons sinking into its skull.

Suddenly, Tal froze in place, as a strange series of squawking noises came from up above. Something flashed by overhead, and a moment later, Tal felt the strangling hold on his throat and tongue ease—not much, but enough for him to speak? At least he wasn't chasing Ardis anymore!

"Ardis!" he croaked. "Ardis, something's turned me loose! For a moment!"

She stopped what she was doing and held perfectly still.

"I'm in the spell, the magic—" Each word came out as a harsh whisper, but at least they were coming out now! "It's like a shell around me, forcing me to do whatever it wants. I think it's using the pen—not the knife, but my pen—I think that's how it got hold of me!"

She nodded—then moved, but not to run. She closed the few steps between them faster than he had ever thought she could move and began taking things away from him, virtually stripping him of anything that might be considered a weapon, starting with his belt-knife and the pen. As her fingers touched the pen, he felt something like a shock; as she pulled it away, he felt for a moment as if he'd been dropped into boiling lead. He screamed, the focus of the worst pain he had ever experienced in his life.

Visyr was a hunter; more than that, he was an angry, focused hunter, one who had pursued difficult game through the twisting caverns of the Serstyll Range. And he was not going to let this particular piece of game get away from him again.

He narrowed the gap between them, until he was close enough to snatch a feather from the tail of the Black Bird. It wasn't squawking now, as it tried desperately to shake him off its track. It was saving its breath to fly.

But Visyr the hunter was used to watching ahead of his prey as well as watching the prey itself, and he saw what it did not yet notice.

It was about to run out of places to hide.

A moment later, it burst out of a maze of gables into the open air above the river.

It realized its mistake too late. Before it could turn and duck back into cover, Visyr was on it.

Two hard wing-pumps, so hard he felt his muscles cry out, and he had his hand-talons buried in its rump. He executed a calculated tumble, which swung it under, then over him, and brought its head within reach of his foot-talons. One seized its skull; the other seized its chest.

He squeezed.

And a moment later, he landed safely on the docks amid a crowd of shouting, excited humans, with his prey safely dead, twitching, beneath his talons!

Of all of Orm's calculations, these events had not entered into them.

He had been watching from the safety of the recessed doorway of his own rented warehouse, figuring that Orm the spice-merchant had a perfect right to be in his own property, and a perfect right to investigate anyone rattling about in the alley. From here he could not see the pile of bodies, so he wouldn't "know" there was anything wrong. This was a good place to watch for the moment when Rand took over the Church constable; when Rand was completely occupied, Orm would have a chance to flee.

But then everything went wrong.

The constable got taken over, all right—but before he could do anything but chase the High Bishop around a bit, there was a flash of black overhead, followed closely by a flash of red, blue, black, and gray. Orm had seen *that* particular combination before.

It was the bird-man, and it was after Rand. Rand, who could *not* duck down alleys too narrow to fly in, Rand who was subject to exactly the same limitations as the creature who was chasing him, and who did not have that creature's sets of finger-long talons to defend himself with. Oh, he had that long, spearlike beak, but the bird-man had a better reach, and besides, Rand wasn't used to defending himself physically. The only things he'd ever used that beak on were helpless human women, not six-foot-tall predators.

The two Church officials were out of sight in the cul-de-sac, but Orm knew what was happening: Tal Rufen was no longer being controlled by Rand. The High Bishop would free him in a moment—and she would have the pen in her possession in another. Nothing he could do or say would take away the fact that *he* still had Rufen's pen in his room, and traces of *his* essence would be on the pen in Rufen's hand. Ardis was famed for being able to dig the true facts of a matter out of people who might not remember them. None of Orm's alibis would hold up against her investigation. Once she began unraveling his web of deceptions, it would fall completely to pieces. Rand might die by the talons of the bird-man, but Orm would be taken by the Church constables, and—

And he'd heard rumors about what they did to prisoners. Look what they'd done to Rand!

Nothing he had planned had included the High Bishop surviving Rand's attack.

His luck had run completely out. He could not run far or fast enough to escape the Church's justice with Ardis in charge.

But for a little while longer, at least, Rufen would not be able to move. Until Rand was actually *dead,* Rufen would be frozen in place. There was only one hope for Orm, only one way he could buy himself enough time to flee.

Kill them both. *Now.*

He had learned a lot from Rand. It would be easy. First the woman, then the man—she, while she was held in frightened shock, he, while the spell still imprisoned him. Humans died so very easily; a single moment of work, and he would be safe.

Lightly as a cat, quickly as a rat, he dashed from shelter, his knives already in his hands.

Just as the spell broke and freed him, Tal heard the sound of running footsteps behind him; he did not wait to see what it was or who it was.

He could move; that was all that counted. Freed from the force that held him, he flung himself between Ardis and whatever was coming. His body answered his commands slowly, clumsily, but he got himself in front of her just barely in time, and turned to face what was attacking them.

That was all he had time to do; he wasn't even able to get his hands up to fend the attacker away.

He felt the knife more as a shock than pain—the attacker plunged it into the upper part of his chest, in a shallow but climbing uppercut through his chest muscles, glancing off bone, too high to do any mortal damage. Tal had been through too many knife-fights to let that stop him.

He thought he heard shouting; he ignored it, as everything slowed for him and his focus narrowed to just the man in front of him. The attacker—a thin, supple, ferretlike man—still had another knife. Ardis was still in danger. He had to deal with the attacker; he was the only one who could.

Cold calm, as chill as an ice-floe, descended over him.

The wound began to hurt; the pain spread outwards through his body like an expanding circle of fire. Hot blood trickled down his arm and side. None of that mattered; what mattered was the other man. He pushed the pain away, pushed everything away, except his opponent.

As time slowed further, Tal watched the attacker's eyes flick this way, that way, then focus over Tal's shoulder. Ardis. He was going after Ardis. His shoulder twitched. His upper arm twitched. He flipped the knife in his hand, so that he held the point. He was going to throw that second knife.

There was more shouting. Tal ignored it.

Tal distracted him for a crucial second by making a feint with his good hand, then lunged for the attacker, knocking him to the ground and landing on top of him. Tal grappled him while he was still stunned, keeping him from using the knife, then used the advantage of his greater weight to keep his attacker pinned. Then Tal shoved a knee into his chest, seized him by the chin with his good hand, and began pounding his head into the ground.

Now anger took over, and the red rage completely overcame him. He continued pounding the man's head into the dirty ice, over and over, until he stopped struggling, until the body beneath his grew limp. There was a growing red smear on the frozen ground of the alley, when he realized that there was no more resistance *or* movement from the body beneath him.

It was over.

There was more shouting, but suddenly Tal was too tired to pay any attention to it.

Time resumed its normal course.

Tal fell off their attacker's chest and rolled over onto his back, and stared up into the gray slit of sky above the alley.

He was tired, so very tired.

His shoulder and chest hurt, along with most of his body, and he rather thought that he ought to close his eyes now. . . .

"Ardis!" Fenris shouted, pounding into the cul-de-sac ahead of his men. "High Bishop!"

"I'm all right," she managed, getting to her feet and stumbling in the direction she'd last seen Tal. "There's been some trouble—"

By that time, she had seen where Tal and the assassin had ended up their battle.

Oh, no—

She ran the last few paces, and knelt quickly at Tal's side, feeling the cold and wet of the melting ice seeping through the thick wool of her robe where her knees met the pavement. He was unconscious, but nowhere nearly as hurt as she'd first thought. She made a quick assessment of his only obvious injury, his shoulder and chest. *He's still bleeding, but he'll be all right,* she judged. He remained unconscious, but it was because of shock, not from any significant damage or bloodloss.

But as her hands touched him, she braced herself, expecting a shock to the heart. There should have been such a shock.

There was the sick sensation she always had when she encountered a wound created by human hands—there was concern, and relief that the injury wasn't life-threatening—

But no shock. No heart-shattering moment that screamed, *The man I love is wounded at my feet!* Just the same feelings she would have had if it had been Talaysen who lay there, or Kayne.

And that was as much a shock in its way.

She rose, wet robes clinging to her ankles, as Fenris reached her side.

"Someone take care of Rufen, he's hurt," she ordered and, striding through the mud, turned her attention to their attacker. Once again, she knelt beside an injured man, but this time it was with a feeling of grim satisfaction that she should probably do penance for when she returned to the Abbey. It was obvious without much examination that *he* wasn't going to be doing anything more; Tal had managed to cave in the back of his skull. He was still breathing, but Ardis didn't think he'd live for much longer.

Fenris had already gotten four of his men to rig an improvised litter out of two spears and two coats; they were lifting Tal into it as Ardis straightened.

"Take him to the Abbey," she said, her mind already calculating where and what to look for to trace the foul magics back to their caster. "Keep a compress on that wound, and keep him warm."

"Stop at the inn at the corner and requisition a warming-pan full of coals," Fenris elaborated. "Get one of their cots for a litter, and borrow the dead-cart to carry him."

The four men carried Tal off, and as soon as they were out of sight, Tal was out of her thoughts as well as out of her hands.

Ardis turned her attention and her concentration back to the scene of the attack. Fenris didn't ask what had happened, but Ardis wasn't going to leave him in suspense any longer.

"Help me gather up some evidence before it disappears," she said in a low voice. He took the hint, and followed her to the back of the cul-de-sac where she had been tossing items she'd taken off of Tal when he froze in place.

"Something back here was carrying that same spell we talked about," she said quietly, as he picked up items using a silk glove she supplied and dropped them into a silk bag she held out for him. "It took over Tal, and he started after me. Then—for some reason, he got out a warning, then froze. I don't know whether he managed to fight the magic successfully, or whether something else happened, but he got control of his voice enough to tell me what was going on, and I started stripping him of anything that could have carried the magic. He said, and I think—" she said, fishing the pen out of a pile of refuse and holding it up "—that this is it."

Fenris frowned at it. "Visyr came tearing overhead chasing something black," he told her as she dropped the pen into a separate bag. "I sent men off after him."

She nodded. "Right after I pulled these things off Tal, *that* man came out of the alley with knives. You'll want to ask Visyr, but it looks to me as if he bears a pretty strong resemblance to the fellow *he* saw." She smiled humorlessly. "It's a good thing that Tal was pounding the *back* of his head into the ground, or we wouldn't be able to make that identification. Anyway, Tal got between me and him, and he wounded Tal. Then Tal fought him off and got him down, and took care of him."

She didn't have to add anything; Fenris saw the results for himself. More footsteps out in the alley heralded the arrival of one of Fenris's men.

"Sir!" he shouted as he came. "The bird-man wants you, quick! The High Bishop, too! He's killed something!"

Fenris gave her a quick glance that asked without words if she was fit to go. She smiled, crookedly.

"Let's go, Captain, there's work to be done," she told him firmly. "This case isn't over yet, although I think . . . the killings are."

Tal had been hurt before, and it wasn't the first time he'd come to in an Infirmary. He knew the sounds, and more importantly, the smells, pretty well. He stirred a little, trying to assess the extent of the damage *this* time, and apparently gave himself away.

"Well, the sleeper awakes."

The voice was amused, and quite familiar. He opened his eyes, expecting a headache to commence as soon as light struck the back of his eyeballs, and was pleasantly surprised when one didn't.

"Hello, Ardis," he croaked. "Sorry, but I seem to have rendered myself unfit for duty for a while."

"It happens to the best of us," she replied, and reached over to pat his hand.

The touch sent a shock through his body, despite weakness, dizziness, and the fog of pain-killers. But no sooner had the shock passed, then a chill followed.

That had *not* been the gesture of a woman to the man she loved. A caring sister, a mother even—but not a lover.

And when he looked into her eyes he saw only the serenity of the High Bishop, and the concern of a friend. Nothing more. Nothing *less,* but nothing more.

Had he imagined that there had ever been anything else there?

If there had been, it was gone now.

Ardis went on, oblivious to the tumult in his heart. "We got the mage—and there won't be any more murders. If it hadn't been for you, I would probably be dead, and the murders would still be going on, because I rather doubt that Revaner would have stopped with me—"

A low voice Tal couldn't quite hear interrupted her; she looked up, listened for a moment, and nodded. He tried to turn his head to see who it was that had spoken to her, but it was too much of an effort.

"The Infirmarian tells me," she said, with a quirk of her mouth, "that if I don't leave you alone to rest, he'll bar me from the Infirmary. He told me that you'll be well enough in a day or so to make your report, and that until then I'm not to bother you."

"It's—no bother—" he began thickly.

She reached out again, and laid her hand on his. "Rest," she commanded. "You saved my life, Tal Rufen. The least I can do is let you have a little peace."

Once again, he looked deeply into her eyes—but what he hoped to see was not there.

If it ever had been.

Then, she was gone, and it was too much effort to keep his eyes open anymore.

"—and that, more or less, is when I fell over," Tal concluded.

Ardis nodded. It was very good to be sitting in her chair, knowing that there would be no more dead women to deal with. Across from

her sat Kayne and Tal, both of them much the better for an uninter-
rupted night's sleep, Tal bandaged and a little pale, but in good spirits.
Ardis wrote down the final word of Tal's statement in her case-book,
and leaned back with a sigh. "So," she said, closing it, "that's the
last that we'll ever know."

"I wish we knew more," Kayne said fretfully. Tal said at the same
time, "That's more than enough."

She smiled wryly at both of them. "From now on, between the two
of you, I ought to have a completely balanced set of opinions on
everything."

Kayne made a face. "All we know is that Revaner *didn't* die, he
escaped. We don't know how. We don't know how he got where he
was when he started killing people. We don't know *why* he was killing
people, we only guess that he needed the energies for magic. We don't
know how he met that other fellow, or even *who* that other fellow is,
really. We don't know how he persuaded the man to help him!"

"But we do know that he was the one behind the killings," Tal
pointed out quietly. "And we *do* know why he was doing them, and
why he chose the targets he did. We know he was building up to take
revenge on the people he felt had gotten him into the situation he was
in; nothing else explains behavior that was completely irrational. The
fellow he chose for his accomplice was probably a criminal, and there
was plenty of money on him; the easiest way to persuade a criminal
is to offer him a great deal of money." He turned to Ardis. "I also
think that if he'd had access to female Priests, he'd have murdered
them the way he murdered female musicians; in my opinion, gathering
magical energy was secondary to him, and what he really wanted was
revenge."

"I suspect you're right," Ardis agreed, as Kayne shuddered.

"I'm just glad I never leave the Abbey," the novice said. "I could
have been one of his victims!"

Ardis put her hand on top of the book, glad to have it all over and
done with. "Tal is right," she said. "We know enough. We know
who, how, and why. We might even know enough now to catch someone else who follows the same path. We mustn't let this knowledge
be lost; though may God protect us from another one such as Revaner."

"May God help us to *prevent* another one such as Revaner." Tal
rubbed his shoulder, and nodded. Ardis wondered if it was hurting
him, or if the gesture was only habit. *Well, if it is, he's bright enough
to take himself to the Infirmarian and have it dealt with*, she thought
dismissively.

And that was not the reaction of a woman in love.

Her peace of mind and heart was back, as surely as if it had never deserted her. After she had gotten back to the Abbey, with the body of the Black Bird and all of the evidence in hand, she had not thought of anything else until she had the bones of her solution in place. After that, she had assigned the rest of the investigation to other Justiciar-Mages, so that all of the loose ends could be neatly packaged up with the appropriate evidence. She looked in on Tal long enough to assure him that the long quest for the killer was over. Then she sent word to the other Orders in Kingsford to begin ministering to the souls of the murdered dead and the bereaved living, and had gone to bed to sleep deeply nearly twice her normal hours.

When she awoke again she worked like a fiend to catch up on some of the work she'd neglected all these months, and only when she had done a full day's work did she look in again on Tal. It was at that moment that she had realized her work, her vocation, and her duty were more important to her than Tal was—and that what she had felt for him might well have been attraction, but it wasn't a passionate love.

One could be attracted to a colleague, or a friend, but that didn't mean one had to go and make a lover out of him.

I am as I thought I was, and what we have been through has not changed that. I am still Ardis, High Bishop of Kingsford, and true daughter of the Church. And that is good. There will be no more sleepless nights. If he felt any different from that—well, she could feel sympathy, even pity for him, but that was nothing she had any control over. He would not die of an unrequited passion, and if it went unrequited long enough, it would surely fade. Meanwhile the surest relief for it would be work.

"I hope that the end of this hasn't made you reconsider, and that you plan to stay on as my Special Inquisitor, Tal Rufen," she continued. "I won't hesitate to tell you that I'm counting on your help from here on. There will still be more than enough work for you—as Kayne can tell you."

"Work!" Kayne rolled her eyes. "There's work enough here for ten Special Inquisitors, and it's only going to get worse as Kingsford grows."

Ardis spread her hands wide. "There you have it."

Tal looked at Ardis solemnly and searchingly, and evidently was satisfied by what he saw in her eyes.

"Thank you," he said simply. "I would like to stay."

* * *

Since his shoulder was still bothering him, Tal Rufen returned to his bed in the Infirmary at the Infirmarian's orders, and drank the potion he was given as obediently as even that worthy could have asked.

"Well?" Infirmarian Nord Hathon asked. "Is everything tied up to everyone's satisfaction?"

"Everyone but Kayne," Tal told him, as he lay back down into the soft embrace of the bed with a sigh. "Revaner is rightly tied into all the murders and the names of his tools are cleared of any wrongdoing. She's arranged for special services to be held for their souls, and the souls of the more obvious victims. So now we can all go back to normal routine."

"You aren't satisfied?" the Priest asked shrewdly.

"It's somewhat bitter justice, but Ardis claims that the families get some comfort out of it." That was true, so far as it went; Tal did not intend to confess the rest of his mixed feelings to this particular friend of Ardis's.

I must have been mistaken when I thought I saw some sign of attraction. No—no, I couldn't have. After all, she's a Priest; her first and deepest love is for her service to the Church. It is the way things are, and should be. I was deluding myself. Or it was the stress of the case that made me see things that weren't there? Were my eyes tired or my mind distracted, making me see expressions and glances that weren't what I thought they were? No, this is for the best, I think.

When he'd looked into Ardis's eyes, he hadn't seen anything there except confidence in him, and simple regard. When he'd come to himself for the second time in the Infirmary, she hadn't been there, and hadn't made any inquiries about him for a whole day.

Granted, she'd known he wasn't that badly hurt—but a woman in love would have been out of her mind with anxiety until she saw for herself that he was all right. A woman in love would have held a vigil at his bedside; she wouldn't have busied herself with work and only dropped by long enough to wish him a cheerful good night.

"The High Bishop wants me to take the position with her permanently," he continued. "She says there's plenty for me to do."

"Will you take the offer?"

He nodded, his eyes closed, while Infirmarian Hathon laid his hands on the wounded shoulder, and a soothing warmth spread from them into the shoulder-joint. This was another good reason to stay on; no secular constable ever got the benefit of magical healing!

"I've got no reason to want to go back to being an ordinary constable again, even though Fenris offered me a place with his force in

Kingsford," he said. "This will be interesting, I'm going to learn a lot about magic, and at least Ardis will believe in my hunches."

"Well, Ardis has seen enough to know that what you call a 'hunch' is merely the result of adding together many, many bits of information based on years of experience," the Infirmarian murmured. "I believe you'll be happy among us. And when you finally do retire, you will certainly never need to worry about your pension. The Duke's certainly going to see to that."

Tal laughed. "Maybe the Duke was a little too enthusiastic when he wanted to reward all of us." He chuckled. "However, I'm personally glad that Ardis persuaded him to give the special medals and ceremony only to the Haspur. The old bird deserved every bit of being made out a hero—and as for me, I will be a lot happier if every miscreant in Kingsford is not personally aware of what *I* look like!"

The Priest chuckled as well, and removed his hands. "Now the Duke will have to make sure he has a Haspur in residence at the palace from now on, or the people will never be happy! There," he finished. "Now you'll sleep."

Tal yawned. "You're right—about—that—"

He fell into slumber, only to be awakened by someone shaking him—carefully.

"Wha—" he muttered, peering up at a lantern held in one of Kayne's hands. The other hand was shaking him.

"I hate to do this to you, Rufen, but Ardis needs you," Kayne said apologetically. "There's been a murder—not in Kingsford, but outside it. This one is going to require more than Fenris can supply. One of Arden's Sires was found in his locked study with a knife in his back, and the Duke has especially asked for you and Ardis to come look into it."

Another murder under mysterious circumstances? So soon?

And the Duke asked for us?

Now he knew what an old war-horse felt like when he heard the trumpets calling the troops to battle. Energy surged into him, and excitement galvanized him; he was wide awake, and even if his shoulder had still been in poor shape, nothing would have kept him from Ardis's side at that moment. He swung his legs out of bed and pulled on his tunic.

The excitement and anticipation he felt at that moment told him something he had not really known consciously.

Maybe it isn't Ardis that attracted me, it was the job and the challenge, and the chance to share both with a clever, swift-thinking colleague. I think—this situation isn't something I'd ever considered, and maybe that's what made me read things into it that weren't there. Ardis is a law unto herself. But I have a friend in her, a real friend, the first one I've ever had. Maybe it's love of a kind, but it might not be the romantic kind, and not the sort that needs anything physical to seal it. And anyway, that's clearly how she *feels. That's hardly bad.*

He was old enough and wise enough to take what he was given and be pleased with it. He wasn't going to pine away and die because Ardis wasn't in love with him, and she wasn't going to run off with him like some daft young idiot in a play. He would always envy people who had romantic love, the kind the Bards made songs about. But that kind of love was not for the High Bishop of Kingsford, and especially not with her Special Inquisitor.

Partners. That's all I can be to her, and that is not bad at all. Two hounds in double-harness, that's us, sniffing out the scent. Even if that's all it is, it's the best thing I've ever had.

He had a place where he was needed, the job he was best suited to, and people who valued him. And right now his harness-partner was howling for him!

And what would the High Bishop of Kingsford have said if she knew he was comparing her to a dog?

She'd probably laugh and say that more than one man has compared her to a prize bitch. Then she'd point out that Justiciars are always called the Hounds of God and ask when I was planning on taking Orders, that's what she'd do.

Kayne would have been shocked if he laughed, given the gravity of the situation—but he whistled all the way to Ardis's study.

There was work to do, the work he'd been born to do, and in the end, that work was more important to him than anything else. The game was afoot, and his life was better now than he ever would have believed possible. He was ready. A wrong had been done, the Hounds had been called, and once again the hunt was on!